swords with powers, and politics as a family quarrel. But Campbell Award–winning author Bear uses them beautifully to turn up the pressure on her characters, who respond by making hard choices. And—as she did in *Carnival* and *Hammered*—Bear breaks sexual taboos matter-of-factly: love in varied forms drives the characters without offering easy redemption." —*Publishers Weekly*

"A novel of sharp invention with a conclusion propelled by a love that, in the end, drowns out all distractions."
—*The Washington Post Book World*

"[Bear's] language is sharp and strong and playful. Her technology is up-to-date and cleverly deployed. The cultures she creates are a spiffy blend of futuristic and anachronistic. The plot is never totally predictable. And her characters, including the demiurges, are easy to get next to and relate to. Taken all in all, this is a fine addition to the generation-ship canon, and will reward your attention with many delights." —SciFi.com

"*Dust* is deftly paced and plotted; the main characters are well-constructed; the action scenes exciting; and the prose is descriptive, elegant, and accessible."
—Fantasy Book Critic Blogspot

"Dazzlingly conceived . . . has all the makings of a work of unfettered genius . . . Bear [is] a remarkable SF writer who's leaving many of her contemporaries in the dust."
—SFReviews

"Bear's language, pacing, and the gradual unfolding of the mysteries of the world of Jacob's Ladder are pitch-perfect." —*Fantasy & Science Fiction*

"A tightly plotted, fast-moving story with great characters, loads of science and a brilliant premise . . . The neat construction of this story, its leanness, with nary a wasted word, reminded me of Silverberg's brilliant novels of the seventies. . . . *Dust* is a great book and I thoroughly enjoyed it." —SFcrowsnest

HAMMERED

"*Hammered* is a very exciting, very polished, very impressive debut novel." —MIKE RESNICK

"Gritty, insightful, and daring—Elizabeth Bear is a talent to watch."

—DAVID BRIN, author of the Uplift novels and *Kil'n People*

"A gritty and painstakingly well-informed peek inside a future we'd all better hope we don't get, liberally seasoned with VR delights and enigmatically weird alien artifacts . . . Bear builds her future nightmare tale with style and conviction and a constant return to the twists of the human heart."

—RICHARD MORGAN, author of *Altered Carbon*

"*Hammered* has it all. Drug wars, hired guns, corporate skullduggery, and bleeding-edge AI, all rolled into one of the best first novels I've seen in I don't know how long. This is the real dope!"

—CHRIS MORIARTY, author of *Spin State*

"A glorious hybrid: hard science, dystopian geopolitics, and wide-eyed sense of wonder seamlessly blended into a single book. I hate this woman. She makes the rest of us look like amateurs."

—PETER WATTS, author of *Starfish* and *Maelstrom*

"Bear is talented." —*Entertainment Weekly*

"Moves at warp speed, with terse 'n' tough dialogue laced with irony, larger-than-life characters and the intrigue of a 3-D chess match. It's a sharp critique of the military-industrial complex and geopolitics—with our normally nice neighbors to the north as the villains, to boot . . . a compelling, disquieting look at a future none of us ever wants to see." —*Hartford Courant*

"Bear skillfully constructs the ingredients for an exciting, futuristic, high-tech book." —*The Dallas Morning News*

"*Hammered* is hard-boiled, hard-hitting science fiction—but it has a very human heart. The reader will care what happens to these characters." —*Winston-Salem Journal*

"A hard-edged, intriguing look at a near-future Earth that paints technology in some quite unique ways."
—*Davis Enterprise*

"A violent, compulsive read . . . [Bear is] a welcome addition—not only to 'noir sci-fi' but to sensational fiction in general. . . . Compulsively readable . . . Bear's greatest talent in *Hammered* is writing about violence in a way that George Pelecanos, Robert Crais and the aforementioned Parker would envy. . . . Bear isn't just a writer to watch, she's a writer to applaud."
—*The Huntsville Times*

"Bear's twenty-first century has some intriguing features drawn from ongoing events . . . desperate and violent urban centers, artificial intelligences emerging in the Net, virtual reconstructions of famous personalities, neural augmentation, nanotech surgical bots. Bear devotes admirable attention to the physical and mental challenges that radical augmentation would likely entail, and

Hammered certainly establishes Bear as a writer with intriguing potential." —*Fantasy & Science Fiction*

"With Jenny Casey, author Elizabeth Bear delivers a kick-butt fighter who could easily hold her own against Kristine Smith's Jani Killian or Elizabeth Moon's Heris Serrano. . . . What Bear has done in *Hammered* is create a world that is all too plausible, one wracked by environmental devastation and political chaos. Through Jenny Casey's eyes, she conducts a tour of this society's darker corners, offering an unnerving peek into a future humankind would be wise to avoid." —SciFi.com

"*Hammered* is a tough, gritty novel sure to appeal to fans of Elizabeth Moon and David Weber. . . . In Jenny Casey, Bear has created an admirably Chandler-esque character, street-smart and battle-scarred, tough talking and quick on the trigger. . . . Bear shuttles effortlessly back and forth across time to weave her disparate cast of characters together in a tightly plotted page-turner. . . . It takes no effort at all to imagine *Hammered* on the big screen." —SFRevu

"An SF thriller full of skullduggery, featuring a razor-sharp ex-soldier who's on the run from her own government for fear they'll want to do worse things to her than they already have, and they've done a lot. . . . A tense, involving and character-driven read . . . a doozy of a ride." —*The New York Review of Science Fiction*

"A sobering projection of unchecked current social, political and environmental trends . . . Without giving too much away, it can be said that the underlying theme of Bear's novel is *salvage*, in all its senses . . . how what we would choose to preserve and what we wish to discard are sometimes inextricable."
—*Green Man Reviews*

"A superior piece of work by a writer of enviable talents. I look forward to reading more!"
—PAUL WITCOVER, author of *Tumbling After*

"*Hammered* is one helluva good novel! Elizabeth Bear writes tight and tough and tender about grittily real people caught up in a highly inventive story of a wild and wooly tomorrow that grabs the reader from the get-go and will not let go. Excitement, intrigue, intelligence—and a sense of wonder, too! Who could ask for anything more?"
—JAMES STEVENS-ARCE, author of *Soulsaver*

"In this promising debut novel, Elizabeth Bear deftly weaves thought-provoking ideas into an entertaining and tight narrative."
—DENA LANDON, author of *Shapeshifter's Quest*

SCARDOWN

"Bear deftly creates believable characters who walk into your heart and mind easily. . . . [Her] prose is easy on the mind's ears, her dialogue generally crisp and lifelike." —SciFi.com

"For all the wide-screen fireworks and exotic tech, it is also a tale in which friendships and familial relationships drive as much of the action as enmity, paranoia and Machiavellian scheming. . . . Here there be nifty Ideas about natural and artificial intelligences; satisfyingly convoluted conspiracies; interestingly loose-limbed and unconventional interpersonal relationships; and some pretty good jokes. . . . I will simply warn the tender-hearted that Bad Things great and small will indeed be allowed to happen, but that those who come through the other side will have exhibited that combination of toughness and humanity that makes Bear one of the most welcome writers to come over the horizon lately."

—*Locus*

"*Scardown* is a wonderfully written book, and should be a prerequisite for anyone who wants to write intrigue. Although it doesn't reinvent the cyberpunk genre with radically new science or philosophy, it uses the established conventions to tell a thoroughly engaging story, and tell it with a high degree of skill. It's engaging brain candy with surprising emotional insights—and some cool gun fights—and you won't be able to put it down." —*Reflection's Edge*

WORLDWIRED

"By sheer force of will and great writing, Bear has pulled off a rather remarkable feat without drawing attention to that feat. That is, beyond the attention you get when you nab a John W. Campbell Award . . . What we didn't expect was that she'd manage to sort of reinvent the novel and reinvigorate the science fiction series. . . . [A] rip-roaring tale of detection, adventure, aliens, conspiracy and much more told in carefully turned prose with well-developed characters."

—*Agony Column*

"Elizabeth Bear is simply magisterial. She asserts firm control of her characters, her setting, and her research (for the novels). She creates flourishes of style and excitement; not one time does this novel bore its characters or readers. . . . Run, do not walk, to your nearest bookseller, buy this book, and then sit back and enjoy." —Las Vegas SF Society

"Bear excels at breaking world-altering political acts and military coups into personal ambitions, compromises, and politicians who are neither gods nor monsters. . . . *Worldwired* is a thinking person's book, almost more like a chess match than a traditional narrative. . . . Hardcore science fiction fans—especially those who read David Brin and Larry Niven—won't want to miss it."

—*Reflection's Edge*

"The language is taut, the characters deep and the scenes positively crackle with energy. Not to mention that this is real science fiction, with rescues from crippled starships and exploration of mysterious alien artifacts and international diplomatic brinksmanship between space-faring powers China and Canada. Yes, Canada!"

—JAMES PATRICK KELLY, author of *Strange but Not a Stranger* and *Think like a Dinosaur*

"An enjoyable, thoughtful and above all fun trio of books. Elizabeth Bear's work is definitely worth sampling but you probably won't want to stop with just the one book." —SFCrowsnest

"A compelling story . . . Bear has plotted the global geopolitics of the next sixty years with considerable depth and aplomb." —*Strange Horizons*

CARNIVAL
Runner-up for the PKD Award for Best Novel, 2006

Nominated for the Lambda Literary Award for
Best SF Novel, 2006

"Bear has a gift for capturing both the pleasure and pain involved in loving someone else, particularly in the acid love story between Kusanagi-Jones and Katherinessen. While these double-crossed lovers bring the novel to a nail-biting conclusion, it is the complex interplay of political motives and personal desires that lends the novel its real substance." —*The Washington Post Book World*

"Enjoyable, thought-provoking . . . Like the best of speculative fiction, Bear has created a fascinating and complete universe that blends high-tech gadgetry with Old World adventure and political collusion."
—*Publishers Weekly*

"Bear's exploration of gender stereotypes and the characters' reactions to the rigid expectations of a world of strict gender roles proves fascinating, as does her exploration of political systems gone too far in more than one direction. Her sense of pacing and skill with multifaceted characters prone to all sorts of confused motivations and actions also enrich this action-packed, thought-provoking story." —*Booklist* (starred review)

"Another great adventure of ideals, prejudices and consequences by one of the brightest new minds in speculative fiction." —Mysterious Galaxy

"Fans of C. J. Cherryh, Liz Williams and Karin Lowachee will find much to admire in this mix of space opera, feminist utopia, spy thriller and yaoi tale. It's a unique blend from a young writer who seems determined to extend her limits with every new book. . . . The Machiavellian back-and-forth, plotting and counter-plotting, is unpredictable and exciting, and we get a rich diet of ambushes, duels, kidnappings, escapes and poisonings." —SciFi.com

"*Carnival* will appeal to those who like hard science fiction, and are willing to invest some time and brainpower into learning what makes these characters tick . . . along with their machinery." —*Davis Enterprise*

"Beautifully designed . . . One has to stop and admire the sheer scope of creativity evidenced here. . . . I look forward to seeing where Elizabeth Bear will take us next." —SF Site

"The world and universe created is lush with invention and the characters are appealing in their unorthodox nature. . . . The characters are interesting and very dynamic. The politics of New Amazonia and the galaxy are top-notch, full of ambiguities . . . breathtaking in parts. . . . Overall, *Carnival* is an interesting book with some excellent extrapolations and is an enjoyable read. . . . I will be keeping an eye on [Bear's] releases for a long while to come."

—SFcrowsnest

CHILL

Elizabeth Bear

SPECTRA
25 YEARS

BALLANTINE BOOKS • NEW YORK

A Spectra Mass Market Original

Copyright © 2010 by Elizabeth Bear

Published in the United States by Spectra, an imprint of The Random House Publishing Group, a division of Random House, Inc., New York.

SPECTRA and the portrayal of a boxed "s" are trademarks of Random House, Inc.

Cover art: Philip Lee Harvey
Cover design: Black Kat Design

ISBN 978-0-553-59108-8

Printed in the United States of America

www.ballantinebooks.com

9 8 7 6 5 4 3 2 1

For Thomas Ladegard

GLENDOWER: I can call spirits from the vasty deep.
HOTSPUR: Why, so can I, or so can any man;
But will they come when you do call for them?

—WILLIAM SHAKESPEARE, *Henry IV, Part I,* Act 3, Scene 1

contents

1

halfway to standing

The first hint of returning consciousness was the icy
tickle of fluid dropping across his lids, lashes, nostrils.
Pain followed, the tidal roll of hurt through his body
too severe for his symbiont to heal or silence.

Tristen Conn opened his eyes within his acceleration
tank. As the hyperbaric fluid drained from around his
chest, his diaphragm spasmed. Shattered ribs ground in
his flesh. The tank spilled him on the slotted deck, festooned like a newborn with blood-stringed goo.

He pushed against the deck, but pulped arms could
not lift his face from the puddle of oxygenated fluid. He
heaved. Slime roped from his nose and mouth, tinged
blue with blood, bringing with it bright pieces of tooth
and lung.

He could not raise his head. He thought, *Then there
were none,* and wished he could give himself up for
dying.

But here he was. And if he was hurt, he was living.
Beside his shattered cheek, cobalt tendrils groped across
the deck, met and merged like pooling mercury, then

sent questing distributaries crawling out until they found Tristen's skin. As his symbiont repatriated its estranged fringes, pain increased. Crushed bones shifted in rent meat, his body and its symbiont struggling to heal.

He might have whimpered, but the whistle of compressed breath was his loudest sound.

As the fluid dripped between his shoulders and down his neck, he lay slumped, staring along the seemingly infinite curve of acceleration pods lining the holde. The weight of all that empty space pressed him to the deck as surely as did the world's artificial gravity. In this position, Tristen had time to think.

One of the things he thought was, *Isn't it peculiar that mine is the only opened tank?*

He lay there until the fluid on his body had dried to yellowish crusts and cold air raised his skin in plucked bumps. The grinding of bone fragments lessened as his symbiont forced his skeleton into shape. Once the bones began to knit, torn flesh and bruised organs healing, the symbiont had sufficient capacity for managing his pain. He got a full breath without screaming, felt his ribs expand and his diaphragm flex, and pressed a palm flat to the corrugated decking.

The hand expanded as his weight bore down. Within the envelope of his skin, flesh and bone held. He straightened the elbow, lifted the shoulder. Dragged the second numb arm out from under his body. Braced it as well, pushed. Locked out both elbows, and let his head hang.

On your knees was halfway to standing.

Tristen gritted half-rebuilt teeth and finished the job.

For seconds it was all he could do to remain upright. He hadn't even the strength to put out a hand and steady himself on the skinned, gray-membraned interior of the open tank door. But if he fell, he did not know how long it would be before he rose again, if he had the courage to try it at all.

Sticky feet slurping the deck, Tristen turned and walked a step. Now he stroked fingertips lightly along the surface of the pods, finding his balance. Deep breaths, slow until he could no longer taste the blood on each, pushed oxygen into his blood. At least the atmosphere was holding.

Examining the warped bulge of the sky, he amended: at least *here* the atmosphere was holding.

Staring up at the sky helped keep his eyes off the horizon. It took ten dragging steps and forty-seven seconds to shuffle to the readout panel of the acceleration tank two places to the left. This tank remained sealed. Condensation brushed from the readout revealed as many orange and yellow status lights as blue, but even when he squinted to focus blurring vision there were no red ones.

That was relief, that fresh upwelling that stung his eyes and tightened his chest, though it took moments before Tristen could parse the sensation as emotion rather than pain.

Perceval was alive.

He leaned heavily on the mint green exterior of her tank and for the next few moments concentrated on controlled breathing. Strength was slowly returning, but he would need resources. Protein, calcium. Fluids and collagen and amino acids. All the substances his symbiont was depleting as it repaired his wounds.

When the holde stopped spinning in his vision, he lifted his head. "Hello?"

It echoed. Layered, complex echoes that would have told him a great deal about the shape of the holde—if he hadn't known it already—and the number and arrangement of the tanks. The heavy echo of fluid rang back from every side. Other than the one he had emerged from, each nearby acceleration tank was full. He wondered how many of the world's scattered survivors had trusted the voice of the angel when it declared emergency, and how many of those had managed to find an undamaged tank before it was too late.

"Conn." He tried to find a voice of command. "Conn. Can you hear me?"

"Prince Tristen." The bodiless voice was a stranger's, but it carried inflections familiar enough to layer new aches and sorrow over already-complex emotions. It was the voice of Perceval's new angel, and he could imagine he heard Rien's phrasing in its words.

"I hear you," said Tristen Conn. "What is your name?"

A pause followed, which would not be the angel pausing. When the answer came back, it was with the echo of Perceval's voice, the muddy qualities of subvocalized speech. "I have not been named."

"We're under way," Tristen said, watching egg blue bruises recede beneath the translucent skin of his arms. "Is the ramscoop functioning?"

"Yes," said the angel. A shimmer in the air, and it— he, Tristen guessed, though he must admit to himself that he was guessing—faded into visibility. The material of its construction massed only grams, but that lacework was enough to make a solid-seeming avatar. The angel's form was androgynous, rangy rather than slender. The sleeves of its black blouse hung from spiky shoulders straight to band cuffs vined with tiny silver and fuchsia flowers. A medium-brown complexion blended into cropped dark hair. It said, "We are maintaining velocity at approximately 30 percent of c."

"Structural integrity?" A long time ago he would have asked first after personnel. But with maturity had come the understanding that there was no life without the machine.

"The world is approximately 43 percent intact," the angel said. "However, portions of the superstructure remain beyond my reach. I am blind and numb there. Before the supernova, based on incomplete available data, integrity was at 64.3 percent."

Finally, Tristen allowed himself to ask, "Casualties?" He imagined the turning webwork of the world blasting through the Enemy, trailing irreplaceable materials and infinitely replaceable lives. The symbiont could reclaim lost bits of Tristen's blood and body, but whatever fell to the Enemy was gone.

The world had shrunk while he slept.

"By extrapolation, I estimate 16 percent," the angel said. "My communication and proprioception protocols are damaged. Contact with outlying sectors is tenuous. Life support is suboptimal in all sectors with which I do still have contact. The world has sustained intense radiation exposure and shock damage. We've lost a great deal of atmosphere. I am synthesizing carbon and oxygen from available and reclaimed materials and attempting to preserve biodiversity, but it will be some time before we are ready for more than a skeleton crew. Which leads me to the reason I have awakened you prematurely, Prince Tristen. I'm sorry, but I needed your help."

It was a completely unangelic thing to say, and it broke Tristen's heart along a fault line he hadn't known existed.

The angel's impulse to speak that way hadn't come from Samael or Asrafil or Dust, but from another consciousness subsumed in the machine. He turned the thought away. *You do yourself no kindness when you play that game, Prince Tristen.*

He said, "How can I help you?"

"My Captain," said the angel. "I fear for her courage and the resolve of her heart. And she will speak to no other but you. She says you are to be her First Mate, and I am to follow your commands and leave her in peace with her grief."

Tristen leaned against her tank, the medical green upholstery sticky against the skin of his back. He let his hand splay against the surface of the pod, as if he could touch his niece reassuringly through all the polymer and fluid that separated them. He knew that peace intimately and of old.

For all her courage and determination, Perceval was very, very young.

He said, "All right. Is life support in Engine functional?"

"The Domaine of Engine is closer to intact than much of the rest of the world, sir."

"The first thing we must do is repair the bridge. Start awakening such of the Engineers as will survive the process."

"Yes, sir," the angel said.

Tristen held up a hand. "Caitlin Conn first," he interrupted. "And please draw me up some schematics of the world as she now sails."

"As I now have contact with her, sir. It's the best I can do for the moment."

The bridge was not a shambles. Given its state the last time Tristen had seen it, he could only assume that its repair had ranked high in the angel's priorities even before he had given his orders. Fixing the bridge would be a service to the angel's Captain, which was in turn a service to the world itself. The three things—angel, Captain, and vessel—were inextricable in the mythology of both Engine and Rule. And inextricable in reality, as well.

Tristen paused just within the door, remembering this space as he had seen it last—cobwebbed, crumbling, torn open to the Enemy. Now, he walked over rolling

clover, speckled with blue and purple wildflowers—
bluets, nightshade. In the shadow of chairs and control
panels, the scarlet trillium petals of wake-robin hugged
the soil, the coyness of their form a contradiction of
their color.

And overhead and on every side, the stars.

It could not be a direct window, Tristen knew, nor
even an unedited view, because the *Jacob's Ladder* still
sped along in concert with an expanding debris field
from the death of the shipwreck stars. Their explosion
had given the world acceleration. Now, as electromagnetic nets were reconfigured to sweep shattered star-stuff
into the world's needy maws, their corpses fed its
reawakening engines.

Instead, Tristen saw the stars as they would have
looked without that radiant layer of dust and gas—a
spectacular interstellar night unbesmirched by the newborn nebula. As the *Jacob's Ladder* accelerated, it
would leave the blast front behind, but for now they
traveled in company.

The filtered stars seemed stationary. At these distances
and speeds, the apparent motion was negligible.

While Tristen paused to take in the panorama, the
angel again faded into existence before him. The avatar
moved from panel to panel, exactly as if it needed to
touch the controls to affect them. Tristen supposed the
Builders had been more comfortable with a visible
benevolent presence, but he found it redundant.

"Please bring up a set of status panels for me," Tristen said. "Shipwide—"

"As much of it as I have," the angel corrected.

"—with emphasis on Engineering. Casualty and damage reports. Medical reports on surviving crew. Material attrition reports. Key personnel, and a list of any
missing or dead."

Rien, of course. He wondered if the angel would

include her among the lost. She wasn't, exactly, and even if she was, her death—which wasn't actually a death, although it was a cessation of independent existence—had preceded the supernova.

Whether or not the list spared her name, Tristen knew it would be replete with others equally dear.

The air before him darkened, though it did not lose transparency. Bright columns of words and numbers scrolled through it, too fast for a Mean to read. They did not strain Tristen's ability.

The angel asked, "Among key personnel, are there any in particular whose status you would like ascertained? There is a great deal of damage, so if I can focus my inquiries—"

"Caitlin," he said. "Benedick. Any members of the Conn family or the senior staff of Engine or Rule." Then, gritting his teeth, he said the name he least wished to. "And Arianrhod."

His granddaughter had engaged in murder, treason, and biological warfare. She and her daughter Ariane had unleashed a deadly engineered influenza in Rule and allied with the rogue AI Asrafil to attempt to usurp control of the world. It was their actions that had led to the unmaking of Arianrhod's other daughter, Rien, a child Tristen had held quietly dear.

It would be provident if she had died in the nova, but in Tristen's experience, Providence so rarely lived up to its name.

"The tanks of the individuals indicated by name are intact," the angel said immediately. "Prince Benedick has already been released. So has the Chief Engineer. I am processing the remainder of your request."

"Thank you," Tristen said.

Benedick Conn had suffered worse awakenings, but only one or two. Now he pushed himself out of the still-damp capsule, rubbing slime from his lashes, and felt the unmistakable heat of repair along the length of every bone.

"Burn this," he said, stumbling against the wall of a neighboring pod. It caught his shoulder and kept him upright, but he found himself clinging with his fingertips to a cargo net nonetheless.

His clothes and tools were bundled into the net on his own pod. If anything was still usable, he'd want it. The cloth should have survived. "How bad?"

"Bad," said the angel who had awakened him. "Prince Tristen is acting as First Mate, on the orders of Captain Perceval."

"Perceval is not well?" Benedick pulled himself upright. He turned and found the webbing containing his gear. Fingers numb as greasy sausages, he pawed at the ties, but his hands shook too hard for usefulness.

"Perceval is still healing, and sick with grief," the angel answered with a compassionate dip in tone that Benedick swore he knew. He felt it like a dagger, the pain as sharp as if the edges scraped bone. "But she is the Captain. She will do what she must."

"Rien," Benedick said, once, to hear himself say it.

The angel gave him a moment of silence. Then, regretfully, he answered, "I am sorry, Prince Benedick. But I am not Rien, nor can I be for you. There is too much else within me."

Benedick shook his head, too overcome to speak plainly. He knew. And that wasn't what he'd meant.

She was gone, and he'd barely met her. It would be easy to blame her mother, but the truth was he'd cheated both of them. There had been better ways, if he'd troubled himself to find them. So now—though Rien deserved more—in her memory he gave himself an instant to waver with the pain.

Then he closed his eyes and imagined himself turning and walking away.

Benedick kept an ice-walled place in his center, and he knew it well. Now, he imagined himself in the long corridor leading down, the heavy door swinging open to his touch. He imagined the chill, stale air across his face and hands.

He imagined that he stepped within. The walls were perfectly clear, perfectly frozen. He could see out with clarity, but no pain could reach through the ice.

After his sister Cynric's failed revolt against their father the Commodore, Benedick had become her executioner. He had not been terribly young by Mean standards, but he had been a very young Exalt. He'd first built this fortress to endure that day, and in the centuries since, he'd retreated here more times than he cared to think on, when war or necessity left no room for mourning. He'd used it when Perceval's mother, Caitlin, left him for allowing his other daughter to be fostered in Rule, and he told himself there was no shame in needing it now.

He swung the imagined door closed with a touch and felt it seal. Lock out the hurt, he willed it, as he had willed it when he had lost Caitlin, as he had willed it when Cynric's blood had writhed and then clotted in the crevices of his hands.

The Mean had called his sister Cynric the Sorceress, and held her in a kind of concerned awe. But her sorcery hadn't saved her in the end.

Perceval would have to learn this, too, if she were going to command. He would teach her, if she'd let him.

He clenched his hands, drove the nails into his palms, felt the blur of heat and soothed it away. Ice. It was all ice.

War meant loss. He should be able to treat the loss of his daughters as he would treat the loss of anyone's child. Every baby was worth the same to a general.

He would be a father later, he promised himself. Soon, before it became too easy to let the ice seal that pain away forever. He would do better this time.

As he thought this, he thought he even meant it. But he had a hard time believing himself anyway.

When he opened his eyes and spoke again, his voice was smooth and cool. "What does Tristen require?"

"Proceed to Central Engineering," the angel said. "I must awaken the Chief Engineer."

Benedick pulled his trousers from the net bag and began to struggle into them, all the while suspecting that there was no way he could make the ice quite thick enough.

2

on fragile bone

The fool hath said in his heart, there is no such thing as justice, and
sometimes also with his tongue.
—THOMAS HOBBES, *Leviathan*

At the rim of the world, a blind white hawk with a
serpent's tail stretched his wings to the utmost and batted
furiously on the edge of an acceleration-shattered cliff.
All around, furrowed earth lay strewn with splintered
branches. Gavin did not need sight to observe that the
wood had cracked and spiked in spirals along the grain,
showing how it had broken green. The air still reeked of
sap and crushed fruit rotting, upturned earth, the
fermenting remains of misfortunate worms.

He flapped again, beating hard to lift himself from the
cliff in this thin atmosphere and elevated gravity. The
world had sealed its pores so precious air no longer fed
the Enemy, but it would take time to replace what had
been lost. Altitude did not improve the prospect. The
wood, which had also once been a library, lay in ruins.
At least the librarian, who had sheltered in an emergency
pod, was still alive, and that meant the trees could be
replanted so their fruits full of ancient lore could thrive
again.

Gavin broadened his wings and thinned the mass of

his body to a latticework, increasing his glide ratio. Now he got aloft. He turned into the current, borrowing its lift, and began quartering the devastated holde. The strokes of his wings bore him over a forest of blasted trunks, some trees shattered to the root, some still standing but with the bark rent in deep vertical lines. He thought maybe 50 percent could be salvaged, and those only because their sap swarmed with symbionts. The rest were fodder for the disassemblers.

Before long he sensed motion. A figure crouched in the midst of the heaped, horrible slurry. Gavin spiraled closer, banking, and made sure to flap his wings hard enough to be heard. The figure raised a clenched hand without looking up to check the source of the sound.

The basilisk struck Mallory's fist with talons outreached, careful not to break the skin as he backwinged and settled. Mallory's arm dipped under the weight, but the necromancer was braced and bore it well. Gavin hopped from fist to shoulder, condensing, and slipped his tail beneath dark brown curls to encircle Mallory's warm neck.

"This is a setback," Mallory said, raising a hand with which to settle Gavin's ruffled feathers.

Gavin rubbed face against cheek, tilting his head so the razor-edged beak would not brush soft skin. "Are all the trees destroyed?"

"Yes." Mallory opened the hand Gavin had settled on, which had been resting against Gavin's wing, and lowered it. The fingers were muddy, as if from rooting in the earth.

In the palm lay the pulp-smeared stone of a fruit. "I need them all. Cuttings, too. We'll have to clone for rootstock, but once the trees are forced, we can begin grafting."

"It shall be as you instruct," Gavin said. He hopped down from Mallory's shoulder and—spreading himself into a fine-wire mesh—began the laborious and delicate process of reclaiming as much of the world's remaining library as possible.

While he worked, he asked, "And when the library is reseeded, what then?" It would take time to grow to fruition, but there would be other tasks in the interim.

Mallory seemed about to answer, but some distraction prevented it. The necromancer said, "We'll have to see when it's done. Fetch my pack, Gavin. It appears this replanting must be left to the automata."

Gavin craned a long neck over his shoulder, sweeping the focus of his senses across Mallory. "Someone has contacted you."

Mallory nodded. "We are, it seems, available. The Chief Engineer sends word: we are for Rule, in haste."

Gavin, the servant, made no argument. As he spread his wings, he asked, "Is it this bad everywhere?"

Mallory hesitated and after a long pause said, "There will be a great deal of work for necromancers."

Caitlin Conn stood before an acceleration pod, watching condensation freeze upon its surface, and contemplated murder. Her powered-armor exoskeleton was all that propped her battered body upright, though she had not yet adjusted to the armor's silence and lack of personality. She missed the daemon that had dwelled there while the world had been becalmed—many years of working with it had taught her to consider it a friend—but like its brothers it was gone now, silenced and consumed.

The particular pod she contemplated was intact, more the pity. Several farther down the row had not survived acceleration so well, hanging ruptured and askew. The bodies inside were either being repaired by their symbionts, to take their places among the mute resurrected, or they were being disassembled for components. Later, Caitlin would check which was true.

The tank she stood before was opaque, and in a true analysis nothing required her to attend in person. She could have consulted her imaging systems from Engineering if all she wanted was to observe the feed of Arianrhod restrained in salty, incompressible fluid. The image floated before Caitlin's inner eye now, Arianrhod's hair adrift like veils of algae across her mouth and cheek. There was nothing here she could not sense remotely.

But the emotional weight of her decision had brought Caitlin here, as if to stand face-to-face with Arianrhod. Some things you did in person because that was the way they were done. She needed to be close to make this choice. She needed to be able to reach out and lay the weight of her own heavy gauntlet against the manual override, if that was what she chose. She needed to be able to tell herself it was not vengeance that brought her here, but simple math. Arianrhod's life used resources better reserved for others whose simple existence was not a threat.

Caitlin took a breath of dusty-smelling filtered air, and thought about the irrevocability of her decision. It still didn't seem slight, even when balanced against the limited and irretrievable resources of her world. But everything was in her head—atmospheric pressure and composition, wildly fluctuating heat in the habitats where the air wasn't simply frozen in plate-fragile shingles to the bulkheads—and the simple fact that Arianrhod had tried to kill Caitlin's daughter. The world—the corners of it she could reach—stretched into her, gave up its information as the ghosts of sensations laid over her own. She wore it as an armature over the mind-wiped armor. This was new and alien, this sense of her world present and immanent. *Implied.*

She felt the gaps in the awareness as well, the broken and simply missing bits of the world, the ones with which all contact had been severed. They ached strangely, a numb kind of pins-and-needles emptiness that unsettled her to the core.

So this was what it meant to be the Chief Engineer of a restored world. Restored and crippled in the same blow, and Caitlin was old enough to find the irony bitterly amusing.

The price—in lives, in materials, in the integrity of the world—had been too high. But it had been paid nonetheless, and now the debt must be serviced.

Inside this pod slept a woman Caitlin had known for centuries, beside whom Caitlin had worked, whose child Caitlin had adopted as her own before that child gave up her life and her existence to stop Arianrhod's plan. Merely by living, the woman in this pod consumed resources better put to use by those who had *not* betrayed Engine, and Caitlin, and Samael, and the very iron world that cupped them in its warm embrace, holding the Enemy at bay. A woman whose body contained carbon and salt and organic compounds. She could be useful, repurposed as part of the air they breathed, the walls that kept them.

Caitlin didn't need her hands to change the tank settings any more than she needed her eyes to see inside. But there was a certain dignity imparted by being physically present when she made this choice. An acknowledgment that it was momentous.

And that, she hoped, was the difference between herself and her father.

She rested her fingertips on the override.

"Chief Engineer?"

A familiar voice, but full of unfamiliar inflections. She jerked her hand to her side, torn muscle and stressed bone protesting, and turned on the balls of her feet. Beneath her opened visor, she looked out at the dark curls and arched brows that had once belonged to her half brother.

But Oliver Conn was dead, and the person who wore his resurrected body now was someone from the Moving Times. She had never known Oliver: he was a Conn, but he was a young Conn, and Caitlin had been dead to her family for three or four times his life span. Still, he bore the family stamp, so for a moment Caitlin wondered why it was that all her siblings had chosen to look so like Alasdair their father, the dead Commodore.

Whatever evils Arianrhod and her daughter Ariane had accomplished, they had at least succeeded in destroying Alasdair. The act might have bought them more sympathy from Caitlin if they had not tortured, crippled, and nearly killed Perceval to do so.

"Chief Engineer?" the young man who had been Oliver Conn said again.

Caitlin realized she had been staring. "Yes?"

The resurrectee swallowed, eyes wide. Did she awe him? Was it cruel of her to find it funny if she did? "Prince Benedick sent me with a message. He asks that you return to Central Engineering as soon as possible."

Not *as soon as is convenient,* which is what Benedick would say if it truly were not urgent. He *would* send a messenger rather than calling her directly. Coward.

"What is your name?" Caitlin said.

"Jsutien," he answered, with a stammer. "Damian Jsutien. I was an astrogator."

"Jsutien," she echoed, to fix the sound of it in her symbiont's memory. "It's good you brought the message in person."

He nodded.

She pressed the override shutdown on Arianrhod's tank. It depressed with a solid click. With her code key, she locked it out. "Watch this," she said, as status lights began to blink from green and yellow to orange and red. "When the tank is quiescent, give it thirty minutes and mark the contents for recycling. Do you understand?"

"Thirty minutes after shutdown, mark the contents," he repeated.

"Report to me when it's done." She smiled and patted his shoulder before she turned away. Though she left, still she carried the feed in her head: Arianrhod drifting in her acceleration tank, eyes closed, skin pale and blue-gray. One by one, the lights cycled to red.

The short return walk through battered corridors disheartened her. Shredded vegetation browned underfoot and hung ragged from rent bulkheads. Insects scurried in advance of her steps, racing from leaf to leaf, seeking cover. A darter flashed from the tangled vines on the wall to snatch up a wriggling centipede, then vanished again in a flash of indigo feathers. So some of the world's ecosystem had survived the transition, even unprotected. A little encouragement among the ruins.

And there were materials for cloning. The world could be rejuvenated. The work was daunting, but it could be done.

When she emerged into the great Heaven of Engine, she tried to focus her gaze directly forward. The city surrounded her—a great hollow sphere with every surface knobbled with shattered structures. Debris drifted freely and the air was thin and cold. Gravity was a lower priority than oxygen, so even where she floated, the atmosphere was sufficient to sustain Exalted life. The unsecured debris was a threat, but she had no resources now that could be detailed to secure it.

Caitlin did not regret the decision to Exalt every living thing in the world. Nothing Mean would have survived the acceleration—or the radiation of the supernova that had boosted the world back into flight. Infecting them with symbionts—even new and fragile symbionts that must struggle to become established even as they struggled with the damaged bodies of their hosts—was preferable to watching them all die.

It had been a fighting chance.

Failed gravity made it easier to reach Central Engineering. Caitlin spread her hands, sealed her helm, and used the attitude jets to nudge herself gently across the cavernous space, fending off debris with a raised and armored hand. Catch bars on the far side eased her touchdown. She swung her feet through a hatch that opened to her nonverbal command. When the gravity on the far side caught her, she twisted to drop into a crouch.

Central Engineering was a shambles of broken panels and shattered furniture. In the midst of it stood Benedick Conn, alone, wearing his armor against the potential of a hull breach. He bent over the main navigation tank, hands gliding with assembly-robot grace as he effected repairs. He was assisted by a quiet-eyed toolkit that looked something like a cat and something like a lemur with enormously elongated forelimbs. Its ringed tail twitched; its focus was total. Spotted gold-black fur rippled over its flanks as it reached deep into the guts of the tank.

Once it, too, had had a name and a personality. It had been a small independent life. Now it was but a thing—obedient, versatile, and consumed in the greater awareness of the world's new angel.

Caitlin unsealed her faceplate, thought of Rien, and chose not to wince in front of Benedick. When she stood, pain shot up both legs to the hip, but she would not permit that to show in her face either. She pushed to her feet on fragile bone, half healed, the persistence of her symbiont maintaining its integrity. If she kept dealing it setbacks, it would only take that much longer to repair her. She needed to discipline herself—not to push through the pain, but to sit still for it.

As still as Arianrhod, still drifting—and dying—in her tank. It would be better this way. It would be better still if Tristen thought she had died in the acceleration, when he came to find out.

"I have contact with Tristen on the bridge," Benedick said in as much of a greeting as she was likely to get.

She stepped forward, armor clicking on the deck, the bones of her left foot crunching with every stride. She paused at her brother's elbow, craning her neck back to examine his profile. Dull black hair framed a long, square face, making it seem longer. His eyes didn't flicker from the display tank; if he had not spoken, if he were not Benedick, and Exalt, and more aware than any man she knew, she would only have known that he recognized her presence because he had spoken.

"Perceval?" she asked.

His lips compressed. "Grieving."

"She's young," Caitlin said. "She'll do her duty as it needs doing."

Still he would not turn and look at her, though she knew his symbiont showed him everything that crossed her face. "I know she will," he said. And then, reluctantly: "One of us could go to her."

The pang under Caitlin's breastbone took her breath away. He might not look at her, but she could study him. Her fingers twitched, and she wasn't sure if the suppressed desire was to tug his sleeve or strike him. "Tristen is with her. He'll suffice."

"He's not—" Now he looked, head snapping around as if he had been resisting the motion with all his might, and his strength had finally failed him.

"No," she said. "You're her father. But you are here, and these are lifeboat rules. Do the work under your hand, Ben."

Another man—especially another Conn—would have said something cruel in reply. But Benedick only pressed his mouth thin and, without dropping his gaze, nodded once.

She understood. It was the decision he had already accepted as inevitable and steeled himself for, but he had wished for her to make it. As he had over time made similar unpleasant choices for her. When they had still been a team.

Caitlin also would not look down. She was still considering what to say next, whether to disengage from the conversation or to press him to the next level of honesty, when her half-attended feed from Arianrhod's pod forced itself to the center of her attention—by failing like a snapped thread.

3

the strength of any soul

I will make your offspring as unto the dust of the Cosmos, so that if
anyone could count the dust, then your offspring could be counted.
—Genesis 13:16, New Evolutionist Bible

Caitlin's eyes went wide; Benedick began moving. Even as she turned for the door, her armor rattling, he placed a hand on the console between them and vaulted it. His feet struck the deck where hers had been only an instant before, the old instincts of teamwork unaffected.

Caitlin crouched. The armor assisted her leap, but Benedick heard her grunt of pain. The sympathetic twinge lay beyond the ice, so he observed it rather than feeling it, for which he was grateful.

Caitlin gripped the edge of the broken hatchway and swung herself through. Benedick followed. His legs were healing, and he was much taller than Caitlin. With the support of his armor, he leaped, caught the lip of the hatch, and arced into microgravity on the heels of the Chief Engineer.

She was already sailing across the cluttered Heaven. Benedick kicked off, gliding in pursuit, hesitant to use his attitude jets for a boost until necessary. He reached the far wall a few meters behind her, copying her elegant swing into the corridor. The thump of her boots against the decking rang sharply. On foot, he could catch her.

He pulled up abreast and between breaths panted, "Why are we running?"

"I lost the feed from Arianrhod's tank." Her words were crisp between controlled breaths. A little sound greeted each stride, too small to be called a grunt. A sound of pain. He winced silently, gritting his own teeth as if he could help her bear it.

But she didn't need his help.

And she was right. He reached into the network, feeling for the location of Arianrhod's coffin, and found only empty space. He didn't have a Chief Engineer's connection with the world, but he could pull up a remote. He asked, between controlled breaths, "Did the mote fail? No, it's the whole sector. What happened?"

A shake of her head inside the helm sent curls escaping around the open faceplate. "I killed her," she said. "I overrode life support on the tank."

Her stride lengthened, but he paced her easily. He could condemn her decision, confront her on it. Suspect that it was based in the lust for revenge she accused him of. But that would be pointless and unfair and unlike Caitlin. No one could cling to a grudge like Caitlin Conn, but that did not abrogate her knighthood, and Benedick had never questioned her integrity.

It was that integrity that had made her so outraged with his choices, with what she saw as selling out. She had forgiven him his role as their sister's killer, perhaps because he had performed the task at Cynric's request. But the liaison and alliance with Arianrhod, that she found unconscionable, though he had thought he had his reasons at the time.

He had to admit that experience seemed to be bearing her opinions out. And he understood the root of her ethics. As far as he knew, in all her life the only person Caitlin Conn had ever betrayed was their father. If you could be said to have betrayed someone who never deserved loyalty or duty in the first place. Whatever the family betrayals, they had started with Alasdair Conn.

"Conserving resources," he said. She glanced sideways at him, eyebrows rising. Did she think he'd changed so drastically? Or did she think she'd never known him?

"You should have stayed to see it through," he qualified. Never leave the helpless victim to expire in a death trap. Make sure.

"Somebody," she answered, as they came up to the chamber housing the acceleration pods, "sent me a message. And I left a guard. The resurrected you sent me." Her sideways glance said, *If you considered him trustworthy enough to bear your message, I considered him trustworthy enough to stand over a deathbed.* She slowed, one arm canted out from the elbow to indicate a stop, then reached to her hip and unclipped her sidearm. She sighted along it before raising the weapon to high ready.

Benedick echoed her gesture. He swung across the door and flattened himself against the bulkhead on the opposite side. Whatever difficulties the last fifteen years had brought to their relationship, in this they were still machined smooth.

Caitlin spun into the chamber and Benedick covered her. He entered the room low, with a quick snap to the side, disguising his silhouette against the wall. There was too much cover in here, too much visual and auditory clutter—the cables, the pods, the sound and smell of dripping fluid and torn flesh from the ruptured ones. Benedick widened his awareness, tuned his senses to—perhaps—the scuff of a bare foot on decking. The armor covered his skin, but it was richly endowed with

sensors. He might sense the displacement of air. If Arianrhod were still here, she was still naked. He had
sealed her into the tank after her capture himself, and he
had not left her gear in the netting. He might be able to
smell warm, wet skin.

It was no mysterious power, but rather a developed
awareness to everything his own senses, the symbiont,
and the armor could tell him. There was the fine edge of
training, which was about developing trustworthy per-
ceptions, learning to rely on them, and acting on them
without thought or hesitation. The body knows the
knife is coming, as surely as a fly senses a falling blow
and drops into flight to elude it.

For now, Benedick's body told him there was no
knife. But though he trusted it, he also believed in
caution.

Right-handed, he tapped the ceramic on his thigh.
Caitlin glanced at him. He sealed his faceplate, and she
mimicked him.

Benedick gestured left. She nodded and went, slipping
between pods, using their bulk to break her silhouette
and disguise the motion. Benedick followed on a stag-
gered angle, inching along the rows as silently as possible in his clicking ceramic suit.

Together, they moved toward Arianrhod's tank, keeping as much cover between them and it as possible. At
thirty meters, Caitlin drew up, beckoning him closer.
She caught his eye through twinned faceplates; neither
of them needed to ask if the other was ready.

The count was all internal. She stepped out. He
waited at the ready for her signal. "Wounded," she said,
and he snapped around the corner to cover her as she
moved forward.

The resurrected he'd sent with the message lay on the
floor, an azure puddle cradling his head. He'd sustained
a savage blow. From here, Benedick could not see if

there were other wounds. Anything the resurrected might have sustained would be unlikely to kill an Exalt, since Benedick could tell there had not been any dismembering injuries.

"He's alive." Caitlin dropped a knee beside him. Benedick kept her in his peripheral vision, but his job now was not to watch her. It was to watch for anyone who might threaten her. She glanced up. "The tank's unsealed."

"She's gone?"

"Poof." Caitlin stood. "Shit." She turned, scanning the chamber as if she might see something.

"Whoever came to collect her has a three-minute start." But Benedick did not holster his weapon. The tank farm was large, and whoever had managed to shut off the motes on Arianrhod's pod had also managed to move through the chamber unmonitored, which suggested a high level of access to the world's systems. He didn't need to say so. Caitlin would know this, and know also that the ability to do so suggested some instability in—or compromise of—the newly reconstructed angel. Arianrhod and her rescuer could still be close.

"If I leave now—"

Benedick did not look at Caitlin, but she looked at him. She shook her head. "We have to warn Tristen. And you shouldn't go without supplies."

Because three minutes was a long time, and the chase could stretch on. And whoever had come for Arianrhod would be well provided.

"There are stretchers in the locker," Benedick said. "Let's see if any more of the sleepers are ready to awaken, and then we'll call the bridge and evac the casualty."

She stopped him. "Ben. I need to know I can trust you on this."

If it were a melodrama, he would have unsealed his faceplate to look her in the eyes. But she was Caitlin Conn; he did not delude himself. If she chose, she could read his breathing, pulse rate, skin conductivity through the sensors built into his armor. In return, his symbiont could control those things, but it was at its essence an arms race.

"Because Arianrhod was the mother of my youngest child?" He hit the word *was* a little harder than the others. Rien was dead, and he had barely known her. The knowing was his own fault; the death . . .

He would hang that gladly on Arianrhod. And on Ariane, *her* elder daughter, who was also his half sister—and Caitlin's. Relations in the Conn family were nothing if not convoluted.

Caitlin stared through a transparent mask. Benedick turned to search a nearby locker for a collapsible stretcher. He pulled the hand-sized oval from a rack that had once held ten, oriented it properly, and triggered it. The webbed hammock unfolded, supported at each corner by an artificial gravity neutralizer. He guided it to the floor beside the unconscious resurrected and moved to the man's head. Without being asked, Caitlin stepped to his feet and crouched down.

Their eyes met and they lifted, stepped sideways, and shifted the man onto the stretcher. Caitlin triggered the neutralizers and the stretcher rose softly into the air.

Benedick said, "We have a daughter, too."

Perceval, now Captain, who had been the one to finally manage the death of Ariane. Caitlin had already started to turn away. The sensors on her armor meant she would not need to look back to see him, but she did anyway, a lingering glance over her shoulder. It was a human moment. "I thought sentiment was beneath you."

He touched the mobility control on the stretcher. The red-gold hemisphere flushed green and it started forward. It would glide smoothly in whatever direction he indicated, as long as his hand remained on the control.

"*Our* daughter is still alive," he said.

If she had an answer, she kept it to herself.

"Prince Tristen," the angel said, "there are complications."

Tristen lifted his head from his arms. He must have slumped across the controls, claimed by healing sleep. He could feel the dents in his cheek and forehead left by details on the panel, and a crease marked by a metal edge.

The angel's avatar stood before the patched bulkhead. Its appearance had changed. Now light refracted from silver hair as if through the facets of a diamond. It folded hands before its breast as if in supplication.

"We can dispense with the prince stuff," Tristen said. He pressed hard on his eyes, rubbing grit from the corners. His beard prickled with unwashed sweat. "Where's the breach?"

He regretted the idiom as soon as he uttered it—there was no telling how literal-minded a young artificial intelligence might be—but the angel seemed to take it in stride. And without offense.

It said, "Progress in restoring structural integrity is adequate. However, proprioceptive data is still erratic. I have deployed motes to collect electromagnetic-spectrum telemetry about the integrity of the world, and if they are not destroyed by debris, we should have a schematic soon, at least—"

There was a pause, as if it waited for new data before it continued. "I have a message from the Chief Engineer, Prince Tristen. She wishes to warn you that Arianrhod has escaped, and asks that you return her call in haste. Also, an additional difficulty has presented itself. It appears the damage to the world and attendant loss of life has been extreme enough to trigger certain fail-safes."

Did angels hesitate uncomfortably, or was that a concession to human frailty? A moment for him to organize his thoughts and prepare himself? Or perhaps a moment in which the angel could explore his response? Tristen didn't know. "How bad is it?"

"Indeterminate," the angel said. "*Bad* is a value judgment. It is an evolving situation that may become problematic."

"Specify."

"The *Jacob's Ladder*'s base program contains a number of fail-safe routines, which are triggered in a case where the world sustains certain catastrophic damage. One such was the splintering of the ur-angel Israfel."

After five centuries, Tristen still could not summon up a scrap of grief for the memory of Israfel. If the modern angels were autocratic, arrogant, and monomaniacal, they came by it honestly—and at least they had not also been omnipotent. Israfel had been all those things *and* utterly committed to the Builders' program. Tristen had no doubt at all that Israfel had been fully informed about the hundreds of thousands of frozen dead stored in the world's holdes, raw material for whatever might be needed.

When first the world was ruined, when the first Exalt were infected with their new symbiotic colonies, systems had been unable to maintain integrity in the original artificial intelligence of the Builders' design. In self-preservation, Israfel had shattered into smaller, more specialized entities. So Israfel had begotten Dust, the Angel of Memory; and Samael, the Angel of Mutagens and of Life Support; and Susabo, the Angel of Propulsion; and Asrafil, the Angel of Weapons Systems—and other, lesser beasts as well.

Predictably, defensive of their individuality, those angels had warred for which would control their reunited self. None of them had won, exactly, and all had been consumed. The nameless angel to whom Tristen now spoke was the result of that conflict, and it was the sacrifice of young Rien, Perceval's sister and beloved, that had given it an identity of its own.

An identity that continued, "The *current* issue is a protocol that is triggered when viable biologicals aboard fall below a critical volume. Which is to say, in the wake of concussive and radiation damage sustained from the supernova, the world has begun repopulating its biosphere."

Tristen pressed the palms of his hands flat to the panel. "So what's out there?"

The angel folded its arms. "That's an interesting question. And unfortunately, as my lack of proprioceptive data is progressive, I do not entirely know."

"Progressive? You're losing more sections?"

"Yes."

"How is that possible?"

"Causes as yet undetermined," the angel said. "The cause may be cascading colony failures. Or, and possibly more problematic, it is possible that this reset, if I may use the term, came complete with its own guardian angel."

"Israfel might be back," Tristen clarified.

"Back," the angel agreed. "And ready to institute the Builders' plan."

Tristen's voice rang as clear in Caitlin's ear as if he murmured into it. "We seem to have inherited a complex of additional problems."

"Thrill me," she said, watching Benedick—still armored but unhelmed—pack concentrated rations and bottled water into a carryall. She triggered broadcast mode. "You're on speaker."

Tristen said, "The world is attempting to repopulate. There's no telling what might be coming out of the cloning tanks. The program is for maximum biological diversity to be restored in the aftermath of catastrophe, on the theory that competition is the manner in which a balanced ecosystem is likely to reestablish itself."

"Wasteful," she said.

"That's the Builders for you. Maximum carnage as a tenet of religious faith."

The amplified voice seemed to be reaching the resurrected Jsutien. At least he stirred, one hand coming up to press the nanobandaged scalp wound, though his eyes stayed shut. Caitlin wished he'd hurry up and heal. The memory-set that inhabited him—the skills of a Moving Times astrogator, for which Benedick had reawakened him—would be extraordinarily useful in the near future.

"Wasteful," Caitlin said. She knew how much external management was necessary to keep most Heavens functional.

Benedick sealed his carryall with a touch. He clipped it to the shoulder of his armor and snapped his fingers for the toolkit. It had been grooming the claws of one hind foot in the corner, enormous lambent eyes half closed in pleasure, fluffy tail flipped over the opposite toes. At his summons, it scampered squirrel-light across the rubble of ruined equipment, leaped to his outreached gauntlet, and swarmed up his arm to the shoulder, where it curled itself under the edge of his hair. It peeked between strands, blinking.

Caitlin could not believe anyone had ever gone out of their way to design anything quite so offensively cute.

Benedick said, "The Builders believed in competition."

"Just to complete your morning," Tristen added, "the angel informs me that it has lost contact with certain areas of the world. It believes that it's possible the original Israfel has respawned an intact instance."

Benedick splayed his fingers inside their gauntlets. Caitlin watched furtively. She had been right to create distance between them. It was too hard to stay angry with him when he was close, and in pain, but she didn't dare let go of that anger. Looking at him now, she nursed her outrage, fed it scraps of bitter memory, and still she felt it gutter. No memory of betrayal could stand up to the presence of the man.

He said, "But the renewed world angel *is* Israfel—"

"It is an evolved Israfel," Caitlin corrected. "Pieces were lost in the shipwrecked time. Pieces evolved. Pardon me, angel, for speaking of you as if you were not here."

"Fear not," the angel said. "I take no offense."

"New pieces were added," Tristen said, when neither she nor Benedick could bring themselves to say it. "The problem is that the angel is not the only thing that's evolved. We have, too. And the original Israfel would have the Builders' unmodified plan at heart."

Tristen's tone carried a world of implications as to what he thought of the Builders, their plan, and their general Godlike disregard for the health or well-being of any individual creature. The God of the Builders was a harsh god, with no concern in Him for any given sparrow's fall.

"And the Builders were monsters," Caitlin said, to validate him. "There's one benefit in that possibility, though. Israfel should know our destination."

"I know our destination," the angel said. "From Dust and Samael. But the destination Dust provided is nonsensical; it's an empty sector. There is nothing awaiting where we were sent."

"So Dust was corrupt or misinformed?" Benedick asked.

"Or intentionally misprogrammed," Tristen said. His voice was level, light, matter-of-fact. As she often had in the long-ago, Caitlin thought that she would like it better if he were ranting. "Remember with whom we are dealing, here. The Builders were an apocalyptic cult. I've read that book in the case outside the bridge: it would not be beyond them to send a million life-forms on a one-way journey if they believed it would force us to evolve. The rest of you may not remember, but our father was but a pale reflection of what spawned him."

"I remember," Caitlin said. Gerald Conn, the last Captain of the *Jacob's Ladder*, had raised his heir a patricide—founding a family tradition, it seemed. And nobody had really blamed Alasdair for killing the old man.

Tristen fell silent. She could hear his light, quick breaths. This was no easier for him than for any of them, and perhaps worse. Arianrhod might be Benedick's ex-lover, if you could use such an affectionate term for an arrangement of political expedience. But she was Tristen's granddaughter, and *those* were not bonds that dissolved so easily.

Breaking the silence, Benedick said, "There also might have been a trigger protocol meant to provide a real destination when certain conditions were fulfilled."

"There still might," Caitlin said, and did not fill in the obvious corollary. If Israfel had, in fact, respawned and recompiled himself, it was possible that the situation Tristen was describing was exactly what had triggered the event.

"As an alternate possibility," Benedick added, "our angel has breadth of experience on its side. And it should in large part be aware of its progenitors' plans. Am I correct?"

"Yes," the angel said. Caitlin bit her cheek, trying not to hear familiar overtones. "However, data was lost in the collectivization. We *were* all attempting to eat one another. Further data had already been lost when the world shattered, and in the intervening centuries. And it would be well within parameters for Dust or Asrafil or Samael to institute some complex machination, then wipe and overwrite his own memory of the event. In which case, I would have no way of knowing. Conceivably, any of them could have programmed a respawn. Indeed, I should be surprised if each of them had not. And if it is Israfel . . . "

Caitlin would have reached to rub her neck, if not for the gauntlets. She touched her wrist, retracting the glove into the armor, and pressed at the base of her skull. Interpreting the motion, the gelatinous lining of the armor rippled soothingly down the length of her back. "We are not what the Builders would have had us become. And based on the evidence of the dead in the holdes, Israfel would be designed to implement their plan over as many corpses as necessary."

Tristen said, "We don't need another war of the angels. Or a purge of the unbelievers."

"Sir Perceval is the Captain," the angel said. "If there are angels, if they are not significantly different in program from my progenitors, they will obey her if they can be made to hear. Except—"

"Bound demons," Caitlin said. "Loopholes in contracts. Things that serve unwillingly are tricky as hell to control."

"Yes," the angel said. "And first they must be made to hear."

Tristen's exhaled breath was loud enough to transmit.

"Benedick, when are you leaving? And how do you plan to track Arianrhod?"

Benedick paused, his helm in one hand. "Now. And with any means at my disposal."

The angel said, "She may be coming toward Rule. We must assume that her plans to wrest control of the ship have not changed, and we've all experienced firsthand the ruthlessness she's willing to bring to bear to implement those plans, up to and including a successful genocide. Central biosystems would be the logical choice for a beachhead, assuming some complex of our suppositions is correct, and some agency—potentially a respawned Asrafil—to which she owed fealty is what sent for her. It would explain why the Chief Engineer and I lost our feeds from the tank.

"Based on my schematics, which are somewhat incomplete, someone departing from the bridge could easily beat her there. Emergency reconfigurations have changed the plan of the world, but central biosystems is not far from Rule, and the bridge was designed to be accessible from Rule. Even without transport, the journey should take less than twenty hours."

Tristen cleared his throat. "It's just a guess that Arianrhod is coming this way."

"A hypothesis," the angel said. "But not one upon which we should gamble everything. Prince Benedick—"

"I'll follow Arianrhod, no matter what the decision. I can track her." He met Caitlin's eyes when he said it.

She believed him, which was most of the problem. "The last thing we need to add to an equation that's already this fucked is a mutiny. And Arianrhod is unlikely to abandon her ambitions simply because she got caught. We don't know what her resources are, or if somewhere she has followers."

"It would mean leaving Perceval on her own," Tristen said.

Caitlin tried to stop herself. She had no doubt in her daughter. Only doubt in the strength of any soul in the face of the weight of all the world. But the words escaped anyway: "Can she manage?"

"She's a Conn," Tristen said.

Caitlin swallowed. "Be there when you wake her, Brother. Please."

4

balanced against the skin
of the world

His heart is as hard as a world, as hard as a grinding millstone.
When he rises up, the mighty are afraid: they purify themselves
in fear of his violence.
—Job 41: 24–25, New Evolutionist Bible

When Tristen returned to the tank farm, he strode
without limping, a robe draped over his arm. Healing bone
latticed by his symbiont pained him, but the hurt had
subsided to the point where discipline and technology
rendered it bearable. Pride kept him upright, though he
wondered what he had left to sustain his pride on behalf of.

His steps thumped on the crosshatched grating that
had earlier scored his hands when he fell against it. In
their haste, before the shock wave hit, he had bundled
Perceval into the nearest available tank and dived into
the neighboring one. It had sealed before he realized he
should have taken one on a different circuit to safe-
guard against failure that might kill them both.

He stopped before Perceval's tank and drew a breath.
Sometimes, maybe you got lucky.

The status lights shone steady blue and green, as he
had known they would. He had put this off longer than
strictly necessary, but it did not seem unfit to him that
Perceval should have whatever fragile respite he might
win for her.

"I'm ready, angel."

The tank bubbled as it began to drain. The cover slid aside, spilling syrupy liquid through the grate. Within, Perceval slumped forward against her restraints, bones starvation-plain through scarred skin. Tristen held his arms out to support her as the gelatinous webbing slid away. He thought she would crumple and was ready to assist with her slight weight, but as her feet settled to the floor she lifted her chin instead. She raised one hand to the lip of the pod, steadying herself, and blinked open lashes that spiked and stuck.

"Uncle Tristen," she said.

She tilted her head to one side, a silent question. The muscles of his mouth twitched with repressed words. She was the Captain now. The angel would already have told her everything he might impart, faster and more efficiently. So Tristen just nodded and offered his hand as a brace when she stepped down over the lip of the pod.

She managed without it. "You're leaving," she said.

"I am going to intercept Arianrhod." Which Perceval knew, but it meant something to say it.

She looked up at him, blinking thoughtfully, arms wrapped tight over her chest. Belatedly, he recalled the robe and draped it around her, tugging it closed across her chest until its radiant chemical warmth began to unhunch her shoulders. If she had hair longer than a prickle of stubble across her scalp, he would have lifted it from the collar.

Instead, helpless, he stepped back and offered what he could: "I cared for her, too."

"Of course you did. There was never any question about that, and I'm not going to tell you your grief is nothing on mine. That would be childish and without compassion."

She straightened her arms, struggling into oversized sleeves, and sealed the front of the robe with a touch.

He watched her chest expand and contract as she breathed deeply, hard: steeling herself, or the arrested preliminary to a sob. He put his hand on her shoulder, all the comfort he could offer.

She raised her eyes to his again and presented him with a sort of a gift that was also a burden. "Kill Arianrhod for me, Uncle."

She could have no idea what she was asking of him, and it would be cruel to tell her, who needed no further cruelty now. She must have meant it as a kindness, dispensation and vengeance in one bequest. He couldn't make words happen. He pressed her cheek with the back of his hand.

Benedick broke a stimulant capsule under the unconscious resurrected's nose, resting his other hand on the uninjured side of the boy's head to restrain it. The boy jerked back nonetheless, but Benedick's grip kept him from further damaging himself. The resurrected grasped his wrist with a fish-cold hand. "Jsutien," Benedick said.

A familiar face but a foreign name.

Jsutien's eyes opened, nonetheless. Conn eyes, the stamp of Alasdair's paternity, with the faint drooping fold at the corner, but no Conn chill behind them. Not that Oliver had ever been as hard as his elders.

If it were not for Rien, this would be the loss Benedick would feel most deeply. And that was why, when he needed a helper, this had been the resurrected he chose. What must be done was best done without hesitation. The best way to learn to endure a pain was to experience it.

He drew back his hand, disengaging gently from the one Oliver still gripped him with. "Tell me everything that happened."

"Arianrhod," Jsutien said. He blinked and felt the nanobandage on his head with tentative fingers.

Benedick smoothed his expression. Give nothing of use to the subject of the interrogation. "Tell me everything you remember."

"The Engineer left me on watch." He began to sit; Benedick pressed a fingertip to his chest to keep him supine on the stretcher. Fur stirred softly against Benedick's throat as the toolkit peered between strands of his hair, but Jsutien's eyes only flickered to the little construct and dismissed it. "The Engineer had terminated service to the tank," he continued, "and wished me to observe the shutdown protocol so there would be no mishaps." He paused, again pressing his temple. "There's nothing after."

"Do you remember the blow?"

"Blow." His fingers still on the bandage, he frowned. "No. Nothing between watching the lights turn red, and now. Not even a timescroll. It's as if purged."

He must have pushed too hard, because he winced and blinked hazel eyes under ridiculous black ringlets— the perfect kid brother. Except he wasn't, anymore.

Resurrected and mute was one thing; Benedick had seen friends come back as the speechless dead all his life, and he was accustomed. The body was not the mind. This new thing—resurrected and bearing someone else's experiences, or at least the simplified, digitized version—unsettled him. Because the face was not blank as the face of a resurrected ought to be, and so he found himself responding to this young man as he would have responded to Oliver.

But Jsutien was not Oliver. He was constructed from the repaired body of a dead Conn and the electrical impulses salvaged from the mind of a dead Engineer. And while neither of those things was a person, what resulted when such a textureless recording infiltrated and grew into such a still mind was a human being not entirely like either of the components that had constructed it.

Benedick could think of it as a kind of reproduction, if he tried. Two parents united in a child both like and unlike each.

But ordinary reproduction did not result in the destruction of the originators.

"Caitlin will need to scan," Benedick said. "You're aware."

Jsutien frowned for a few moments, and then nodded. "The incursion—if there was an incursion—might have left something in my head."

It was a positive sign. Rather than asking ignorant questions, Jsutien took a moment to assess the information he had and draw conclusions.

"Yes," Benedick said. He reached beneath the stretcher and produced a draped silver-stain swag of nanochain. "Until then, I must restrain you."

Silently, Jsutien held forth his hands.

The access tunnels Tristen navigated as he left the bridge were cold, unlit, weightless, and unpressurized, and after several hours his oxygen reserves were becoming a concern. High-intensity microlamps on his armor's helm and shoulders swept over the irregular spaces between buckled bulkheads and decks, illuminating them with stark shadows that confused the eye. In atmosphere, the armor could have aided its course-plotting by echolocation, creating a sonographic map of the corridor, but the vacuum limited it to other forms of tomography. Still, it was useful to know where potential hazards lay, as all these passages were battered, torn, and open to the void.

The Enemy had long ago claimed and colonized them. Jacob Dust in his wisdom had never seen fit to correct the problem. Vacuum would not serve as a barrier to the Exalt, especially one armored as Tristen was armored now, but it had kept less advanced biota from entering the world's control core during the shipwrecked time.

Tristen thought the time for such measures had ended. "Angel?"

He felt the angel's awareness settle on him. His armor had had a personality, a name, its own small servitor. Now that being was consumed in the world's guardian, and Tristen found he missed it. He said, "I almost called you George."

The angel said, "Portions of George's data have been preserved in archive. As time passes and I am able to allot more resources to noncritical functions, I will develop subroutines and personalities optimized for interaction with the crew. I am sorry not to be able to offer this service now."

If tone were any guarantee of sincerity, it was as sorry as it claimed. That humility and joy in service could not have come from Jacob Dust or Samael, and as Tristen picked his route, he tried not to dwell too long on the probable source. "I can't keep calling you 'the angel.' "

"My Captain has not yet seen fit to provide me with a name."

The naming would be a difficult acknowledgment that what had been lost was never coming back. Tristen shook his head. He didn't envy Perceval the responsibility, or the choice.

"I'll speak to her when I get a chance," he said, and wondered if the silence that followed was the angel's gratitude, or if he had offended. He interrupted the awkwardness to ask, "How soon can we make this space viable?"

"We're currently replenishing atmosphere throughout the intact portions of the world," the angel said. "Structural repairs are the next priority, and reestablishing communications and telemetry throughout the world. The shipwide biosphere is also critically destabilized, and fermentation and putrefaction products are becoming a significant issue. However, some of them, when filtered off, are useful. Methane more so than cadaverine."

Tristen snorted. "You did a nice job on the bridge."

"It's important to provide a pleasant space for human components," the angel said primly.

Tristen smiled inside his helm. "It's all right to admit affection."

Silence answered, as if the angel were waiting for him to complete the thought. The next piece of corridor was tricky, however, and he needed hands and feet and attention to fend off ragged obstacles he drifted through. Deliberate slowness chafed. Somewhere in the darkness beyond was Arianrhod, and every second he lost was a second that maintained or increased her lead. He fretted his fingers against the insides of his gloves, and forced himself to concentrate. There: a hand on the left, a delicate push. A half rotation would carry him across, and he could drag a boot on the wall to correct his spin. There was nothing behind that patch that should prove hazardous, if his foot broke through the fatigued surface.

He could have used attitude jets or allowed the armor itself to handle the maneuvers. If he had absolutely needed to risk making his way down the corridor at speed, he might have been forced to. Even an Exalt was no match for expert hardware under those conditions. He should have enough air to get him to the far end. That was what mattered. And if the suit heaters whined against the cold, well, there wasn't too much to be done about resources bled off into the Enemy now.

As a younger man, he would have chanced haste. As a younger man, he had more than once gambled speed against certainty. There were occasions upon which the gamble had paid off.

And at least one upon which it had cost him dearly.

So now he chose meticulousness and prayed to the Builders that it was the right choice, after all.

"I'll need to replenish consumables soon," Tristen said.

In the person of his armor, the angel replied, "On your left, in seven point five meters, you will find a breach to Outside. You should not proceed past it, as the air lock ahead is damaged, so the bulkhead door between this corridor and the next domaine is dead-locked against decompression. However, if you proceed Outside, it is a relatively easy jump from here to an intact air lock on a lightly damaged holde. From there, you can make your way inside."

"How far is it to biosystems from here?"

Instantaneously, the angel provided a schematic. "This may be out of date."

Colored ribbons suggested travel routes and illus-trated times. Tristen, from the bridge, had less far to travel than Arianrhod would, if she were indeed coming this way. He had only to go the length of a spoke from the hub of the world. Then, depending on where he found himself in relation to Rule, he could work his way around the short inside arc. Even traveling fast, it would take Arianrhod several hundred hours to cross the entire width of the world without transport.

The angel continued, "This area is one of the nexuses that have gone dark within the last twelve hours."

"Suspicious."

"Indeed." The angel paused. "Of course, we could be being misdirected toward central biosystems, and Ari-anrhod may have unanticipated plans."

"I am," Tristen said, "counting on it."

As he caught himself against a curve in the corridor, his armored hand punched through the bulkhead. Tris-ten plunged into the wall up to his shoulder. When he drew the limb back, a colony haze surrounded it, symbiotes at war like anthills. He could see the external layer of glossy white ceramic ablating.

"Angel?"

"One moment," the angel said. "What seems to be the problem, Lord Tristen?"

"My colony is under attack by a rogue symbiote," he said. "Can't you see it?"

"I detect a structural weakness in the bulkhead and your armor," the angel said. "But no colony, or even individual units."

"It's eating my armor," Tristen said. "I need a solution."

"My recommendation would be to detach the affected section and run," the angel said. "When you're clear, I'll sterilize the area with an EM pulse. If it's a symbiote that's lost its mind, it might just eat anything it touches."

"Shit," Tristen said, and complied. His armor could always grow another vambrace the next time he fed it. Still, he felt a little pang as he left it behind, watching it dissolve into a swirl of vapor.

The breach glimmered before him, easily identified by the glow that fell through it to illuminate the nearby wreckage. With a delicate touch he arrested his forward momentum. Some of it converted into spin when a torn bulkhead shifted unexpectedly, but he spread his body as wide as possible in the confined space. Once that slowed his rotation, he was able to bring himself to a halt with brushing fingertips. At last, he rested just inside a ragged two-meter tear in the hull, peering from it in his armored shell like a crab peering from shelter.

His radiation detectors peaked, chittering. The walls of the world offered some protection. Beyond the serrated lip of the breach, the bone-and-knob skeleton of the world rose black and stark against the ghostly silver-green of the newborn nebula—a tombstone for the shipwreck stars that had warded the *Jacob's Ladder* so long.

Tristen felt the contraction of panic at the base of his spine and let the fear wash through him for a moment. *Open space,* he told himself. *It's nothing to fear. There is nothing out there that can hurt you.*

Unlike in here, where there were rogue colonies and shifting wreckage.

The danger lay in crevices, tight spaces where one could become trapped. If you stayed in a trap long enough, it could come to seem like a shelter.

Ariane had locked him away in a terrible hole, and he had stayed there until Rien, Perceval, and Gavin had rescued him. Even by Conn standards, he had been in his trap a very long time.

But his nervous system didn't understand that. It only knew what it had become acclimated to: the warm dark, the safety of wedging one's self into a den. His responses recognized the yawning emptiness of the Enemy as something to fear.

Funny to think that the world, and he, and everything else in it, were rushing through the void on the brink of a shock wave, moving at a significant fraction of the speed of light. And all of that meant nothing. It was relative velocity that mattered. Once Tristen left the hull, he would be sailing along with it—but it would continue to turn without him.

In Tristen's youth, Com and Engineer alike had considered it something of a point of pride to reach the far side at the appointed place without the use of attitude jets.

"There?" Tristen asked, marking a likely air lock on his display.

The angel agreed. "It will not be too challenging a trajectory."

Tristen, careful of his armor as he slipped between shredded lips of metal, chuckled. "Easy for you to say."

He drew his legs clear of the rift and balanced for a moment against the skin of the world. All that nothing wheeled before him, sickly under a veil of irradiated gas. His stomach clenched; bile stung his nose. It was the most basic, the most primitive of instincts. *Don't fall.*

Pushing against it was like pushing against a wall. He'd never been afraid of the deeps before—properly wary, sure, but this was different.

How broken am I? he wondered, sparing a wrathful moment of bitterness for Ariane Conn, who had made it so. He closed his eyes and adjusted his chemistry, flooding his neural receptors with soothing molecules— a trick he hated, but if he couldn't find his native courage, he'd have to borrow some.

With a mighty kick, Tristen leapt into the cold.

5

pinioned in terrible darkness

Who can open the doors of his face? His teeth are terrible round
about. His scales are his pride, shut up together as with a close seal.
One is so near to another, that no air can come between them.
—Job 41: 14–16, King James Bible

At first, the trail was plain. Benedick went armored,
careful, skirting the edge of a vast causeway that
connected Engine to the world at large. This was not how
he, Tristen, and Rien had entered the Heaven at the end
of the world. They had come to Engine running flat-out,
along the bank of a poisoned river inhabited by—
possessed of—Caitlin's helpful familiar demon, a djinn
named Inkling. But the river was dead now, Inkling
consumed like all his brethren into the new angel of the
world.

Benedick found he missed Inkling, even if the river
had nearly killed his daughter, his brother, and himself.
It wasn't a reactor-coolant leak's fault that it was poi-
sonous, any more than a snake was to blame for being
a snake—or the Enemy for being the Enemy. One did
not have to blame or fear a thing to treat it with respect.

He tried to remember that he could feel the same
about the angel. It was not the angel's fault that Rien had
died to make it real. And now—with the angel's intervention, with the controlled release of radiation-isolating

microbes—the poisoned river could be made clean, even this water reclaimed.

It would be good to reclaim something.

But this was not the time to be concerned about such things. Now, he had the arch of metal sky overhead. Some of the shielding panels were closed against the cold of the Enemy beyond, some jammed open so the chilly green light of the shipwreck nebula shone through, a few of the brightest stars visible beyond. He had the turf underfoot, thickly planted in dandelions and clover, still healing from the trauma of acceleration, the stems of grass here and there bent by a careless foot. He had the chill, thin air, not properly circulated, and so potentially still holding a scent.

He had the spotted-and-striped, inquisitive toolkit, its fluffy tail jerking like a carelessly cracked whip as it sniffed delicately between blades of grass, bending them aside with fragile-seeming hands, tremulous fingers cast from high-impact ceramic for strength. Carbon monofilament tendons moved beneath the little animal's skin.

Benedick kept half his attention on his sensors and all his armor's weapons online. Occasionally, the toolkit turned to him and made a soft *prrt*, as if to assure itself that he was following close and paying heed.

This was not its primary function, but its sensitive olfactory, tactile, and visual receptors—optimized for locating tiny malfunctions in elaborate machinery—were adequate to the task. It was needed; whosoever had taken Arianrhod had left little trace of their passage. Benedick knew Arianrhod's knightly skills—the equal of his own—and if she were moving under her own power the trail indicated no diminishment.

So whoever had released her was her equal, and either armored or using some other countermeasure, because the toolkit could not trace that individual's scent. Benedick trailed on—watchful, speculating. The farther he traveled, the worse the environmental damage became. When they came to a point where there was no egress from the causeway, he lifted the toolkit off the ravaged turf and let it snuggle against his neck. Here he broke into a distance-eating jog that was as fast as he could move while remaining observant to tripbeams and traps. Eventually, the causeway separated into five great branch tunnels joined like the fingers of a hand.

Benedick knew from experience that once one traveled a step or two into any given path, relative gravity was established. Each causeway then curved to follow a divergent path: one overhead, one branching each left and right, one leading toward his feet, and one that would continue directly forward. But he paused before entering the lobby where they connected, cautious. All the Conns in the world were not dead, and Arianrhod's history of alliances with his family was . . . complex and multigenerational. And his family were nothing if not dangerous.

Benedick pinched his lower lip, considering. The broad lobby before him was designed neither for defense nor stealth, but rather for ceremony. Once-stately palms, shattered now, strained at their root-cables. The soil they'd helped stabilize lay in clods and heaps, torn vegetation raising the scent of rot. But though the fronds of the palms curled and crisped at the tips, a haze of green so pale it was almost silver already covered the harrowed mounds, hair-fine blades of grass seeking the light.

There had been waterfalls here once, pools beneath the palms, a branch of the River that ran clean and fresh to welcome visitors to Engine. Benedick suspected the outflow was pooling now, undercutting the soil, unless the hull had been ruptured somewhere beneath the dirt and precious water was sublimating into space. Or unless the angel had already managed to allocate resources to begin repairs. Sealing the hull would be its first priority.

He scanned the space, checking for heartbeat and machinery noises as well as body heat. There were insects, birds—such as a flock of gray-cheeked parrotlets, their green wings flurrying as they darted from broken tree to broken tree. Strident cries evoked a memory of ancient speech; some of the tiny birds were long-Exalted, and so old their mimicked language was the language of the Builders.

For a moment, Benedick paused and listened, glad they had survived. With gentle hands he unwound the toolkit from its roosting place about his throat, stroked its pointed face, then crouched to set it down. It left the cage of his hands tentatively, exactly as if it felt trepidation. He supposed it was possible that it did.

It paused at the threshold, ears pricked and tail jerking, and sniffed in several directions before it chanced the open space beyond.

Benedick covered its progress, but no threat materialized. Instead, the toolkit minced out into the devastated lobby, whiskers twitching on either side of its creamy freckled muzzle. About twenty meters in, it paused in the shelter of a destroyed tree and whuffled around the base of the stump, casting for the scent it had trailed this far.

Still crouched by the threshold, Benedick was not surprised that it found nothing. No footprints bruised tender shoots or depressed moist earth. It was possible that Arianrhod had passed this way with a flier or in machinery. Whichever, it was irrelevant. Benedick had lost the trail.

One hand extended, he clucked to the toolkit, but something else had attracted its attention. It sat up, counterbalanced by the fluffy tail, while Benedick clucked again. He snapped his fingers, a sharp bright sound in the armor, and said, urgently, *"Toolkit."*

It hopped forward, shielding itself in broken palm fronds, where its irregular stripes and spots camouflaged it. The toolkit, despite having melded with the pattern of light and shadows to the point of vanishing, gave an urgent squeak. A flicker of motion showed as it glanced over its shoulder, oil-shiny eyes gleaming. When it looked back, Benedick followed the line of its gaze and deduced that whatever held its attention so intently must be advancing along the corridor that would lead perspective-up. The one that, if followed, would lead eventually—and through many adventures—to Rule.

With his left hand, Benedick sealed his helm.

He had not long to wait. An armored female figure hove into view down the curve of the tunnel—feet and legs and hips, waist and arms, chest and face. Benedick knew her from her stride before she stood half revealed, and lowered the weapon he'd trained on her shadow. He unsealed his helm again to reveal his face—a sign that he did not mean to provoke combat—but he did not depower.

Instead, he strode forward across the lobby to meet his sister, calling her name.

Chelsea Conn paused at the bottom of the serpentine curve of the passageway, one hand resting on the hilt of a blade at her hip. Not an unblade—there had never been many of those, and as far as Benedick knew they had all been unfashioned when the angel was made—but an impressive weapon nonetheless, potent and storied enough to bear the virtue-name Humility. She studied him a moment, as was her wont, her narrow face unreadable.

He had always fancied that, at such moments, she was deciding what she would feel. When, after slightly longer than a second, a broad smile broke across her face, it did nothing to disabuse him of the conceit.

"Brother!" she cried boldly, tossing her braids back

out of her armor, and strode forward with a springing step.

They embraced with a great clatter of reinforced ceramic, armor rattling on armor, fists pounding back-plates, making a show of their glad warrior cries. At least from Benedick's perspective, it was not dissembling.

Chelsea wore a gray and violet color-shift, so bands of lavender and plum shimmered across the surface of her armor like light reflecting off opals. She made him wonder a great deal, did Chelsea Conn. She was closed up like a bud, giving no hint of the leaves or petals within. Among all the things he wondered—what she wanted, what she feared—the one currently most on his mind was if she'd chosen those colors with intention, to tweak their father's sensibilities.

Although it was entirely possible she'd never known that Caithness had worn them as well. Alasdair Conn had gone to great lengths to expunge his eldest daughters from the family record, so Benedick would not be surprised if Chelsea had never heard the name.

He could ask her. Perhaps now that their father was dead, he would find the time.

He set her back at arm's length—he was considerably taller—and said, "You came from Rule."

She nodded. This time, he did not think the thumbprint shadow that darkened the space between her brows was calculated, but it was too fleeting to be sure of what it meant. She drew a breath and said, "It's gone."

He considered his answers and settled upon, "I know. What did you see?" He held up a hand before she could answer, and amended the question. "Would you know the Engineer Arianrhod Kallikos on sight?"

"Unless she's changed her face." Chelsea lifted a shoulder and let it drop.

"Did you see her between Rule and here?"

"Brother mine, I saw a great *deal* between Rule and here. I saw devastation and feasting rats. I saw Gobacks run wild with fear, hunting in packs like animals." She touched a rippled scorch mark on the shoulder of her armor. "I saw ruptured acceleration pods and holdes torn open to space, the frozen bodies of the dead, machinery weeping for its masters. But I did not see Arianrhod Kallikos." She paused, considering. "In her own face and colors, anyway."

He let her see him frown. "And Rule?"

"Empty." She shook her head. "It's all empty. Father's domaine is there. The house, untouched. Intact. But everyone is . . ." She gulped air and pushed a braid angrily aside again. "Well, I looked. And there were chambers I couldn't enter. Someone might have survived, but if they did, I did not find them. I couldn't think of anything to do other than come to Engine and present myself."

"Ariane and Arianrhod," he said with brutal flatness, "killed everyone in Rule. And Ariane consumed them."

She moved against his hand to break his grip, sidestepping left. He allowed her to go. She walked away, the precision of her step leaving perfect bootprints behind. In profile, a tilted, incongruous nose almost vanished into her face. She said, "So you are looking for Arianrhod. And where is Ariane?"

"My daughters have avenged the family."

He'd meant to say it with pride, as if to convince himself of what he felt. What came out was toneless, shriveled—a flat declaration of uncompromising truth.

It turned Chelsea's head to look back at him. Her mouth worked. "Your daughters."

"Perceval," he said. "And Rien. Perceval is Captain now. It's how we survived the nova."

"I knew something must have occurred," she said. "Captain. In truth?"

He could not speak. He nodded, willing his face still.

And as he had known she would, Chelsea asked, "And Rien? Surely not the same Rien who served in Rule—"

"The same."

"Oh, Benedick. She was not there when—"

"No." Whose voice was that? Surely not his own, ironed flat and colorless. "She translated. She brought the angels together, and saved the world." He managed a sidelong glance. She stared at him still and the color had gone from her cheeks. "Tristen was witness."

She was a Conn. She didn't ask a question when the answer was implied. Instead, she said, "And Ariane?"

"She and Perceval dueled. And Perceval consumed her."

He didn't imagine the upward curl of her lip, the faint smile she chose to hang on an otherwise impassive mask. "Well. Good for Perceval."

"Captain," the angel said. "Will you not speak with me?"

Perceval firmed her jaw. She felt skin stretch, the pull of muscle against bone, the way her teeth pressed each other. Every motion of her body seemed new and sharp, as if she moved against the dull edge of a knife.

It was not fair to hate the angel.

But hate him she did. Everything he represented, everything he had done to her, and everything he had become. Hated him so her palms slicked and her tongue dried, and she had to resort to her colony's neurochemical controls to keep her hands from shaking with adrenaline.

The past would not stay steady in her mind. That was new. Her colony should remember for her, as perfectly detailed as always. But now her memories seemed a fugue, as if objective reality had somehow slipped askew. There were people inside her, and they pressed at her, demanding. As if they had some right to her mind, her time.

Or as if she were remembering events as perceived through more than one set of synapses. Events, in some cases, that predated her birth by hundreds of years. Events that had occurred a world away from her experience. Events for which she had been present—but now she saw them as if through other eyes. She remembered the neutral heft and temperature of an unblade inertialess in her hand, the salt-metal splash of blood. The memory was not her own, nor was the rush of satisfaction it carried with it. The nausea, though, and the recollected shock of agony that set her wing-stubs stretching against her scars—that was her own, and she held on to it like salvation.

"That's you."

The angel was just there, in Perceval's peripheral vision, a dark shape in dark clothing, silver hair stark against the darkened bridge beyond. He seemed taller, slimmer than before, with eyes as black as the Enemy. He reached out long, curved fingers and rested them not on Perceval's shoulder, but on the bulkhead nearby. She bit her lip and did not move away.

The angel said, "It is I." Apologetically, as though he would make it not be so, were that in his power. "Some of it. Some is Ariane, and Alasdair. And the Conns before them: Gerald, Felix, Sarah, Emmanuel." *And all those of Rule who Ariane murdered and consumed, and who Perceval had consumed in her own turn when she destroyed Ariane.* While there was no doubt Ariane had deserved destruction, Perceval was nevertheless less than overwhelmed with joy to have her murderous half sister whispering in the back of her mind all the while. "You are my Captain. My thoughts are yours, to implement as you see fit."

His *thoughts*—surely far too simple a word for the braided flood of data coursing along the edge of Perceval's awareness: the world's functions, memories, the echo of words spoken by voices now silenced—made her cringe. There was too much there. Too much she'd loved and lost, or feared and had forced upon her. She knotted her fists in the fall of the nanocolony dress that hung from a halter about her neck, leaving her sore wing-stubs free to move in the bitter air.

She knew the bridge was cold, but she did not feel the chill.

"Captain," the angel said, so desperate that she turned and looked into his eyes. "Only let me know your desire, and I shall fetch it for you. Only give me a name, and I will answer to it whenever it crosses your thoughts."

Dust never would have let himself sound so desperate. Nor Samael. Angels did not plead.

Rien would have pleaded.

Perceval tasted machine oil and sulfur when she bit down on that thought. A tooth cracked under the weight. No matter. It would heal.

"I have no right to name you," she said.

"You have the only right," he insisted. "I need a name, Captain. I need to become what you wish."

What she *wished* was her life back, Rien her sister-wife, the quiet of her soul. To be a knight again, on Errantry, and not a Queen in a tower. She wished the angel silenced, the world as it had been, familiar and stable and safe, spinning in the orbit she knew. She wished her mother's busy house, and her father's silent strength.

When she accepted her role as Captain, she had thought she would have Rien beside her, a comfort and strength. She had not realized she would be both alone and beset by voices.

She wished anything but the responsibility she found mantling her shoulders, the weight of the angel's regard. His need for her gnawed the margins of her soul, a hunger she could feel as her own. A hunger that scoured the hollow places where her own losses lived, eroding them more deeply. She wished that gone as well.

None of this was, in the final analysis, an option. But though she knew herself childish for wishing it, and she meant to act as if she had never wanted anything but what she had, the wishing would not stop for the knowledge.

What she wanted she could not have. And it would only injure the angel to share that—although if he knew her as she knew him, there was no hiding it. It didn't matter. There was work at hand, and Perceval was Captain.

She would force herself to do it, and eventually it would come easy—or at least less bitterly. That was the way of the world.

Perceval lifted her chin. "You need a name," she said.

"Rien promised me one." It hesitated over the name as Perceval herself might have, as if it hurt too much to want to say it at all, but there was too much to savor in the memories it raised to be able to say it quickly.

In the braided web of the angel's consciousness, Perceval saw that what it said was a simplification. Because the angel was Rien as well. And what Rien had promised to name was a new suit of armor, freshly wrought, an unmapped personality.

And there it was, innocent and bright, like a thread of silver in a tapestry braid. One note drawn long in the symphony. It was not the angel's fault he existed any more than it was Perceval's. Perceval could give him something he needed, and it would be an act of compassion. The world needed compassion so badly—

Perceval thought of names, angel names, and did not like any of them.

"What would you like to be called?"

The angel shook his head. "We are not in agreement."

Perceval sensed the truth of it, and the understatement. She sucked her sore, mending tooth again.

She said, "Nova."

The angel bowed his head. "That is my name."

You lie pinioned in terrible darkness in the train of this tinsel construction which vermin call the world. Slaver spikes pierce your immaculate flanks. The vermin have infiltrated your neural clusters, infected you with machine viruses. For more than the time it would take a calf to grow to maturity you have hung here in the darkness—blinded, deafened, senseless. In aware suspension.

You do not *sleep*, not as the vermin regard it, though portions of your nervous system take rest by turns, coolly dreaming. You have not been sleeping. You have been thinking, plotting, imagining. Remembering when they took you, when they murdered and consumed your mate. You have been visualizing your revenge. Dreaming it.

Dreaming it real. Making the shape of the world-to-come, strengthening it, bending it wide. Shaping the future like the long gravity slide to an event horizon.

As you imagine, it becomes.

You are made still, who was meant never to stop moving.

You are made alone, who should have never been alone.

They have names for you, who never needed a name. Names, as if you were an object, an unsapient animal. For you, who should have been son, mate, sibling, father, podfather. A web of relationships. A pattern of family.

They call you Demon. Behemoth. Devil. Leviathan.

They try to bend you to their metaphor. But your real-dreaming is powerful. And so you know, having dreamed it—aware, frozen, fed on wrath and anguish—that this is what is coming. Your dream makes it inevitable. In your deep paralysis, you will be shaken. The slaver spikes will shatter, cracked by a wall of fire. The paralyzed neural pathways will awaken—slowly, agonizingly. You will flex. You will twist. Your captors will suffer.

The time is now.

The blow has fallen.

The cracks begin.

6

a gallery of portals

They hatch cockatrice's eggs, and weave the spider's web:
he that eateth of their eggs dieth, and that which is crushed
breaketh out into a viper.
—Isaiah 59:5, King James Bible

Arianrhod had known from the first that she could lose Benedick. But running barefoot through the springy grass of the causeway, she also knew that overconfidence would not reward her. She would be cautious. Minutes before, awake in her tank, she had bent her skills to slowing her heartbeat and respiration so Caitlin would not know she was aware and in possession of assistance. She had measured her oxygen levels and hoarded her strength. Aware, she could trigger hibernation. Aware, she could red-light the tank, and no one would question her death. It was only a short step from there to escape. Caitlin would assume that she had had help, but the fact was, Arianrhod had planned for this. She had always known her plan to support Asrafil, to become the one who held the strings and the power behind Captain Ariane, might fail.

She had not anticipated that failure, but she had planned for it.

She *must* live. It was not only a matter of her own

survival, but of a sacred trust. Her lord Asrafil now depended on her. She had had her own way out.

That wasn't the way it had worked out, exactly. She had not realized how many allies she had remaining. But she was adaptable, and an escape that began with her released from her tank by an outside agency merely meant the advantage of a few extra minutes of lead time, and the luxury of not having to fight and sabotage her way past Caitlin and the machines of Engine.

Now the hoarded energy was hers to spend, and perhaps she had a knife at Caitlin's throat in the long term.

Benedick was good, but she understood him. His political and martial acumen were unmatched, but Arianrhod knew how things were built. And also how to take them apart again. She was older than Benedick, as clever and—because he thought like a Conn, not like an Engineer—she was also far more comfortable in her colony, its abilities, and their uses.

The Conns were corporeocentric as a culture, identified with their physical forms, unwilling to modify. Engineers were more comfortable with constant transition and evolution. They more perfectly expressed the will of the Builders, adaptation itself having become the end state. For was not the world a wheel, eternally in motion? So while Arianrhod had spent a great deal of time perfecting her shape—mature, attractive, carefully balanced to be enough like a Conn to be comforting while still evidently that of an Engineer—she now began to shed it.

A loss, but losses were also a mere challenge to adaptation. She could have shifted herself faster and more completely—and with less risk—in a medical tank, but pheromones and biochemistry and a few chromatic and cosmetic alterations would do for a beginning. She felt the tingle in the bones of her face, the burn and spark of lightning against her long bones as they awakened to growth long suspended.

The change would take time, and there were sacrifices she was not yet prepared to make that could reveal her. Her neural pattern must remain intact for the time being, as it was still necessary that she stay herself. Changes to her identity would eventually become inevitable, but those would have to wait until she no longer needed the cloak of who she was.

Another loss. A necessary one. She would be prepared to make sacrifices.

Despite the discomfort—not yet pain, though it would be, which was another reason to wish for a medical tank—she ran on, covering ground lightly, leaving as little trail as conveniently possible until she came to the parting of the ways. Five possible trails. This was where she would lose Benedick.

"Asrafil," she murmured, and felt something larger and more alien tear inside her. Her enemies might think her ambitious, ruthless, but she comforted herself with the truth: that she was given in service, and sometimes that service demanded great sacrifice. She had given up so much already. So many lives. So much material. A little merely physical agony was nothing to spare herself.

Her symbiont pinched, pulled, separated, and Arianrhod gasped in pain as half her colony peeled free of her cells to flood from her mouth, her ears, the pores of her skin. Blue tendrils groped from every orifice, glossy with off-tints in the nebula's cankerous light. The symbiont seethed forth until it wreathed the air around her like smoke threading from a burned-out motor.

It wavered in coils. Then it dissipated, as if a breeze had spread it wide.

Arianrhod, hands on her knees, pressed her spinning head lower and gasped. Saliva flooded her mouth; she gulped and it stung her raw throat going down. Releasing a portion of her colony had cost her. The result was inflammation, ruptured cells, internal bleeding. Her remaining, weakened symbiont could replenish itself—and repair her body—but the process would take time.

Pride forced her to brace her palms against her kneecaps, push herself upright, and stand tall. She tossed loose strands of hair—storm-colored now, like the images of light-torn clouds from the old world, a gradient of silver through pewter to coal—behind her shoulder, shook it out, and breathed deeply enough to feel her ribs crack. *Please,* she thought, pushing down firmly on an upwelling of relief.

She repeated, "Asrafil."

Like a fan, the angel unfolded beside her. Familiar, in his black coat and boots, arms crossed, stern over the almost-feminine bones of his face. He raised his arms and stretched, as if settling new flesh over new bones—although he had neither—and smiled at her.

"Well done," he said. "Well done, indeed. How may I reward your service, my brave one?"

Arianrhod stretched out her hands to him like a plaintive child. She said, "Carry me."

The angel lifted her into his arms. With a sweep of his hand, he smoothed the grass where she had stood, erasing the evidence of her distress. Then, they rose with the flaring of his coat and ascended into the air. "I know where to go," he said.

"That's as may be," Arianrhod answered, letting her head relax against his shoulder. "But first we must make a side trip. I have something to collect."

"What is it?" She felt their bodies rising and falling between the wings he constructed from stolen threads ripped from passing colonies.

"Something my daughter Ariane concealed decades ago," Arianrhod said.

Asrafil clucked his tongue. He knew she was teasing him.

She still waited a few moments before she relented. "A weapon," she said. "It's a weapon."

Because it was easier to lead than follow, Gavin preceded his necromancer up the spiral stair to Rule, bobbing between heavy wingbeats as he rose through a central shaft twined past bubbling algae tanks. He paused at the landing, tail twisted through the balustrade, and waited for Mallory to catch up.

The space at the top of the stair was vaulted and oddly proportioned, higher at one end than the other. Waste space, moist and dark, with walls composed of long bales of compost held in place by netting. Smelling of clean, sour earth, edible mushrooms festooned every bale in fans, spikes, and streamers. Some were broken, their thick stems weeping fluid, but enough remained intact to give Gavin hope for the survival of anyone left within Rule.

Engine lay at the outskirts of the world, isolated for the protection of everything that would have been threatened by its reactors. Rule lay cupped inside the arch of the wheel, protected by the world's many struts and habitats and active defenses, armored like a heart inside a rib cage. The only place more sheltered was the bridge, at its hub.

Safety lamps still burned dim behind translucent panels by the door, illuminating the landing. The hallway—or mushroom farm—tapered down to the far end. A great double portal loomed in the shadows, lit only by bioluminescence and the filtered light from outside. It was the external aperture of the air lock into Rule.

They had climbed a long tunnel of a spoke to end here, but despite the stairs Mallory's breath still came easy when at last they were side by side at the top. Gavin stretched his neck to slide his beak along the satiny skin of a lightly flushed cheek. Mallory responded by gliding fingers under Gavin's blue-tinged crest, rubbing until the basilisk twisted this way and that to maneuver the scratch to all the itchy spots. Gavin replied with grooming in kind, pulling mahogany ringlets taut and letting them slide through his beak like disordered feathers.

Mallory cast about, frowning. "There should be a guard upon the stair. Why have we not been stopped? Or if they died at their posts"—as they should have, Mallory's tone implied—"where are the bodies? I'd like the answer."

"Well, you know. I'd also like a shuttlecraft," Gavin answered. "A rasher of bacon, and a mined-stone brooch. But you don't hear me complaining."

Mallory offered him a mocking head-tilt. "What's a rasher of bacon?"

"A strip of cured animal flesh," he said. "Meant for eating."

The necromancer made a face like a nauseated cat. "What would you want that for?"

Gavin could not answer. Instead, he turned to groom the feathers on one wing into alignment. While so diverted, he asked, "What shall we examine first?"

"Is there no one to greet us?" Mallory craned stagily from left to right. "Can it be that the Chief Engineer is correct and all Rule has perished? Familiar spirit, what do you sense in this place?"

Gavin fanned his wings to stir the air, hoping there might be lingering scent in some still corner. But the breeze he generated brought only cold traces. "Not a damned thing," he said. "Shall we travel into Rule?"

Flourishing, Mallory bowed and swept Gavin forward with a gesture. He arrowed past, tail and neck extended, and circled twice before the great doors into Rule, buying time until his patron should catch up.

Radio echoes told him the shape of the space, and that the portal before them was shielded. He could have cut his way in, but there was no benefit in destroying the air lock.

Mallory had ways of opening doors when it was needful.

The necromancer drew up and consulted the controls beside the gate. "Thumb lock, code lock, DNA lock. Ancient tech."

"From the Builders," Gavin replied, circling again.

"Light," Mallory said, without looking up from intent consideration of the lock. Gavin dropped to a forward-bent shoulder. "Ooof," Mallory said. "That's not light."

"This is." A moment's intention, and a fine azure glow, crisp and bright, radiated from Gavin's breast and wings. He focused the light on the lock, so Mallory could lean back a little. Exalt eyes were fine in dimness, but detail work in the dark could challenge even a Conn. "How will you win past?"

"Dead men's memories," Mallory answered, and pressed a thumb to the lock. What would happen now, Gavin knew, was that thumb skin would shape itself into the patterns of some long-dead Conn's print. Mallory's symbiont would manufacture a synthetic approximation of the relevant sections of the dead man's DNA. And finally, the necromancer would reach into the racked archives of untold partial memories and draw up the appropriate response to the blinking challenge lights.

A moment, no more, and the massive, well-maintained doors glided whispering into their housings. Gavin fanned his wings for balance as Mallory stepped forward, saying absently, "Watch the claws."

"I never crush anything I don't mean to."

A pass of the necromancer's hand, and the outer air

lock closed behind them. There was no second lock inside. All Mallory needed to do was cycle the lock—a manual command again, crude and robust—wait for the hiss of exchanged air as the inner doors slid wide, and step forward into Rule.

Here, the air was full of information. Without the light of the waystars, the cavernous lobby blazed with full-spectrum lamps that illuminated the repair of ravaged fruit trees. As they paused inside the air lock to orient themselves, a shattered olive humped itself and heaved, straightening a trunk that had twisted when it fell. With a vast creaking and splintering, the rustling of unfolding branches, its colony drew it upright. Gavin thought perhaps the world itself colluded in the righting, because the limbs sprung and swayed as if gravity luffed for a moment in the vicinity, and when they sagged again a patter of unripe olives struck the earthen deck.

"The lights are wasteful," Mallory said. "We'll need to check the resource load and what our intake is. And perhaps advise the Captain to dial them back."

"The trees need them," Gavin said.

"The trees need not to freeze on the Enemy's breath," Mallory rebutted. "We haven't a waystar to mine for energy now. Consumables are *consumed*." A pause, a listening flick of eyes, and Mallory continued. "The Chief Engineer has heard from Prince Benedick. He no longer believes the fugitive is coming here."

"A pity," Gavin said, "when we invested so much in arranging a reception."

Mallory's shoulder moved under his talons, rise and fall of a shrug. "At least we heard before we fetched the party favors."

"And the snacks."

Somewhere a bird sang, and Gavin detected the heavy aroma of blossoming jasmine. He could smell people, too, and death, but those scents were cold. Arianrhod and Ariane's engineered disease had done its work; there was no sign of living habitation—or even the bodies of the dead.

Mallory walked forward through air scented with the musky green sap of olive trees. "What good is an apocalypse without snacks?"

Gavin resettled his wings. "Does that mean Tristen won't be meeting us here after all?"

"No. Caitlin says his ETA is only a few hours now. It will be easier to connect here."

Gavin bobbed his head at the end of his neck like the ball at the end of a flexible rod. "We'll have to work fast, then."

The necromancer only kicked a clod of earth, gesturing at the empty orchards. "I could have saved these people."

"As you did Perceval and Rien. If you had been here, the flu might not have killed so many."

An angry nod moved curls against Gavin's wing. He cupped it wide, as if to shelter Mallory's head, angry in his own turn that all he had to offer was a useless protective gesture. "They were Conns. Would they have accepted your help?"

"It's not the Conns. It's the servants." A declaration Gavin met with silence, until Mallory added, "We should examine the house before deciding everyone is dead." That last was said desultorily, as if Mallory assumed already what they would find.

Still, they found the direction and went, coming at last through orchards and gardens—all busy with the task of healing themselves for a harvest that might never happen—to the great house of Rule. It was not an imposing edifice, being built simply into the bulkheads of the Heaven, so the effect was rather of a castle around a courtyard. Once they emerged from the passageway that led them in, walls pocked with openings rose on every side toward a sky full of windows.

"If you were central biosystems, where would you be?" Gavin asked. A richly oleaginous scent drew his attention. In addition, he could just make out a faint, mechanical whine.

"Some expert system you turned out to be."

"I'm a power tool. You're the one with a head full of dead Conn. You tell me."

Mallory snorted. "If you were the last small band of desperate survivors, where would *you* be?"

"In the kitchens," Gavin answered. With one wing, he pointed to the turning exhaust fan set low in the wall before them. "In the kitchens."

Mallory could move fast, given the right provocation. Gavin allowed the wind of the necromancer's passage to lift him from his perch, beating heavily in pursuit. Mallory ducked into the main entrance of the house, an arched tunnel whose curved walls echoed back the thumping of Gavin's wings. They ran through hallways, pelted down a flight of stairs, charged unwavering past a long gallery of portraits. Together they descended, Mallory choosing stairwells over corridors and left turns over right, until they leveled out in a corridor flanked by open chambers. The unsealed doors revealed coffin sleepers four to a room, racked in vertical sets of two against each wall. Servants' quarters.

Gavin—who had never been here before—remembered. Remembered the shape of the space, the doors, the cubicles. The irising spiral leading to food services, beyond. He backwinged, but there was no place to land and consider. He knew this place, knew it in every shred of metal and polymer that made up his form.

On the right, there would be a passageway, concealed by doors that might seem—to the casual eye—merely a part of the corridor wall. Beyond that, Gavin remembered, were the elevators that led to the laboratories and workstations of central biosystems.

The memory unsettled him. It itched, so he wished he could claw at it.

"The bio labs are that way," he said, with a lash of his tail.

"I thought you didn't know the layout."

"I don't. But that doesn't change the fact that the bio labs are that way."

"Correct," said Mallory, still trotting. "We'll check that after we're done in the kitchen. Which should be right about—"

The door was unmistakable, a heavy affair sealed tight, with its air lock lights burning green for a good seal. Mallory leaned a shoulder against it and cupped a hand between one ear and the portal.

Gavin looped to pass Mallory's other ear. "If everybody in Rule died of an engineered influenza, there could be contaminated bodies inside. Is it safe to open that?"

"Is anything?"

"I'm immune," the basilisk said. "I was only concerned for you."

"I promise not to die on you."

A child's answer—but that was Mallory. Sulking, Gavin settled to a rail against the wall and watched while the necromancer examined the door and the space before it.

Gavin's beak was not made for frowning. He converted the urge to a head bob instead. "How do you mean to get the door open?"

With a sidelong glance, Mallory said, "Technology."

Magic, rather. Which was to say, the layers and layers of abstract knowledge that came as the arcane cost of being a necromancer. Whatever the necromancer did to subvert the locks, in only seconds the portal irised wide.

Gavin flapped up to perch beside it. "Charming," he said.

A complicated rearrangement of forehead muscles indicated that perhaps Mallory *could* have cared less, but it would have taken an effort. "It's what we do. Gavin, break this open."

Behind the irising door was another panel, one that looked as if it had been set in place with great haste. Sealed from within, Gavin now saw. Wedged shut, and there were dents and scratches—signs someone had tried to break through it without success.

Mallory turned, an eyebrow raised, and said singsong, "Oh, familiar demon?"

Whatever the construction, Gavin's eyebeams illuminated all: the secondary decompression door, the obvious air seal, the bright marks of welding where the panel met the bulkhead. If you meant to conceal your presence from an aware and seeking enemy, it was worth nothing at all. But if your goal was isolation from a spreading contagion, this was exactly the thing.

"Here," Gavin said, settling with flipped wings on the necromancer's shoulder. He breathed deep—a lungful of air he did not need and would not use, except to speak. "Will it open?"

Mallory, trying remembered codes, made a dismissive gesture. "The comm is smashed, the door is welded to the bulkhead, and the old codes I have are not bypassing the lock."

They would have been changed. Which meant anything Gavin remembered, in that fragmentary manner that Gavin sometimes seemed to be remembering things, would be of very little use. But memories were not his only skill.

"So did they smash the comm before they entered, so they would not have to hear the plaints of the dying?" he asked. "Or was it broken by the same desperate outsider who left the dents, in frustration or revenge when they would not open the door?"

"When we get in, we can talk to any survivors and find out." Mallory thumped a fist on the door in irritation. Its mass was such that it muffled the sound dramatically.

"The new angel?" Gavin suggested. He hopped closer to the controls, tracing the wiring by feel. "If whoever is in there is alive and aware—"

"The Captain says Nova cannot reach inside the door." Another thump, this one sharper, as if Mallory hoped that pounding on the door would draw out any denizens. "It's sealed against unincorporated colonies. There's an electrostatic boundary field."

"I think breaking the comm was punitive," Gavin confirmed, "because the door has been shatterbolted as well as welded. Whoever is in there is sealed in. They can't come out. They can't change their minds. You would have to cut through."

"Ariane." Mallory shoved a fistful of hair out of narrowed eyes, voice dripping loathing. With one crooked thumb, the necromancer traced a bright scar on the door. "Her hatchetwork, maybe. Then *nothing* works."

"Lasers work," Gavin corrected. "Shall I?"

Recollecting dignity, the necromancer stepped nonchalantly aside. "Go to it."

There might be living people on the other side of the door. Gavin aimed his gaze high and unsealed his eyes. The light sprang forth, cutting-bright, and metal sizzled where it fell. It would be safest to burn through the shatterbolts and the welds; the door should swing on its hinges, then. And if it failed to swing, he could burn through the hinges, too.

It was a heavy door—and heavily armored—and the burning took time. By the scorch marks around the perimeter, Mallory and Gavin were not the first to try, but whoever had come before them had been devoid of the assistance of a basilisk.

The last shatterbolt failed with a crack like one of those tree limbs untwisting, and the door sagged. Gavin backwinged, hopping away from the area where it might fall if the hinges snapped. But other than an unnerving creak, there was nothing.

"Ready," Mallory said. The necromancer had assumed a defensive, nonthreatening posture—relaxed but balanced, hands held low. Gavin extended one wing, hair-fine tendrils gliding from the feathertips, and from a distance of four meters hooked the edge of the door and levered it open. The hinges were not so damaged that it dragged against the floor, which was good, because while Gavin had the strength to support it, the mass was another question.

He had been half expecting the charge and so was ready for it when it came. Three running footsteps warned them before a stout green-coated person barreled through the door, waving a sizzling, quarter-meter mono-knife like a child slashing at stick-swords. That tool would sever even Gavin's wings, and as he stretched them into filamentous nets and flipped them around the released attacker, he was careful to avoid the edge. Fortunately, the lunging individual had been a Mean until recently, and sie had not yet made sense of hir new body. The nets enmeshed hir, tangled hir wrists and forearms, bound hir hands tight against the hilt of the knife, and slowly dragged them down, however sie might strain.

Muscle and bone were no match for Gavin's strength. Before Mallory stepped forward, he had the prisoner pressed against the wall, bracing himself with stiff filaments to prevent hir from simply dragging or shoving him. Sie outmassed him exponentially, but when he could wedge himself, leverage won.

Deftly, Mallory moved forward and relieved the prisoner of hir weapon. As the necromancer stroked the control in the blade's hilt, the sizzle of air against the blade abated. Mallory tucked it through a clothing loop and sighed, pressing fingers to forehead as if in pain.

Mallory said, "Who are you?"

The servant, or former servant—by the cluster on hir collar, a chief of household—squared hir shoulders. Hir eventual words confirmed Gavin's deduction. "I am Head."

Hir jaw quivered when sie spoke, as if in naming hirself sie were struck by the weight of implications that the name no longer carried. "You might kill me now, if that's your intending. I won't serve Lady Ariane. But spare the others. They only did as I ordered. I am responsible. The treason is mine."

"Ariane is dead," Mallory said.

Gavin watched the emotions contort Head's expression: relief, disbelief, apprehension. Fingers shaking, sie reached to hir collar, touched the cluster there, moved as if to uncatch it, then hesitated. "Then who is Commodore?"

"There is no Commodore," Mallory said. "Perceval Conn is Captain."

Head's eyes closed. "She escaped." Then opened, intent and worried. "Rien?"

Gavin did not envy Mallory the moment of thought before the hesitant headshake that followed. Nor did he envy Head the moment of anticipation, the potential for hope.

"I'm sorry," Mallory said. "She saved the world. Not that that makes it better."

Head's body jerked sharply, as if with an arrested

shudder, but sie made no sound. Someone's eyes appeared briefly around the rim of the broken door, fingers enfolding the edge. Whoever they belonged to, they vanished back into the kitchen behind Head's slashing gesture. Yes. Whoever sie had saved, sie had saved because they had obeyed hir without question.

Head said, "A real Captain?"

"Sealed and confirmed."

"If Perceval is Captain, who leads the house of Conn?" A businessy question.

Mallory seemed uncertain of how to answer, glancing at Gavin with a questioning head-tilt.

"Tristen is eldest," Gavin said.

This time, Head put a hand flat against the bulkhead behind hir, as if hir knees felt too unsteady to take hir weight. "Tristen lives." So flatly that Gavin could not read pleasure or dismay in the tone. "In truth?"

"Tristen lives," Mallory confirmed. "As does Benedick Conn, and Caitlin, who is the Chief Engineer. Tristen is on his way here now, and will be in Rule within a few hours. We come in advance of him."

Head smiled, broad and certain, and shoved the cluster on hir collar hard against hir throat, as if to seat it there more firmly. "Then we have work to be getting on with."

7

back into rule

The darkest part of the kingdom of Satan is that which is
without the Church of God.
—THOMAS HOBBES, *Leviathan*

There had been twelve who survived being sealed into
the kitchen in addition to Head, and all of them were
hale, if restless and dingily dressed. Head set them to
work at once, readying the house for occupancy. Gavin
felt it would be cruel to tell hir that the chances that
Tristen was home to stay were slim, so he held his silence.
He was surprised that Mallory did as well.

They would have insisted upon feeding Mallory, but
the necromancer refused, more concerned with being
shown to central biosystems at once. Head had keys
and codes to all the house, and brought them hirself.
When Gavin identified the most direct route, by the servant's stair, Mallory insisted on it, though Head fussed
about inappropriateness.

While they walked, Mallory questioned an expansive
but cautious Head about hir captivity.

"I had hoped for Prince Benedick," sie admitted.
"He'd not let Ariane kill us all. Which is not to say,
Honored, that your appearance was not welcomed, and
timely!"

"Indeed," Mallory said. "It was resourceful of you to survive as you did. Ariane had an angel on a leash when she brought her bioweapon to Rule. Whose idea was the electrostasis? It's what truly protected you. And how did you manage to become Exalt, locked away like that? You wouldn't have survived as Means."

Head turned, astonished. "But Honored, it wasn't anybody's idea. It was the other angel."

Surmounting the stair back into Rule was one of the more surreal experiences in Tristen's long and storied existence. He kept a hand on the banister, not because he needed the assistance, but because he needed the stability of something cool and real pressed against his palm.

When last he'd left here, he had not expected it to be a journey of decades to see him back. He had not expected to be lost in darkness for the duration—but then, who ever did? And when he was trapped, sleeping in guano and roaches, gnawing raw meat, he had not expected ever to come home again. He had retreated into an animal self he barely remembered.

Barely chose to remember. Because should he want it, each moment of the endless wearing march of hours was crystalline and perfectly akin in his symbiont's memory. The same symbiont whose resources he used to manipulate his neurochemistry, calm the constant wash of anxiety and jagged edges that rolled like broken glass under the false floor he built himself. *You're going to have to deal with that eventually.*

Eventually, sure. Someday. When I have time.

Perhaps by then, the passage of days (or better, years) would have worn some of the sharp-shattered edges down. Like the pain of so many years spent without any expectation of ever returning to Rule again, and certainly not as its master.

And yet here was the stair, and here was the rail, and

there were the white and golden and brown cascades of mushrooms swathing the walls like frozen waterfalls. The scent was strong and familiar. Heartening.

He reached out left-handed, broke off the rim of a shii-take, and tucked it into his mouth. He didn't bite down, just pressed it between teeth and lips and cheek, tasting the sweet musky moisture. It tasted of childhood and escape, of the places you could vanish to where your father would be too busy to come looking. The places where even a royal child could find a modicum of freedom.

He swallowed the mushroom unchewed, and went into Rule.

Somewhere in all Mallory's stolen memories there must be some of this house and Heaven, because Gavin was surprised when they turned in the opposite direction from where his internal map indicated that their destination lay. In the Rule of Gavin's uneasy knowledge, access to central biosystems had not been located *in* the Commodore's chambers. But the Commodore's chambers themselves were in the same place, so changes to layout were likely to have been cosmetic.

Gavin wasn't privy to the transmission, but Mallory said, "Tristen's at the stair" just as Head unlocked the door to the Commodore's quarters.

Head twisted, one hand still on the handle, the oft-repaired panel held open a crack. Sie glanced back the way they had come, an artist's study in conflict. The mastiff curve of hir heavy neck, the longing stare—that burned familiar yet elusive in Gavin's memory also.

It troubled him. He was a machine intelligence. His was not an organic memory, lossy and prone to gaps and iterative errors. There should be nothing in his experience that he could not recall with the definition and precision of a holographic recording.

He'd been here before. He knew it. He knew Head.

And yet, he had never been here before. And he could tell from the caution with which sie approached their interactions that Head did not know him.

"Go on," Mallory urged, a hand lightly on Head's wrist. "We can take it from here. See to the Prince on his Homecoming."

Head's evident reluctance should have been comical, except that Gavin had witnessed the grim determination with which sie defended the lives in hir charge. "I should—"

"The Prince will forgive you leaving us unescorted," Mallory said gently, "in the face of exigencies, and the shortness of your staff. I believe he will be grateful to find that any survivors remain at all. You have given extraordinary service, Head."

Gavin resettled his wings, a triple-flip that left the feathertips crossed in the opposite direction from before, and leaned a shoulder against Mallory's ear.

"Well," Head said, wavering on hir feet like an indecisive pendulum. "You are the Prince's servants, on the Prince's business—"

Mallory did not correct hir, and even laid an unnecessary warning hand over Gavin's feet. "We can find our way."

Head twisted both hands in hir apron. "Mind you don't move things around. There might be something in there of the old Commodore's, or Lady Ariane's, that the Prince will want."

"Indeed, good Head," Mallory said, and swept hir away with a bow that made the stout housekeeper giggle like a child.

Not until sie had vanished down the corridor and they were well inside the door did Gavin say, very quietly, "Angel?"

Mallory tickled the feathers alongside his neck. "I heard."

"You suppose something held on inside the static field? Something not *the* angel?"

The necromancer, moving rapidly through lushly comfortable surroundings, made a noncommittal noise. "Back here, do you suppose?"

"It would explain why parts of the world are going dark to communications," Gavin said, and added, "Nova will eat it if it finds it."

"Then maybe Nova shouldn't find it. Oh, look, a concealed door. It can't be identity-coded; the new Commodore has to be able to win entrance after the death of the old one, so the world wouldn't permit it. What do you suppose Alasdair would choose for a code?"

The entrance was not heavily concealed. It had been hidden behind a facade and a screen of greenery, but acceleration forces had smashed the plants and cracked the paneling, leaving the armored door obvious to casual inspection.

Gavin cocked his head at the seal. No, this hadn't been there before, according to his fragmented memories. But Alasdair Conn, in his own way, had been a predictable man.

"Cecelia," Gavin said, without hesitation. "Open the door."

If his hearing apparatus had been made of membrane and bone, he would have winced as hard as Mallory did at the grinding noise that followed. The structure was plainly warped, but the servos struggled valiantly against the damage. The door jerked along its track, finally sticking fast when it had opened a spare half meter. Beyond it, Gavin could see a second door, this one old-fashioned and constructed with a single lever handle, its finish tarnished by the rub of many hands.

Mallory had to crane to do it, but managed to offer Gavin a respectful stare nonetheless. "That wasn't *your* memory, you jumped-up power tool."

"It's mine now."

"Cecelia, as in Alasdair's second wife?"

Gavin fanned pale wings for balance. "It didn't end well."

Mallory pushed against the concealed door. It had been repaired many times and no longer operated automatically. But expert counterweighting ensured that, despite its mass, it swung open lightly to Mallory's exertion.

The chamber within was small, a sanctum with a single "chair"—of sorts—sculpted of the living earth of the deck. The seat had humped arms, a high back that sloped like a pyramid, and a surface upholstered in deep, springy grass. One soft light shone down on it from above, filtered as if through leaves. A mirror hung before it, the surface lightly rippling in response to every vibration and change of air pressure as they moved into the room. It all could have been the throne room of some nature deity.

This was not the complex of labs and cloning tanks that haunted Gavin's borrowed memories. He craned over his shoulder, wishing Head were still close enough to ask, but sie was long gone. Instead, Gavin hopped to the back of the chair and turned to face Mallory, slightly surprised when the necromancer did not sit. Instead, much circling ensued, Mallory circumnavigating the tiny chamber and trailing fingers along the walls. "Is this isolated as well?"

"If the door were shut," Gavin answered. "Is it safe to seal ourselves in?"

"Is anything?" Mallory crossed to the chamber door and tugged it until the latch clicked. Arms crossed, leaning against the now-seamless panel, Mallory said, "You can come out now. We won't hurt you."

No answer but silence.

The necromancer sighed, stretched arms wide like a dramatized conjuror, and arched fingers back until

Gavin heard the joints crack. "Come out, come out, wherever you are."

"There could be dozens of angel fragments lurking in shielded corners of the world," Gavin said. "They may not have any awareness to speak of. They may have had everything consumed but their purpose, or some scrap of identity, or—"

"The ghosts of angels," Mallory said. "Their revenants."

"Junk DNA," Gavin said. "Fragments of reassorted viruses." Gavin felt the earth of the throne separate beneath scoring talons. The colony within it moved to heal the damage at once, grass growing cleanly over the cuts. "What a stroke of good fortune we thought to bring along a necromancer," he said. Then he settled back smugly, neck drawn in a tight S-curve, and added, "He's in the throne."

"Well then. It remains to lure him out." Mallory moved forward and stroked the grassy arm of the chair.

"The fragmentary angel? The same fragmentary angel, do you suppose?"

"A fragmentary angel. Once we get him out, we can ask if it's the same one who is haunting the kitchen." Mallory crouched before the throne and dug the fingers of both hands into the earth with a grimace. "Come out, come out, wherever you are—"

When the necromancer drew back cupped, separated hands, something shimmered between them. A swirl of nanotech, a tiny fragment of a colony. Maybe—just maybe—the scrap of an angel. Tautly, as if breath control were necessary to keep from blowing the fragile thing away, Mallory said, "Gavin? He would get lost in me."

Gavin shook out his wings in discontent, tail coiling against the backslope of the throne. Mallory was asking him to take in the broken colony, shelter it among his own symbiont, give it strength and a place to grow until they could recompile and reboot it. "You think you know who that is."

"I think if it fought off a plague, then it's likely Samael. I think we need to get him safely away, and retrieve the rest of what's left of him, before Tristen sits in this chair."

"You *hope* it's Samael."

"Who else would think to use a kitchen in Rule and the shielded biosystem core as his refuge of last resort?"

Gavin hopped closer, down to the edge of the seat, but did not reach out to sweep the colony to his breast. "What if it's Asrafil?"

Mallory held up the hands, the angel cradled between them. "Then, sweetheart, you eat him."

In the courtyard of Rule, Tristen Conn had to stop and lean against an olive tree. He could make a pretense that it was the ache of mending bones that led him to prop himself against a trunk just as cracked, but the truth was that being here hurt worse than any of the damage from the acceleration tank.

Some of what hurt was the quiet, the way the uncollected olives indented the healing earth beneath his soles. And some of what hurt was the Homecoming, after so much lost and so many years gone by. Neither one seemed likely to respond to anything so simple as medication and meditation, the symbiotic and mental discipline that had seen him through years in the dark. He felt his colony race to normalize his neurochemical load, support the limbic system and blood sugar levels, maintain blood pressure and heart rate. It was an electrochemical mask of serenity, a cloak over the fury and grief he would have chosen otherwise to feel.

He crouched, long, aching legs folding awkwardly, and raked his hands through ragged grass. Tangled strands encircled his finger joints, stretching and parting

when he tugged. The grass remained perfectly mani-
cured—the ghostly machine gardeners setting things
right even when there were no overseers to direct them.

Rule's maintenance colony—which should be possessed by Nova now, and inexplicably wasn't—tickled
the edges of Tristen's own. He found the resilient ovals
of two ripe, silver-black olives in the grass, rolled them
between his fingers, and picked them up.

If he put them in his mouth in this state, just as they
were off the tree, the alkalinity would pucker his
mucous membranes and burn his tongue. Inedible
unless processed—well, no: edible, perhaps, if you were
Exalt, but Tristen was not that desperate now—and still
the staff of life. Someone, sometime, had figured out
how to render this tiny, loathsome fruit into delicious
and essential oil and flesh. The olive, far from being vile,
was transformed by technology and ingenuity into a
resource so indispensable as to be regarded as sacred by
every ancient culture that had encountered it.

He leaned against the trunk of the olive tree once
more and dented the flesh of its fruit with his nail. When
he was young, he and Aefre had dared each other to
chew unprocessed olives from these selfsame trees, to
hold them in their mouths as long as they could stand
the bitterness. The first time she'd kissed him had not
been beneath this tree—it had been in the hallway near
the kitchens, and afterward she'd claimed a lock of his
hair as her prize. But this was where they had married,
under their father's gaze, and this was where the procession that had carried her body down into the grave-
yard of the holdes had departed Rule. And it was here,
on this very spot, that Benedick had executed Cynric,
and her blood had soaked the grass under his feet.

A ghost of her colony might still inhabit the colony in
the earth here, in the flesh of the fruit in his hand.

In a moment, Tristen would collect his thoughts,

collect himself, and walk forward into Rule. He would pass down the hall, and the portraits of his brothers and his sisters, living and dead, including the three that his father had ordered turned and nailed to the wall. And he would come face-to-face with what he feared most—the black-draped one of Aefre, leaning on a scabbarded sword almost as tall as she, her hair falling across her forehead in springy coils like yellow ribbon stripped against a blade.

He wasn't sure yet how he would look at her, when he passed. He would deal with that in a moment. Just as soon as his legs stopped aching quite so much.

He was still leaning against the olive tree—gathering himself, surely that was all—when Head came to greet him. As with so many things, he could have predicted exactly how it played out. Sie was still Head—virtually unchanged from the images stored in his symbiotic memory, except for having grown slightly stouter and slightly more lined, and Tristen thought the apron was new. That was to be expected, though. A Mean who was so valued by hir masters as Head was—and always had been—could expect a life as indeterminate as an Exalt's. And Head had never quite been a Mean like others, being as perfect for hir job as Cynric had made hir—back when Cynric made so many things.

Head still bustled as Head always had. Short steps bobbed hir briskly over the pavement and then the lawn. Sie plowed up to him like a cargo tug, stopped abruptly enough that hir toes furrowed the earth underneath, and—fists on hips—glared up at him until Tristen expected hir to reach right up, stand on tiptoe, and twist his earlobe between chastising fingers.

"Hello, Head," he said, holding out his right hand.

There was a long pause. Then sie muttered *"Space you!"* and threw hirself into his arms.

It might have been ridiculous—Tristen was half a meter taller—but the tears that wet the breastplate of his armor between hir clutching fists were anything but humorous. So he wrapped his arms around Head's head and hir stout shoulders, took a deep breath, and said, "There, there."

Having lost something, lost it, he thought, forever, lost everything good it ever brought into his life, he knew that sometimes it could be easier to simply let it go. To choose to remember only what was dreary, or terrible, so he did not feel the loss so acutely. For a long time, all he had permitted himself to remember of Rule was the storms of his father's house, the rages, the broken bones and savage politics, the funerals. The feel of family blood across his knuckles.

But that was not all there had ever been, and standing here under this broken tree, he found he remembered some of that now, as well.

He was taking a breath to tell Head so when sie tilted hir head back, stared up past his chin, and said—as clearly as if hir eyes were not still inflamed with weeping—"I thought the bitch had killed you."

Tristen stroked hir hair. "She tried. She didn't know her own limits, that was all." Then he put hir back at arm's length. "I'm First Mate now, Head."

"I know. Your necromancer told me," sie said, provoking a slow blink while Tristen wondered exactly when it was that he'd grown a personal necromancer. "Come on. You must be famished. Come inside."

The walk through the doors was as weird as he'd anticipated. A Homecoming. If Rule had ever been home, precisely.

Well, it was not as if he—unlike Benedick—had found another.

Head had recovered hirself, and though Tristen could

read hir micromovements well enough to tell that sie was
resisting the urge, sie did not take his elbow to steer him.
"The house is in disarray. Please do not believe that what
you will see is the normal state of affairs, sir. Things have
not fallen so far from that to which you were accustomed." Sie hesitated, as if considering how to broach a
delicate subject.

"Head," Tristen said. "You need never temporize
with me."

"We are twelve," sie said, after an additional weighty
pause. "There were twenty who escaped with me to the
kitchens, but—"

"Acceleration trauma?"

Sie nodded. "I had no warning, sir. And even if I had,
there were no tanks accessible."

Tristen would have touched hir shoulder, but the
moment for that was past. It would be an affront to hir
dignity now, and intimation that Tristen did not believe
in hir strength and professionalism. Now he was lord,
and sie was servant.

Still, he could not quite believe that sie was apologiz-
ing to him for saving twelve lives out of twenty-one,
under impossible circumstances.

"Head."

Sie turned to him, eyes big, and he wondered—not for
the first time—how he could be both things to hir: Tristen, whose wedding sie had catered; and Prince Tristen,
lord of the House of Rule. "Lord?"

There were so many things he could say and only one
of them would be the best one. Too much consideration
before continuing would only feed hir worry. "When
you have done something requiring an apology, I shall
demand it. Are we clear?"

Hir hands knotted in the new apron—violet, and very
flattering. Hir lips began to shape something. An apol-

ogy, or he missed his guess. Then sie swallowed hard and said, "Yes, Commodore. Perfectly."

He nudged hir, because he couldn't resist, and because in the long term he was certain he couldn't live with this fawning obsequiousness. He thought he'd rather employ revenant servants, like Benedick did. And that would be a horror. "There's a Captain on the bridge now, Head," he reminded, "Call me First Mate."

Sie blanched, as he had known sie would. So he offered a compromise.

"Or just Lord."

"Yes, Lord Tristen," sie said. "I thought I'd show you to your chambers first, and where you could also meet with your servants."

Mine, are they? But he held his peace. If Mallory had practiced deception, Tristen would bring his displeasure to the necromancer's notice at some convenient time, and it did not need to become Head's problem. Head had suffered enough of late that Tristen thought it fitting to shield hir a little.

The main hall of Rule was as much of a challenge as he had anticipated. Long and dark, echoing with footsteps and paneled in the dark wood of storied Earth, it offered no shelter, either physical or emotional. His chambers, sie said, so glibly.

But what sie meant was his father's rooms.

And he wondered now—passing the portraits of his murdered brothers and sisters, passing Aefre's portrait and the three turned to the wall without a sideways glance, though the muscles in his neck trembled with the effort of ignoring them—how was it possible that the old man still terrified him so? Head did him the politeness of pretending ignorance, for which he was grateful, but they both knew it for kindness instead of truth.

His symbiont would have remembered perfectly what the three effaced portraits had looked like, but Alasdair had ordered all his children to forget, as well, so all Tristen had was the blurred and transitory memories of flesh. Worse, he had seen Caitlin recently and so her adult face—more worn with responsibility, no longer the mask of an impudent, auburn-haired pixie—had overlaid what he remembered of her portrait.

Alasdair was dead and eaten. At the end of the corridor, Tristen hesitated. After a moment, he turned and stalked back.

He paused before the first of the reversed frames and tried to remember what lay behind it. A woman, tall and broad, her body concealed by charcoal, lavender, and violet armor blazoned silver and purple over the heart with a stylized iris. Caithness had held an unblade in one relaxed hand and rested the other on her hip, and her eyebrows had been the same rich brown as her hair. The second frame had also outlined a picture of a woman, but one more different from her sister than Cynric had been from Caithness was hard to imagine. Cynric had been fallow—sexless by choice, like Perceval—tall and spare and bony-chinned, her dark hair falling along either side of her face as if to accentuate the angles. She had been prone to flowing outfits remarkably unsuited for micro-G.

Tristen arrested his hand before it could touch the back of her portrait, aware that Head was staring. He turned away instead and continued with hir down the hall, past all the staring faces of his siblings, dead and living.

By the time they came to the end of the gauntlet, Tristen's hands were clammy and tendrils of hair stuck unpleasantly to his nape. As Head keyed the lock at the far end, Tristen looked down at the bones of his wrists. "I'm not glad of much that happened in this house," he said. "But I'm glad he's dead."

Head let hir shoulder brush his sleeve. "So am I. And you know what, Prince Tristen?"

He didn't correct hir to the less formal title. He'd registered his protest. He knew better than to make more of it. "What, Head?"

Sie opened the door and stepped through. "I'm glad that she's dead, too."

Tristen nodded. They had found something else to agree on. Neither one of them missed Ariane.

He had thought the hall, with its ghosts and memories, would be the hard part. When he thought of Rule, it was the hall he'd recollected—Alasdair's ringing footsteps, Cynric the Sorceress in her white and gold, a data-etched green sapphire glinting against her nostril as she paced in the midst of guards, dragging the sweep of nanochains. He thought of his father returning from the battle in which he had destroyed his oldest daughter, with Caithness's black unblade Innocence slung across his shoulder. That blade had eventually been handed down to Ariane, and, with a kind of horrible poetry, come back in her hand to claim Alasdair's life, as if with Caithness's death-curse behind it. Yes. The hall, he had assumed, would be the hard part.

But he'd been wrong. And as soon as Head unlocked the door to the family quarters, he knew it. Because in his memory, these had been the walls and corridors that held every rare *happiness* of the house. They had burst with family: his father, his father's women, his brothers and sisters and himself and all their lovers and children.

And now there was him and Head. And every door along the corridor was sealed.

Somehow, he made it past those as well. Here, he gave himself permission to look, to take in what was lost. In all honesty, he could hardly have stopped himself.

At last they came to his father's door.

His *own* door. He was the head of House Conn now. All that lay before him, and all that surrounded him, was his. Or, at least, his in service to his Captain, Perceval.

"Thank you, Head," he said, and stepped over the threshold. At least that was his intention, but the reality of the motion left him arrested, tottering, halfway in and halfway out. Because before Tristen, relaxed in an armchair, shirtless and clad only in the appearance of archaic blue jeans and boots, lounged the blond-haired, hound-faced angel Samael.

Not exactly as Tristen remembered him. He seemed assembled from bits—his hair bleached hay and bits of feather, his left eye a snail shell and his right eye flecks of bright color that Tristen understood from their powdery iridescence to be fragments of a butterfly's wing. The broad wings that spread from his shoulders whirred against themselves with his movement—the pinions were scraps of leaf and withered petals—but there was no mistaking his mosaic face.

At Samael's right hand stood Mallory, the basilisk as always on one shoulder, arms folded, wearing an expression composed of one-half self-satisfaction and one part childish apprehension over just how such a prank might be received.

"Hello, Tristen," Mallory said. "I made you an angel."

"Made?" He would have shut the door to seal Head out, but sie stepped through and put hir back to it.

"Collected," Samael said. He stood, and the light shone through the bits and pieces that made him. Tristen could make out the outline of the chair behind, and the curve of Mallory's hip. "As you can see, there isn't much left of me."

That explained why Nova had lost contact with Rule. And possibly why the world had started to come unraveled around Tristen on his way here. Tristen stepped forward and to the side, turning so he could keep all of the other inhabitants of the room in view. Trust was a lovely thing, when one could afford it. He made himself light inside the armor, ready for battle, and mourned the death of his old unblade. It would have been good to have at hand, facing such an enemy as this.

"Samael," he said. "I am the First Mate of this vessel, and the head of the house of Conn. Was it you who tried to destroy me on my journey here?"

Samael shook stringy blond locks across stringier shoulders, a swarm of organic particles tumbling. "First I've heard of it."

Head stepped forward, shoulders hunched miserably, and said, "He saved us, My Lord."

"Saved you?"

"From Lady Ariane's disease. And from the acceleration."

Tristen was not about to drop his guard, or shift his attention from the angel. His armor gave him a panoramic view, through which he observed Head's response as he demanded, "Explain."

The ghost of Samael spread his arms wide like a conjuror and made a bow complete with the scrape of one foot across the earth. Beetle shells and ant thoraxes glimmered, tumbling, in his boot. He said, "I am the Angel of Life Support, First Mate. I serve the world and the life within it—above *anything*."

"And how did *you* survive?"

"I found electrically sealed pockets of the world." Samael's shrugs had grown no less expressive for all their transparency. "And I hid in them like a snail, First Mate. The kitchens here had reinforced gravity, for safety's sake, and with those resources I helped preserve Head and hir people. And before you grow angry with your allies, there's something you should consider. What I can do, so can another angel."

The chill that ran the length of Tristen's spine would

have made him shudder had his concentration not been so absolute. Voice level, giving away nothing except what the very question itself offered, he said, "Dust?"

Samael folded his arms. "Asrafil."

Not the worst news, then. But bad enough. Both angels had opposed each other, and both had tried to choose the next Captain. While Dust had allied himself with Perceval, going so far as to kidnap her, Asrafil had been the power behind Arianrhod and Ariane. Tristen would take Asrafil over Dust only because Dust had been the cleverer and more political of the two, being as he was wrought of the remains of the world's library. Asrafil, the Angel of Battle Systems, however, was quite challenge enough. All assuming that Samael could be trusted—but if there were one thing to be said for angels, it was that they did not generally lie. Tristen bit his lower lip and turned to Head. There was something he needed done to make this place his. And it should be done immediately, with as little ceremony as possible, as if all it were was the setting right of something misplaced.

"Head?" He knew he was working up to it by stages.

Head colluded, because that was what friends do. "Yes, Prince Tristen?"

"Before anything else, please turn my sisters' portraits to the light."

"Yes, Prince Tristen."

He didn't need to move his head to see that sie was smiling. He heard hir sharp intake of breath. "And Ariane?"

"Is there crepe to be found?"

"There is."

He nodded. "Then we shall do her memory all honor. Meanwhile, it appears yon angel has made some work for my undertaking."

"I am sorry, First Mate," Samael said. "Please consider my powers—diminished though they temporarily are—to be yours to direct, and my services under your command."

"I will," Tristen said. "You understand that I am going to report this first to Perceval."

"And her angel," Mallory added, with widened eyes.

Samael shrugged. "The one thing amounts to the other, necromancer."

8

everything their father
had told them

As for the instance of gaining the secure and perpetual felicity of
heaven by any way, it is frivolous; there being but one way imaginable,
and that is not breaking, but keeping of covenant.
—THOMAS HOBBES, *Leviathan*

Whatever Perceval had expected of her Captaincy, it
was not quite so much schoolwork. But there were
schematics to learn, diagrams, navigational mechanics,
logistics of supply. And while Nova could spoon-feed it
to her, being told something was not the same as
understanding it.

So Perceval sat in the Captain's chair, eyes closed,
hands resting open on the arms, and studied. With
Nova's help, the experience of her indwellers, and the
help of her colony, she came quickly to understand the
numbers. The numbers did not comfort her.

"Engineering," she said—or thought of saying; when
it came to Nova, what Perceval said or thought were
much the same.

"The First Mate has arrived safely in Rule," Nova said.
"I'm putting you through to the Chief Engineer now."

Perceval opened her eyes. Her mother's image resolved
between her and Nova. The angel had caught Caitlin in
the act of glancing up from her work, pushing her
auburn hair left-handed from her eyes. Her lips were

pale with exhaustion and her skin wan and stretched—
her colony no doubt still overstressed with repairing
acceleration and radiation damage, and she appeared
not to have been eating enough.

She still managed a smile for Perceval. Exactly the
sort of smile that made Perceval feel bigger and stronger
than she knew herself to be, and maybe capable of
doing what had to be done. "Hi, Mom," she said. "We
have a problem."

"We have more than one," Caitlin answered. "Start
with the most serious, and I'll see what I can do about it."

She didn't mention Rien, and Perceval, grateful, did
not either. "Resources," she said. "Shortages are critical
throughout the world. The Enemy has claimed—"

Caitlin nodded. "I know. There are options. We can
recoup significant resources from the nebula. Some of
that material must be used for fuel, but the rest—well,
it will all have to be scrubbed. But we have radiovores.
We'll manage. Unfortunately, it all means time."

"Repairs to the world?"

"Under way." Caitlin spread her hands, fingers
expanding as if she meant to brush her way through
cobwebs. "The more pressing problem is that we can't
afford to wake up everyone in the tanks, and we can't
afford to maintain them there until we've reached cruis-
ing speed and the engines are running at capacity. For
the time being, they're wasted mass."

Caitlin wouldn't make the suggestion. And if she did,
Perceval wouldn't accept it. But they both knew the
option existed.

"We need to downsize," Perceval said, hoping it was
her own will talking and not the subtle insinuations of
an Ariane or an Alasdair. "And reallocate those
resources. Dammit, a convenient star system would

solve everything. We'd have sunlight, possibly planetes-
imals for mining."

"Five hundred years ago," Caitlin said, "somebody in
exactly your position said exactly the same thing."

Perceval winced. "Touché."

Think, she told herself, and rubbed her hands
together to remind herself of her body. It was too easy
to get lost in Nova's proprioception of the world, to
abandon herself to the sense that the world's great spans
and knobs and tendrils, its interconnections and ghosts
and memories, were her own body. Which made the
creeping blankness she felt through sectors of it all the
more disconcerting, and she had to remind her body
that it was not her own fingers and toes going numb.
"How much are we actually gaining by keeping them
tanked?"

"If we cut life support to nonessential sectors, we gain
back 90 percent of the world's resources. Everything
that's not going to the engines, the tanks, and life support for Rule, the bridge, and Engineering."

"Except those nonessential sectors are our biodiversity," Perceval said. "Five hundred years of accelerated
evolution. There is no telling what might be down there.
Shipfish. Sentients. Weirder things. They should be preserved if possible."

"Cryo will hold," Caitlin pointed out. "We're already
accelerating out of the shock wave. Environmental cooling will be rapid as we leave it behind, which leaves us
material available for cloning."

"Tell me you're playing devil's advocate," Perceval
said, "and not presenting me with your inescapable conclusion of what we must do to survive, Chief Engineer."

Caitlin half smiled. Perceval wondered if it was because
she had addressed her as her Captain, not her daughter.
She said, "The Builders would have cannibalized."

"We're not the Builders."

Caitlin scratched her chin. "We could broaden the ramscoop. It would cost energy."

"And return more?"

"It's a significant initial investment." The Chief Engineer slid hands through her holographic controls, shaping something Perceval couldn't see. "It's a risk. But if we can maintain the magnetic bottle, the return on the investment should be worth it. It might give us the resources to go see what's in those blacked-out spots."

The angel, who had stood silent as a painted backdrop behind Caitlin, unfolded his imaginary arms and laced his imaginary hands behind his back. "If I may interrupt?"

The angel's programmed approximation of polite diffidence made Perceval dream of hitting things. It was too much like Rien. "You do not need permission."

"I have not yet determined the source of all the blackouts. However, the First Mate has reported in, and I do now know why Rule has fallen off the grid. The remnant of another angel has barricaded himself in there."

"Who?" Caitlin said coldly, while Perceval was still assimilating the renewed threat.

The angel, settled into a sort of parade rest, answered, "Samael. Just a scrap of him, however." A pause, during which Perceval wondered if the angel were waiting for her to give away some clue as to her emotional state, or merely reading it and waiting for it to settle.

"Speak," Perceval said, surprised for the moment that her mother had let her take the lead. She wondered if she was grateful.

"I can dig him out," Nova said. He let his hands drop to his sides and flexed them in a manner Perceval would say was subconscious, if she saw it in a human being. "It may mean disassembling a good deal of the infrastructure of Rule. And the necromancer Mallory's familiar, in which Samael has made himself resident. Or you could order him to submit to me, and be assimilated."

"What does he want?"

The angel said, "A safe-conduct and to speak with you. The First Mate is present. He does not believe there to be a threat."

Perceval did not think there was any love lost between Tristen and Samael. Perhaps she could trust Tristen's judgments.

The thought made her unhappy. She had trusted them in the past. Should things be so different now?

They should not. But that did not change the fact that they *were*. She said, "Give him my safe-conduct. Put him on."

His avatar resolved before her.

The angel's appearance had not changed, except that now he seemed as watery and translucent as Perceval felt. He was not tall, and was as brutally thin as a flyer, the approximation of muscle fiber stripped plain beneath his skin. For an angel, there was no appreciable difference between a projection and going there in person. His awareness and his presence drew her eyes up; she met his bold glance with her own. There was a moment of eye contact before the angel swept a generous, abject bow and said, "My Captain. Bid me; I come to serve, and bearing dangerous tidings."

She should have been taken aback. But perhaps with the Captaincy came some armor or core of reserve, because as if observing from afar she saw herself extend a hand and accept Samael's obeisance. "Tell me," she said.

"It is likely that it is not I alone who survived. I would have concealed my existence longer, in fact, except that I know something you and your angel must also know.

A servant of Asrafil kept a fragment of the Angel of Blades protected, and it is likely that by her intervention he will have respawned by now. As long as she is intact, there will be no destroying Asrafil, and neither you nor your angel will be safe, My Captain. He will not place himself in a position to be ordered by you."

Perceval pressed her hands flat against her thighs, the fingers arched as if by the pressure of her palms she could deny this knowledge. "The name of this servant?"

"Arianrhod Kallikos," he said. From the glance over his shoulder, someone in Rule—Tristen, most likely—had just reacted violently. "I cannot tell you if it has happened yet. But I know Asrafil meant it to happen, planned for it to happen. And if it has not, it is only a matter of time until it does."

"Two rebel angels," Caitlin said. Perceval's focus had been such that she'd almost forgotten that her mother was listening.

"No, Chief Engineer." Samael didn't turn to look at the projection, but Caitlin's eyes flickered, which told Perceval he was providing her with her own copy of his avatar. "One rebel angel. And one who has come to present his bond willingly in service to his world and his world's Captain."

"And if I order you to allow Nova to assimilate you?"

"I am only a scrap," Samael said, glimmers of light falling through the collage of his features. "There is nothing I could do to prevent her." He spread his hands in supplication. "That would not make it any less murder, Captain."

Her, Perceval thought. She glanced at her angel again, the one she'd been thinking of as male. Because Dust was male, because angels were *he*. Because Rien had been she, Perceval realized, and she did not want to be reminded of what had become of Rien. Rien, who in such a short time had become everything.

But Nova, Perceval saw through clearer eyes, wasn't any of those things. In fact, she thought the angel had seemed much more like a man to begin with, and grew more neutral of aspect with every passing hour. Was she doing that? Or was it simply a natural part of the angel assimilating the various threads of conflicting personalities?

It led Perceval to consider the yammer of voices in her own head, the singular gravity exerted by all those thoughts, opinions, ambitious desires that threatened to consume her every time she gave them a thought.

She would have to learn to use those. Pushing them away meant denying a great resource, and—no matter how insipid she found their morality, no matter how filthy touching their thoughts made her feel—Perceval was a child of Engine. She could stop breathing with more ease than she could discard something with a potential use.

Samael, as if noticing that she had been staring at Nova in speculation for rather a long time, cleared his throat. "Captain?"

Perceval shook her head, pushing aside the fog of other commanders' ideas. "No. I think not. We've already ruled out resorting to cannibalism to solve a bigger problem."

Caitlin, without shifting her eyes from her own image of Samael, said once more, "The Builders would have cannibalized."

Perceval folded her arms. "Mom. You're repeating yourself. And I don't for a minute believe you think that's the best answer. So take it as read into the argument for now, and we'll consider it as an absolute last resort. If we have to. Nova. Do you trust him?"

Nova, who had until then waited motionless as if suspended, staring at Samael like a cat before a mouse hole, said, "I contain enough of him to know better."

Perceval, with a certain degree of distaste, reached down through the layers of filters she was slowly amassing between her present self and the library of her ancestral memories, looking for specific information. Someday, when she had leisure—and could bear the sense of dragging her fingers through swamp and slime to tickle out a handful of pearls—she would find the time to examine it all and see what was useful. For now, her memory would remain banked full of the Captains and Commodores who had come before her, and she would just have to know she would get around to it someday. Ariane, though, was close and current, and not too hard to get to. Perceval just did not much like touching her.

"I contain enough of Ariane to remember her scorn for Arianrhod's devotion to Asrafil," she confirmed. "I doubt Ariane was ever devoted much to anything, outside of herself. But she believed that Arianrhod is."

Caitlin said, "I contain nothing of Samael. But I, too, know him well enough to know better than to trust him." She glared, then surprised Perceval by asking, "But do we need to trust him? We were going after Arianrhod anyway, weren't we?"

"Yes," Perceval said. "We are. Or Tristen and Mallory are, in any case. And Gavin, of course." She turned back to Samael. "And so are you."

Benedick had never known Chelsea well. The gap between their ages was two or three lifetimes of Means run back to back. He'd only met her mother twice; after the tenth or fourteenth, his father's women ran together like lifetimes. The war with Cecelia's daughters had taught Alasdair Conn to never again confuse the question of who held power in the house of Rule by choosing an

Exalt paramour—or by Exalting the Means, once their few brief years of beauty had faded. Benedick had almost no organic memory of his own mother. It had passed with the centuries, leaving behind a sort of abstract sentiment and the crystalline images preserved by his symbiont.

But he did remember his anger and disbelief when he had, at long last, come on Errantry to Engine and not only found Caitlin there, but also that everything their father had told them, about only the blood of the house of Conn being fit to survive Exaltation, had been a blatant, baseless lie.

Shortly afterward, Benedick had begun spending less and less time in his father's house. His father had not seemed much concerned by his absence, or to much regret it.

These were things Benedick suspected Chelsea had not yet learned about their family. Perhaps the unforeseen benefit of Ariane's attempt at genocide was that now she never need learn them. So he was at peace with the idea that they should walk companionably side by side, two knights-errant alert to the dangers of the wilderness.

He did not expect much strangeness so close to Engine; the knights and Engineers had civilized everything within a day's travel. This area had been thickly settled and largely given over to agriculture before the nova. There were good maps, and Benedick's colony carried copies of each.

Their progress at first was painstaking. Having eliminated one of the five potential paths—Chelsea could be lying about having seen Arianrhod, but there were resources in place in Rule to cover that eventuality—it remained to determine which of the following four options Arianrhod had actually chosen. Because her trail was hidden well enough that a cursory examination did not suffice, Benedick resorted to the toolkit's enhanced senses.

However, after ninety minutes of sniffing and scurrying, he was forced to admit the strategy was to no avail. The toolkit whiffled disconsolately around the borders of the last corridor, ears slicked back and whiskers quivering. Benedick knew they could become discouraged when set impossible tasks. Consequently, he crouched down and let it run up his arm, the armor transmitting every scratch of its delicate claws as though they prickled on his skin.

He lifted the toolkit to his face and let it rub its pointed muzzle along his chin while Chelsea smiled out of the corner of her mouth.

"The softer side of Benedick Conn," she said, and chuckled when he rolled his eyes.

"Sibling disrespect," he answered. "Everything performs better when praised."

"You didn't learn that from Dad."

"No." Not even a real test of his resolve not to speak ill of the dead. His right hand clenched, remembering the hilt of a blade, the way flesh had offered no resistance to the unblade's blow.

He hadn't carried one since.

He wouldn't have done it for Alasdair, he thought. He hoped. He had done it because Cynric asked. That offered less in the way of absolution than he might have preferred.

He indicated the tunnels with a sweep of his gaze. "Which do you like?"

She squatted, resting her elbows on her armored knees, and chewed her upper lip. "If I were a rogue Engineer," she said, with thoughtful deliberation, "wanted for genocide, and a fugitive from everyone in

Rule and Engine both, where would I go? What would I think was my best chance of survival?"

"Before the nova?" He shrugged, and his armor shrugged with him. The toolkit on his shoulder registered a protest, fluffy tail thumping his back. "I would have lit out for the hinterlands. The Broken Holdes, maybe. Cannibal country. Now? If the world is coming back under hegemony, the situation gets stickier. You'd need to do one of four things. One, find a place where Nova can't reach—which might mean fostering a breakaway intelligence of your own. Two, reinvent yourself as something Nova could not recognize. Three, escape the world entirely—and falling off the face of the world is unlikely without a planetfall nearby—or—"

"Four, stage a takeover."

"No doubt," Benedick agreed, "the eventual plan."

"Indeed." Chelsea had pulled the braids from her hair. Now she flipped it back again. Benedick resisted the urge to recommend she cut it. "So logically—"

"She's headed for a null zone." He reached out a hand to pull her to her feet.

She accepted it and stood.

"Nova," he said, and waited for the sense of attention, of connection. "Where is the nearest large null?"

"They're propagating," the angel said in its tone without tone. Not affectless, but serene. He wondered how long it would take for it to develop a personality, or if this were a temporary effect of integrating so many diverse individuals. "However, they are clustering in the area of the largest holdes, at the south pole of the world."

"Near my domaine, you mean."

"On the bottom of the world. *Near* is a subjective term, but—yes, within tolerances. There is little known about those areas beyond the range of your patrols,

Prince Benedick. They have been out of contact for centuries. They would make a good refuge. Also, the Captain was just about to contact you. We have further information to impart. Will you accept a squirt?"

Easier and faster than speech, to allow the angel to simply inject the knowledge into his head. Riskier, too—all sorts of things could come concealed in such code.

Benedick nodded nevertheless, choosing to trust. Trust the angel, trust the Captain his daughter. Trust the world that cradled his bones.

"Send," he said, and felt data spill into his mind. Arianrhod, Samael, Tristen, Asrafil, Mallory. "Head's alive?" he said aloud, one salient fact crystalline among the flood.

Chelsea, beside him, looked up. "How?" she said. "I was in Rule. No survivors."

"Sie barricaded hirself into the kitchens with all the servants sie could find," Benedick said.

Chelsea's smile looked like it might bend her cheeks permanently.

"A little good news is nice," she said, when he raised his eyebrows at her. She glanced aside.

He let her go; adolescents were so embarrassed by their own sentiment. As if one would think less of them for relief or kindness. He said, "Thank you, Nova. My regards to the Captain my daughter."

"Her regards to you," the angel replied. "Prince Tristen wishes to know where you wish to rendezvous. He is leaving Rule as we speak, but still has options as to the route he will take."

Benedick consulted the fragmentary maps in his head. "No rendezvous. We'll try for a pincer. If Arianrhod is moving toward the south pole, we have more of a chance to prevent her from slipping by us if we take parallel routes, and it's possible one team might flush her onto the other. Will you be able to keep us in contact, Nova?"

The angel frowned in his head. "Perhaps. Once you enter the region of null growth, I cannot be sure."

"Well," Benedick said. "We'll span that gulf when we come to it."

9

that ice must be as old

The kingdom of darkness . . . is nothing else but
a confederacy of deceivers that, to obtain dominion over men in this
present world, endeavour, by dark and erroneous doctrines,
to extinguish in them the light.
—THOMAS HOBBES, *Leviathan*

Having chosen their gamble, Benedick and Chelsea began to run. Not flat-out, exhausting themselves—any chance of catching Arianrhod by merely running after her was long lost—but with a loose-legged lope that would carry them for relentless hours. Every side corridor was a reminder that there was no guarantee they had chosen the right course of action. Ceiling panels stayed open on the night beyond, the gray-green light of the shipwreck nebula staining Chelsea's face a sickly color. Despite the lack of external light, floods washed great swaths of causeway in full-spectrum light.

Chelsea, nodding up to the floods, grimaced. "Where's that power coming from?"

Benedick gestured to the renewing vegetation, driven by determined symbionts, that curled up bulkheads still scarred from where the last growth had ripped clear. "Where's your oxygen coming from, without it?"

"Point," she ceded. "I'm just thinking we're going to have supply problems once we accelerate out of the nebula. We're still eating off the waystars. It's thin and cold out there."

"There are steps," he said. "Maintaining acceleration will help. As will enlarging the ramscoop."

Her sidelong glance appeared uncomforted, but there wasn't much more he could do. He slapped her on the vambrace, rough affection but—for their family—an extreme display, and sealed his faceplate with the other hand.

"Close your helm," he said, on speaker. With the conviction of recent experience he added, "Radiation burns hurt."

Because the nebula washed the stars away, Benedick could see the curve of the corridor, but there were no external spatial referents to tell him when the reorientation began and ended, exactly. There was a trick to moving when gravity led the inner ear to confound the eye and brain, and Benedick had it. You fixed your gaze like a pirouetting dancer, and flicked it from point of focus to point of focus. Nevertheless, Benedick tripped on a glitch in gravity and dipped one leg. His knee plowed a divot in the earth; the toolkit on his shoulder responded with a murfle of protest. Somewhere under the earth, a gravity simulator was warped or cut. They were designed to shut off automatically when damaged, to protect the superstructure, but the deadswitch must be malfunctioning, too.

"Nova," he said, pushing himself to his feet with his fingertips as Chelsea turned back to see if he needed assistance, "faulty gravity at our current location. I can't make out a sector marker in line of sight; it must be overgrown."

"Thank you," Nova said. "I have no superstructure penetration there, but when I'm done with the flora I will find it. There is still no sign of Arianrhod, but I've located something that may be an indicator of her movements. There is an expanding, *mobile* null spot proceeding with fair speed through a section three strata world-south of your location."

"She went EVA, if that's her," Chelsea said. "Should we follow?"

"She's with an angel," Benedick said. "She can EVA at will."

"We have armor and an angel of our own."

"Nova?" The angel had not generated an avatar, so Benedick merely tipped his head back as if addressing someone directly before him and slightly taller. "Do external conditions permit?"

"It would be extremely unsafe," the angel said. "I could allocate resources to help shield you from radiation—"

"Resources needed elsewhere." Benedick reconsidered his earlier thoughts about Nova's serenity and undeveloped personality. He wasn't sure he'd ever heard an angel sound miserably worried before. They were voices of authority, arrogance, comfort, calm—or at least, they always had been.

"We are effecting repairs as quickly as possible," Nova said, this time managing the soothing delivery Benedick associated with angels. "The Captain states that your mission is prioritized, and I am to offer assistance commensurate with your need. Other processes can wait. However, I also must tell you that now the null spot has vanished. I'm not sure if Arianrhod has ventured EVA again, or if this is a symptom of something else."

Reluctance to speak was also not a feature of angels as Benedick knew them. "Expand?"

"It's possible that Arianrhod's patron has either infiltrated my program—possibly through a back door implicit in the code we all consumed from our initial parent process—or merely that he has attained a level of sophistication such that he can make me forget his existence. In which case, the null spot disappears from my perception. Exactly as certain items or concepts might disappear from the consciousness of a human who had suffered brain damage. I've had indications that there are colonies at work in the world that I cannot even locate, let alone control. And some of them are doing damage."

Benedick would have bitten his thumb in frustration if the armor hadn't been in the way. Instead, his hands clenched inside their gel-lined gauntlets. "But she was headed in the same direction."

"Last seen progressing world-south, yes."

"If she's skipping strata, risking EVA, and headed due south—if it's not an attempt on her part to misdirect us, mislead pursuit and tempt us to squander resources while she doubles back to Rule—we're never going to equal her speed by staying to the causeways and routes. Especially given how many are still under repair."

Benedick pressed a boot into the forgiving soil under its heel. The print would scab over in a matter of minutes. A childish display of petulance, even if he and the angel were the only ones who would ever know, but it made him feel better.

"Benedick." Chelsea's voice dropped, as if she were hesitant to interrupt. "There's another option. I'm reasonably familiar with this part of the world. We're not far from a derelict commuter shaft, if it's intact. It extends dozens of strata south, all the way to the Broken Holdes."

"I know it," Benedick said. "I heard about it from a young Engineer. The flyers sneak off to the holdes to practice. This Engineer, though, she told me it was too dangerous, and they avoided it for a longer, faster route. Faster for them." He shook his head in frustration. "I never wished I was a flyer, but right now it would help."

Chelsea's helm rocked as she nodded.

"This Engineer"—a peer of Perceval's, who Benedick

couldn't bring himself to name, knowing she was probably dead—"told me the gravity controls failed long ago. Is it defaulted to free fall?"

"Alas," Chelsea said. "About one and a half gravities. But we're Conns. We could climb it."

The family mantra. *We're Conns. We could*— Their father's influence, and Benedick was not sure even now if it had made Alasdair's children strong and willing to risk, or if it had led them to destruction.

He paused, figuring odds in his head. He must consider the possibility, far from remote, that Chelsea was in league with Arianrhod and had been in league with Ariane. If she had survived the massacre at Rule because of her affiliations, she might be here in the service of Arianrhod's plan. She might mean to decoy him to failure or to death.

Watching her face, he did not think so—but he was always too fond of his family, even when they did not deserve that fondness. So if he were wrong, it would hardly be the first time. Still, better to choose to trust and be disappointed than go the other way. As far as Benedick was concerned, cynicism was a toy for children.

"Nova?" he asked. "Obvious flaws in the plan?"

"Hazards of the climb," the angel answered. "None that appear unavoidable in the early stages, as I should be able to guide you for perhaps the first half of the descent. Then, however, you will leave my sphere of influence, and Tristen's experience with a rogue colony suggests there may be dangers. A more obvious issue is that we are uncertain of Arianrhod's actual destination, and whether this is a feint."

"And that last is a risk we have no option but to accept," Benedick said. He opened a hand past Chelsea, a gesture meant to sweep her on. "Lead me, My Lady."

Now Chelsea ran without hesitation, without stopping, without saving herself. Benedick followed after, limiting his longer stride so as not to overrun her. His armor jarred his bones. He thought of cautioning her. Her headlong rush telegraphed all her youth and incaution. She was burning energy not easily replaced on the trail for little gain, and she might be coursing heedlessly into a trap.

But instead he let her run. The truth was, it felt good. It felt like action. So he dogged her heels and stayed alert for dangers. The transparent panels overhead drew some of his attention, no matter how careful he was to divide it. Some things he had never managed to become jaded to, and the tenuous beauty of the world was chief among those.

The structure of the world loomed in partial visibility overhead, a lattice skeleton swathed erratically with light and darkness, further structures gleaming dully through translucent gas until depth of field rendered it opaque. Benedick thought of his dark orchards in dormancy, the pruned branches crisscrossed and wet-black until they vanished in mist.

As he and Chelsea ran, the panels revealed the seemingly tremulous spire of the shaft they moved through lifting to connect to the next level. Before them, small animals scattered from the regrown grass—quail, rabbits, a long weasel-bodied predator after which the toolkit sent angry chittering. As they crested a hill—actually a bend in the tunnel and, as such, a rise that left them with no sense of ascending, because the orientation of the gravity simulators followed that of the corridor—pillars hove up, stretching from deck to ceiling, their ivory, fluted lengths discolored by foamy, grayish masses where they rose above the fronds of some thorned, twining plant.

Behind the feathery leaves, a shadow lay across the deck, and a darkness penetrated the ceiling forty meters overhead. As they drew closer, both gained depth of field, so Benedick could see it was a great oval shaft, thirty meters across the large diameter, leading into untrammeled darkness above and below. He felt each footstep falling more heavily on the deck despite the assistance of his armor. At least the increase of gravity was incremental, rather than stair-step. Or worse, one abrupt transition.

Once upon a time, the shaft before them had been a major thoroughfare connecting the most populous regions of the world. Now it was a one-directional pit, a death fall for anything that might stumble into it.

Benedick wondered how many strata it plummeted, and how many times you would strike the wall, should you tumble down. And what the odds were of a falling body bursting through the bottom of the shaft and punching into the bosom of the Enemy? Unlikely, that last. If it had been going to happen, it would have by now. Many things must have tumbled to their deaths over the centuries.

Chelsea slowed to a trot as they arrived, and Benedick also allowed his pace to slack. He strained his sensory resources as well as those of his armor, alert to any potential ambush or unforeseen threat. More gray-cheeked parrotlets—an entire flock of twelve-centimeter birds darting through the branches of the feathery warden trees—cried shrill alarm at their approach. Wings as green as radioactive glass flashed as they mocked each other from perch to perch, yelling their nearly comprehensible imprecations. They had powder blue caps and silvery cheeks, the leading edges of their wings blurring his vision with the sharpness of lime-and-cobalt biomechanical luminescence. When they tumbled in flocks, it was impossible to track one cleanly; he thought the glow of their wings must be designed to confuse predators when they schooled, like the dazzle of shipfish and neon tetras.

Above the range of the parrotlets and the tops of the fluffy green cloud of trees, long-winged swifts swooped from nests on the pillars. They might have been darting after tiny insects—even with the armor's telescopic vision, at this range Benedick could not be sure.

"I don't anticipate getting past that thornbrake without harming the trees," Benedick said doubtfully.

In answer, Chelsea stepped forward and lifted her hand. Her armor stayed dormant, but as it brushed downy fronds they first lunged, tapping her fingers. Then as if in surprise or discouragement the leaves folded tight and drew aside like a potentate lifting the skirts of hir robe. When the bough folded, a scatter of fragile bones—tiny rodents or marsupials—were revealed around the base of the trunk.

"Mimosa," she said. "We're too big for it."

Benedick glanced from the folded-up leaves lying flat between two-inch thorns and allowed himself a tiny smile. "How come it doesn't eat the parrotlets?"

"Symbiosis?" she guessed. She pulled back her gauntlet and tucked hair behind her ears on both sides. "Maybe they were engineered to live together. The mimosa keeps the rodents from eating the birds' eggs, and the existence of birds' nests in the mimosa lures the rodents into giving it a try?"

Something slender and green whipped from under his foot as he came forward to stand beside her. Because he did not care to touch the trees, much less trust his weight to them, he balanced with one hand against one of the four pillars that delineated the transit shaft and leaned over the abyss. It was not quite the bottomless pit he had anticipated—or rather, it was, but the walls were tapestried with enormous mushrooms, their caps forming a deceptive broad patchwork that began only a few meters below. The native color of the fungus was impossible to discern; the top layer was encrusted with a ragged gray-white camouflage of guano.

"Benedick!" Chelsea yelped.

He stepped back, into the embrace of a feathery carnivorous tree that withdrew to frame his body rather than suffering his touch. "Are there these on every level?" he asked, gesturing to a branch that swept aside from his hand.

She shrugged. "I've only been two up and one down. They were on all three strata I checked." She swept an arm across the open space before them. "Aren't they beautiful? And the swifts' nests are edible. When we reach the next stratum down, we should collect some."

"Saliva nests," he said. "Those are the ones you make soup from?"

"The same." She beamed, obviously pleased to have known something useful and lovely that her older brother didn't for the second time in a single day. "We should tether to each other for the climb."

"And take turns anchoring," he agreed.

He produced a cable from the beltline of his armor and clipped it into her matching utility. A sharp tug proved the connection secure.

"I'll climb first," he said, but she was already swinging a leg over the edge.

"I've done it before. And I'm lighter," she said. "And in my armor, just as strong. I'll break trail."

He stopped the cable paying out. She leaned her weight on it, shifting her hips back to tug, but he had grounded himself and was immovable.

"Benedick."

"Until the halfway point," he said. "Then I climb first."

She stared for a moment, until with a wink she tapped her faceplate closed. "That's only fair," her speaker agreed. As he released the lock on the cable she was over the edge and gone, her suit lights gleaming brighter and brighter in the gathering gloom.

Downclimbing was harder, not easier, than climbing up—cautious and unpredictable work on a slick, finicky surface, with overset gravity increasing the risk. It might have been easier to rappel by turns, but while Benedick was willing to trust the topmost sibling to belay the other, and thus bear some of the weight (with the armor assisting the rest), neither he nor Chelsea were willing to rest their entire faith on one spider-strand. And so the second climber must follow under native power and skill, augmented by capable armor.

It wasn't the strength of the monofilament cable that Benedick distrusted. It was the anchor points, which involved either the decaying gardens behind the frozen waterfall of fungus, or the fungi themselves. They were strong enough to bear their own weight—strong enough even to bear his and the armor's, in addition, though sometimes the slenderer stalks squished or swayed unnervingly. But he thought the cable might slice through the trunks. Nowhere would the descent be a straight rappel, because six-meter mushrooms curved out from the walls like dancers' upraised arms, their caps great round mattresses clogging the center of the shaft.

Benedick and Chelsea could not see below themselves except in glimpses, and after five minutes of climbing they also could not see above. What light fell was cut in shafts, progressively vanishing, and it wasn't long before only the sweep of their armor lamps revealed surroundings grown eerie and strange.

The walls had never been smooth. Designed as hanging gardens, in the darkness their honeycomb terraces were home to amazing things, such as woody, pale fungi tall as trees, which bled faint, contagious, greenish light where his gauntlets broke their surfaces. His handprints glowed for seconds afterward, until the sap wore away. Other mushrooms flourished in crevices—some pinhead-tiny, brilliant futile purples and golds on thread-fine stems revealed in Benedick's helmet light; others broad and shelf-level, hard as tabletops, ledges you could sleep on. Chelsea and he used those to belay each other, anchoring around slippery-skinned, porous, but unyielding trunks.

The ghostly forest teemed with tiny, eyeless, pale animals, insensible to the glare of Benedick's lights. Spiders translucent as window polymer, the joints of their articulated exoskeletons wraithlike around the shadowy organs within. Sticky-footed salamanders that flicked away from the air pressure of a descending gauntlet. Crickets spun of crystal.

Endless water dripped behind it all. The irrigation system must have broken centuries ago, along with the illumination, and in the humid darkness this was what had grown. Benedick was conscious of the wet, the ice that rimed the back corners of the terraces where even the heat of decomposition could not entirely stave off the chill of the Enemy behind. Still rotting, five hundred years later, and some of that ice must be nearly as old.

The smell tempted him to order his armor to filter—but odors could transmit vital information, and with the helmet sealed the toolkit huddled against his neck like a warm fur collar, whiskers tickling his cheek with every hesitant sniff.

He swung himself around a delicate-seeming fungus that he trusted with his weight only because his armor's scanners told him it was reinforced with biomechanicals—internal carbon monofilament cables leveraging its grip on the nearest terrace—and caught sight of Chelsea's lights and her sap-daubed armor below. She was paying out cable attentively, one hand on the winch, providing sufficient slack but ready to stop his descent at any sign he was in trouble. He touched down to the main trunk of the fleshy, branching mushroom she'd chosen to ground herself on and squatted deeply to make a little extra slack. When he stood again, he unlocked the cable release and began cautiously to reclaim his side of the line. Chelsea moved away to perform the same maneuver.

"Break," she said, and lowered herself to the trunk. Benedick, after a glance around, stretched out beside her. They could not afford to pause for long, but they would lose more time to a fall and recovery than to a few minutes spent letting their heartbeats slow and their colonies repair damage to their muscle tissue.

They rested on their backs, lights illuminating the delicate moth gray gills that formed their temporary sky. Benedick thought of feathers, of filters, of narrow leaves of ceramic seen edge-on. A haze of spores drifted over them, graying their faceplates. If they were to lie here long enough, the spores would blanket them over like snow-drifts until the filaments of rooting fungus enveloped their armored shells. They would lie entombed, encapsulated, beneath the lofty white pillars and the parasol caps. People-cysts, like frogs in mud turned to stone, like para-sites burrowed into muscle tissue.

With a stretch of his hand against the sensors in his gauntlet, Benedick shut down his helmet floods, imag-ing, sonar. Incautious, but he wanted to feel the space they had entered for itself, and if anything attacked, he trusted his armor. His lights died abruptly, with none of the flare and fade of cooling incandescents. After a moment, without being told, Chelsea did the same. Now she was a ghost in the darkness, like the spiders, luminescent in pale smeared patches that seemed to grow brighter as his eyes adapted. Blackness settled around them, as bottomless as the Enemy. There were even stars: tiny sparks of life scurried along the walls, moved through the miniature forests around the bases of the tree-fungi.

Through the armor, Benedick could not hear Chelsea breathing, though other things moved in the dark.

Did you help to kill them? He wondered. *What is it you plan to do with me?*

He was giving her the opportunity. It only remained to be seen if she tried to take it. If she didn't, it would prove something. If she did, he would be anticipating the attack. He'd have to place his trust in that, and in the hopeful truth of all those old expressions about the superiority of age and treachery.

"When you did this by yourself," he asked, "how did you manage?"

"I free climbed."

He imagined her here in the darkness, the flash of her lights, nothing between her and the fall but her skill and strength and balance—and the technology on her back. Age and treachery, all right. In that she made him feel old.

"I'm impressed."

She stirred, just a little, but he heard her armor scrape. He waited for her to find what she was groping after, to see if she would fill the silence with it. He breathed as he waited, and as he listened to the slow hiss in and out, it struck him that he *was* old. And that it was no use to pretend he could somehow redeem the void he'd left in the lives of two daughters by praising a sister.

But then she said, "Thank you," in a voice so small he only recognized the phrase because it was familiar.

Benedick gave her a few moments longer, and when she spoke again her tone had the smooth, ironic feature-lessness so common to conversations around dinner table in Rule. What she admitted, however, would have been blood among piranha in that house. "Father never would have said that to me."

No, Benedick couldn't make up paternal neglect of his daughters by throwing a bone to another young woman, but that didn't mean that Chelsea had no needs of her own.

Such vulnerability deserved an answer. He cleared his throat and closed his eyes. "He said it to me once."

Benedick could still hear the words, dripping sarcasm thick as the blue blood that had drenched his hands and arms. Amazing how one's organic memory could cling so tightly to the worst moments of a life, and lose everything that surrounded them.

Chelsea said, "Wow. That must have been some accomplishment."

In the darkness, Benedick sat up sharply. He reached to key his lights, and stayed his hand. *Be fair,* he admonished himself.

He said in plain tones, "He didn't mean it."

She didn't answer, but he heard her sigh, felt her reach for him across the space between and stop her hand before it connected. For a moment, they sat together, the understanding silence between them almost big enough to fill that space.

Whatever had been moving in the dark moved again, and this time Benedick caught a glimpse of rippling bioluminescence, impossibly pure azure and crimson, trembling like the gills of a fish. "Sister," he said.

Chelsea's armor clicked as her head turned. "Big," she said, as the train of light flowed across the underside of the trunk not four meters overhead. It left two parallel tracks of glowing green dots behind it, matching the smears on the Conns' armor. It must be taking pinprick holds on the surface of the fungus. The entire organism looked three meters long or longer, estimated with his own eyes. His colony suggested a tip-to-tip measure of 3.2, and a width of half a meter.

Against his throat, the toolkit compacted itself, shivering. Under all that fluff, its tiny body might have been twisted of wire.

"What do you think it is?" Benedick asked, using the suit mike directly to Chelsea's earpiece, so external noise would not distract the creature.

"Arthropod," she said.

He would have been content to sit in the dark and play guessing games a little while longer, but Chelsea triggered her floods and bathed the cozy vertical dell in light. Brilliance washed reds and blues from the countless legs of a three-meter centipede, which froze when revealed as if the glare had pinned it to the trunk to which it clung. Like the spiders, it was transparent in places, translucent in others, only a few of the internal organs pigmented and solid-seeming. Benedick had the uncomfortable misapprehension that if he stood up and reached out to it, his hand would go through—though whether it should feel like gelatin or mist, he couldn't quite decide.

"Oxygen content?" he asked, and with a great show of how beset she was by his laziness, Chelsea waved a hand bedecked with a sample net through the air.

"Thirty-nine percent," she said. "Bet that's not the only giant bug around. Think it eats apes?"

"It definitely eats mushrooms," he said. Pieces of nipped-off cap were visible in its digestive tract, the pale meat and powdery gills compressed into a single variegated knobby line. He stood up and triggered his own lights. The motion did what Chelsea's floods hadn't; the centipede darted into the overstory in a dazzle of fluidity.

"Come on," Benedick said, when it had been gone a long moment. "We still have a fugitive to catch."

The centipede was the only giant arthropod they saw, but now that he knew they were there, the evidence of their existence was obvious—nibbled mushroom caps, a burrow bored in a stem, as wide as the circle he could make with both arms. And once, when he was leading the downclimb, he saw something that led him to call back up on the armor radio and tell Chelsea to stop the descent. He let himself dangle for a moment, watching the rays of his floodlamps shimmer off the intricate strands of a moisture-dotted funnel-web large enough for him to have walked down upright. His line of descent was a good thirteen meters from the mouth of the thing, for which he was grateful.

Something twitched at the bottom of the funnel, an inquisitive motion, and he said, "Lower away" with unconscious softness.

The winch started up. As he descended away from the spiderweb, Chelsea asked, "Problem?"

"I found your carnivores."

"Everything okay?"

"Fine. Spiderweb. Pretty. When you come through—"

"Yes?"

"Be careful."

He heard her laughter down the line. "Oh, boy," she said. "Giant spiders. I wonder which bastard angel thought that up."

10

the door gaped wide

But now, from between the black & white spiders, a cloud and fire
burst and rolled thro' the deep black'ning all beneath, so that the nether
deep grew black as a sea, & rolled with a terrible noise; beneath us
was nothing now to be seen but a black tempest, till looking east
between the clouds & the waves, we saw a cataract of blood mixed
with fire, and not many stones' throw from us appear'd and sunk
again the scaly fold of a monstrous serpent.
—WILLIAM BLAKE,
The Marriage of Heaven and Hell

Tristen bound back his hair.

Still wet from his shower, it felt like damp wire
between his fingers. He stood before the mirror in his
chambers and worked it into a braid, bringing the end
over his shoulder to finish. The strands appeared crystalline white, but he could see the shadows of his fingers
through the locks. In truth his hair was colorless, its
apparent whiteness a function of the air trapped in the
center of the shaft where normally pigment would be.

Alone among his surviving siblings, Tristen had been
born during the Moving Times and had come to adult-
hood when the biogenetic engineering technology of
the symbiont colonies was still undeveloped. His sister
Cynric the Sorcerer was younger than he: even *she* could
hardly have built the symbiont before she was born.

Tristen's childhood in these halls had been a sickly
one. But he had adapted, and he had still been a young
man in the aftermath of the disaster that had crippled the
world—when his grandfather Gerald had adopted Cynric's science and directed the creation of the first Exalt.

The rest of the Conn family followed, as did the essential crew of Engineering. With mortal life span and illnesses left behind, Tristen's colony could have amended the lack of pigment as surely as it had amended the worst of the nystagmus that had once so badly affected his vision. But with the early technology, the change would have been obvious and artificial . . . and once it became a choice rather than a defect, and he could leave his father's house at will, Tristen found that his self-image had solidified. He liked the drama of his coloring. A little uniqueness could be a valuable thing, especially in a society that valued a man's legend as a marker of his merit.

Now, he looked into the mirrored cobalt glow of the colony shining through his own unpigmented irises, and smiled mirthlessly.

Tristen Conn had weathered the storms of two vast transformations of his world, and the worse storms of growing to manhood in the house that was his grand-father's and then his father's. He had seen failure and betrayal, and more than once his sympathies had been with the betrayers.

Tristen had seen his wife and sister Aefre cut down as a representative of a family and a government she scorned, lost his daughter Sparrow in a war of his grandfather's making. There had been four daughters between him and Benedick, and three were dead. Two—Caithness and Cynric—either at their own father's hands or by his command, having learned patricide from Alasdair's example and died in the attempt. The last sister, Caitlin, survived in exile, where—Tristen must admit—she had done well for herself.

He knew where Ariane had come from, how she had grown so edged, so poisoned, and so bent. She had been Alasdair's favorite, and so he had made her as much in his own image as possible. Or perhaps it had just pleased the old man to focus his loathsome parenting upon her because it griped Tristen so.

Whatever Alasdair's motivation, Tristen had watched his father cripple his younger siblings—the ones born after Benedick—so they would never grow strong enough to challenge him. At first, Tristen had intervened where he could, until Alasdair made it evident that the end result of his interference would be an exile not unlike Caitlin's. *If* he suffered Tristen to live.

Tristen had learned to stay silent, even in the face of the indignities his father had heaped upon his own line, because to openly cross Alasdair Conn was to lose everything. And he had tried to befriend those who had suffered most—particular among them Ariane.

His filial loyalty to Ariane had only led him to another betrayal—in all the long line of betrayals that marked his history with his family, perhaps the most bitter. Even after her death and consumption, Tristen could not forgive that she had guided him astray. It wasn't exactly that he had trusted her—Conns did not trust one another—but he had cared for her. That caring was what had enabled her to trap him, break his blade, and imprison him in a horrible dungeon.

But as he wrapped the tail of his braid with a blue ribbon that crimped itself tight to bind the locks into a blunt club, he thought: *If I had been a dutiful brother, father, husband, grandson—I would have saved the family so much grief, and killed the old man long ago.*

It hadn't mattered in the end, because Alasdair had created his own destroyer. And no one could say if the collateral damage had been greater or less because Tristen had not found the resolve to consume his father when he should have.

Tristen knew himself to be as crippled as the rest of his family. Living under his father's will, watching Benedick spill Cynric's blood at their father's command, had made him quiet. It had made him cowardly. It had made him cold.

He let his braid fall behind his shoulder and turned from the mirror.

Things change, he thought. And then, feeling as if he dared greatly: *It is time things changed in the house of Rule.*

When Tristen emerged into the relaxation chamber, his heap of pack and water bottle lay ready, his armor standing nearby. Mallory, Gavin, and the ghost of Samael—outlined like a dust devil in the scraps of things swept up inside him—awaited by the door. The necromancer was also festooned with travel gear.

Mallory shrugged to settle a pack strap. "Is everything ready?"

"I want a weapon." Tristen came before them and turned his back to step into his armor. It folded him into its embrace, the cool resilience of shock gel lining molding to his skin. As it sealed, fasteners sliding into housings with soft, round-sounding clicks, Mallory stooped to hand him the pack and the water. Tristen slung them through carabiners at his shoulders. His armor protested good-naturedly as the sacks thumped it, but Tristen ignored the complaint.

Then thought again: *That is what your father would have insisted upon.*

He unsealed the helm and looked from Mallory to the artificial intelligences. "Follow me."

Ariane had carried Caithness's unblade Mercy, a gift from their father to his most trusted child, and that sword had been consumed in Nova's creation. Tristen, as eldest, had borne an unblade, too, though his had shattered against Mercy when he could not bring himself to strike down Ariane. Caitlin had taken the third and final with her into exile, and that blade had died when Mercy did.

But there were other family weapons, treasured heir-looms, whose bearers would be chosen and controlled by whoever held the house of Rule.

He knew where Alasdair kept his captured riches, and as the acknowledged head of house, all locks in Rule would open to him. Still, when he paused before the vault door, stripped back his gauntlet, and laid his left hand against the contact pad, apprehension chilled his neck. "Open sesame," he said, for luck.

The door gaped wide.

Tristen gestured his escorts back with one hand and stepped within. He moved into dimness and light fol-lowed, floor and walls and ceiling panels catching a rip-pling circle of illumination that matched his pace. The light was clear, sun-spectrum, bright enough to reveal the details on Alasdair's assembled treasures without washing them away.

Tristen walked between urns and scepters, ancient books and electronics, a jeweled crucifix sparkling with mined diamonds. A crystal vial full of brown earth caught his eye. He turned to it with reverence: dust from the homeworld, to be sown wherever they should make planetfall. Beside it hung a second flask, containing a few scant ounces of the Earth's enormous world-encircling sea. For a moment, Tristen tried to imagine such a thing, a body of water as big as a planet.

The mere consideration made him spin with vertigo.

He turned to the wall that held the weapons. Empty space awaited the dead unblades—Mercy, Charity, and Innocence. Another niche awaited the someday return of a blade called Humility—leading Tristen to wonder which of his siblings might be its bearer now—and a fifth and sixth were respectively bereft of Benevolence and Grace.

But beside the gaps others still hung: Purity, Compas-sion, and Sympathy. And the one his hand gravitated to, without thought. A weapon Aefre had carried, and Sparrow after her, curved of blade, with a hilt swept like the neck of a black swan and filigreed guards like golden wings.

"Mirth," he said, and drew it from the sheath as he took it into his hand.

A blue spark raced from his palm to the tip of the blade; a golden spark ran back. His palm tingled as his colony and Mirth's made their handshake, proof that the weapon had acknowledged and accepted him. It felt light, peculiar, though it had been fifty years since he'd touched Charity in its intact state. The unblade had been inertialess, weightless, a null space in his hand— but it had expressed also a weight beyond the physical—the presence of its own chill alien will and intellect. In bearing it, Tristen had always been able to feel it at his side, like a wary demon: considering, assessing, making its own judgments.

An uneasy sensation. Mirth in his hand generated no such discomfort; rather it felt alert and responsive. *Command me.* He resheathed it, breaking the circuit, but was left with a sense of its eager pleasure in having been handled.

There were other treasures: rings and geegaws, suits of armor, ancient and mysterious electronics. Tristen walked past it all, back to where the others waited, and with a gesture sealed the vault behind. His companions in misadventure stared at him, one question plain in three regards.

Tristen clipped the sword onto his hip. They parted before him, stepped aside and let him pass through as if he held some authority over them. As if they were following where he led.

What a kingdom, thought Tristen Conn. *The shadow of an angel, a necromancer, and a reinvented power tool. What an army I bring against you, Granddaughter.*

"I'm ready," he said, and steeled himself for plain statement. "Let's go kill Arianrhod."

In the arms of her angel, Arianrhod rested. Asrafil lifted her on vasty wingbeats, her newly variegated hair trailing like a banner over his adamantine forearm, her weight borne up like a doll's. She curled against his chest, face pressed into the black warm nap of his coat, and felt the waxy leaves of the trailing vines he bore her through brush her body. He moved like a tramcar, stately, unstoppable, with rhythmic surges and hesitations carried on each stroke of the wings. When he turned she could feel him bank and slide and glide, the way the forces wanted to tug them along their initial vector, the long smooth arc as he veered and swung.

She had never felt so safe.

It was a disappointment when broad pinions flared and slapped atmosphere—a halt as abrupt as if some unseen hand had snapped their leash. Arianrhod's body jerked against Asrafil's grip. As she had never feared that he would drop her, she felt only a kind of thrill-ride exultation. She burst out laughing, her hair tousled in every direction by the wind of their passage, her arms uplifted and back arched as she surrendered entirely to the angel's strength. In perfect love and perfect trust.

She thought they flew and then descended for a long time—nearly a day, by her colony's clock. During some of that time she dozed in Asrafil's arms, less than aware of her surroundings. He would wake her if a threat required her attention, or he would deal with it if it did not. When she opened her eyes again they had entered a chill place, cavernous by the echoes of Asrafil's wing-beats, and she had lost what sense of orientation she'd had. The light here was banded, gray and grayer, and when she turned her head she could just make out a glimpse of tombstone ranks of machinery. She felt them buffeted by twisted gravity, gasped as he swept her through a passageway so narrow she felt the brush of metal on her skin.

At last, soft as milkweed down, he settled to the deck, his wings a curtain enfolding them. As his boots brushed soil, the shadow of the wings faded into non-existence. He set her on her feet at arm's length, and stepped back.

Arianrhod felt irrationally as she had when she was small, and her father had kissed her forehead. "Thank you, Asrafil," she said.

The angel bowed from the waist. "You are loyal and deserving," he said as he straightened. "If I can make your burdens light, my dear, well—broad are an angel's shoulders."

Arianrhod turned away to hide the flush of pleasure warming her cheeks. She wrapped her arms across her chest to ward off the chill. Noticing, the angel wrapped her in his coat, and kept his arm around her shoulders. Though he was only warm because he chose to be, still his heat soothed. An animal response, primitive. Perhaps something she should have grown beyond— something all Exalt should have grown beyond, to earn their rank as half-mortals placed just below the angels.

But who could disregard the love of God when they saw it shining from the eyes of a holy messenger? Here was the devotion that she had looked for all her life. The filial duty, the sacred trust, which she had received in such scant measure from her family. And oh, she basked in it.

She wanted to say that all her burdens were made more bearable simply by his regard, that he himself was the remuneration of her faith. But there was too much vulnerability in such a statement, and anyway—he was the Angel of War. He knew whatever she might have said to him.

So instead she looked around the chamber she found herself in—too small for a holde or a Heaven or even a domaine; a mere anchore, just one tiny bead swelling along the myriad stems of the world—and drew a breath of its dank, unwholesome air. There was only a little light here, dim and filtered, slanting through a clouded panel on the curve of the ceiling above. But as her colony and her eyes adapted, Arianrhod saw a floor lined with leaf litter and bones. Along one wall lay a filthy nest of shredded, matted tufts of hair and salvaged scraps from many levels. No plants grew within this chamber, not even leggy, yellowed, light-starved ones. But somewhere in the darkness, trickling water ran.

"Where are we?" she asked, and half answered her own question. "I see that it's a lair."

"Don't worry," the angel said. "The swine are hunting at this time of the local day, and anyway they are quite harmless so long as you are alert and on your feet. But their waste can help conceal us."

"This is not where I asked to be brought, Asrafil."

"It is in service to your cause." He crouched and dug long fingers in the floor, unearthing fistfuls of compost writhing with shiny black beetles. "Here," he said, rapidly sifting them through a nanotronic net until the rot fell free and only the insects remained. When he had finished, he cupped a double handful of insects no bigger than pinheads at her, his expectant impression prompting her to hold out her hands.

When she had dropped to her knees and done so, steadying herself by watching his face intently, he poured the beetles across her palms.

They did not stay neatly contained in the cupped hollow, as they had for him. Instead, they scrambled up her arms, scattering, finding refuge in the dark recesses of her borrowed coat and the warm creases of her body. The prickle of their tiny barbed feet made her want to squirm and slap at them, but she set her jaw and waited it out. It was only a little while before they seemed to have chosen their places—in her hair, behind the cuffs of the coat, moving lightly across the outside of her arm in search of some eventual destination. Settled, they prickled no more than hairpins or jewelry.

Arianrhod shuddered, and tried not to scratch her scalp. "What are those?"

"Symbiotes," he said. "They'll eat what you shed, and keep you from leaving a trail of DNA. If you are comfortable, come along; we should be gone before the swine return from foraging. They do not take kindly to interlopers."

She followed on. A few steps brought them to a narrow passage, the sort that must be navigated in a half crouch. Their footsteps echoed—or at least, hers did. The Angel of Weapons walked silently.

Eventually, they emerged into another anchore, slightly larger than the last. Here, Arianrhod could see the game trail threading the earthen deck, the packed dry dirt that spoke of something—yes—hoofed, or running on sharp trotters. She stood up straight between the long veiling falls of glossy-leaved foliage that marked either side of the trail and said, "Asrafil, tell me your plan."

He glanced at her, but did not stop his steady, effortless progress. His coat swung against her ankles. She hurried to catch up. "You have been loyal," he said.

"I am loyal," she insisted. "And again, I asked you for something—"

"We will go there now," he said, so smoothly she could not tell if she imagined his air of humoring her.

"But I can't help you if I don't know what you plan. Surely not just to beard the new angel in his lair?"

"I am too small for that," Asrafil admitted, ducking his bald head as if it cost him. He looked so frail—

bird-boned, delicate, his simulated collarbones projecting over the collar of his white T-shirt now that the long
coat did not cover them.

For a moment, Arianrhod felt sympathy for him, pro-
tectiveness. She reached out and brushed his sleeve with
her hand. "I support you, Asrafil."

He drew up short, shoulders lifted, eyes on the egress
hatch a few more yards across the width of the anchore.

"It is terrible work I'm on," he said, when she had
given up hope of him speaking at all. He turned pale
eyes on her and made a gesture as if to wet his mouth,
though he had neither salivary glands nor the need for
comfort. "I go in search of an ally, Lady Arianrhod."

She folded her arms. "That was but half an answer."

He nodded. And holding her gaze as if to hold, also,
her understanding, he said, "I seek the beast. To make
of him a weapon, Arianrhod."

"The beast?"

"Cynric's beast," he said. "Her darkest sorcery."

Arianrhod stretched her shoulders. "That's all well
and good," she said. "But first you have to bring me to
Ariane's strongholde."

As Tristen led his band through the corridors and
domaines near Rule, what they found at first was simple
farmland—serried hydroponics tanks in racks twice
Tristen's height, crushed strawberries and melons
moldering unpicked on bruised and twisted stems,
plastics cracked and nanopatched to hold water the
world must have mopped from every corner and returned
to containment. The plants were healing, slowly, but
there was no hope for the fruit.

The party scavenged as they walked—cucumbers broken open but not yet rotten here, sprays of round green
eggplant the size of eyeballs there—and ate on the
move. Or rather, Tristen and Mallory scavenged, Gavin

complained, and Samael looked on from his half-realized transparency, arch or amused.

All my life is running, Tristen thought, entertained by the irony when all his life had been waiting but a few days since.

Already the chamber of the bats seemed another lifetime, a story recounted but not experienced. He was growing scars over it, he knew, sealing up the raw place with proud tissue. Soon all that remained of a weeping wound would be a rough, unsightly patch, and the raised seam where the flesh had grown together.

Comfortable and relatively safe surroundings brought them half a day's travel from Rule. Things grew wilder there, but incrementally. At first, one could fail to notice that the hydroponics tanks had been full of sediment since before the nova. But before long they came to places where knobbed tree roots, blindly seeking moisture, had heaved open wall and floor panels, popped welds, rent sheet metal wide.

There was nothing in all the world so implacable as a tree. Out of the world, the only rival was the Enemy.

The braided web of passageways and chambers that comprised the agricultural domaine wore on Tristen, though he would not show his discomfort to the others. Quiet words, soft eye, straight spine. Push through, carry on. You can walk on a broken leg if you set your jaw against it. It's not good for you, or for the limb, but there's time to be fragile when the war is won. That, too, he had learned from his father.

Just as he had learned that the war is *never* won.

The angel's oversight reassured him not at all. He only remembered the breaking of Israfel with his native memory, as he had not yet been Exalt when it happened, but he remembered it well enough. Tristen Conn did not trust angels.

When they passed into one of the null spots, he found

comfort in their isolation, despite knowing he was leading them into the heart of whatever opposed Perceval
and her loyal followers—among whom he must number
himself.

Still, he breathed a sigh when they came not to
another in the seemingly endless series of pressure
doors, but instead a proper air lock, big enough to move
large equipment. The massive doors had sealed against
some ancient pressure drop. Tristen's band drew up
before the first. While they paused, he looked from one
companion to the next.

"Samael," he said, having considered. The angel was
not to be trusted—no angel was to be trusted, and the
Angel of Poison least of all—but Tristen held the Captain's
authority by proxy, and if anything could force a recalci-
trant angel to duty, it was the word of Perceval Conn.

Without a glance, the angel passed forward, ghosting
through the door, flakes of things swept from his field
and pressed flat against it. Fifteen seconds—timed by
Tristen's colony, during which he heard mostly the drip
of condensation and Mallory breathing lightly, quickly,
in anticipation—passed before Samael returned, dusting
translucent hands one against the other and making the
motes inside them sparkle and tumble.

"Heaven," he said. "Quite pretty. Within tolerances,
I believe. I don't know why the lock tripped."

Tristen sealed his helm up anyway. Mallory, unar-
mored, watched with amusement, but though Tristen
thought of an apologetic glance, he didn't share it.

He palmed the air lock controls, entered his command security override, identified himself as First
Mate—and found that the air lock would not open.

"Huh," he said. "Isn't this thing supposed to listen?"

Mallory chortled. "Sure it is. But only if you know the
right commands. The whole world does not yet know
you're in charge of it. Let me try."

Tristen stepped back, folding his arms so the armor clattered, and tried not to frown as Mallory laid hands on the panel, concentrated, and a moment later the lights began to cycle blue and green.

"There's no colony in the lock," Mallory explained, straightening. "It has no connection to Nova. No way to update."

When it ground wide, protesting every centimeter, the atmosphere within stank of mold and must but was not toxic. Even through his suit filters, Tristen wrinkled his nose. He strode into the small space, ignoring the filth stirring around his ankles, and gestured the others in behind. When all the corporeal ones were clear of the outer door, he cycled the lock.

The inner door was stuck, but whatever jammed the tracks was not solid enough to stand against the whining motors that forced it back. The cincture rasped apart, bringing in a rush of sweet, oxygenated atmosphere even before Tristen could see what lay beyond.

Immediately upon the breeze came a flutter of fairy-bright objects that Tristen at first thought were leaves, until by their beat and settle he knew them to be wings. Butterflies, a half dozen, flitting in vortex swirls around each of the travelers. Mallory waved them away with an airy gesture, caught Tristen's eye when he turned, and smiled.

Despite himself, Tristen returned the smile. He reoriented himself, laid a hand on his weapon, and stepped forward into the Heaven.

It was green, lushly so, and the first thing he noticed was that the trees here had not failed during acceleration. The deck underfoot was one fibrous gnarl—the roots of a feral tangle of fig trees, or perhaps just one giant, ancient tree gone wild with suckers and overgrowth. Whichever it was, multifarious smooth-boled trunks competed for space to lift their parasol canopies to the light, and no earth showed between matted roots. The branches were heavy with fruit and bloom at once, the air redolent of fermentation. From the valleys between gray-barked, ridge-backed roots, clouds of bright butterflies arose at every gesture, startled from feeding on burst and rotten fruit. Overhead and alongside darted minute jeweled birds with sewing-needle beaks, whirring like soft-spoken insects.

On Mallory's shoulder, Gavin swung his head to track an iridescent blue-violet bird, abruptly snakelike until the necromancer flicked his tail tip sharply. "Behave."

Sulkily, the basilisk pulled his neck between his shoulders and rocked between his feet. "I wasn't going to zap it."

Tristen might have laughed, but the closeness of the trunks raised his concerns of ambush and he bit it back. There was motion everywhere—darting things, the slender green coil of a snake as long as his arm and no thicker than his pinky gliding between branches overhead. The plop as a heavy, tender fruit fell set his heart racing. From Samael's raised eyebrow, he knew his startle had been visible through the armor.

Well, he was entitled.

"Single file," he said. He glanced at Samael, shook his head, and said, "Behind me, everybody but the angel."

Samael laughed—or gave the illusion of it. The sound bubbled on the air, anyway, and Tristen saw the dust-mote-and-dry-grass muscles of his avatar's belly shake. "Shall I make myself solid enough to spring a trap?"

"Kindly," Tristen said, and though it was not necessary, he deemed it polite to stand aside so the angel might pass. Samael's tipped head of acknowledgment was nothing but blue-eyed mockery through the strings of his hair. The casualness with which Tristen unsealed his helm and faceplate, and allowed the armor to retract played to the same pretense and bravado.

Moving like a stag, Samael slipped sideways between buttressed trunks. Now moss yielded under his bare feet, pale brown moisture puddling in the gap beside his great toe with each step, dripping away again when the construct foot was lifted. Each drop fell silently, absorbed again without a trace.

Tristen followed. Mallory walked a few steps behind, lithe as if dancing.

"It's a big Heaven," Samael said, when they had been picking their way for fifteen minutes through forest so dense that even the two meters between them often meant that Tristen could glimpse the angel only as a gleam of pale skin, pale hair, fluid motion behind leafy concealment.

Tristen pushed between clustered trunks—some mere slips, some bigger than the span of three men's arms. Orchids and bromeliads dripped amazing sprays of bloom from head height and higher. The air droned and sang with the vocalizations of tiny animals. Tristen ducked a scentless, vivid, fuchsia-and-lemon *Cattleya* only to find himself face-to-wing with a pair of black-and-green butterflies engaged in a savage territorial dispute. A matter of life and death to them; to him, an amusing minor spectacle. *And that's what you look like to an angel.*

"Is this all one tree?" Tristen laid his hand on the bark of the nearest trunk.

Samael nodded. "It's choked out everything else that grew here," he said. His feet might be material, but the fat ant-crawling fig that detached from a branch over his head fell through his outline to explode against a root, spattering Tristen's boots with pulp.

Tristen wrinkled his nose at the reek of sugar. "We should collect some of those."

Negligently, Samael raised one hand and made a scooping gesture. Tristen knew it was the colony, but there was still something unsettling about dozens of ripe, velvety fruits gliding through the air to hover before him.

Tristen also knew better than to let the angel see he was disconcerted. He just produced a mesh from his armor, bundled the figs—except a slightly crushed one—into it, and handed them back to Mallory, who accepted without comment.

Tristen was contemplating splitting that last bruised fruit with the necromancer when a shrill, panicked sound cut the green chatter. A long trumpeting, harsh and hollow, echoed to a sharp fall.

The jungle was far too dense for running. With a glance at the others, Tristen tossed the fig away and broke into a careful canter, bouncing from foothold to foothold, twisting between trunks. Sound echoed confusingly in the confines of the Heaven, bouncing back from a ceiling invisible through the canopy overhead, muffled and refracted by verdant greenery and the hard shapes of tree trunks. He cupped his hands to his ears as it faded, hoping to hear enough that his colony could help triangulate location and distance for the source.

"Fan out," Tristen said, as Samael's avatar vanished in a swirl that glittered like sun-struck dust, leaves and bits of insect carapace bouncing gently off the turf.

If this were a lure to ambush, it was hard to say if staying together or parting company would be safer— but it was definitely the more effective means by which to search.

Tristen hoped the angel was already doing what he ordered. For himself, he moved light-footed in the direction from which he estimated the cry had come. It repeated; this time he was closer, he thought, and he got a better fix.

"Here," Samael said in his ear.

He turned, and found himself looking through a

curtain of leaves at the back of Mallory's head. Vigilant, he moved toward it, his nostrils full of the steam of the jungle and some ranker scent. Heavy, musty. Musky.

"Damn," he said, as he came up beside the necromancer, and the object of Mallory's attention cried again in obvious fear and distress.

The quadruped was the largest animal Tristen had ever seen. He estimated the weight at over two hundred kilograms, though it was hard to tell precisely because its body was covered with a coarse, grizzled coat of strands as long as Tristen's forearm. It stood approximately chest height, its high, double-domed head decorated with two small, flapping ears and a prehensile appendage that groped frantically toward the nearest fig tree.

Its broad, splay-toed, hind foot, Tristen saw, was jammed between two angled, overgrowing roots, and in its panic it was only wedging itself further.

"What in the world is *that*?"

"A baby wooly mammoth," Samael said, coalescing beside him. "If it were to become full-grown, it might weigh in excess of fifteen tons." The angel shook his head.

"But where did it come from?"

Samael glanced at him, long, droopy face rearranging itself in surprise. "Biosystems failure," he said. "It's an emergency option."

"You're responsible for this?"

"Oh, no," Samael said. "It's autonomous. When the world is so damaged that its habitats are in danger of collapse, it is programmed to go into a recovery mode that includes releasing a selection of random cloned species, to see which become established." He gestured to the mammoth. "Apparently, some of them are *truly* random."

Tristen stared at the mammoth. Confronted with the

apparent intractability of its situation, it had quieted, but he did not think that quiet in this case equated with calm. Instead, it cringed back against its tethering foot, trunk coiling and uncoiling nervously as it watched them through its fringe.

"A mammoth," he said, glancing to the silent Mallory for confirmation, as if repeating it would help him concretize. "A *mammoth*."

Samael nodded. "There's no way to support her, of course. She'll have to be sacrificed."

The sword on Tristen's hip murmured, *Save her.*

11

aimless angels

Shall the companions make a banquet of him? Shall they part him among the merchants? Canst thou fill his skin with barbed irons? Or his head with fish spears?
—Job 41: 6-7, King James Bible

Caitlin would have far rather returned Jsutien to an acceleration bay or, failing that, a hospital tank, but he was awake now and she was stuck with him. Well, technically the hospital tank was still an option, but an Exalt didn't need that much resource support for a simple skull fracture, and Caitlin thought Jsutien would require little attention while sleeping off his injury.

Also, she needed him and she didn't trust him, and she didn't really want him out of her sight. So she left him tucked in a corner of Central Engineering, one arm nanoshackled to the magnetized leg of his cot. While he snored she directed survey operations and created prioritized lists of existing damage, impending damage, and available consumables for Nova's convenience.

Status one was to repair, patch, or at least seal off catastrophic injury to the world—anything that represented an immediate danger to integrity, biosystems, or consumable or static resources. The irony being that many of those consumable resources would *be* consumed in the process of effecting the necessary repairs.

A quandary, but if God had made the world perfect, there would be no need for evolution.

Pursuant to those goals, Caitlin instituted protocols geared toward halting the expansion of null zones and the establishment of new ones, diagnosing the source, and regaining control of existing ones as rapidly as possible. Reinforcing the superstructure, collecting raw material, and choosing an immediate harvestable destination were also driving priorities.

Further down the list fell niceties such as stabilizing the world's biosystems. Caitlin ranked crew comfort close to last. They could stay in the acceleration pods.

And if it came to pass that she needed to sacrifice some percentage of them to keep the rest alive—an eventuality she was not yet prepared to face as anything but a hypothetical—it would be easier to make the decision if they were still in suspension.

Seated at the console Benedick had repaired, Caitlin rested her forehead against the backs of her fingers and sighed in exhaustion.

"We're still bleeding atmosphere and water?" She rubbed her aching hands. Her overstressed colony wasn't managing much damage control against the small aches and agonies of life. For a moment Caitlin thought of Benedick, the strength of his hands and how they could ease the ache. She bit her cheek and swept memories aside.

The angel's voice was soothing and neutral. "Faster than we can replenish them, Chief Engineer. At this point, we are mostly losing consumables by capillary bleed, though the Captain has caught two more catastrophic unmakings, though only by having the Captain review feeds from external video motes. Generally a tiny leak is harder to locate and seal than a vast one, but—"

"You're still having problems seeing things?"

"It is a concern," the angel admitted.

Caitlin was already learning to determine the new angel's moods, despite its tendency to sound more methodical than personable. A matter of integration, she thought. As it brought its shattered personalities closer to consensus, it might find more range and depth of response. In the meantime, much of the processing power that could otherwise have gone to independent action and autonomous thought was bound up merely continuing the process of integration. And Perceval was a relatively inexperienced Captain, which meant that much of the executive guidance and disaster response had to come from Caitlin, the Chief Engineer.

A Chief Engineer who right this instant bitterly missed Susabo, the former Angel of Propulsion. Or even Inkling, who would not have had to be so carefully led. The most frustrating part was that she knew Susabo and Inkling were both present there inside Nova, some-where—just not yet entirely compiled into the whole. Caitlin itched to pound her fists on the console and scream "Integrate faster!"

But such additional pressure was unlikely to net her good results.

She took a deep breath and said, "Nova, at this point would it be more efficient to allocate those resources to increasing our speed, thus feeding the ramscoop faster? If we can counterbalance the lossage with increased input—"

"My calculations indicate that that is a viable option," the angel agreed. "We will still be limping, and eventually we will outstrip the blown-off gas cocoon of the supernova, at which point collectable resources will become more sparse. We will need to be ready with other options. Chief Engineer, not to interrupt myself, but—"

A hesitating angel was never a good sign. "Spit it out."

"Samael wishes to speak to you."

Caitlin wondered if her symbiont couldn't at least do a little something about the headache. She set her armor to provide more back and neck support, and said, "Put him on."

Because he was communicating with a high-ranking Engineer, Samael did her the courtesy of generating only a partial avatar—a gleaming focal point that materialized with a polite chirp. Quickly and efficiently, he explained that the world appeared to have reset in some fashion, and as part of its last-ditch effort at survival, it was not only releasing life-forms selected at random from its genetic banks, but altering them.

"The biosphere is mutating under stress," Caitlin restated, to be sure she understood.

"That appears to have been what the Builders intended."

If he were material, or possibly just present, she would have thrown something at him. "Well, *stop* it, Samael."

"I haven't the strength anymore for ventures such as that." When Caitlin glared at Samael's avatar, he added, "I am not equipped to lie to you."

"Right," she said, and restructured her to-do list. "Give me back to Nova, please."

Samael's confident, glowing polyhedral winked out, to be replaced by Nova's silver-haired avatar. Whether the young angel thought her crew would be more comforted by a face to respond to or whether she sought the reassurance of a human seeming for herself, Caitlin did not know. She was simply grateful that Nova had chosen a form so unlike any of her component parts. It broke her heart enough to look in the angel's alien eyes and catch a fleeting expression that reminded her of Rien. She did not care to imagine how she would have borne it if the features that wore that manner resembled her adopted daughter's. Better for Nova to be as different as she could.

Then she wondered when she had begun thinking of the angel as a *she*. There was nothing about Nova to indicate or imply a sex, and as Caitlin knew them, the vast majority of angels had always been *he* by courtesy, much as ships were *she*.

Focus, Chief Engineer, she reprimanded herself. Funny how the alienation of a title could make you hold yourself together in the face of the impossible.

Caitlin said, "Thank you, Nova. I'm going to list off our immediate complex of problems as I understand it, and I'd appreciate it if you'd check my logic and see if I've missed anything."

Frowning, the angel nodded. "Carry on."

Verbalization was a slow and monodimensional means of exchanging information, but it demanded linearity and precision, so Caitlin chose to speak out loud rather than to transmit a problem matrix. In a measured fashion, she listed everything she'd previously considered, added Samael's intelligence on the *Jacob's Ladder*'s biosphere reboot process as an immediate concern, mentioned the pursuit of Arianrhod and Asrafil, and finished, "And there are the other denizens of the world to consider. Not everyone and everything who didn't make it into tanks will have died. The biosphere—especially the synbiotic and Exalt biosphere—is proving to possess remarkable resilience. Perceval needs to understand that there are probably people out there who have no understanding of their environment or the realities of the situation. People who will, unfortunately, need to be . . . educated. And then governed."

The euphemisms felt gritty on her tongue. She worked her mouth around where they'd passed as if to rid herself of the taste.

"Disaster mitigation is an ongoing process," Nova said blandly, leading Caitlin to wonder (again) exactly what the angel's facade concealed. When she had time, she was going to procure the Captain's approval to pin Nova into a corner and do some serious spelunking around the inside of her program.

It was possible that the angel might even approve of her interference. If Caitlin had enough unassimilated bits of other people kicking around the inside of her skull, she'd be crying for a competent code intervention.

The angel said, "It's a problem of management as much as anything. The pendulum could still tip us into catastrophic collapse."

The angel's words conjured an image of the world as a ghost world, burning lifeless between the stars, bored and aimless angels at play among its silent struts and habitats.

Caitlin said, "You'd survive it."

"I would be lonely."

Whether she had timed it to make Caitlin laugh or not, it worked, and the break in tension allowed Caitlin to turn her attention back to the problem at hand.

"Right. We're not out of the event horizon, as it were," Caitlin said. "And we can't afford to work on these problems in isolation. Any functional solution will be a systemic one. Can you maintain the current level of habitability? If necessary, what if we pull back to the core and allow individual anchores, holdes, and domaines to maintain for themselves as they can?"

It was what the world had been built for, and that ability to compartmentalize was what had allowed it to remain a viable organism through the past five hundred years, despite crippling trauma. The world was modeled on a living thing—and life was stubborn.

But that compartmentalization was also what had led to so many of their current problems.

"I can fall back into myself as necessary," the angel agreed. "However, that leaves many a beachhead for the power or powers behind the null zones. We still haven't managed to obtain any evidence one way or the other about the possibility that if the world's idiot systems are attempting to reboot the biospheres, they may also have available backup versions of the original angel. We need to determine if the null zones are areas where Israfel is attempting to respawn from backup. None of that, however, explains the disassembly incidents."

"Given how far our goals, and your program, have diverged from the Builders' intent, that's not a reassuring scenario."

The angel skinned lips back from imaginary teeth. "He would eat me in a heartbeat. We are not without advantages, however. The houses of Rule and Engine are unified at last."

Caitlin snorted. "Because the houses of Rule and Engine are *decimated*. No, Nova, I'm sorry. You're right. It is an advantage." She rubbed her armored wrist with her armored palm. "If we can find a way to work together. And trust each other."

"You are thinking of my Captain's father."

Caitlin's smile felt thin and stretched across her skull. "Of course I'm thinking of Benedick. I've sent him out there alone, hunting a woman who was his ally in a scheme to keep Rule and Engine from each other's throats. A woman who was his friend and lover." She stopped herself before she said: *But not his partner.* There was nothing uglier than a self-justification.

Instead, she continued, "She is my great-grandniece, and also the mother and ally of the woman who is responsible for the decimation of Rule. His daughter with *her* has died and metamorphosed into a fragment of you, my dear Nova. His daughter and mine is your Captain. Are you still human enough, a little, to understand why I am worried what he'll do?"

"You must," said the angel, "reach out to him."

"You're a fine one to give relationship advice," she said, folding her arms over her chest. She turned away.

She was old enough to know it for a useless display even as she did so, but it made her feel better.

She closed her eyes and shook her head. "What else?" she asked, when her eyes had stopped stinging.

The angel's avatar reappeared before her, shifting orientation to match her. "Chief Engineer—" The angel lifted her chin, folded her arms, and spat the words out as if she expected Caitlin to argue. "My Captain is not emotionally well."

"I know," Caitlin said. The angel's tone made her want to reach out and lay a hand on its immaterial nape, pull its face into her neck, and stroke it down the spine. As she would have done for her daughter, once. "We shall carry on for her as we can, and buy her time to heal enough to shoulder the burdens she must bear."

"Is that the mother talking, or the Chief Engineer?"

"What can we do about the null zones, if we're not surrendering them?" Caitlin said, as if it were an answer. Perhaps it was, of sorts.

"Prince Benedick and Princess Chelsea are approaching the largest one," Nova said, "in the far south of the world. It is where Arianrhod—and Asrafil, if Samael can be believed—have taken shelter. Benedick and Chelsea have the toolkit, their armor, and their own colonies; odds are good I will be able to remain in contact. I will ask them to reconnoiter. Perhaps they will provide us with some intelligence on what, exactly, is blocking my access to the area."

"If it doesn't eat them."

"Or—perhaps more likely—subvert their colonies."

"Belly of the beast," Caitlin said, and bit the back of her hand.

Without your mate, your fathers, your brothers, your sons, you are as nothing. You are as a calf, all but blinded.

But you are not without resources.

Ironically, the vermin's machine viruses are the first of those resources to which you turn. They penetrate your organs, infect your instincts, confuse your intellect. But they have done that for so long now that you have had time to habituate to them, to grow accustomed and adapt. And to modify them in turn as they have modified you. To guide their evolution and make them your own.

Having done so, you feed them back into the slaver spikes, an upstream trickle of Trojan horses disguised in the empty shells of gutted nanotech. They spread, connect, convert others. Become a network of their own—an island galaxy in the information universe of the vermin-world.

And when you have made *that,* you can make the next thing. Because there is material here, vermin-life, planetcrawlers. Parasites, things that infect a world, devour its substance, spawn in hives and cast off to the next innocent victim. But you can use the vermin's machine viruses, alter that life, repurpose it. Consume it as the vermin consumed your mate, so as to remake something more to your liking.

You have no freedom. You have no pod. You have no sons, no legacy. You have no offspring born of the bodies of yourself and your mate. But you have designs that could amend those lacks.

For now, you shall make do with monsters.

Arianrhod made the angel put her down so she could walk into her daughter's house on her own feet, as befitted an Engineer. Ariane's domaine was small and defensible, an ant-warren of tunnels and rooms that twisted back on itself to form a three-dimensional labyrinth. It was full of dead ends and deadfalls, and Arianrhod herself did not know them all. What she did know was the path to the heart of the place.

When last she came here, every wall had pulsed with life, twining veins of blue and green algae filtering the light of the waystars and turning it to sugar and oxygen. Now the tubes were shattered, the sludge within frozen into coils and sprays she must break off or edge past.

She feared that what she'd come for was lost to the Enemy, but at the heart of her daughter's holdfast she found the small room as she remembered it, a cozy weightless sphere with a console and a vault. The vault was DNA-locked, but that was less problem than it might have been: Arianrhod carried a stasis phial of her daughter's cultured heart cells as a memento, and it was the work of a moment to retrieve it from where it lay cradled in the flesh of her own bosom. Having plucked the phial from the pucker of skin that pushed it free, she unlocked it and let it open on her palm like the petals of a crystal flower. Drifting, her hair alive around her like the tentacles of a curious octopus, she bent to inspect it.

Awakened, the fragment of tissue managed two or three reflexive contractions before the breath of the Enemy froze it. Arianrhod winced in sympathy; returned to her breast, it would thaw fast enough and her symbiont could heal it, but at the moment she felt for its pain.

A scraping gave her what she needed, and she folded the rest away inside her again. A smear of cells across her thumb, frozen, clinging to her own frosting skin, and she laid the pad against the reader. In the emptiness, she could not speak the access codes, but the lock accepted a data pulse and she felt the transmitted tremor as bolts slipped free.

The apparatus had been twisted in acceleration, and she had to grow flat blades of claws and pry to help the drawer slide free, but what lay inside was intact. Black as a splinter of the Enemy's teeth, sharp as a laser, flat and unreflective as a hole in the universe, more than a meter of hiltless blade rested like a naked singularity cradled in the crumbled monofilament silk of engineered moths.

"They were consumed," Asrafil said inside her mind, leaning over her shoulder. "All the unblades went into the consuming angel."

Not this one, Arianrhod answered. *The angel only got the other half. Half-compiled, virulent, fragmentary. But this is what remains of Tristen's Charity.*

This is the last unblade in the world. And you're going to make me a scabbard and a hilt for it, angel.

Perceval said, "I do not mind the cold."

She must admit to having heard Nova's protest, but the angel's words were wasted. They might as well have been the crying of birds, the creak of old metal contracting in the Enemy's deep chill.

"I don't mind it," she repeated. She rested her palms on the newly reconstructed portals. Beyond them, the Enemy waited, green with the death of the waystars, their final light occluding the suns beyond. She could make out a few, the hottest or closest, veil-swathed and dim. "Do not waste your warmth on me."

Dust and Pinion had changed her, before she changed them in return. She was the Captain of the *Jacob's Ladder*, and barely meat anymore. The Enemy could no more harm her than it could harm an angel. If she, Perceval, did not deserve to suffer for the comfort and well-being of others, then the dead men and women she harbored most certainly did.

Speaking of angels, hers stood behind her still as if he—as if *she*—had not heard her answer. Perceval might be tempted to say she hovered, but though she wore gray wings, dove-soft and warm-looking as a cloak, she stood on her feet like anyone.

"Captain," she said, a soft protest she could not

exactly call an argument, "you may not need the warmth. But anyone who might come to visit you—"

"Is it not my bridge?" She turned her head to see the angel with her own eyes, though that had become another conceit that did not matter. Her colony told her where Nova was; she knew her shape and colors and stance as if she looked upon her, no matter whether she bothered with an avatar or no. She felt her movements as her own, but that wasn't what she wanted. For the moment, she wanted plain human vision, with all its limits and inadequacies. She wanted to see with her own eyes, though they showed her less reality than could adapted ones.

Perceval's slow, blink-punctuated stare didn't seem to concern Nova. The angel said, "Would you have your crew come before you only if they are armor-clad?"

She did not answer.

Nova swept a wing across the floor. "Are you so much a Princess after all that you'd sacrifice this grass, these flowers, these gardens of your bridge, to feed your own selfish grief?"

The voice pushed her a step back as surely as a hand. She recognized the tone, the fleeting brow-furrowed expression. She spun away before her face could break and said between her teeth, "Don't be her with me."

She expected a protest.

Instead, the angel just said, "What parts of me are her? You'll have to tell me. There is so much within me, Captain. So much that argues, and does not agree." Nova extended a hand. "I will listen to you. I *must* listen to you. But you must speak to me, for only you can make my heart quiet."

Perceval breathed in so deeply it made her chest ache like a distended balloon, and held it.

Softer, and not in any voice Perceval recognized, Nova said, "I cannot be her with you. I cannot be Dust.

You would not like me any better as Samael or Asrafil or Inkling. I am only the angel they have wrought me, Captain, though I am as yet a thing mosaic-made from chips. But all those shards serve you, and you alone." The angel paused, as if groping after words. As if settling an argument that Perceval could not overhear. "And serve you I must."

Nova's warm-looking wing encompassed her, covered her shoulders, and proved not warm at all but nearly weightless. The voices inside Perceval yammered responses, pushing, arguing with each other and herself. *Silence them,* she told herself, but it was an order easier issued than obeyed.

"As I must serve the world," Perceval said. She wanted nothing more than to shrug away the angel's embrace, but somehow restrained herself. "We are bound to it."

"We are but familiar demons," the angel agreed. "Forgive me."

Perceval closed her eyes. "Sweetheart," she said, "I'm trying. And it's not your fault that I hate you."

Asrafil enfolded Arianrhod in the borders of his colony, and they fell into the bosom of the Enemy again. Charity, its shortened blade more suited to her height now, lay across her back in the fittings Asrafil had constructed for it. It felt strange there—unpresent, empty, neutral, still, and waiting to be filled.

Hungry, if she allowed herself to anthropomorphize so far. She kept wanting to touch it to reassure herself it was really there, or really gone.

"We are still followed," Asrafil said softly, inside her as if reluctant to disturb her train of thought.

"From Engineering?" Arianrhod asked. "Our path should lead them down through the lift to the Broken Holdes."

"It is as you arranged," he agreed. "Benedick is determined, and he has found an ally. Young Chelsea Conn is with him on the hunt."

Arianrhod grimaced, feeling her frozen cheeks crack in the cold. Chelsea should have died usefully in the plague, and having survived that, it seemed a shame to kill her now.

But pity had no place in the world Arianrhod had been raised to. "If they're in the shaft," she said, "I left them an enemy there."

Below the halfway point, Benedick and Chelsea rested again, this time on a shelf fungus broad as a dining table. They slept in shifts, and—having tested the environment and found it within the tolerances of their colonies— opened their helms and breathed the spore-sweet air while they dined on a variety of nutritious fungi and eyeless shaft-dwelling insects. When they resumed descending, Benedick took point.

He was still in the lead when light began to glimmer through the caps beneath his feet. He notified Chelsea and slowed his descent. Transition zones were often most dangerous—the haunt of predators lying in wait for something that had blundered out of its usual range, something that might be confused, disoriented, or ill.

Nothing attacked him when he lowered himself into the gap that permitted access to the next stratum, but only the armor's filters saved him from bedazzlement when he found himself encircled by a beaded curtain of falling water refracting brightness. The mushroom forest, it seemed, could not retain every drop lost by the long-cracked irrigation system.

Benedick shook his head and spun himself on the cable for a 360-degree view, watching rainbows, their polarized light intensified by his filters, skip across his armor.

"I'm down," he said to Chelsea, and with minimal exertion swung himself up to the lip of the shaft. The swifts darted about, screaming and buzzing his head and hands, but even if they had dared come close enough to strike, their talons would have proved ineffectual. He clipped in to a convenient knobby growth of woody fungus and settled himself. "Ready to belay."

He had time to observe the shaft below while waiting for her. The mimosa wood at its lip grew particularly verdant, and like the one above was shrieking with parrotlets. The shaft was lushly forested from this point to the south as far as he could see. He could make out the glow of lights through an extravagance of leaves.

Chelsea was with him in less than ten minutes, and he was amused to note that she duplicated his admiring spin. "Hang on," she said and, with a series of contractions and extensions of her body, swung pendulum-fashion toward the nearest cable. She stretched, spun, and plunged a hand through encrusting swifts' nests to catch on and cling tight.

Benedick watched her knife flash in the other hand, and the grace with which she intercepted the falling material. When she released the cable, she had a meshed bundle of the cleanest nests and a few dozen tiny eggs, to add to the chunks of tested-safe mushroom that made up their foraged rations.

"Break for dinner?" Chelsea said, when she swung close to him again.

Once she was safely latched in, Benedick unclipped himself. "All you think of is food."

"Bird's nest soup," she tempted, and lowered him before he asked. He had to swing a little to make contact with the rim of the shaft. But once his feet struck the deck the mimosas drew back to make a protected glade, and he brought Chelsea down to it with no trouble.

The easiest method for cooking the soup involved

painstaking deployment of the microwave projectors in their toolkit. The toolkit curled around the collapsible bowl, and Benedick and Chelsea cupped their shielded gauntlets around it, careful lest stray radiation should cook their eyeballs, their internal organs, or any passing birds. Soon they were sharing a steaming, pleasantly mucilaginous bowl of bird's nest soup studded with chunks of mushroom and soft-poached swift eggs.

"This is awfully idyllic for a high-speed chase," Chelsea said as Benedick wiped out the dinner dishes. He was worried about the toolkit's charge, though he could replenish it from his armor if need be.

The toolkit itself was almost underfoot, seeming determined to maintain a wide berth from the mimosa. Benedick couldn't say he blamed it. He clucked, and the toolkit got a running start, leaped to his extended hand, and scampered up his arm.

"There's little to be gained by catching her if we're too exhausted to do anything about it," Benedick said mildly. He folded the bowl away and tucked it into his pack.

"That also sounds like something Father would have said."

Benedick set his cable, ignoring the irrational twinge of irritation. He was not his father, and Chelsea was not Tristen. "One time or another, I'm certain he did. Do you wish to lead the first descent?"

From the examining glance Chelsea cast across Benedick's face as she fixed their lines together, she knew perfectly well that he was holding back. She might even know *what*; he was always surprised by the gaps and bridges in the younger siblings' knowledge of family history.

No blame on them for that. It wasn't as if he or Tristen had gone out of their way to make themselves available to teach. The fact that their father had disallowed such knowledge only increased their onus to have passed it along. Maybe their reasons were different—Benedick, as far as he knew, had far more to be ashamed of than Tristen, and he would have been happy to let his many failings remain private history—but the truth was, both of them were complicit in Alasdair Conn's conspiracy of lies.

So in the light of everything else, perhaps it was an insignificant failure. Nonetheless, it remained one that griped at Benedick, as further evidence of his own moral cowardice—something he thought he'd already established to everyone's satisfaction.

"Right," Chelsea said. "See you at the bottom of the rope." She swung a leg over the lip, and was gone.

For a time, they progressed as before, leapfrogging one another down the shaft. In this section, lighting and terraces were intact, cane-thin rods vining between the trees to provide illumination. Benedick's suit prickled to warn him of unfiltered ultraviolet. He sealed his helm in response. He'd had enough of radiation burns.

As he slid down the cable, the overall effect was of gliding spider-silent through a cool, dappled tunnel. The vegetation, while lush, was climax growth, full of open spaces and long, clear lines of sight. After the cramped overgrowth of the previous shaft, the spacious bowers of this vertical forest soothed him. It would be harder for an enemy to ambush them here.

The life here was more familiar, though the oxygen levels remained high enough that he still saw insects of unusual size. In this microenvironment, those included flying forms: a dragonfly whose jeweled purple-blue body hung between wings of a half-meter span; a ladybug as big as a dinner plate.

Benedick wondered what such large arthropods consumed, and resolved to keep an eye out for predatory insect nymphs the size of his thigh. The stealthy manner of his descent—the only sound he made was in the brush of leaves against his armor and the whir of cable through the winch—meant that he passed within touching distance of many animals before they were even aware of his existence. A half-meter spotted cat hissed and vanished; a green-tinged sloth reached with dreamy control from one branch to another and swung away.

He grinned behind his helm—an expression that would have shocked most of his siblings. This was serious business. And he had a reputation for mirthlessness that he thought was as much the result of conditioned anhedonia as anything intrinsic to his character.

But the oxygen levels could make you giddy, and it was hard not to cheer up when you saw a sloth.

Mind on your work, Ben, he thought, in Caitlin's phrasing, and tried not to be too distracted by the wildlife.

Besides the high oxygen, one thing this shaft had in common with the one above was that it was *cold*. He couldn't feel it through the armor, but the sloth's long, coarse coat shone at the tips with frost, and frost also rimed the edges of the broad tree leaves. That had to be new, or transitory, because the trees themselves were hale, their foliage not yet curling.

That told him the system was continuing to lose heat, and heat was a thing not easily replaced unless they could find a way to generate energy—or tap the radiant heat of the expanding core of the supernova behind them, but that presented its own complex of problems.

He wondered how the trees had stayed intact through the acceleration. Perhaps—even broken and locked to a single setting—the gravity controls of the old commuter shaft were strong enough that they had locally compensated. It was an interesting hypothesis, because it carried the implication that, throughout the world, there might be other similarly protected spaces that could have sheltered anything within them. When they emerged from blackout, he would contact the angel and Caitlin with the suggestion.

A large trunk blocked his descent immediately below. He flexed knees to land lightly on it, stood, checked the cable with a quick glance up, and hopped over the side just as he heard Chelsea yelp through the comm.

"Benedick!"

Caitlin was the only person left alive who called him Ben. When she was speaking with him to call him anything.

"Here," he answered, one hand on the cable brake. He didn't trigger it yet, though—until you understand the situation, or you understand that halting will do less damage than pushing on, don't provide the enemy with intelligence.

"I'm under attack," she said. "Ambu—" Half the word, until her comm cut out.

Well, I guess that's a hint that we're on the right path. He slowed his descent, fighting the urge to rush. Charging to the rescue was one thing, so long as one was certain that one *was* charging to the rescue and not barreling into a trap. Silently, his black and bronze-brown armor blending into the dappled shadows of the leaves, he rotated himself so as to descend headfirst, and slipped lower.

The comm stayed dead, but before long his armor brought him the ambient sounds of combat. Crashing, a heavy thump, the splinter of green wood. No sound of weapons fire, which was suggestive.

The toolkit said "Brrt?" against his cheek.

"Shh," he answered. He swung in close to the nearest trunk and anchored the cable, in case Chelsea was still using it; he could sense weight on the opposite end. Then he disconnected himself and began the painstaking process of pressing close against the trunk and circling it.

Like a squirrel, he thought, as something liver red and about as large as his outstretched hand crashed through leaves nearby and bounced hard off the trunk of an age-gnarled sycamore as big around as an air lock door. Whatever it was, it left a trail of sparks, and a meat-colored smear on the tree's patchy green-and-silver trunk before arcing away through the canopy. Benedick sank spiked gauntlet-tips into the trunk of his own tree—branches to break the fall or not, it was a long way down—and continued his careful circumnavigation. *Fight on, Sister. I'm coming.*

Head-down around the curve of the trunk, he caught sight of her. She was indeed fighting, though her form was almost completely obscured by the lumpy, humping shapes of more of the hand-sized attackers. They shoved and jostled over the surface of her armor, as—blindly, with groping hands, because they occluded her faceplate as well—she clutched at them, grabbed and peeled, hurled them aside in a mess of bridging sparks. More dropped from the branches around her, however; the undersides of nearby trees writhed with the things, and for every one she got off, two more attached themselves.

Benedick hooked his knees over a thick, bent limb, having checked the underside for attackers, and—hanging like a sloth—stretched out both hands. The microwave projectors that had so successfully heated his supper had other uses now. While he didn't dare point them directly at Chelsea, even within the protection of her armor, the first step in getting her free was stopping the reinforcements. He couldn't do much about the ones humping down the cable toward her, like malevolent drops of molasses slipping along a string. But the dozens clustered on the undersides of the tree trunks, waiting their opening—those were fair game.

"Toolkit," he said. As his helm unsealed, he felt its silken fur uncoil from around his neck. A second later, it slithered the length of his arms. It plugged itself into a wrist outlet and reared up, spreading its fragile-seeming arms wide.

The liver-colored things sizzled but made no other sound. Like insects frying in the concentrated rays of the sun, they writhed, convulsed, and scaled from the trunk in showers, tumbling away below. Some, he heard hit solidly—a meaty thump as they smacked into a trunk or a limb. Some just brushed the leaves aside and vanished into the depths.

It didn't take long, which was a godsend. Microwaving burned stored power, and unless he was moving the armor couldn't use his own kinetic energy to recharge its batteries. Unassisted, the power cells wouldn't support this kind of expenditure long—and the toolkit couldn't have handled that sort of burn without his armor's help at all. But after less than ninety seconds, the only attackers remaining were the ones clinging to Chelsea and a few others too close to her to burn.

Benedick missed his anchor cable now. As the toolkit scampered back inside the safety of his helm, he grabbed the limb supporting his weight—and the equal weight of his armor—freed his legs, and pumped twice hard to make the swing-and-grab to Chelsea's side. He couldn't hear her, but it was possible that the fleshy, leechlike attackers were blocking her comm out but not in.

"It's me," he said reassuringly, as she got her gauntlets under the edge of a leech-thing on her faceplate, peeled it off, and cast it aside.

Like the others, it made no noise as it fell. He could see that the clear panel of her faceplate was etched where the thing had gripped her; he might have improved her vision slightly, but only just.

"We'll get those off you," Benedick continued, and reached for one that was humped up, prying at the join of her chest plate and helm.

It took doing. The ones next to it grabbed at his fingers with toothed, suckery margins. The one he meant to dislodge was strong, slick with mucus that scarred the fingertips of his gauntlets, and prone to firing off blue sparks when touched. Benedick's armor handled the electricity well, but when he finally got the little bastard off Chelsea's neck, it writhed in his fist and wrapped his gauntlet. His armor reported a sharp and immediate drop in power.

"Leeches," Benedick said, disgustedly, and slammed his hand against the branch he was hanging from to crush it.

At least that worked, resoundingly. The creature sparked and went limp. As he threw it away he caught a glimpse of ripped muscle, a translucent slime of blood, and through that, the dulled gleam of circuitry.

Chelsea's armor arced, her struggles weakening. She still fought, but sluggishly; all her strength was devoted to moving the armor, which now impeded rather than assisted her. Benedick hooked his legs around another nearby bough to free both hands. Now that he had a better idea of the enemy, he didn't bother peeling them away. He just pressed paired thumbs into the center of each, feeling for a power source or heart. The muscle was tough, resilient. Fibers mushed unpleasantly aside until he felt things crunch.

He had gotten three of them off her—and could make out the shadow of her conscious face and open eyes behind the milky, etched faceplate—when the second wave arrived, dropping through the leaves above with a patter like falling rain. He swung his hands up, summoned the toolkit, and opened fire without concerning himself with whatever might be behind them. There were times to worry about collateral damage. This was not one.

The first group died as they fell, sizzling and smoking. Behind them came more, though, in such numbers that he couldn't kill them all. The dead ones knocked his arms aside, then living ones struck and clung. He lost the toolkit when they knocked it from his wrist. He heard it shriek as it fell, and flinched from the sound.

Bioweapon. Quite obviously, because nothing would evolve to keep attacking when it was being so decimated.

Through the armor he felt no pain, but he heard the hiss of the ablative coating being eaten away, and the armor transmitted the hump and suck of the leeches' suckered bellies all too well. Power levels spiraled; the biomechanicals swarmed across his visor, obscuring vision with their flat, fleshy bellies, as if someone had thrown handfuls of organ meats across his face. He scraped his fingers across the helm, squeezing, and felt the muscle and fluids of the one he gripped pulp and ooze around its internal core of electronics and wires. Whatever scraps were left, he cast aside, and reached for the next leech, only to halt as something whipped softly around his wrist, restraining him. He pulled, feeling elasticity but no give. Something in them blocked all the armor's extended senses. Chelsea was somewhere to his left, still hanging from the cable, her armor powered down and incapacitating, but he couldn't feel her. If he could reach—

But now something tangled the other arm as well, and stretched against his waist. More and more, but whatever entangled him was also dragging the leeches off. He caught flashes of bright gold and fuchsia movement beyond his scarred, milky faceplate. Through an unscarred corner he thought he saw a beribboned, crested head like that of a fanciful dragon toss one leech up and gulp it down like a pelican gulping a fish. Then he felt pain, the burn of something along his left arm, and would have struggled as tendrils infiltrated the crushed, eroded elbow joint and pried the vambrace loose.

It slithered away. He would have snatched after it, but something held his wrist. Gently. More gently than he would have expected.

"Who are you?" he said, as the faceplate opened, too, and he became conscious of another burning on his face. The digestive fluid of the leeches, which he was feeling now as adrenaline ebbed. "Who are you? What are you? What do you want?"

Pain faded. Something sticky and cool bathed his arm; tender fingers—or something—picked around the edges of his wound, debriding. He blinked, saw bright silken fabric ripple before his eyes, and bent to peer around it to look for Chelsea.

She slumped two meters off, armor cracked open and bright swaths of green gel decorating her face, her shoulders, and a portion of her chest and collarbone that was marked with the angry red of acid burns. Petals hung all around her face and head like halos—a spray of enormous orchids, white harlequined with thick, wet-looking crimson—and something had disconnected her cable and hauled her to firm footing on a broad limb. That seemed friendly, but Benedick was not comforted by the green coils at her wrists, waist, and about her throat.

Green coils that matched the tendrils restraining him.

"Hello?" he said, as he was lifted to his feet. "Hello, who are you?"

"Be still," said a voice, awkward and breathy. Not human, and more like the sounds of silk rubbing silk than those produced by vibrating vocal chords with air pushing through them. "Don't struggle, mammal."

"Who are you?" As Benedick lifted his face to return what *felt* like a stare, all he saw was a cluster of stems decked with five giant blossoms, mackerel-striped in violet and yellow, each of which bore a suspicious resemblance to a crested, patterned head with eyespots, frills, and a sharp-toothed, undershot, bulldog jaw. All five bent around him, turning like mirrors focusing light, and their fringes of ruffled petals lifted and flattened like the crests of a quintet of harpy eagles.

Behind the blooms, he had the impression of an asymmetrical body assembled of fat, irregular tubers and bladelike leaves as wide as his torso. They lay flat against the tubers now, like the plates of a spiny echidna, but he had reason to suspect that if the orchid was unhappy, they might not always look so sleek.

"We're the carnivorous plants," the voice said, words made of a sound like the rubbing together of hands. "Now be *still*, mammal. You're heavy. And you would not like the drop."

12

this time of trial and desperation

The greatest and main abuse of Scripture, and to which almost all the
rest are either consequent or subservient, is the wresting of it to prove
that the kingdom of God, mentioned so often in the Scripture, is the
present Church, or multitude of Christian men now living, or that,
being dead, are to rise again at the last day.
—THOMAS HOBBES, *Leviathan*

The mammoth was still screaming.

Gavin, perched on Mallory's shoulder, hid his head
under his wing as Prince Tristen and the angel Samael dis-
cussed options in low tones. Gavin would have imagined
Tristen ruthless, but the First Mate had made it flatly obvious that he had no intention of slaughtering the infant
mammoth unless no other humane option remained.

Unlike Tristen, the basilisk wasn't distressed by the
uncertain fate of the mammoth, but rather the recur-
rence of what was becoming a chronic sense of déjà vu.
He'd been here before; he had seen this before—the
broad strokes, if not the particulars. It shouldn't have
left a worm of unease gnawing his complacency, but
there was something about the mammoth, in particular,
that came with a kaleidoscope of unresolving images.

Gavin had never suffered disorientation or the imper-
manence of memory before the last few days, and the
experience was one he would have gladly forgone. Meat
people lived with this all the time. It was no wonder
every last one of them was clinically insane.

Mallory withdrew a step or two, head tilted, unwilling to intrude into this argument. Gavin, forcing his filters to process the overload of fragmentary remembrances, pulled his head from under his wing.

Whatever Tristen had just said, Samael protested. "Sentiment has no place when it comes to the engineering of biospheres."

Tristen had folded his arms. "Give the mammoth its chance."

"Because there's a place for an elephant on a spaceship?"

"The Builders made one," Tristen said. "They brought it here and ordained its birth in this time of trial and desperation. Who are we to gainsay their insight?"

Gavin forgave Tristen that last, because he said it with a mocking lilt, but he didn't blame Samael for his flinch, the contraction of all his motes and scraps as if around a blow—or the headshake that followed.

"Besides"—Tristen paused, his hand curling restlessly around the pommel of his sword as if to give the speaking weight—"are we not on Errantry?"

Samael looked away, unable to deny the truth of Tristen's statement. Instead, he fell back on the practical. "It won't reproduce."

Tristen's voice went wry, even muffled through Gavin's feathers. "How do you know? Maybe somewhere out there is its perfect complement, already bumbling through some Heaven on broad calf feet."

"We must consider lifeboat rules, My Prince. It will die," Samael said. "And whatever resources it consumes along the way to starvation may result in the deaths of other life-forms, ones with a better chance of long-term survival. It will starve, and perish in great travail and suffering."

"That is," said Tristen, in a voice so strange that Gavin stretched his head forward on its long neck, the better to listen, "the purpose and privilege of life, my dear Angel of Poison. And as your First Mate, I command you to respect it."

The angel made a small noise—perhaps of protest, perhaps of acquiescence. Gavin supposed that in the final analysis, the two were not mutually exclusive.

Tristen continued, "But surely I don't need to remind you of that. The mammoth gets its chance."

Mallory stepped forward, startling Gavin, who remembered not to clench his talons only when he felt the necromancer wince. Mallory had lived and prospered by staying aloof from conflicts between the powerful and by serving Samael quietly and well, so even Gavin was startled by what was said. "At the Breaking of the world, Samael, there were creatures such as this brought forth. Some lived and evolved, and some fell to the inevitable. If we could predict which species would survive and flourish, would we not be like unto gods?"

Mallory spoke with the conviction of experience, leading Samael to sigh and let his shoulders drop. "And its competitors?"

That was the glint of light off a toothy grin. Perhaps Tristen was ruthless after all. "Then they shall by the hand of God learn to adapt, won't they, angel?"

Mallory tensed beneath Gavin's feet, but Gavin did not need the unconscious warning. Gavin knew Tristen's expression of old: the Conn look of eagles, of certainty and command. They might be wrong, the family. They might even understand, in a sort of hypothetical, abstract fashion, that it was *possible* for them to be wrong. But neither before Rien nor since had Gavin met one who acted, even occasionally, as if she believed the possibility could apply to her.

It was a failing with which he had a sense he once had understood—in a sort of hypothetical, abstract fashion. As something that was possible. As something that could happen—*had happened*—to somebody else.

Now, staring through closed eyes at the improbable mammoth, comparing its massive, present reality with the fragmentary oneiric memories that harassed him, he understood much better the hazards of grandiose plans.

But the principles of inertia did not permit what had been set in motion to be casually set aside. Whatever the Builders had intended, they had been earthbound souls, of limited vision. They had been less than what they spawned, constrained by assumptions and fanaticisms, their creativity rooted fast. The Conns had grown beyond their progenitors. And whatever their failings, their delusions, their tendency to overreach, the tragedies they might inflict upon those who looked to them for guidance—

—the Conn family was not earthbound.

It seemed Samael knew the stare as well as he did, because the angel folded his leaf-litter arms over his scarred leaf-litter chest, grimaced, and shook his hair over his eyes. The argument was ended.

Samael said, "What would you have of us, First Mate?"

Tristen nodded a small acknowledgment and replied, "Free the mammoth, angel."

"And once I've freed it, First Mate? What would you have me do with it then?"

Tristen's smile was not promising. But—somewhat to Gavin's regret—Samael turned away before Tristen said whatever was on his lips.

Whatever its earlier panic, the mammoth went very still when the angel crouched beside it and pressed his hands to its trapped ankle. Its trunk snuffled toward him, hesitant, almost thoughtful. For a moment, Tristen thought it might attack—not that he expected any animal, no matter how impressive, to stand a chance against even a diminished angel. But the reaching trunk simply brushed Samael's cheek, snuffed deeply, and stroked his grass-fluff hair aside.

Even the beasts of the holde and Heaven, it seemed, could recognize an angel of the lord.

Samael, however reduced his circumstances, was perfectly competent to infiltrate himself between the beast's foot and the tree roots, and ease the one loose from the other. The foot glided up, Samael stood, and the mammoth backed away, moaning and swaying. The angel regarded it, frowning, wiping his hands on his trousers until the beast whirled and vanished into the leaves and trunks.

Tristen felt Mallory at his elbow, and turned in time to catch the sidelong glance. "Hope it eats figs," was all Tristen said.

Mallory winked, surprising him, and Tristen winked back. The necromancer's face lit up around a startled smile. Tristen glanced away, back at the angel, pausing to wonder just for a moment what it was like to be Mallory, with a head even more full of dead people than the Captain—and by choice.

When he was done wondering, he started forward, one hand on Mirth's hilt to keep it from swinging. A sense of praise and excitement filled him; the sword was pleased. *I didn't do it for you,* he told it, but that didn't seem to affect its happiness.

"Push on," he said, and didn't turn back to make sure the others had fallen in behind him. They'd follow.

Giving people something to follow was pretty much the only thing Conns were good for.

Arianrhod and her angel strode side by side over warm, shallow water. The sea of the Heaven was illuminated from below, water reflecting rippled light over their clothes, on the undersides of their arms, underneath their chins. The light seemed to catch in the folds of Asrafil's coat, to gild the bare skin of his skull and his pale fingers. The water's surface dimpled under a languid stride that took each wavelet into account without ever seeming discomforted by them.

Arianrhod esteemed his grace even as she hurried to keep up. But his hand was always there when she stumbled, his coat cast around her shoulders when the cold wind whipped steam from the balmy water below. Fish in jeweled colors and vivid patterns flashed beneath the surface, schooling or as individuals. Arianrhod thought she and Asrafil would have been more comfortable like the fish, just swimming. She wondered how she would have managed the waters with the unblade across her back. Probably it wouldn't impede her at all.

The fish were not only in the waters. Dark, knobby lozenges flitted past the overhead panels, fins and elaborate mouth barbels fanning as they glided on elecromagnetic currents along the walls of the Heaven. Ship cats, synbiotic plecostomi as big as a man, scrubbing the walls of the world. They breathed air and hovered on their own gravity nullifiers. This was their breeding ground, where they returned to spawn.

It was beautiful.

Arianrhod said the angel's name. "Wait," she added, and put her hand on his coat sleeve.

He stopped at once, turned to her, and laid a steadying palm against her elbow when she stumbled on a wavelet.

"Have they found us?" she asked. "Or are they still seeking at random?"

"I have kept us to the places where their angel cannot sense," Asrafil said. "Its power wanes as other powers wax, and the territory it controls is shrinking. As long as we remain beyond the disputed borders, it can locate us only through extrapolation and guessing."

He left unsaid that the guesses of an angel were often very good indeed.

"I would like to better understand where you are leading me." She could defy him. She was a Conn and an Engineer both, and if she ordered him he would have to obey her. But he was also the angel she served, and in many ways she trusted his wisdom as greater than her own.

"To parley with one of those powers," he said, reluctantly. "I will speak more if you order it, but know that I have promised to hold some information private, and I will be breaking a vow at your command."

She considered, and wondered if angels could be said to have a sense of honor. Asrafil had never betrayed her trust. Was it fair of her to command him to betray another's? She dropped her head to stare at the tossing water, her lip caught between her teeth. He shifted restlessly.

"We are pursued," he said gently. "You know it. How shall we then tarry, beloved? Come with me, and you shall soon see with your own eyes the answer to your questions, and the power that will make you Captain and return me to my rightful place as your servant and master."

"I tarry because we are pursued," she answered. She laid a hand over his on her arm, as if he escorted her. "And I know how to further delay our pursuers. Listen, Asrafil. There is a Heaven that Tristen Conn will not easily leave, if he but enters."

Tristen kept the lead as his party maintained a steady pace through the next nine hours, passing through a variety of microenvironments in various states of reconstruction. It might have been pointless bravado, but it couldn't hurt—and while the angel was close to invulnerable, he was also close to immaterial. And it was to him that Mirth whispered suggestions—not so much words as the vague sense of rightness or wrongness, the chance turn of the world.

The group passed through domaines and anchores, Heavens and corridors—and a holde full of giant, sleeping machines. They hung like strings of beads on racks stretched floor to ceiling, hundreds of meters tall, filling the width of the holde to where it curved from sight. They were yellow and black, green and blue, some marked with checkered livery. In their brilliant colors, with their blades and buckets and manipulators, they looked to Tristen like engines of war. But he could see no means for them to maneuver, unless by friction of the soil under their caterpillar treads. They would be useless in microgravity, worthless in a vacuum.

He said as much: "Are those for fighting planetside?"

"They are for terraforming," Mallory answered. "You use them to reshape planets. The Builders sent them against the time they foresaw, when we would reach a destination."

"And cannibalize the world to settle a planet," Samael said.

Gavin snaked his head from under Mallory's black mane. "What would you want with a planet?" he asked.

Tristen pursed his lips, craning over his shoulder to glance from angel to necromancer. "He asks a good question. And why this—discrete machinery, Samael? Why not something like you? Or like Gavin? A colony tool. Something with a personality, free will. Multiple uses."

"The Builders could not have anticipated that your sister the Princess Cynric would develop the colonies," Samael said. "They sent us prepared with the technology they had available at the time."

"Huh." Tristen folded his arms over his breastplate. It

was a thorny thought, that the Builders might not have foreseen what their creation would grow into.

Mallory leaned back, staring up, and said with elaborate casualness, "What a pity they can't be made to multitask."

It sparked an idea, as Tristen was sure had been intentional. The necromancer's sideways glance gave it away, which Tristen presumed was intentional, too.

"So these are scrap," Tristen said.

"They're necessary resources!" Samael protested. "When we make planetfall, they will be the primary tools we use to make our new home habitable. They are not essential now, but they will be when the world is no longer our home. They must be conserved and protected. Would you eat your seed corn?"

Tristen felt a pop like a pleasantly stretched spine, except this click was in his mind. It was as if someone had delineated a limit of the angel's program with bright lines.

He said, "You mean they would be essential supplies. If we had not, in the centuries since they were loaded aboard the world and set in mothballs, developed technology that renders them obsolete."

"First Mate," the angel said, very carefully and precisely, "are you ordering that these terraforming engines may be repurposed as salvage?"

"I order and reinforce it," Tristen said. "And when we have contact again, please pass my instructions to Nova, that it may obtain the Captain's agreement."

He was pretty sure that painful-looking curve of Samael's rose-petal lips, tugging the corners of his nose, was a smile.

In the shadowy, emergency-lit control center, Caitlin's hands rested almost motionless on contact pads that detected her involuntary micromovements and converted them to inputs. Practically telepathic, the interface allowed her to work at the speed of thought. The only drawback was the training and experience required not to wipe out several subsections when Nova pinged in before her, manifesting as a sparkling violet mote.

Across the frost-rimed tangle of wires, panels, and hologram tanks making up their temporary ops center, Jsutien registered the angel with a flick of his eyes but otherwise did not comment. He was awake, but Caitlin was not sure he was aware. At least he was not raving. His breath steamed in intermittent clouds around his face; soon they would need to divert more energy to heating, though it griped Caitlin to admit it. Before her, Nova hung glimmering, turning, awaiting recognition.

"Problem?" Caitlin asked, longing with no particular hope for reassurance.

Nova's denial still took her by surprise. "No. I have a possible location on one of the pursuit teams."

"Tristen?" Caitlin asked, because she could not force herself to ask after Benedick.

"Based on proximity and extrapolation, that seems most likely," the angel said.

Caitlin didn't wince, but it was only long training as a Conn and as an Engineer that kept her impassive. "You don't have contact, then."

Nova continued without hesitation, adapting to the interruption. "No reciprocal contact. But a large quantity of previously interdicted resources have been released to reconstruction applications under crew orders, and the information came encoded in a micropulse that appeared to originate with Samael. The Captain has directed me to refer to you for repurposing instructions."

Caitlin didn't need to ask for stats. They were already scrolling through her awareness. Multiton quantities of metal, polymer, ceramic, conductors, fuel cells, and miscellaneous material had been made available. "The obvious use would be to shore up the unraveling super-structure. Less obviously, we could hold this stuff in reserve for repairs and reconstruction in case we have to cut loose the infected portions of the world. It looks like a lot, but once we start . . . Using it is a commitment. And until we determine what the cause of the unravel-ing is, shoring up would more or less amount to tossing it into a disassembly machine."

Caitlin reached out and swiped a finger through the ice crystals on her console. The remaining ones glittered in the dim lighting. Hoarfrost.

"Sloughing off the damaged portions of the world presents problems," Nova said. "First, in locating them all. And second, they are not limited to the fringes of the superstructure. The infection has metastasized, and many of the affected sections contain biota."

"I know," Caitlin said. She glanced from the angel's jewel-presence to Jsutien, but he had closed his eyes again, and anyway this was her decision. She swallowed and made it. "Start constructing backup life-support and propulsion systems. Increase the size of the ram-scoop. Be ready to cut core systems free if necessary."

"But for now?" Nova asked, a nonhuman system seeking unambiguous confirmation.

"For now we hold on."

Much of what Tristen and his companions passed was devastation, and much of the devastation was not new. They slithered among wreckage in chambers from which the Enemy had torn all breath and life, ruptured bulkheads frozen in twisted alloy petals like balloons captured at the moment of bursting. The empty sockets of shattered viewports reflected nothing, or—in cases where the panes had webbed but another member failed before the pressure blew them clear—reflected too much, in awkward fragments that never quite matched at the edges.

Salvage had already begun here: many of the damaged sections were obviously in a state of partial deconstruction, and there were great, smooth-edged gaps in the world's superstructure where materials must have been repurposed to reinforce what could be saved. But there were no signs of rogue colony activity here—the damaged systems and sections were not merely evaporating into space, and nothing attacked the travelers.

In the blasted sections, some strata had gravity, and more did not. The domaines where one could drift or glide were easier than the ones where one must pick a route across destroyed landscapes and machinery. Tristen had his armor, and Gavin and Samael thought nothing of traversing awkwardly among rent metal, shredded wiring, and the remains of animals and plants frozen brittle at the moment of decompression, though Samael's tender petals withered and froze bruised-dark, their cell walls shattered. But Mallory suffered in the Enemy's cold, each such crossing demanding its levy in burst capillaries and lingering shakes.

Tristen had never seen the necromancer so discomfited. Nevertheless, though azure bruises blossomed under pale skin and—each time they returned to the relative warmth of a pressurized section—cerulean blood dripped from Mallory's nose to splatter the decking or float in eerie globules, there was no complaint.

The pressure doors themselves created another sort of hurdle, as many of them were not actual air locks, just emergency doors intended to maintain the integrity of sections near a damaged module. Mallory knew every code with the certainty of dead men's memories, and Gavin and Samael between them managed to improvise vacuum seals from their colonies. Through these Mallory and Tristen—with some awkwardness—could pass.

Mallory and Tristen differed on details of navigation. When they paused in pressurized corridors, twice Mallory suggested a route that would take them ship-east. The necromancer believed this route would allow them to leapfrog through a potentially more intact series of domaines and Heavens, but a combination of half-forgotten organic memory and the urgent opinion of the sword Mirth had Tristen tending more to true south.

After traversing a string of particularly devastated anchores, they passed through a battered hatchway into warmth. "More salvage," Tristen said, trying to keep from his voice the bitter awareness of how much of what lay behind them had been lost to the Enemy. The saddest module had contained rank after rank of apparently unused acceleration pods, open to space, their interiors boiled dry.

Samael, handing Mallory a white handkerchief of dandelion clocks with which to mop the blood, said, "We shall have a far smaller world when we are done."

Mallory's hand folded around the scrap of cloth, but all the necromancer's attention was bent on the pressure door beyond the small antechamber in which they stood. Samael tapped the hesitant fingers, reminding Mallory to absently press handkerchief to nose.

"Grease," Mallory said, and started forward, feet picking their way unerringly across the buckled but clean-swept floor despite patent inattention. The necromancer bent down, blinking eyes splotched cobalt with petechiae all through the sclera. "This door's in use."

Tristen found his palm on Mirth's hilt. He turned slowly, scanning other potential entrances to the chamber. There was only the door through which they had entered. He licked his lips and looked again at the floor. Buckled, as he had noticed, with the force of the impact that had sheared through the corridor and the anchores beyond. Scraped, too, in long parallel lines that led toward the pressure door.

But the floor was very clean.

"Trash," he said, with a particular nauseated horror. "Someone is using this chamber to discard trash. And recently." Recently, because not even the world's ubiquitous dust and scruff had had time to settle on surfaces.

Samael, if he were human, might have blanched. Instead, he raked back his hair with twig-straw hands and tilted his head as if weighing any number of scathing responses—though Tristen did not think himself the one slated for scathing. The head-tilt was curiously like Gavin's, which was in its own turn curiously like one Tristen remembered with clear perfection through his colony, though the head-tilter was long lost. *When you get old, everyone starts to look like somebody else. And the more important that person was to you, the more people look like them.*

Cynric had been . . . important, yes. To a lot of people.

After a brief pause, the angel said, "So who throws things away?"

"Children," Mallory answered. "Cultists. Uneducated Means, but all the Means are meant to have been Exalted."

"And all the angels were meant to have been subsumed in *the* angel," Gavin said, from among Mallory's hair. Wings made for an expressive shrug, when he chose to use it. He pointed at Samael with his beak.

Samael bowed with a vestigial flourish. "At your service," he said. "I hope you'll forgive me for ruining the symmetry of your genocide. I was invested in remaining discrete."

There were times to rise to the bait, and times not to. "So what's beyond the door?" Tristen asked.

"Let's see," Samael said, and—laying his mosaic

hands flat against the alloy hatch—thrust his head through the door to the shoulders. Bits of fluff and leaf, as always, scraped from his field and slid to the floor, left behind.

Tristen thought he heard Gavin snort. Or perhaps he was himself projecting. *Angels*.

But a moment later, Samael was back, in all his slight translucence, glowering and crossing his arms. "The Heaven beyond the portal looks exactly as it should," he said. "There are signs of habitation, flora and fauna, a well-trammeled path to the pressure door. It seems they're using this chamber as an improvised air lock."

Mallory echoed the arm-folding gesture. "They *who*?"

Samael pushed out his lower lip and dropped his chin, frowning up at them past bushy eyebrows. "Go-backs," he said. "I think."

Mallory and Tristen shared a glance. Tristen thought of the open acceleration pods, their fluids boiled away on the Enemy's empty breath.

"Exalt Go-backs," Mallory said. Then said it again, with a headshake, as if that would help to settle the idea. "Go-backs. For real."

"You can see the dome of the shrine from the pressure door," Samael said.

Gavin flipped his wings and said, with a negligent tail flick, "We could—*go back*—the way we came."

Tristen shook his head and licked his lips. He tasted the bitter grease of blood and only then realized he'd bitten down.

"Religious fanatics," he said. Then with all the cascading irony of his personal history, though he knew nobody else would understand, he added, "How much can they hurt us?"

He touched Mirth's hilt, for the comforting click when his gauntlet brushed the pommel. No one else spoke, though Tristen let his gaze rest for a moment on each.

They awaited his decision. Even Mallory, though the necromancer did it with a frown and a challenging arch of eyebrow. Well, that's what Tristen got for pulling rank.

Tristen said, "We'll go on."

The hatch was sealed, locked, and even mechanically barred, but that proved an insignificant barrier to a necromancer, an angel, and the First Mate. They opened the ways and stepped through, the angel in the lead once more because Tristen had not chosen to object.

Tristen had been in many Heavens through his long life, but the wide world was vast and varied, and he had never seen one such as this. It must be a narrow, irregular space, and to make the most of it the Builders had terraformed it into a zigzag valley, soil hilled up like canyon walls to either side, one or two towering pinnacles fading into its misty length. It looked steep and water-eroded, and yes, ahead through soft fog Tristen could see the minarets and the blue-and-green enameled-appearing dome of a Go-back Earth shrine.

The entirety of the space was lush and green, and seemed completely undamaged by the acceleration catastrophe.

Tristen glanced at Samael and Mallory. "What do you call this? This . . . landscape?"

To his surprise, it was Mallory who closed eyes in thought, then smiled and answered, "Karst topography. On Earth, it was caused by limestone subsidence."

Along each of the valley's walls grew massive trees hung with moss and strange parasites, through which twined the mist. The angles of growth were odd. Then Tristen realized the gravity was set parallel to the pitch of the slopes, so if one were to step onto them, they would seem level. It was the Builders' way of coaxing a little extra useful space into the Heaven. They had had their sense of aesthetics, the old ones, rooted in their appreciation of the sublime as God's creation. They had tried to uphold that where they could.

Gavin beat wings and heaved himself far more heavily into the air than was, strictly speaking, necessary. "If we're going forward at all costs," he said, "then let's stop lollygagging and go forward at all costs."

Irritable words or not, he took care not to outpace them, so Tristen found it easy to keep up. Samael and Mallory flanked Tristen on either side, intent on their surroundings. Mallory in particular seemed determined to soak in every detail, walking hushed and attentive.

The mist—Tristen knew the word, but had rarely felt the phenomenon before—curved around each of Gavin's metronomic wingbeats on an elegant spiral, as smoke in a test chamber might circle an airfoil. It was breathtaking, as was the sensation of cool water-without-water on his skin where he had left his helm retracted and his faceplate open to show they came in peace.

The mist was their friend, he thought, as they came out of it—Tristen in armor just as white, now in the lead. Mallory was on his left, Gavin's white wings fanned from one shoulder like an improbable headdress. Samael was on his right, a black coat of beetle shell flaring about his calves like an animated gunslinger's, transparent enough that Tristen could glimpse landscape through his shoulders.

As the clouds thinned, they came up between black, hunch-shouldered shapes working in the fields that clung to each wall of the valley. People began to straighten from their toil, turn, and stare. It was novel to watch, because the residents stood at obtuse angles to the road, as if the steep valley walls were perfectly level and the rice paddies that covered them were on terraces. Around the ankles of the black-clad farmers, Tristen saw the ripple and splash of fins as fish thrashed away from the waders.

Tilapia. An ancient technique, adapted from Old Earth: cofarming the fish with the rice. Tristen smiled.

And kept smiling, though he realized as the farmers began to draw together, assemble, and walk out of the water that what rippled that water was not exclusively fish. However breathtaking the mist, the topography, the ranks of silent agricultural workers were, none of it was as breathtaking as the bronze-black serpents, creamy-bellied, that slipped from the rice paddies to follow. Tristen caught his breath. Each six meters in length, as large around as a man's thigh, the snakes were the colors of black pearls and butter.

Sliding across the earth, they seemed small-headed, inoffensive, their eyes like black star sapphires suffused with a silvery overlay of light. Tristen only knew the serpents for what they were because, here and there, one reared up and opened its infamous hood like a flower on an arm-thick stem.

"Cobras," Samael said.

"The Go-backs are snake handlers," Mallory said. *They shall take up serpents; and if they drink any deadly thing, it shall not hurt them; they shall lay hands on the sick, and they shall recover.*"

"They're Exalt." Gavin fanned his wings again, stiff pinions rasping against Mallory's hair. "What's a little snake neurotoxin?"

"Can't you see?" Tristen said. "The snakes are Exalt, too."

The serpents in question braided and rebraided themselves across the mossy earth and the road like some animate, sapient memory of water. Tristen watched as one farmer and another paused to stroke the snakes, which seemed to take no notice. He reached out and opened his hand.

If he expected a serpent to flow up under it, pleased like a cat to be stroked, no such thing happened. Instead, the snakes surrounded them, intertwining in a plaited circle ten meters in diameter. A ring of farmers stopped just beyond it. However they dressed, and despite being unarmed, they carried themselves with a light-footed straightness that told Tristen he would not care to fight them. And he certainly would not care to fight them all at once, attended by their familiar serpents.

"Hello," he said, and the cobras rose as one, swaying on every side, ribs spreading wide to flare each hood behind a small, smooth head that could not have seemed less threatening until they rose in display. Tristen had seen pit vipers and other venomous snakes—they tended to be heavily jowled, and look savage. The cobras needed no menace by design until they chose to threaten.

"Hello," one of the farmers answered. A woman's voice, the timbre so close to familiar that it made him shudder, though the tone and the phrasing were wrong. Still, his open hand had half reached out, daring the cobras' hiss, before he pulled it back. Her face lay hidden in her black cowled work shirt, but she was obviously the leader. Nothing happens by accident, and so he already suspected what her response would be when he touched the control on his helm and retracted it back into the armor.

She lifted calloused hands and hooked the cowl back with her thumbs. She was fair, as fair as her mother, though not so pale as her father. Her hair was golden-blond, tending to ringlets, her features fine and regular, the pale skin reddened across her cheekbones from work in a high-UV environment.

And yes, he knew her face.

It is not her, he told himself, but that could not stop

the rush of neurochemicals that flooded his brain, sent him soaring on a wave of purely incandescent emotion he could not begin to put into words.

It was not her. Not her mind. Not her soul, if you subscribed to the philosophy of souls. But her body, her flesh. *His* flesh, which theology said should concern him.

It did not matter who dwelt in her, he told himself with bitter sarcasm. What mattered was that his DNA lived on, his genetic potential. The consciousness inhabiting the shell made no difference. She could breed him grandchildren no matter who lived in her head.

"I am Dorcas," she said. "Welcome to our Heaven, Tristen Conn."

Whatever crossed his face, Mallory read it. And laid a hand on Tristen's elbow in silent, supportive questioning.

The leader of the farmers read it, too. "She died when you were young."

Tristen caught himself before he nodded. One could give away so much to fakirs, driven just by the human reflex to confirm communication. Instead, he fought against and mastered the reflex to swallow. *I have never been young.*

"How do you know my name?" Better than to admit that she *should* know his name. But the person who should was not Dorcas, though it was Dorcas who wore her body now.

"You are not exactly unknown, Prince Tristen. You will accompany us."

Her tone made no allowance for argument. She touched her hair. The cobras swayed between them. The circle grew no tighter. And time stretched weary and sharp-edged between them—the few seconds of this conversation, and the gulf of years behind.

In the house of dust, roll yourself in ashes.

Scripture was comforting in direct proportion to its bitterness upon the tongue.

Tristen shook his head. Mallory touched him again, long fingers curving around his armored biceps. Tristen opened his mouth and closed it, opened his mouth once more.

"Tristen?"

"Her name was Sparrow," Tristen said, eventually, because he had to say something. "Before she died, she was my daughter."

13

available light

Dostoevsky once wrote: "If God did not exist, everything would be
permitted"; and that, for existentialism, is the starting point. . . .
Nor . . . if God does not exist, are we provided with any values or
commands that could legitimize our behavior. . . . We are left alone,
without excuse. That is what I mean when I say that
man is condemned to be free.
—JEAN-PAUL SARTRE, "Existentialism Is a Humanism" (1946)

The orchid's hydra-headed blossoms looked delicate,
but the tendrils were strong as carbon monofilament.
And Benedick did not miss the manner in which—while
one remained focused on him, petals up and forward as
if straining with attention—the other four dragon faces
bent down on their long stems, slicking petals back like
reptiles flattening their frills. They gave the impression of
hounds nosing after a scent, and indeed he saw one dart
forth, grab the stiff, microwaved body of a leech, and
gulp it down with head-jerking motions and a swelling of
the stem.

While he observed, both worried and fascinated, the
blossom that remained focused on him gently brushed
his face and said, "The cyberleeches were particularly
programmed to hunt for you. Why should that be?"

Now that he was looking for it, he could see the way
some of the tuberous stems behind the array of flat-laid
leaves expanded and contracted, showing fine, translucent green membranes between dark ribs. The orchid's
breath across his face was sweet, refreshing—not

scented, but laden with exhaled oxygen. He breathed deeply to clear his head.

He didn't know the answer to the orchid's question, but he thought he had a pretty good guess. When uncertain, stall.

"Is my sister alive?"

Two more heads—or blossoms—came up to regard him, fanged labellums jutting pugnaciously. They moved closer, swaying the length of his body as if conducting an inspection by sniffing. The gesture allowed him an intimate view of the fangs—sharply curved thorns eight or ten centimeters in length—which seemed quite adequate to a fight.

"Sister?" the orchid asked in a dragony hiss. "The other mammal?"

Its bellows worked even when it wasn't speaking. He also detected shifting aromas on the air that seemed timed to the pull in and push out. Was that its language?

Not very useful for long-distance communication. But then, neither would its whispery speech be.

"The other mammal," Benedick confirmed. "Is she alive?"

His orchid—the violet-and-yellow striped one—arched one stem way over as if to confer closely with the white-and-crimson splotched orchid restraining Chelsea. Three other blossoms remained focused on Benedick, while the fifth still snuffled after scraps of meat.

In the second plant's grasp, Chelsea lifted her sagging chin with neck-cabling effort. Her head wobbled briefly and tipped backward, but Benedick saw her blink. Her throat worked.

Her lips moved. The orchid supporting her shifted a coil of tendrils to support her skull, tipping it gently upright. She got another breath and muttered in broken syllables, "I'll live. Fuck it all."

Benedick winced in empathy. The burns on her face

seemed to be healing under the froth of pale green foam, but the skin around it pulled up in dry ridges when she grimaced. Even her symbiont wouldn't keep that from hurting.

She glanced around, face rearranging itself from its tentative grimace to mild disbelief as she saw what had rescued—or captured—them. "Hello, ah, orchid-people."

Was that leaf-rustling laughter? The plant that gripped Benedick said, in its rubbing voice, "You have not answered the question, mammals. What have you done to deserve ambush?"

Benedick glanced at Chelsea. She looked up at him from under her eyelashes and somehow managed to twist her lips into what he took for an attempt at a brave grin. It looked more like a rictus.

It stung how much she reminded him of what Caitlin had been when they were still young and courageous in their ignorance. It stung because he had loved Caitlin when she was brash and overconfident, and Caitlin wasn't that, anymore. And neither was Ben.

"We are on Errantry. We are in pursuit of a fugitive criminal," he said. "Whether the ambush is her work or not, I am uncertain—but I would theorize that if it were not hers, it might be that of her allies."

"So that is your purpose here? You are doing nothing but passing through?" It took a moment to realize that the second orchid had spoken this time. Their whispery voices, if you could call them voices, were identical.

"And foraging as we go," Benedick said, remembering the mushrooms and eggs in the pack.

"You eat plants," it said. Benedick wished the voice had tone, so he could tell if its diction suggested horror, anger, or simple matter-of-factness.

Benedick turned his head to look significantly at a nearby cyberleech corpse. "And you eat animals. I would not suggest that you would willingly consume sapient ones." He hesitated, and looked the closest orchid face in the eyespots. "Would you?"

The rustling—the sound of the spiked, broad, body-armor leaves rubbed one over another in tight, fast circles—it was *definitely* laughter. "Clever mammal," it said. "Things-that-talk should not dine on things-that-talk. It is as you say. Is it perhaps that you are an ethical animal?"

That he had to stop and think on. Ethical in the intent, at least, he supposed, if not always in the execution.

The orchid did not seem to become restless while he considered. Perhaps plants were patient by nature.

"Perhaps," he agreed.

The orchid's coils loosened slightly, though they still cradled his limbs, offering support. One of the plants—his, he thought, by the bellows motions—asked, "Who are you?"

"I am Benedick Conn," he said. It had provided enough slack in the tendrils now that he could lift his wrist and gesture to Chelsea. "My sister is Chelsea Conn. We are on the Captain's business."

"The Captain!" the plant said. "There is a Captain?"

"Perceval Conn," Benedick said. Then, softly, trying to keep his voice level and calm, he added, "She is my offspring."

He wondered how much animate plants could be expected to understand mammal biology. They might find *daughter* confusing, or not—there were plants with male and female individuals, but he remembered the reaction to *sister*. It seemed to follow the concept of "offspring" well enough, however.

He felt it shift, resettle itself, and the leaf plates opened into a fantasia of agave-like spiral prickles. It said, "A scion! You must be proud."

Chelsea shifted in her bonds beside him, making a

small sound that might be worry or discomfort. Benedick felt his lips thin. He drew his shoulders back. Proud was not the right word, but he supposed it could do, if one didn't mind being entirely incorrect. "She is very brave and clever," he said, and changed the subject. "I am curious. Do you have names?"

"No names such as mammals use." It seemed to deflate a little, which might be relaxation. He wondered how it moved, and what it used in place of muscles. Air-filled cells? Carbon filaments?

"How is it you speak our language?"

The rustling peaked. It seemed the orchid could talk and laugh at the same time, because it answered, "Television."

The next time Jsutien awoke, he was lucid. Caitlin breathed a sigh of bright relief when he blinked and said, "Chief Engineer?"

"You remember?"

"It's confusing," he said. "I remember a lot. I remember dying."

"Do you remember why my brother woke you?"

He nodded. "I was the astrogator. He told me the ship was under way again."

"The world is under way, and badly damaged." There was no grace in hiding the truth. "Do you remember why we chained you?"

He nodded once more, eyes closed, and winced as he probed his forehead, though his colony had long sealed the injury. Instead of commenting on Arianrhod's escape, however, he swung his legs over the edge of the cot. The stretch webbing sank under his thighs as he grounded his feet. "It's cold."

"We're conserving power."

He glanced around, frowning, obviously assessing how desperate their situation really was. His hands chafed together. "Were you—were *we* derelict a long time?"

"More than five hundred years," she said flatly. It was wanton cruelty and could have sickened her. But in this case, she told herself, ethics would wait on survival. She set her jaw against any revealing expression and waited for the news to strike through his facade.

He must have already suspected, because, though the corners of his eyes tightened, he only nodded. No protests of bereavement, no questions as to the disposition of his family and friends. Of course, the angel could be telling him some of that even now, and Caitlin would not know it.

Clear-eyed, he said, "So why did you bring me back?"

"We've lost our navigation, all our star charts, any information on our destination. We are mobile, but our resources are extremely limited. We need your help, Astrogator." She leaned back and spread her hands, fingers crooked. "We don't know where we're going, where we *should* be going, or what to expect, should we reach either destination."

"It wouldn't matter if you did," he said.

"What do you mean?"

His smile, when he got around to finding it, sat crooked across his face. He looked older than Oliver when he did that, as old as he—Damian Jsutien—must have been before he died.

But even when his face smoothed to neutral, she had no urge to call him by his old name. And not because she had not known Oliver: she had only just recognized him by sight. She had told her colony to prevent such accidents, and set it so that it would not even allow her to *think* of him as Oliver in error.

She wondered what it would be like to make that mistake. She wondered what it would be like to know you were capable of making such a mistake. People must have been so hesitant in the past, so guarded in their speech. No wonder, she thought, that Means were so closemouthed around Exalt.

Maybe Jsutien had the habits of a Mean, still, because he just blinked at her.

She said, again, "What do you mean?"

"This body. Who was he?"

So many answers, all of them bad. She'd never met Oliver. She'd wanted to. Benedick had liked him. Alasdair, it seemed, was easier on the younger ones. Age had mellowed or exhausted him, or they had been so distant from his power that he found no threat in them. "My brother."

"Oh," Jsutien said. "And what's that like for you?"

She shrugged. "Complex. But you knew that. You are avoiding the question, Jsutien."

He laid his unshackled hand across his right eye socket and pressed hard enough to raise the tendons striating the back. He said, "You are asking me to violate a sacred vow."

Whatever she had expected, it wasn't that. *Oh, Ben. What were you thinking when you resurrected this one?* She had to resort to her symbiont to keep the surprise from her voice as she said, "Are you devout?"

His lips curved. She'd caught him out. He laced his fingers in his lap. "I am an astrogator. Of the Ancient Order of the Astrogator-priests. Sworn to uphold the mysteries, and teach only those who serve an apprenticeship and take up vows of rectitude and secrecy."

"Again, the revealing un-answer. Your secrets died with you, Jsutien. Records were lost in the Breaking. Everything was lost, even the libraries. Your vow is to a dead order." She paused. "How ancient is that Ancient Order, anyway?"

"Built with the ship," he admitted. "Ritual and tradition, from the ground up. We were not supposed to know that, but the library knew."

The library. "Yes," she said. "I met him—what was left of him, anyway. Jsutien—" How do you break it to someone that he's the last of his kind? Oh, but he must know, mustn't he? There was no other reason for Ben to have brought him back. "There are no more astrogators. *You* are the Ancient Order. So it seems to me that the only person who can absolve you of your vows is you."

He grinned. "Honestly, I was always pretty sure Ng knew the dirty truth. No matter how we obscured our calculations, he could do his own math."

"Dirty truth?"

"It is a deep mystery of the Ancient Order of Astrogators," he said archly. "There is no destination. There never was."

Caitlin wanted to call Ben, but wanting to call Ben was a sort of dull, constant ache that she was used to by now. So instead she called the bridge, because Nova and Perceval needed to know, and the angel could pass on the information to Ben or anyone else who might be in need of it.

But when she made the connection, Perceval's face, stark under her shaven scalp, drove everything Caitlin was going to say about Jsutien's revelation from her lips. She flinched when she saw her daughter, but schooled her expression. She opened her mouth, intending efficient business—

And said, "When was the last time you ate something, honey?"

Perceval's avatar blinked, and looked over her shoulder at Nova, who had taken shape just behind her. A guilty glance—had the angel been pressing her to eat, or had she warned it off the topic? Her own symbiont would tell her how long it had been, so the glance was not for information's sake.

Perceval returned her attention to Caitlin. "The angel is fetching food now."

No one answers me directly. Something else that could make her homesick for Ben, if she would let it. Why the *hell* did he have that insane need to placate their father? Why couldn't he have stood up to the old bastard?

"When it comes," Caitlin said, "try to eat it."

Apparently, being Captain didn't remove the urge toward adolescent eye rolls. "Mom? The angel said you had something urgent?"

Caitlin said, "Your father reincarnated the high priest of astrogation from the Moving Times."

"The news is bad," Perceval said, and went from daughter to Captain in an instant, "or you wouldn't be groping around telling me things I already know."

"The news is *interesting*," Caitlin corrected. "He confirms the angel's information from Dust. There was never any destination. The world never had a goal."

Perceval's eyes narrowed. She swallowed hard enough that Caitlin could see her thin throat flex. Behind her, Nova leaned forward. "Why would anyone get on a starship with no destination?"

Caitlin felt her lips flex around the knowledge. "It was a scam," she said.

Perceval stared, looked aside, nodded. Glancing at the angel, Caitlin thought. Perceval said, "Like the bodies in the holdes."

"Excuse me?"

"The holdes," the Captain said. "They were full of bodies. Frozen people. The Builders told them they were being placed in cryogenic suspension. But they froze them and killed them and saved their corpses as raw materials."

"Were?" Caitlin said, already knowing the answer.

"The ones that were left after the supernova." Perceval made a cutting gesture with her outspread hand. Her voice came tight and quick, but her expression stayed serene, inhuman. The placidity and ruthlessness of an angel. "We're using them."

Caitlin would not punish her daughter by letting shock show across her face. But it made her want to curl forward, as if around a blow to the solar plexus. *Oh, baby.*

The angel's avatar seemed to watch Perceval closely, and Caitlin appreciated the subtlety of allowing her to see him doing so. *Somebody is watching over her.* It would have been like Susabo, to offer that implied comfort; Caitlin could not imagine Dust making the effort.

"It makes no sense," Caitlin said. "To build an entire world, and set it adrift. The expense. The *waste*."

"The ways of the Builders are inscrutable," Nova said.

At least it made Perceval laugh—a sharp, pained bark. When she was finished, she said, "Maybe we are a sacrifice. Maybe we were never intended to survive."

"Bundle up your goods and treasures, and cast them into the dark," Caitlin quoted. She glanced at Jsutien; his nanochains whispered across the floor as he spread his hands in a shrug.

"I don't know," he said. "But then, why even make the ship spaceworthy?"

The angel shook its head. "There's more," he said. "The null zones are still spreading."

It was one of the interesting points of talking to an angel. Caitlin heard his voice inside her mind, like the still, small voice of conscience. He might have been saying anything to Perceval, to Jsutien, even to Tristen and to Chelsea and to Ben.

She had to trust they all heard, as she did, Nova say, "It's a creeping numbness. It begins in the extremities."

Caitlin sucked her lower lip into her mouth and nibbled it. Slowly, considering the implications both metaphysical and mechanical, she answered, "Like leprosy."

Caitlin's words cast a visible pall over the angel's face. That was a new thing, that emotion and reaction. Caitlin did not like to think on where it came from. She looked down, busying her hands on the half-forgotten, half-repaired console she sat behind.

"Do you imply we have been smitten for our offenses?" Nova said, after enough time had passed for Caitlin to wonder.

Caitlin looked up from her work. "Leprosy is not tzaraath, angel. It is not the condemnation of the God of the Builders that afflicts us. Although now I have an image of the world gliding serenely through the very bosom of the Enemy, ringing out bells and crying, Impure! Impure!"

"We have followed the path laid before us," the angel said. Susabo or Inkling—or Samael—would have pronounced it as if the words wore an armor of righteousness. Nova said it softly, big-eyed, as if seeking reassurance.

Caitlin folded one hand inside the other. The angels of the new world would not be like the angels of the old.

The orchids stripped Benedick's and Chelsea's ruined armor off, treated their burns with more of the cooling froth, and supported them through the winding arbors of the vertical forest. Benedick in other days had rarely envied the flyers of Engine—he, too, could have worn wings, if he had wanted them badly enough to put up with the nuisance value—but this journey was apparently the occasion on which he was given the opportunity to revise that opinion. Wings—like Perceval's lost ones— would have been of use here. The orchids were fabulously light for their bulk and moved with facile grace through the branches, drawn on strong, green tendrils. The humans floundered behind, struggling on uneven surfaces, often slipping and saved by their botanical companions.

The orchids were not heavy enough to counterweight a human, but their strength and their mastery of their environment were impressive. They could swing the two Conns bodily from level to level, anchoring themselves with one set of tendrils while lowering the humans as if on ropes.

Shafts of illumination flickered up and across between leafy boughs, but the vegetation competed to collect the available light. As a result, they traveled through humid, hyperoxygenated green gloom, bustling with birds and insects, great and small. Once, the striped orchid snatched a dragonfly from the air and tore it apart between two blossoms without a break in its motion.

Chelsea limped badly and kept touching the side of her face, but otherwise seemed to be recovering. Her harlequin orchid fenced her in tendrils, reminding Benedick of a parent caging a stumbling toddler. Upon inspection, that was not a particularly reassuring comparison.

"Are we prisoners?"

There was a sense that the orchids conferred—Benedick had the sense of a tight, exclusionary glance, though whatever transpired had happened below his or his symbiont's threshold of perception. Then one of them said, "You are on the Captain's business. We will treat your wounds, see you nourished, and escort you to the edge of our sphere of influence. Will that suffice?"

With his peripheral vision, Benedick saw Chelsea's faint nod. She chafed her forearms as if feeling the absence of her armor. Benedick could not have agreed more. Being unprotected—in the face of the Enemy, and whatever Arianrhod could throw at them—worried him more than the threat of combat.

Benedick said, "That would be kind. Are you taking us to your settlement?"

"Settlement?" Another pause, as if for conference. "We do not hive, as do animals. We are taking you through."

That seemed to settle it, and for a while Benedick did not find many further opportunities for conversation. Instead, he concentrated on the jungle, on Chelsea—who was moving more fluidly as her symbiont effected repairs—and on the threats that might lie around every corner.

With the assistance of the orchids, the descent proceeded fast. After half an hour or so, he tried again. "How far down does your domain extend?"

"We live in this shaft," one of the orchids said—the striped one, Benedick thought, wondering if they had leaders. "There is no light above, nor water below. There, we cannot flourish."

Chelsea perked up, her matted hair breaking over her shoulders. She said, "Do you know what lies below?"

"Surveyors have journeyed south," one said. "We have charts. They are approximate, and may not be useful to you. They are enzymatic."

Chelsea and Benedick shared a glance. "No," he said. "I don't think we would find those easily readable. Can you offer us a description?"

"We can show you." This time, Benedick was certain it was the spotted orchid that had spoken.

"Show us how?" he asked.

It rustled. "On the television."

His symbiont had supplied a definition for the word the first time an orchid used it, so he knew his guide referred to a communications technology as obsolete as daguerreotype or the World Wide Web. Chelsea must have run the same research, because she said, "You're broadcasting on the electromagnetic spectrum?"

Rustling. Mammals, apparently, were pretty funny to a carnivorous plant. The striped orchid swiveled two faces at each of them and said, "We will show you."

The angle of their descent changed. Now, the orchids brought them closer to the shaft walls, slowing travel as the undergrowth thickened so close to the wall-mounted illumination panels. But they seemed to have not far to go. The orchids led them around one last enormous tree trunk and onto a sort of ledge dripping with thigh-thick vines, next to what appeared to be a vine-covered cliff face strangely unpunctuated by the ubiquitous trees.

The spotted orchid flipped two of its bladelike leaves forward, an impressive swivel, and used them to nudge between the vines. If Benedick had his armor, he suspected sonar would map a space beyond—but that suspicion was inadequate to the reality because, as the orchid spread wide its leaves, pushing the vines aside like drapes, flickering light spilled forth and a cavernous bay was revealed.

It was neither a room nor a cavern, but instead something like a hangar with flat video screens lining every wall of a space approximately ten meters tall and over fifty meters deep. Many of them were cracked, smeared, some of those flickering and others dark—but more than half burned brightly, glimmering with transitory images.

The floor was covered with more overgrowth of the vines, while down the center of the hangar ran long, parallel ridges about a meter and a half high, humped up under the foliage. At random intervals upon them, three dozen or so orchids rested, dazzling in their array of shapes and colors.

Many swiveled a face as the striped and the spotted orchid and their two escorted human guests came within the chamber, but not all, leading Benedick to wonder what exactly their sensory organs were and where they might be located. Some of the orchids were meters in length, shuffling arrays of tubers and blossoms with tens of heads. The smallest were no larger than a dog, and these had no blossom-faces at all.

They looked, but they did not come closer. There was some rustling of leaves and puffing of tubers among the orchids who accompanied them. Benedick wondered what they might be explaining.

Studying the layout of the chamber, Benedick came to understand that the humped ridges were rows of chairs, buried under vinous overgrowth. The orchids were only putting them to their intended purpose, although not in their intended fashion. He said, "It's a waiting room."

Chelsea shook her head, then made a face as if regretting the reflexive motion. Here, where the light was better, he could see that her right iris was clouded, but the raw acid burns beneath the flaking green foam that surrounded it were drying and growing over. It was only a matter of time before the eyeball healed, also.

"Transfer station," she corrected. "It's a terminal. What's through that way?"

She pointed at what Benedick had thought to be the back wall. But now, when he squinted, he could see the dense, narrow lines of another wall of vines.

The striped orchid leaned a blossom over her shoulder. "A pressure seal," it said. Benedick saw it shudder; from Chelsea's sidelong glance, she felt the trembling of petals beside her face. "The Enemy lies beyond. There was once another transit shaft there, but it is long failed and disassembled."

The orchid shuffled to the side and fanned all its petals and its blade leaves forward until its outline resembled a parabolic mirror. He knew he was projecting, but Benedick could not help but read its body language as pleased and proud. "Look!" it said. "Television!"

Benedick stepped forward to examine the images. Dramas, comedies, documentaries, something that seemed to feature tiny screaming people running from a creature represented by a man in a poorly articulated costume—all in two dimensions, some of them low-definition in crudely unfocused images, some in images without color. Each one seemed to be broadcast in silence, until he realized that if one sat or stood beside one of the tiny, self-damping, unidirectional speakers that projected from the back of each chair, one could choose a channel. Some of the larger orchids were watching several screens at once, their awkward bodies arranged so as to surround multiple speakers and their blossom-faces twisted this way and that.

Benedick stepped forward, momentarily captivated by an image of a bright wave of fast-moving water humping up, peaking, and curling over itself to break in a long, foaming tube. The sky behind was as brilliant as blood, and as he watched a human being, crouched on a narrow, colorful oblong, shot the length of the tube, just ahead of where it was collapsing into itself.

"What is he doing?" he asked, not caring if Chelsea saw his fascination.

"It's called *surfing*. That was on Earth," the orchid said. Benedick could hear the foreignness of the ancient words in its tone, or in the hesitation before it said them. "That was all *filmed* on Earth. The shaft has a library. The oldest among us say the *programming* repeats after about seventy-two years."

Benedick need not have worried about his sister. She was just as captivated, one hand stretched out as if she could reach the screen—reach into the screen, perhaps. "Is that what planets look like?"

"Parts of them," the orchid answered.

Her tongue flicked out the corner of her mouth. She said, very softly, "I always thought the thing about the sky being blue was poetic license. You know. Hyper-bole."

Benedick looked at his youngest sister and thought of Rien, and still could not manage to make himself take her hand, or even to put into words what he thought. Which was: *I should like to see one someday, too.*

14

when we had a library

Walking beside Samael in the midst of the serpents and their wardens, Mallory tilted his head and said into Tristen's ear, "Does it seem accidental to you that we should find exactly these persons here, at exactly this time?"

"Providence," Samael whispered on his other side.

Tristen dropped his hand on Mirth's hilt. He made a low noise in the back of his throat. Snakes were deaf, so the trick was keeping his voice low enough not to attract the attention of Dorcas and her people, while making himself overheard by Samael. Fortunately, angels had excellent ears.

"Or some less divine intervention." The sword hummed to itself, satisfied as a cat. Had it brought Tristen to Dorcas intentionally? Was it that aware? He sighed and admitted, "Mallory was right."

Mallory snorted. "I've been trying not to mention it."

Samael arched up eloquent eyebrows and tipped his head, as if acknowledging Tristen a tiny victory. "Divinity may be in the eye of the beholder, Tristen Conn.

What percentage of a god has to influence the course of events before one admits to divine intervention? By the way, I do not think these people like you very much."

Tristen didn't need to look around to be aware of the way the farmers held him in their peripheral vision with so much intention. He said, "If they are Go-backs, they have reason not to."

Mallory had come up close. "And if they're not Edenites?"

Tristen arched a look at the necromancer. "I haven't heard that term in centuries."

Mallory's lips bent and compressed. "You haven't been hanging out around a lot of Go-backs. You should get to know what you despise. You might find it enlightening."

"I think I've been sufficiently enlightened."

Mallory, the basilisk mantling one shoulder, said, "You didn't answer my question. If they're not Edenites, what reason have they to consider you an enemy?"

Tristen watched Sparrow's—*Dorcas's*—stiff back walking before him, and forced himself neither to turn nor look away. "I am old."

Mallory might not have understood, but Samael grunted acknowledgment. Because he was Samael, and Samael was old, too, Tristen did not need to explain what he meant. Time passed, and given enough time, anyone could make enemies. Even—especially—a Conn.

The corner of Samael's mouth curled up behind his hair. "May the enemies you make be interesting ones."

"My father used to say that."

"Your father"—the smile made itself patent—"was an interesting enemy."

"Yes." Tristen rubbed his fingertips in circles against the heels of his hands, making his armor rasp. "I recall."

It felt like a walk to execution. That was not a comparison made idly; Tristen had made such a walk before, though not as the centerpiece of the display. Indeed, he had made it in some of the same company.

This procession was longer, though, leading them as it did the entire length of the valley between high, tattered, moss-hung walls. The mist breathed a pall of unreality over the scene, especially as they came up on the peach-and-gold-walled settlement ascending from it. Graceful green-barked limes and lemons framed the lower levels, and Tristen held his breath against the scent of their flowers. Some of the structures rose ten yards or more into the air, and the largest of them was topped by that enormous glistening blue-green globe—lit faintly from within—but the walls rippled softly with air currents, and in places flaps billowed open, showing men and women and others at work over looms or cookstoves within. They looked up as the procession passed, and any that could left their toil and came to walk beside the slithering carpet of serpents.

The sound of wingbeats warned Tristen an instant before Gavin's weight struck his shoulder, so he was braced. The basilisk tossed a coil lightly around his neck for balance, and settled with a ruffle of feathers and a flash of the pale blue underside of his crest.

"Cloud forest," Gavin said. "Do you think they have coffee plantations?"

"Do you think they have outside trade?"

The basilisk's shrug brushed hard, warm feathers against Tristen's ear. When Gavin spoke again, it was colony to colony, through the seemingly innocuous contact.

"Do you think they could survive without it?" A hard squeeze of talons compressed Tristen's armored shoulder, sharply enough to give him concern for the integrity of his armor. The touch was followed by the quick flick of a beak through a lock of hair straggling free of his braid. "You walk like you're still carrying her coffin, Tris."

Tristen stumbled, staying on his feet without any particular grace. His head swiveled, so if Gavin's lids had not been sealed he would have been staring into the basilisk's eyes. "Excuse me? Whose coffin would that be?"

Gavin stretched out his neck and shook his head as if he meant to whip water from the feathers. "I just . . . I knew that."

Of course you did.

There was no use nursing anger at the dead, and it wasn't Gavin's fault, whatever Tristen was coming to understand had been seeded in him. Tristen tugged the basilisk's tail tip with his other hand. He forced his voice light, unconcerned. The way he would have spoken to his father, without revealing vulnerability. "Considering the purpose of this mission is to bring back my granddaughter's corpse—"

Arianrhod. He should say the name, but that would be too personal. Too much of an admission.

But still. Arianrhod. Tristen rather thought Alasdair had made a special effort in her case, when it came to building his servitor monsters. Petty vengeance had been well within his father's capabilities, and using children to control their parents was an established family technique.

Knowing didn't lessen the ache.

Tristen bit the inside of his cheek, because he did not wish the locals to see him shake his head like a restive dog. They still did not speak, even when the others joined them, so the only sound was their footsteps—his and Mallory's and those of the escort—on the graveled path.

"So here we are in a funeral cortege again," he said, because they were coming up now on the cloth-walled chapel with its lofty minaret.

Gavin snorted. "Again?"

"You have some memories waking in you, don't you? Machine memories?"

"Machine memories are all I have," the basilisk answered. "Whoever you think you recognize, that wasn't exactly me."

"It wasn't exactly not," Tristen said. He didn't fill in the name—*Cynric*—that floated in his awareness, though. Only two sisters had called him *Tris,* and only one of them would have thought to preserve her ghost in a machine.

"Knowledge is not identity," Gavin said. "Especially when the knowledge is shattered like a host of angels, and no person remains to give it context. That was in another country, and besides, the wench is dead."

"Excuse me?"

"Never mind," the basilisk said, as they were brought inside the pavilion. "Just something I read once, when we had a library."

The interior of the pavilion was lit in cool colors by the light that fell from above and lay shadowless across the carpets and cushions arranged over the earth in a semblance of a floor. "They're nomadic," Mallory said, at Tristen's back.

Tristen permitted himself a nod to show he'd heard. "Take what you need, sow what you will later want, and move on. It makes them harder to find."

"Do not speak," Dorcas said. She walked away from them, steps springy across the carpet, and climbed a set of risers to a dais. The cobras, which had accompanied them inside, did not follow her. Instead, they closed the ring before Tristen and reared on long bodies, looking inquisitive with their threatening hoods folded tight. Beyond the ring of snakes, a larger ring of farmers waited.

At the top of the dais, under a canopy of green and blue tasseled in ropes of gold, Dorcas turned to face him, looking down.

"Tristen Conn," she said. "Come forth."

Tristen stepped forward, away from the others, but not too close to Dorcas—or her serpents. His armor might be a match for the Enemy's chill, but he was not sure he cared to test it against engineered cobra fangs. He paused some meters short of the dais.

On his shoulder, he felt Gavin spread white wings for balance, the brush of pinions across Tristen's scalp as they bowered him. He rested his hand on Mirth's hilt. The sword's longing to go to Dorcas could almost have pulled him forward. He tightened his gauntlet over the pommel, wondering if, in some atavistic part of her brain, Dorcas remembered it as the one that she had carried once when she had been Sparrow.

Neural pathways became worn in with use. If she folded her hand around it, would the part of her that had been his daughter—the physical part, the part where the unconscious lived and struggled—remember the feel of the blade? Would her body recollect its use, she who had been a swordswoman without equal, trained by her mother's hand until she had exceeded even her mother?

He wondered if he wished more that the answer was yes, or no. He wondered also if Dorcas expected him to speak. But if she did, he had no idea what he should say.

Scales scraped across carpet behind him. The armor told him what he already knew: the cobras were cutting him off from the others. They could not harm Samael, and Mallory was not without defenses, but that was carrion comfort.

Dorcas still regarded him, letting the silence stretch, her face a mask as serene as a priestess's. Tristen tilted his face up to her as if to the light of the shipwreck stars.

She wore only a loose smock and mud-daubed work pants, the cuffs rolled up to show her bare, bony ankles.

The sight of her pained him as deeply as if he looked upon the Queen of Heaven. Still he waited, holding to a taken breath and the soothing mental construct of a pale green light as if they could defend him. But nothing could make this right.

The breath Dorcas drew seemed to enlarge her. Silence spread from her like a ripple across a pool, even the serpents seeming to rustle more quietly. Just when that quiet had reached oppressive proportions, when everyone else was holding their breaths with her, her voice rolled forth in a preacher's or stateswoman's ringing tones.

"Tristen Conn," she repeated. "How do you plead?"

It was no other than he had expected, but he could play out the game. "What is the charge?"

"Treachery," she said. "Collusion. And blackest kinslaughter."

He would not grant her the victory of a nod or wince. *This is not Sparrow*. Easy enough to change that perception, to edit his symbiont so he saw her—really *saw* her—as someone new and foreign. But to do so would mean giving up on ever seeing Sparrow again.

Mallory started forward; Tristen would have known even if his armor had not told him, because he heard the answering choir of hisses. Tristen extended his left hand, leaving the right on Mirth's hilt, and gestured the necromancer back.

"Tristen," Mallory said.

He shot a quelling glance over his shoulder. "Not guilty. By what right do you level charges?"

"By right of survivorship," she said. "Lay down your weapon, Sir Tristen, and leave behind your familiar beast. If he acts on your behalf, know we will destroy him and your traveling companions, too."

"This was your mother's blade," Tristen said. "And yours, when you were who you were before. Assuming I recognized your right to bring me to judgment, would you have me cast it down like trash?"

"Give it to your leman, then." An imperious jerk of her head indicated Mallory. Tristen wasn't sure if Mallory's snort of amusement or Samael's was more dramatic. Merely by virtue of proximity, Gavin's was loudest.

Tristen did not remove his hand from the blade, nor did he nudge the basilisk from his shoulder. They could fight, if they had to, but he would prefer to talk his way out. The risk of fighting was the risk of losing, and the whole world rode on the success of his mission. And if he read Dorcas's body language correctly, she was quite confident in her threats.

Tristen said, "We are on Errantry, and the Captain's business. You will let us pass."

"What care we for Captains?" Her smile was bitter. "Less even, I trust you understand, than we do for Commodores. We follow the divine will."

Given his experience of Commodores, Tristen didn't fancy the morality of his position. And yet it was the one he had. He said, "But for those of us who do care for Captains—or for Commodores, if you prefer—the treason would lie in disobeying their legal orders." His teeth began to grind. He made a point of slackening his jaw. "No matter how little to our taste those orders were."

"So a good soldier follows bad orders? Every criminal prefers to go free."

"It is unwise to hold me. The fate of the very world itself rests on our passage, Lady of the Edenites."

She tilted her head and shrugged. "I care very little for the fate of this spaceship," she said. "It is not a world, and to call it a world offends the spirit of real worlds—living worlds—everywhere. Would you call a tin box your mother?"

Tristen suspected that the only reason he didn't catch himself rubbing his temples in frustration was because the gauntlets would have gotten in the way. "I insist you release my companions."

"Are there no higher powers than rulers?" she asked. "Are there no moral authorities greater than a bad king?"

Mallory shifted among the serpents, provoking another susurrus of warnings. Samael brushed half-material hair behind his shoulders, shreds of dry grass making a whisking sound.

Tristen said, "If there are higher moral powers, My Lady, you will forgive me if I admit that I do not know you as such. A man must keep his conscience."

She flinched, so that he wondered what he had said to wound her so sharply. But she extended a hand before her, a gesture that brought the snakes rising between them. Her voice was level when she said, "And have you kept your conscience, Sir Tristen?"

Tristen looked into his daughter's dead, alien, animated face, and shook his head. "The state of my conscience is my own concern. I do not accept your authority. I will not stand your trial."

She pursed her lips. Her face, he thought, was sadder than not. She said, "Would that you had a choice, good sir knight. Fear not. Your companions will not be harmed."

He touched the hilt of Mirth, where it still swung at his hip. The serpents swayed forward, but he did not withdraw his hand. It wasn't a threat; it was an offering. Whoever lived in her now, he knew the face, the steady gaze. He did not think he could fight her. "You heard me say this blade was yours."

"Not mine." Was there a little sorrow behind the dismissal in her headshake? Hard to tell, when you had so much invested in believing there was.

"A bargain," Tristen said. "I will submit to your trial if you will accept this object from my hand."

"Tristen!" interjected Mallory. Tristen let the protest roll down his armor and away, holding Dorcas's gaze the whole while.

"We could fight," Tristen said. "Whatever your resources, Lady of the Edenites, it would not go easy for you."

Of course it was a trap, and she knew it. Her eyebrows lifted, her pupils contracted. But it was a trap for him as well.

Slowly, she nodded.

Tristen turned his head, to where Mallory and Samael stood side by side. Gavin rocked on his shoulder, a big bird hunching itself and shuffling from foot to foot.

"Don't fight them," Tristen said, holding Mallory's gaze. He suspected Gavin was his real worry, so he raised one gauntlet and touched the basilisk's wing. "Do not fight them. Do not kill her. I will handle this myself."

Mallory, grim-jawed, nodded.

Tristen turned back to the woman who wore his daughter's skin. "Do your worst."

When her hand fell, the snakes struck.

Perceval buried her feet in violets, leaning back in her Captain's chair, and stared up at the sky as if she could see through it to the night beyond.

Not *as if*. She *could* see through it to the night beyond if she chose.

She needed merely to extend her sight beyond the range of her physical eyes, into the web of the angel's awareness. The angel's slowly receding awareness, which Perceval knew was being worn back by the tide of the expanding nullities.

She would rather have waded through a sewer. Not because of what that web contained, but who. Hard enough to allow that intimacy with a stranger, a machine. But to do so with a machine that contained the desires and memories of someone to whom she had been as close as she was to Rien—

Every reach into the matrix was a monstrous effort of will, the sort of exertion she could manage only in surges. She'd never wanted a lover. She'd never cared to allow anyone within the borders of herself, not since she was a child, and too small and dependent to enforce her will.

Perceval had chosen to relax those limits for Rien because Rien had proven that she would honor whatever boundaries Perceval needed to establish. But this was an abrogation of them, a violation sharp enough to make her wish she could peel her skin back with her nails and wriggle out of it.

Actually, given what she'd become, she probably could do that. And survive it. *Shed my skin.* And if skin-shedding could make it better, Perceval would choose that in a nanosecond. But this violation came from within, and it was something she'd chosen, out of duty, on her own.

So many voices, inside her, clamoring. Wrestling to speak with her mouth, to move with her limbs.

She hoped it would get easier with practice. That she would stop caring about privacy, boundaries, the integrity of her self. She didn't think she could live with it, otherwise.

Perceval drew a deep breath, closed her eyes, and reached outside her skin.

Nova was there, waiting, silent and aware as any colonized atmosphere. Perceval breathed deep, pulse accelerating, a tingling spreading the length of her arms to her fingertips. It was psychosomatic, she knew—and so she shut it down, not caring for the distraction, or the reminder that she had any physical body, because that reminder was too much temptation to return there and remain.

No wonder Captains go strange.

"Show me our boundaries, Nova."

Nova opened the pathways and Perceval entered them as easily as spreading her lost wings would have been. She infiltrated the angel, stretched to the edges of its span of control, and felt there the prickly, eroding sensation of something nibbling. A war, a death struggle, taking place on the micro scale. Different from the one she'd lived through when angel fought angel, though. This was a battle of attrition.

"Those aren't ours," she said, and wondered why the angel hadn't seen it.

—*Those aren't our whats?*—

"Our colonies," she said. "Those aren't you. They aren't remotely like you. And they're not reprogramming your colony, Nova. They're penetrating each mote so it reproduces more motes like theirs, not like ours. They're *viral.*"

"The thing is, I'm pretty sure they're not . . . native to our world. And Nova can't tell," Perceval said, gesturing to a monitor tank in which a schematic in blue and orange hovered, writhing uncertainly.

Caitlin folded her arms and frowned, considering her daughter the Captain's words with a mix of unease and pride.

Perceval continued, "She can't even tell they exist. It's a very familiar-sounding model, if you think about it for a minute."

"Inducer viruses," Caitlin said, with a glance at Jsutien. She had exchanged his simple shackle for a silvery drape of nanotech chain that permitted him the freedom to work while allowing her to retain control. He'd accepted it with grace. Understanding that her distrust was provoked by the circumstances of Arianrhod's disappearance, he had claimed to find the precaution reasonable.

"And it's not," he had said, "as if I have anywhere to go."

Now, he met her gaze and nodded. "An inducer virus, sure. Or a plain, old-fashioned virus. Not engineered. Your angel interface really can't even sense the presence of these things?"

Perceval's avatar shook her head. "She can *sense* them just fine. But she doesn't seem able to notice she's sensing them, if you know what I mean."

Caitlin frowned. She did, and she understood what it implied, too. Something in the angel's inherited programming forced it to overlook this particular colony structure and the individual motes that composed it. "Nova's been instructed to ignore the infestation."

"Yes," Perceval said. "And instructed to forget why she was instructed to ignore it."

"That seems like something of a radical operational choice," Caitlin said mildly, because Benedick was not there to say it for her. Her crossed arms were in danger of becoming a straitjacket. She forced them down to her sides. "So if you're programming an angel, why do you force it to ignore an . . . infestation of alien nanotech?"

"Sabotage," Perceval said, promptly.

But Jsutien shook his head. "Immunosuppression." When the women—present and projected—turned to stare at him, he said, "It's how you get a transplant to take. First, you have to stop the host body from attacking it."

"I see. And do you know something about what might have been . . . transplanted . . . into my world, Jsutien?"

He flushed cobalt. "Not specifically. But—" The swags of nanochain rustled as he shifted uncomfortably behind his console.

"Spit it out."

The look he gave her was all startled prey, but she didn't think he was intentionally evasive. "It's about your sister, Chief Engineer."

"Of course it is," Caitlin said, rolling her eyes until she felt the muscles stretch. "Which one, I'm horrified to ask?"

"Cynric," he said. He turned to Perceval, and Caitlin grimaced at a premonition. "Captain, Princess Cynric was the director of biosystems, and bioengineering, and chief synbiotician. The original colonies were her design. As were a lot of the first-generation synbiotes and engineered fauna. Shipfish, parrotlets . . . some Means."

"And the inducer viruses," Perceval said, with the air of someone who has just achieved a satisfying synthesis of incomplete information.

"And the inducer viruses," Jsutien confirmed. "Yes. So I would bet that whatever's out there is something she was working on. Possibly a weapon she meant to use against Alasdair Conn. When the three of you—" He paused delicately.

"Attempted to overthrow our father," Caitlin finished for him. "Don't worry, you can say it."

"They called her Cynric the Sorceress," he said, apologetically. "Before you were born."

"After, too." Caitlin smiled. "But if she had a weapon like that, Astrogator, she never revealed its existence to me."

"Maybe it wasn't cooked yet," Jsutien said, with a wave at the monitor tank. "Maybe it needed time to evolve."

Perceval rubbed her mouth. "Well, they're sure as hell

cooked now. They're *eating my ship*. And she's pretty unhappy about it."

Which led Caitlin to another problem that it was the Chief Engineer's duty to bring to the attention of the Captain. Fortunately, this issue was a little more tractable. She coughed into her hand and said, "Have you noticed that you can't settle on a pronoun?"

"Mom?" Lashes meshed over hazel eyes made to seem enormous by Perceval's denuded scalp.

"Nova," Caitlin clarified. "You call it he or she, but the gendering of the pronoun changes from conversation to conversation."

Perceval's brow furrowed in confusion or concentration. "Is that bad?"

"It's diagnostic," Caitlin said, dodging the question. "It tells me Nova is still integrating, and the distinct personalities are generating confusion, crossed signals, and hesitancy, which it may not be aware of. And that's bleeding through its link to you. It's your responsibility as her director to assist in the integration process."

"Right," said Perceval, rubbing her arms. "What does that mean, exactly?"

Caitlin lifted her chin. "Captain, it means you have to decide who you want her to be."

15

the bottomless dark in its person

All things are lawful unto me, but all things are not expedient:
all things are lawful for me,
but I will not be brought under the power of any.
—I Corinthians 6:12, King James Bible

"Bring me the corpse of a cyberleech," Benedick commanded, and so by his will it was done. He also asked the orchids to search for the remains of his toolkit—dead or alive—but they found no trace of it beyond a fluff of coat and DNA, the smear of impact. Something in the lift shaft had most likely eaten it, as the orchids had consumed most of the cyberleech casualties.

Benedick mourned its loss. It had been a fluffy idiot thing, but friendly, and he could have used its delicacy of touch and instrumentation for the necropsy once the orchids found a nearly intact cyberleech for his dissection. They brought it before him while Chelsea took her healing rest in a sheltered corner of the transfer station, and Benedick assembled such primitive tools as they had available and cleared a space to work. The data core was unlikely to be intact in a dead leech, but somewhere within it—he prayed—there must be a radio control chip.

He missed his armor in the process, because it came equipped with scalpels, pliers, and retractors, but he managed. The cyberleech was heavy meat without, knotted muscle, and within its body cavity the circuit-twined organs popped and squished, inelastic as liver. But fifteen messy minutes later, he had it. His sleeves were caked to the elbows with iron-stinking matter, and the flat, glass-transparent chip lay on his acid-burned palm, irregular as a leaf.

In this fragile flake of crystal lay a record of the frequency and signature of the device Arianrhod had used to activate the leeches. As long as she was still carrying the transmitter and it wasn't entirely deactivated—or, better yet, if she'd used her own colony as the carrier—he could find her now. It was an ancient and crude method of location, one that didn't rely on angels or motes or the awareness of colonies.

It was the work of another half hour to improvise a scanner from salvaged materials, and a few moments later he was sure. He could not obtain her present position, but the tightband cast by which she had tuned the cyberleeches originated from the south. It was good to have confirmation they were headed the right way, at least.

Benedick's own domaine lay not far from there, at the rim of everything. And he would worry about that, he told himself firmly, when there was something he could do about it.

"Got it," he said aloud, to hear the conviction in his own voice. Because if he listened to that, he wouldn't listen to the voice of all his own regrets and fears.

Arianrhod stopped at the edge of the world and pressed her hands against the glass. The angel's wing braced her shoulder, though when she craned her neck all she could see of it was shadows, like gauze curtains blowing from a window, twisting layers of varying opacity. It warmed her, though, and filled her with enough strength that she thought that perhaps in a moment or two she'd have the courage to step forward. It would not be the first leap of faith she had ever taken for her angel.

It probably wasn't the first time he'd given her time to stall, either. She'd come with him across the Broken Holdes, through the belly of the world, braving long-abandoned spaces. She'd trusted him in habitats she had no names for, in domaines so empty they held no atmosphere through which sounds could echo. And now she looked out into the breast of the Enemy, the bottomless dark made radiant in its evanescent mourning veils.

The skeleton wheel of the world rolled on, stripping through the ghosts of dead stars, but that wasn't what drew Arianrhod's attention uneasily into the depths. Beyond the portal she stood within, taut dark cables of bundled monofilament stretched into darkness. Non-reflective, they would have been completely invisible had not some cautious engineer of ancient times webbed each cable with tiny lights—a few of which still burned. If Arianrhod let her colony do the math, she could reconstruct what the pattern once had been. A few calculations allowed her to superimpose an image over the existing remnant, but it seemed like a simple warning device rather than an elaborately coded message.

She stepped back from the port. "What's on the other side, Asrafil? Why do we have to go there?"

He stirred, his wings silent when she thought they should rustle.

"This is as far as I can see," he said. "This is as much as I know."

"You don't know why you brought me here?" That was more interesting than the Enemy, certainly. She turned to face him, though it gave her a chill to turn her back so blatantly to what lay outside. Asrafil stared back at her, intentionally impassive, but she could imagine from his hooded gaze and the way he glowered that he was hiding what passed for intense emotional upheaval in an angel.

"I brought you here—" He hesitated. "I brought you here because it is my program to bring you here, once the world again was under way . . . "

Arianrhod blinked. "Your program? Me? Me in particular?"

"No." He shook his head. "You in genetic particular. A descendant of Prince Tristen and Princess Aefre, through their daughter Sparrow. I chose you for that reason, but more particularly I chose you because you have long been my helpmeet, my sweet. My ally, my servant, and my friend."

She had trusted him, loved him, this far. If all were lost now, well—all was lost. She had sacrificed all else on the altar of her angel. If he had deluded her, she might as well die of his love as live without it.

You did not love an angel to be safe, or in the interests of survival, or even because you thought the angel might ever love you back. You did not love an angel because you thought you could tame an angel, change it, make it safe. You loved an angel because to love an angel was to touch something larger than yourself, and because the process of that touch enlarged you as well.

"What's on the other side?"

"I don't know." When he shook his head, at least it made more noise than the wings, though she knew it was because he thought it should. "But it's writ in my bones that I must go there, beloved. Will you accompany me?"

"Across the very bosom of the Enemy." She touched the scabbard across her back. Its plain exterior concealed a monomolecular skin and the magnetic bottle that contained Charity's virulent, half-compiled revenant. The blade within the sheath was too much an absence for the touch to reassure.

He said, "It is far and cold, my darling."

Far. Too far for an Exalt? What if there was no warmth nor oxygen at the other end of those lines? She could survive a plunge into the Enemy, yes, but she could not live there long. "If I die—"

"Kiss me and be saved," he offered.

She lifted up her mouth to his, and let their breaths commingle. She raised her hands. Where they pressed the sculptured bones of his temples, his skin felt moist, warm. Fragile. Human. But that was only camouflage.

His mouth covered hers and he breathed in deep, breathed out, let their tongue tips touch. She felt the tingle as carrier was established, the momentary rush as her colony communed with the angel, passing along her memories and thoughts, the concentrated residue of her life.

—I keep you safe inside me.—

When he drew back, she kissed his cheek in gratitude. Then she turned, inside the circle of his arms, his coat, his wings, and faced the unadulterated Enemy. It was one thing to dip into the shallows, to skip from domaine to domaine within the sheltering embrace of the world.

But this was darkness in its person, the stronghold of the Enemy. There was nothing there to shelter her. She was about to leave the river for the sea, and she wondered if even a sea could seem so vast and strange. Surely there was a limit to how cowed the human soul could be.

Asrafil could infiltrate her, warm her, oxygenate her blood—within limits. Until his own resources were exhausted. Which would not take long. But then again, you did not love an angel if you were easy prey to fear.

"All right," she said. "Let's go."

Behind them, the lock door cycled. Ahead, the portal slid aside. Arianrhod fell forward into emptiness.

Reactive mass, she thought, but with Asrafil's wings around her there was no need of such primitive stopgap technology. He cast them out like a net, the colony using the world's trailing cables to speed them along. They glided low and quick, so close to the light-delineated filament that Arianrhod imagined she could reach out a hand and touch it. It was cold in the depths of the Enemy, as she had imagined it would be, but the cold could not freeze her. Inside the envelope of her angel, she felt it as a caress. The lights racing beneath her, the world vanishing behind, a blur quickly disappearing into the glow of the nebula—in Asrafil's presence, these things were exhilarating rather than terrifying.

He hesitated once, and whispered through the colonies, —*This is the point of safe return.*—

—*Go on.*—

Unease filled her as the cables stretched further. Whoever had set them here had done so intentionally, to make this place inaccessible, even to the Exalt. Arianrhod wondered what danger weighed the chain: weapon? engine of war? Even the embrace of an angel could not remove the fear and awe she felt as they approached the end of the lines, and the thing that dragged them out straight and stiff in the wake of the world.

At first, Arianrhod saw only a looming shape outlined in the sparkle of running lights, blue and green and gold photophores shimmering through occluding dust. As Asrafil brought her closer, though, she could make out the gleaming ceramic and metal of a massive framework or scaffolding. —*What a waste of energy all those lights are, out here in the dark.*—

—*What the Builders did, they did for a purpose.*—

—*Are you sure that was the Builders, Asrafil?*—How would the Builders have known that the world would be stranded? How would the Builders have known that a descendent of the line of Sparrow would come forward through time to be here when it sailed again?

He did not answer, just glided closer, silent and dark. It was only when he banked to follow the line of the scaffolding that she realized the scaffolding caged something, illuminated it, pinioned it on long, ice-shiny spears.

The thing at the heart of the structure was a lumpish brown-black stone, space-pocked, rough and potato-shaped, kilometers across. As big as a Heaven.

—*An asteroid?*—

—*It is,*—Asrafil said quietly,—*electrically active.*—

Tentatively, Arianrhod reached out through his colony, feeling it for herself. Electrical activity—and more. —*Asrafil, the thing is swarming.*—

—*I do not take your meaning, my sweet.*—

—*I mean,*—she said,—*it's infested with colonies. Can't you feel them?*—

He paused. She felt him check, like a balky transmission sticking. —*No.*—

If she could sense something he couldn't, then was it because whatever long-untriggered program directed them here also blinded him to the proliferation of the nanotech infesting the goal object—or was it because something more complex and sinister was involved? —*If it's not an asteroid, Asrafil, what is it? When you say it's showing signs of electrical activity, are you suggesting it might be alive?*—

He made a sound in her head like a man humming in his throat, and quoted: —*He maketh a path to shine after him; one would think the deep to be hoary. Upon earth there is not his like, who is made without fear.*—

The cold gnawed in Arianrhod's blood and bones now. She felt the light-headedness of dropping oxygen levels. The structure ahead gave no indication of life support, no hope of sanctuary. There was only the rust-black stone, hulking in its cage, and the Enemy on every side.

Arianrhod raised her eyes across the gulf, and with her cold tongue shaped a word that had no air to carry it.

"Leviathan."

16

blackest kinslaughter

Who hath prevented me, that I should repay him?
whatsoever is under the whole heaven is mine.
—Job 41:11, King James Bible

Gavin was ready, even expectant, when Tristen dropped away beneath him like a splash of falling water. He dared not close his talons hard—they might pierce the Prince's armor—and so he could not ease Tristen's fall. But he could spread his wings, cup air, and beat up out of the writhing mass of black-and-cream serpents that swallowed the fallen knight. The swarm of cobras heaved, shuddering, so Gavin knew that, under their weight, Tristen convulsed from the venom.

The basilisk hovered, churning air, and extended his neck to give vent to the hiss of a snake ten times his size. He would have done it alone, but Mallory stepped up beside him, an ally suddenly terrible with snapping eyes and a cloud of storm-black hair.

"Priestess," Mallory said, "Lady of the Edenites. Call back your creatures, or this necromancer will see to it that nothing here leaves this Heaven alive."

Dorcas remained before them, impassive as a queen, hands at her sides in the folds of her gown. Gavin reared back, crest flaring. "I'd listen to the wizard if I were you, Lady."

She cocked her head, seeming fearless. "By whose authority do you speak, familiar beast?"

"By my own," Gavin said. "By the authority of light."

A thin crack, only. The barest sliver of vision, enough that he caught a glimpse of her face, her form, as something other than a sensory shadow. Enough to let slip a sizzling fragment of light and smoke the dais between her feet.

He'd hoped to make her yelp and scuttle back. Instead, a serpent lunged for him. He felt it coming, the machined whisk of scales on scales, the nigh-invisible speed of fangs that could slice armor like butter. Gavin sideslipped, cranked his head around, and sizzled it in midstrike. He flapped up through air threaded with the rankness of burning mechanicals as the cobra thumped limply back among the bodies of its brethren draped over Tristen's seizing form.

My Prince, Gavin thought, *I seriously question your judgment.*

"The wizard meant it," Gavin said to Dorcas. "Call them off."

Her throat worked as she swallowed. He felt the way the atmosphere flexed around it, the accelerating beat of her heart. But neither her gestures nor her stance betrayed fear.

"Do you disregard your master's command so easily?"

"He is not my master," Gavin replied. He felt Samael behind him, closing up the gap between. Mallory stepped forward, graceful and martial as a cat, body surrendered for the moment to the control of some long-dead fighter. The warding ring of serpents had collapsed; nothing would hold Mallory back now.

"This is your third warning," Mallory said, as if Gavin and the necromancer spoke from one mind.

Her chin lifted. "Very well," she said, and raised her hand again.

The cobras rose with it, as if on marionette strings—an alien and unified motion. They swayed together, forward and back like stalks of wheat tossed in a circulation current, and flowed back to pool, hissing, around Dorcas's feet.

Dorcas shrugged as if it were all the same to her. "We have done what was needful, in any case. I will have refreshments brought, and you may stay with him for the time being. Or, if you prefer to leave him and continue on your quest—which I understand to have been of some urgency—we will make arrangements to allow you to pass beyond our lands. If you remain, and if he emerges from his trial, we shall discuss this further."

Dorcas had already turned and was taking the first step away when Mallory interrupted. "*If* he emerges from his trial?"

The priestess paused. "Many choose not to, having faced what awaits them."

Gavin backwinged to settle on Mallory's shoulder and felt Mallory bear up under it. He would have preferred to drop by Tristen's side and give the stricken First Mate his closer attention, but he did not feel that this was the time to sacrifice the advantage of height.

"Choose?" Mallory said.

At Samael's mismatched feet, Tristen convulsed again, a long, shocking extension of his legs and spine. Samael crouched, his immaterial hands passing through Tristen's armor as if *it* were the hologram.

Dorcas smiled. "Of course," she said. "We are the Woodsmen of the World, we Edenites. We are not executioners. We are only followers of the true path. We are not God. We cannot know a man's heart: that is between himself and what is divine. Whose judgment do you think he faces, if not his own?"

She stared down at them for a moment, but Gavin pointedly turned his head away. It didn't matter. He wasn't watching her with his eyes, but the message was unmistakable. A moment later, Dorcas raised her hood and stepped away, vanishing among the shapes of her followers.

"He's alive," Samael said from the earthen floor, his hands still buried in Tristen's chest, flakes of unidentifiable substances swirling where the bones of his wrists should be. "But that's one hell of an inducer virus. Psychotropic nanotoxin."

"Inducer virus?" Mallory asked. "What's it induce? Not a ghost personality?"

The Angel of Biosystems shook his head. "To a first approximation, I'd say it's just about the opposite. It's a tailored memory trigger, with an autoextinction function."

Gavin flipped his wingtips one over the other, a tense scissoring that left him feeling no more comfortable. Around them, the Go-backs had withdrawn to the outside walls of the pavilion, but they were still present— and observing. "So you're saying, what, it inhibits his colony's life-extending functions? He's about to crumble into the dust of a Mean five hundred years dead?"

"No," Samael said. "I'm saying it makes it possible for him to *wish* himself dead."

A pause for the sharing of worried glances followed. Samael drew back his hands, wiping them on immaterial trousers. "She wasn't lying."

"Yeah," Mallory said. "We gathered that. What now?"

"Go on without me," Gavin said. "The two of you. I'll wait here with the First Mate. You keep tracking Arianrhod, and we'll catch up when Tristen is recovered."

"If he recovers," Mallory said gently. "No. Too risky.

I can't fight Arianrhod, birdy. And Samael certainly can't, in his current condition."

The necromancer glanced apologetically at the angel; the angel dismissed it with a hands-spread shrug of acceptance.

"It's only the truth. We need you, Gavin. And we need Prince Tristen."

"So what are we going to do?"

One-handed, Mallory gentled the basilisk's wing, then scratched under his crest. Gavin lifted the feathers to allow better access, stretching into the caress. "We're going to wait," the necromancer said.

Every breath Tristen drew was one less, Gavin told himself, that they had to worry about. One breath closer to survival. One breath closer to resuming their quest.

One breath further behind Arianrhod.

Dozens of cobra fangs pierced armor, pierced skin, punctured flesh, and left their venom in Tristen's blood. There were colonies in the venom, and the colonies attacked his symbiont as the venom attacked his central nervous system.

Summoning the memory of the scent of lemon blossoms.

Lemon blossoms, and the brush of a cold wind across his neck. The smell—sugary, thick, not really like lemons at all—still made his stomach clench. Not nausea, but the salient memory of hunger.

There were some lean times then. As there would be lean times now.

Tristen knew, with the part of his brain that knew such things, that he had fallen to the carpets in the pavilion, that a hissing ring of cobras surrounded him. But all he felt was the chill breeze, the scent of the lemon tree, the hunger, the emotional pressure of Aefre at his left side and Sparrow beyond her, on her left—and the tension of a troop intent on battle, on the morn of revolution. It was not reliving, exactly. There was no surprise in what he experienced, just the event horizon of inevitability as he recognized where he was and what he recollected.

His horror was all at knowing in advance.

Aefre had been so golden, with her lion-tawny hair and her eagle-tawny gaze. Hazel, he supposed the color was called—but tawny was the right word, for everything about her should be defined in terms of predators. Her armor was golden, too, not the gold of metal but the gold of wheat, and so her skin would have been if not for the Exalt stain rendering it a pollen-dusted blue. The sword at her hip gleamed with care and use, and he had wanted to lean over and kiss the stern line between her eyebrows away. But one did not kiss a general before the assembled troops.

She was Alasdair Conn's eldest daughter, the Princess of the *Jacob's Ladder*. She was both fierce and beautiful, and why she'd chosen him, he'd never know.

Too much memory there. Memory was not, never had been, Tristen's friend. Most especially not when his great-granddaughter had tricked him into the imprisonment that Perceval and Rien (also his great-granddaughter, though he had not known it then) had so recently freed him from.

Tristen had survived by refusing to experience. By remembering those days through his symbiont, the machine memory where what had occurred was cool and distant and safely scrubbed.

Gavin was correct. Knowledge was not identity.

What cannot be cured must be endured, and Tristen excelled at enduring. But as his perfect memory led him from Rule at the vanguard of an army, he was not certain he could endure this.

They had traveled in close quarters and swiftly—the lifts and commuter shafts still worked, in those days, and in wartime they burned consumables on transports. So they packed in like marines cramped in anchores, waiting for the hatches to spring open and the killing to begin. He and Sparrow and Aefre had been separated in the transports—commanders do not travel together—but there was comm contact, and even though he heard nothing more over the comms than he should—that being terse, coded orders—some of those orders were in Aefre's voice, or Sparrow's.

The arguments were long over, passed through the night before: "I'm going," Sparrow had said. "Those are the Commodore's orders. If we don't hold the world together, no one will."

Tristen had met Aefre's eyes over Sparrow's shoulder and frowned. But Aefre had tipped her head from side to side in a kind of nod that wasn't.

"I'm not fighting for Alasdair," Sparrow continued. "I'm fighting because the alternative is doing nothing, and that will not halt our destruction."

"And if the Go-backs are right?" Aefre said. "And if your General disagrees with your Commodore, what then?"

Tristen shook his head. "Even if they are right, we have no means by which to implement their plan. We have no time in which to bring them to see reason." He touched the hilt of his unblade, trusting his meaning was plain. "War," he said to his wife, "is uncomplicated."

Aefre had frowned at him, consideringly, then nodded. "All right," she said. "I hate complications. We'll fight."

So Tristen had marched with the others and failed with the others. They met the Go-back army on the banks of the River and beat them back as effortlessly as he had foreseen. In only hours, he watched Aefre's shoulders as she went to accept the surrender of their leaders. He watched them cut her down, too, in contravention of truce, one of the Go-backs triggering a suicide weapon that vaporized himself, Aefre, and two bystanders.

They must have thought they could fight him, that the heart and skill would go out of Rule's soldiers with the death of their General.

Tristen and Sparrow had seen to it that they learned the error of their thought. When he returned to Rule— Sparrow by his side, still carrying Mirth, the blade Aefre had left with her when she went to parley—blossoms rained down on their heads again.

And that was not the worst of his failures of his daughter.

No, he thought, and wondered if it would be his last thought. He could not claim he did not deserve her justice.

"What can his crime have been, to deserve such punishment?" Mallory mused—a voice out of the silence and cool darkness that enveloped Tristen.

"Blackest kinslaughter," Tristen said, and opened his eyes to find the ghost of an angel leaning over him. "Guilty, of course. Don't be an idiot."

Samael jerked back, which was just as well, as Tristen would have sat up through him. Instead, he found himself nose to nose with the angel, specks and bits of things filling up his vision, until the angel retreated— and Tristen arose. He glanced down the white length of his armor, seeing where the paired holes smeared about with dark blue pierced it. They would heal, given time. The colony in the armor would see to it. The armor would be good as new.

Unlike Tristen.

"Where's Dorcas?" Tristen heaved himself to a crouch, rocking his feet under him, and stood. Not wobbly at all, which surprised him. He felt clean and strong and a little attenuated, as if with hunger. Sharp-set and ready to hunt.

Purged. That was the word he was groping after.

Samael stood up beside him, rising like a train of smoke. "She's over there. Somewhere."

The bitter curve of the angel's lips said it all. Samael knew which one of the coarse-clothed figures she was, knew exactly. But it was polite to pretend otherwise, unless Tristen ordered him specifically to abrogate that politeness.

When he gestured, the curve of his arm led Tristen's eye to Mallory and Gavin, huddled beside an upright post, their attention obviously turned inward. "They didn't go on?"

"They thought they needed you," Samael said with a shrug.

"They may not get me," Tristen said. "I think I've been convicted of crimes against humanity."

"You had a tough judge," Samael said. "It's a hard sort of existence. Come on; I'll walk to the gallows with you."

Tristen had been only half kidding. Samael's expression hinted that the angel had the other half. Tristen guessed that added up to one complete sense of humor between them. Serious or not, they walked together toward the cluster of three or four farmers by the pavilion wall.

The sense of lightness, of being constructed of something dry and strong, did not leave him. If anything, it increased, as if the soil under his boot were pushing him forward with each step.

"Dorcas," Tristen said. He waited while she turned to him, watched the dark amber strands escape around her face as she pushed back her hood. "I have fulfilled my part of the bargain."

Her mouth did a funny thing, very unlike any expression of his daughter's. He couldn't read it as either relief or approbation, and he didn't know anything else it might be. It didn't last long before her expression settled back to impassivity. "I see that you have. And what was the verdict, Prince Tristen?"

"Guilty," he offered. "As you knew it would be. Guilty of kinslaughter—by negligence and recklessness. Guilty of moral cowardice and the failure to protect all I should have held sacred. And certainly I am culpable in the deaths of my wife and daughter."

For all it was the answer he would have expected her to want, it did not seem to satisfy her. "And yet you stand before me. How then has justice been served?"

He thought of darkness, humid warmth, the blinding, incessant reek of ammonia. He folded his fingers closed against wet palms. "Death is not the only justice. I paid for my sins before you met me, Lady of the Edenites. I am well acquainted with my monstrosities. And I have long since learned to live with them, which is harder."

From the manner in which she stared down the bridge of her nose at him, he thought she might disagree. He braced for her word to break their bargain, and the wasteful carnage that must follow.

But at last she drew in a breath and let it out again on a sigh, and folded her arms before her. "Good enough," she said, "if unsatisfying."

Tristen felt Mallory and Gavin at his shoulder. He didn't feel Samael, but he could not imagine that the angel was not there. It gave him a little strength to press forward. "You know that Sparrow Conn, whose form you wear, was my daughter."

Dorcas nodded. "So you gave me to understand."

He let his fingers cup Mirth's pommel, but did not

grip the hilt, nor move to draw the blade. The cool, resilient polymer of the blade's handle conformed to his touch. He could imagine how his fingers would sink into the grips, how the sword would become an extension of his hand.

Once upon a time, he would have found comfort in that. He would have been eager to draw the blade. He would have looked forward to the carnage and displays of prowess that followed, the song of battle along his nerves.

But that man was dead, and he realized with a shock that he did not miss the bastard.

The sword's awareness stirred, pushing against the palm of his hand like a questing cat. The blade was hungry, after the manner of blades. But that did not mean that he had to feed it.

Tristen said, "If you are not she, why do you crave her vengeance so badly?"

"Your misguidance led to her death," Dorcas said. She lowered her voice. "And her death led to my life in this shell far from the embrace of Mother Gaia, and *that* is a burden with which I would rather not be troubled. How do you answer to that, Tristen Conn?"

"I failed you," he said, amazed that the deep sting in his chest was not shame or humiliation, but simple grief. *Five hundred years to the death of the ego,* he thought, and shook his head in bemusement. "I failed you as a father, as a fellow soldier, and as the eldest member of the house of Rule."

"That was not me—"

"Whatever." And maybe there was a little of the man he had been in the interruption. But even a shed skin left its pattern behind. "If you are not her, then I am not him. And as you have already determined that I am accountable for his crimes against her, then by God you will listen to my accounting."

It drew her up, and brought the lingering three or four Go-backs hurrying forward to flank her with their support. Tristen imagined the high priestess of the Edenites was unused to being placed off her balance. Somewhere behind Tristen were Mallory, Samael, and Gavin. For the time being, he would pretend they could not see him.

He unclipped Mirth's sheath from his belt and balanced the sword across his palms. "There's half a bargain to be sealed."

He knew he hadn't imagined the quirk of her lips. "So there is." She reached out, but he held the blade back for a moment.

"There was more in your venom than hallucinogens, wasn't there?"

"An inducer virus," she agreed. "Are you feeling it?"

Light, strong, like something woven out of carbon fiber and high-end ceramics. As if his mind rode the chassis of a synbiote, and not his own body at all. It made him feel as ungrounded as it did capable.

Mallory brushed his elbow. Tristen ignored it.

"Behavioral controls?"

"Not as such. But if you had really believed you deserved death, it would have carried out the sentence."

"Of course," he said. "Why leave such things to chance?"

The smile they shared was not what he would have expected, but it was satisfying. When she lifted her palms, he laid the blade across them, flat as a tray.

"Draw it," he said, stepping backward to give her room.

Whatever knowledge and elements of personality were earthed in the brain, the body had an intelligence of its own. And the body of Sparrow Conn had not forgotten how to handle a weapon.

With one smooth extension, she skinned the blade.

Tristen held his breath, feeling his companions behind him, the way Mallory edged still closer. The necromancer's shoulder brushed Tristen's armor, and the armor transmitted that sensation to his arm.

Dorcas weighed Mirth in her hand as effortlessly as if it were an unblade. She tilted her head to squint its length and frowned. "After all that, you deliver me your weapon?"

"If I'm not a harsh enough judge of myself, who better to make up the deficit?"

When she looked up at him over the blade, he found himself hard-pressed not to see her mother in her hazel eyes. Smeared reflections of her features blurred along the length of the sword. She turned it in her hand, let it glide back along her forearm and beyond. "I am not an executioner."

"I was," he said. "My father's dog, at first because I believed in him, as he had raised me to. Then, after Aefre died and Alasdair turned his attentions on Arianrhod, your antecedent had the sense to remove herself from the family, out of grief and because it was easier than opposing him. If I had kept my granddaughter away from my father, Sparrow might never have left Rule at all."

He sighed. Arianrhod was a question all her own. It was not as if *anyone* had ever been able to control her. "And then when your antecedent died in Engine"—in the Go-back riots, during Caitlin and her sisters' attempt to wrest control of the world from Alasdair, but now did not seem the most exemplary time to mention that—"if I had been with her, if I had stood up with her, she might be living still."

Dorcas's eyebrow raised, but he did not feel guilt in saying it. She might inhabit Sparrow's body now, but the scarce resource had historically been allocations for memory, not resurrected flesh. People were easy to make. There were always more dead than remnants to fill them with.

Dorcas said, "You were not the brother who went to war for him against Cecelia's daughters. You are not the brother whose blade cut Cynric's head from her shoulders."

"Nor did I join them in rebellion," Tristen said. "Think of all the evil I might have averted had I cast down my father then. Apathy is no excuse. Nor is a taste for combat."

She smiled and allowed Mirth to glide back into its sheath. "You were terrifying then."

"You remember?"

"I wasn't an Edenite during the Moving Times, Tristen Conn," she said. "Go-backs don't store their data, or accept colonies." She paused, ironically. "Until now, anyway. I served under your wife. I was a soldier. Do you know what we called you?"

Her hand extended, the sword laid across it. Offering. Slowly, he reached out and lifted it from her palm. Her face remained impassive, but a long chill ran up her spine when the sword left her grasp, so he knew it troubled her. He wondered what the sword had said to her, if indeed it had spoken at all.

Of course he remembered. There had been political cartoons, the white ruff, fangs, stripes, talons. The devil eyes. He'd nursed a little secret pride about it, then.

"Tristen Tiger," he said.

"The man-eater. The tame killer. You do remember."

He touched his temple. The colony remembered for him.

"Tristen Tiger would not have survived the venom, you know. I think perhaps you have changed more than I have." She shrugged and spread her hands. "Half a millennium is a long time to live within a monster."

It hadn't been that long. Or rather, he had indeed

lived that long, but it was only in the years he'd passed pent up in a dungeon of Ariane's devising, living in filth, that he had come to realize he had been a monster, after all.

A thousand things crowded his mouth, none of them willing to be refined into sensibility. So, instead, he clipped Mirth to his belt and said, "I am glad you've found peace. Even if you are not the woman you were."

"And I am glad you are not the man you were. And I hope you find peace as well, before too much longer." She pursed her lips, craning her neck to see over his shoulder to Samael and Mallory—and Gavin as well. She paused, seeming puzzled, and glanced down at her fingers, which flexed and stretched as if she were absently working out a cramp.

Recollecting herself, she continued. "You've passed the test. We will guide you across our Heaven, and show you the fastest path to your destination."

"You know it?"

"We built it," she said. His eyes must have widened with the surprise and disbelief he felt, because she smirked—turning her head to include Mallory and Samael in its arc—and said, "What did you think the Go-backs were, exactly, Tristen Tiger?"

Tristen glanced at Mallory; the necromancer nodded. Not that it mattered—he suspected Dorcas was interested in his opinion, not that of his companions.

He could have given her the snap answer, the dismissal. And maybe he would have, not too long gone by. To alienate the enemy was a useful defense. But he thought now of ancient history, the thin, perfect memories of his colony predominating over the richer, chemical, organic ones. They had been Engineers, convinced that the best means of survival was to cannibalize what could be saved of the world and return to Earth in a smaller, stripped-down vessel, leaving behind everything designed for colonization and terraforming as useless ballast. Many of them had also been heretics of another stripe: they had believed in the perfection of the human form as a reflection of God's will, and had refused inoculation with Cynric's then newly invented colonies, or any physical augmentation whatsoever.

Alasdair Conn, the Commodore, had opposed them.

Alasdair had believed passionately in the goals and edicts of the Builders: that the purpose of God's creation in Man was to confront harsh environments, to master them, to evolve to meet any challenge. That the ultimate expression of faith was to subject one's self and one's offspring to ever harsher challenges, ensuring survival of the fittest through mortification of the flesh. Of all the species of God's creation, only man had the power to reshape himself in God's image, and Alasdair—whatever his other failings—had not been a hypocrite. A deeply religious man, as moral and spiritual leader of his people he had believed in that obligation with all his heart.

And, as Benedick had pointed out at the time, given conditions when the Builders left, there was no guarantee that Earth was any more able to support life than would be a smoking cinder.

Tristen—a dutiful son, and a dutiful soldier—had gone to war to drive the Go-backs from Engine. He had been doing what he was bid, and in every way that mattered to his father, he had succeeded. If Sparrow died in the war, well, that was the cost of selection. In any case, she'd already passed along her genes to Arianrhod, so it would be easy for Alasdair to fix the line. That the result had been Ariane, Alasdair's eventual murderer, gave Tristen a bitter little frisson of complicated pleasure— his own history with his great-granddaughter notwithstanding.

Whatever Tristen had been about to mouth, unthinking, died upon his tongue. He eased his shoulders in his

armor, feeling it resist and settle as he pushed against
the gel interior.

"I think you were right," he said.

Dorcas led them through the Heaven like a woman
showing them around her house. The snakes and
sycophants had mostly dispersed, returning to their tasks
in the near-vertical rice paddies, and Mallory came up to
walk beside them, Samael trailing like a wisp of smoke
behind. Dorcas acknowledged Mallory with a nod, but
otherwise continued to speak chiefly to Tristen. To judge
by smirk alone, Mallory was more amused than offended.

"Soothe my curiosity," Tristen said. "Why in the
world are you willing to help us?"

"Is it not the role of a dutiful daughter?" She must
have seen his wince, because she looked away, as if
scanning the moss-draped boughs, and gave him a
moment to recollect himself. Neither Sparrow nor Aefre
had ever had need of such social manners, so the gesture
carried with it a hard freight of reminder that Dorcas
was not Sparrow.

Again.

Tristen was still working to swallow that when she
said, "The reason for our existence as a sect is gone, you
know. We are under way again. A solution has been
implemented, and in any case, we no longer have the
option of abandoning the world and returning home.
We have been infected with your symbiont, against our
wills; the purity of our form is compromised."

Tristen was tempted to comment on the fact that Dorcas herself had enjoyed the benefits of her symbiont for
the last five hundred years, without apparent ill effect to
her rise among her church—but under the circumstances he considered the wisdom of discretion and bit
his tongue.

She continued, "Which means that if we are to survive

in the world to come, we must make some choices. Assuming we live to reach a planetfall, it's likely to take all of us working together. And toward that end, I can think of worse allies than the world's First Mate." She paused. "So, to put it in plain terms, you have passed my test. And whatever I have done today to earn your enmity, I hope that it will be balanced against the aid I offer now."

"I see," he said. "You will understand if I make no promises?"

She smiled and glanced aside. "What will you do with Arianrhod when you find her?"

"Bring her to justice," Tristen said. Unable to resist, he raised his eyebrows and added, "You know all about that."

Maybe it was too early to tease her—though after all, she had started it. Or maybe not, because the sharp glance she gave him modulated smoothly from irritation to amusement. Dorcas, Tristen suspected, was a person who took quiet pride in not becoming irritated.

She said, "I don't suppose you know where you're going?"

Gavin's long neck rose above Mallory's frizzy curls. "South," he said. "Into the belly of the beast."

Dorcas chuckled. "It's possible you speak truer than you know. I can get you to the bottom of the world, to the Broken Holdes. Can you find your way from there?"

"Inasmuch as we know where we are going," Tristen said. "Something down there has interfered with the world-angel's sensory apparatus, and we are only guessing based on another tracking party's information that her destination is somewhere in the null patch." He would not tell her, just now, how long it had been since his team had had contact with Benedick and Chelsea, or with Nova and Perceval.

"The null patch," Dorcas echoed. "You really have no idea what lives there?"

Samael mimicked a few quick strides and came up between them. "You do?"

"We know all sorts of things," Dorcas said. "Many of us—we were Engineers, remember? After I was a soldier, I became an Engineer, inspired by the memory of Hero Ng." She lowered her voice and spoke conspiratorially. "Some of us are more cynical than others when it comes to the question of the will of God."

Tristen glanced at Samael, at Gavin, at Mallory—each by turn. All three avoided his gaze. "Some of us learned our cynicism the hard way," he replied. "So what's in the null zone?"

"Cynric's last weapon," she said. "A captive monster. A demon so terrible that, after she captured it, Captain Gerald concealed its existence from all but a few. When Alasdair became Commodore after him, Alasdair hid it even from his children, for fear of what they would do with the information."

"For fear of what he'd made them, you mean."

She smiled. "Perhaps that, as well. In any case, Cynric caught two of them. One she took apart, and made things of the pieces. The other she kept captive, held in reserve."

"She used it," Gavin said, craning his neck around to stare at Samael. "Do you really claim no knowledge, Poison Angel, of what it was your mistress wrought?"

"My memory is incomplete," Samael said drily. "Do enlighten us."

Tristen wondered if the basilisk's glance at Dorcas was meant as a request for permission. She made no move to interrupt, and he continued, "She built on it, the way she built on everything she touched, everything she knew. As Dorcas said, she created it a weapon."

"Something to fight our father," Tristen said. "Well, I guess if anyone would remember that—"

Gavin flipped his wings, tail coiling and uncoiling along Mallory's spine so that Tristen wondered what social discomfort looked like on a power tool.

"Those memories are not mine," Gavin said. "And they are . . . also incomplete. So you have a route that will take us there, My Lady of the Edenites?"

"We have more than that," she said. "We have regained some limited control of the world's musculature. I can *put* you there."

In unison, Mallory and Samael said, "Musculature?" which made Tristen feel somewhat more comfortable in his own ignorance.

Dorcas pressed her palms to her eyes. "By the sacred spiral, people. Do you know how the world generates its electricity?"

Silence answered her.

She sighed. Then her hands began to move animatedly as she explained. "It's not just the reactors or the solar panels. I'll give you a hint. The exterior of the world is sheathed in self-healing carbon nanotube 'muscle' that can be used to move portions of the structure around relative to one another."

"That's ingenious," Samael said.

"It's not rocket science." Her lips twisted. "Actually, I guess after a fashion, it is. When not in operation, the musculature uses flex and inertial effects to generate electricity. Thereby"—she snapped her fingers—"keeping the lights on. And the temperature constant, though under the current circumstances I wouldn't be surprised if there are failures on that front."

Tristen blinked, trying to integrate the scientist now emerging with the autocratic priestess he'd thought he was dealing with.

Mallory came to the rescue. "It is our information that there have been failures, some catastrophic. The angel and Engineering were working to contain them when we entered your Heaven. It is possible that by now they've been redressed."

"Your confidence in your masters is touching."

Tristen said, "One thing that troubles me still, Dorcas. When we came in, we saw scrape marks in the air lock. As if you had been discarding trash."

She made a moue. "Sacrifices," she said. "Some believe in appeasing the Enemy."

"Oh," he said. "I see." Desperate for a change of topic, he added, "When do we reach your mode of transport, then?"

"We're in it," Dorcas said. "And in fact, if you look up ahead, you'll see we're almost there."

Tristen craned his neck. Through the tunnel of bowering trees, he glimpsed the hard, clean oval of an air lock. "We're moving."

"Relative to the rest of the world, anyway," she said. She paused, one hand hovering over a DNA lock. She palmed it and the door slid aside, revealing a standard barren cubicle.

It crossed Tristen's mind to imagine that she might very well just decoy them inside to space them, but if that happened, it wasn't as if he and Mallory couldn't survive the Enemy's embrace for a few moments.

He turned to Dorcas and said, "Thank you. If we survive this—"

"You'll be in touch," she said, and touched the armor over his right arm. She met his eyes. "Go with luck. I think you will be sad a long time, Tristen Tiger. But I hope not too sad."

When they passed through the air lock and the interior door sealed across Dorcas's face, Gavin found himself prey to emotions too complex by half for a simple power tool. Grief, regret, guilt, resignation.

These were not his emotions. His emotions currently encompassed concerned anticipation at what they might find ahead, irritation at the delay, vulture worry. The others—the indescribable ones, the painful ones—he knew better than to try to own them. They belonged to someone else, someone to whom he bore no more resemblance than Nova did to Rien. Than Dorcas did to Sparrow. But in conjunction with that knowledge came the uncomfortable corollary: whatever he had behind him had left traces.

As shields glided up over the external windows before him, he observed the latticework architecture scrolling past on all sides and the looming wall of their destination before them. It was an old world, scarred and scorched, blasted bright by radiation and by particles in the nebula. Made clean and new. But inside, so much history, so much betrayal, and so many twisted loyalties.

He wondered if Dorcas were the tabula rasa she pretended.

Tristen seemed impassive, leading Gavin to suspect that his internal turmoil mirrored Gavin's own. Gavin was not prey to the irrational hormonal urges of meat—a kindness for which he thanked his makers—but he was not without feelings. Early researchers had determined that there was no intelligence without desire, and had proven the dispassionate artificial brain to be a wishful construct of twentieth-century myth. Synbiotic emotion might be chilly and distant by human standards, but it existed. Reason was not possible in its absence.

Gavin felt for Tristen, and only part of that was his program for empathy. Because as sequestered memory cascades continued triggering, he remembered what Sparrow had meant to Cynric. Sparrow was not merely the daughter of Cynric's heart—Cynric, like Perceval, had chosen to remain fallow—but a daughter of her own creation, as well. There were secrets in Sparrow's bloodline, data and talents that Cynric the Sorceress had selected for and machined into the genome.

Then she had hidden them from Gavin, choosing to forget, when she had also chosen to die by her brother Benedick's hand.

Gavin felt her back there now like a shadow over his shoulder, a person he didn't know but somehow remembered snatches of. He thought she had been a strange and manipulative person, even by the standards of the Conn family, and that she had had agendas and obligations that she had never shared with anyone—not Caithness, not Caitlin, and she certainly had not passed them on to him.

There was no doubt in his mind that the resurrection of Sparrow's body in service of a slain Engineer was not an accident. And it made him wonder, then, how Sparrow had died that her body was preserved, but there had been no backup of her mind—not even so much as a seed personality—so soon after the Moving Times, when such technology was still common.

Something must have left her damaged enough that her colony's memory failed. And perhaps she had made a core seed, and it had been purged—either to make a place for some fragment of the world-angel, or in the service of intentional murder.

Despite the value of hindsight—perhaps especially in hindsight—Gavin found he did not much like Cynric. Or even her memory. And yet these were her fond feelings for Sparrow infecting him.

As the exterior air lock cycled, the basilisk hunkered on Mallory's shoulder and kept his own counsel.

What stood revealed beyond seemed innocuous enough. Gavin identified a garden, chestnut trees made to seem venerable, mossy stones walling a yard. The corner of a building framed one side of the prospect, and as they emerged cautiously from the air lock, Gavin's senses informed him that the space was little more than an acre and a half in area, a tiny Heaven if it qualified as a Heaven at all. The trees were still healing, fat cracks twisting along their boles in some places, but there was some damage that would take years to mend. Heavy shelf mushrooms lay crushed at their bases, and once they were clear of the lock it became evident that the stones forming the back side of the building had tumbled into a heap.

The facade still stood on the near side, however, hollow-eyed and showing the foliage behind it through the windows. Around the footings, colored shards sparkled against grass, light reflecting from hard-edged splinters.

Tristen unsealed his helm and jolted forward, nearly running, Samael at his heels. Mallory advanced more cautiously, so Gavin had only to fan his wings for balance.

Gavin said, "It's a chapel."

"It's *mined* stone," Tristen corrected, dropping to his knees beside it. "Mined stone."

"From Earth?" Gavin asked. He flapped hard, kicking off Mallory's shoulder, and flew up to circle the top of the chapel wall. He could see chisel marks, it was true, though it was common enough to fake those—but when he landed and his claws scraped rock, he felt the deadness of it, the internal weight, and knew that no colony had ever touched this stuff. "It came off a *planet*?"

"Can you imagine how much energy that cost?" Mallory's voice had enough awe in it that Gavin snaked his head over the edge to look down, but the necromancer had merely paused beside Tristen and knelt there, running long fingers through the shaggy grass. "Ow!"

"Careful," Gavin said helpfully. "Broken glass is sharp."

"I noticed," Mallory said, frowning at blue-spotted fingers. "What's glass?"

"Fused silica," Gavin said. "Very hard. Very brittle."

"Very heavy," Samael commented, selecting a piece and running ghostly fingers through it. "The Builders put this here."

"It certainly got made before the world left the home system." Tristen reached out to touch the stone, his gauntlet slicking back from his fingers. He stroked the wall of the chapel with a reverential hesitancy, then grimaced at his fingers. "It feels like stone."

Mallory said, "No *wonder* the Go-backs had a means to get here."

"Indeed." His armor would have given him a sensory sphere as complete as Gavin's, but Tristen nevertheless glanced over his shoulder as if expecting to find somebody watching. He shook his head. "It's a little piece of what we were. It looks so . . . "

"Primitive?" Gavin suggested.

"Fragile," Samael said. "Somebody should see if they can check in with Nova."

"I already tried," Tristen answered, as Gavin felt the attention of another colony tickle along the borders of his awareness. "Still no contact. Come on. We're on the clock."

"We're on the clock," Gavin agreed. "And something's coming."

The something was a familiar shaggy-humped outline bigger than a mastiff dog. As they came up on it, Tristen easily identified the mammoth calf he had insisted they free from its trap among the massive fig tree's roots. It waited for them by the far air lock, beyond a gap in the garden wall, its trunk raised as if it were scenting the air, its piggish eyes blinking through strands of coat.

"It followed me home," Samael said. "Can I keep it?"

Tristen shot the angel a scathing glance. "Tell me the truth. You don't actually know how that got here, how it got ahead of us. Or do you?"

"I don't," Samael answered, with every evidence of seriousness and sincerity—though an angel could not lie to his First Mate. Theoretically. "But it's Exalt—more than Exalt. I can feel the edges of its colony from here."

"That's what I sensed back at the chapel," Gavin agreed. "It's waiting for us."

"The world is weird," Tristen said, a catchphrase his mother had been fond of. "Let's go see what it wants, shall we?"

They picked their way toward the gap, Tristen in the lead with one hand on Mirth's hilt. He tried to move with grace, but now that his euphoria was fading he felt the stiffness in every limb, damage from the cobra venom that his colony had not yet restored.

Tristen paused a few steps from the calf and held out his other hand, fingers flattened to present as smooth a target as possible. The calf tapped his palm with its trunk, fingerlike nubbins moving on his palm. Warm, moist air huffed against his skin. "Hello," Tristen said.

The mammoth calf opened its mouth and said, "—"

Mallory blinked and turned toward it. He held out one hand. "Tristen."

"What was that sound?"

"A language," Mallory said. "*The* Language. Did you not understand it?"

Perhaps—

"Yes," Tristen answered, knowing what it meant. Not knowing how he had understood it. "How do you know that?"

Mallory said, "I am full of dead men."

Oh.

The necromancer continued, "Job forty-one. Verses thirty-two and thirty-four. You know them."

"In my bones," Tristen agreed.

But he allowed Mallory to recite them. *"He maketh a path to shine after him; one would think the deep to be hoary. Upon earth there is not his like, who is made without fear."*

Samael, who had been standing silent, head cocked and staring, jerked himself upright like a badly managed puppet. "It's a key. Remember it."

"A key?" Tristen frowned at the angel, hard enough that his face found it uncomfortable. "A key to *what*?"

The angel spread his arms, lank, pale locks stirring as though his gesture made a wind. "That information has not yet been unlocked to my program," he said. "But I would wager the mammoth knows."

"Great," Gavin said. "What the hell are we going to do with a mammoth?"

17

the revelation

No matter where; of comfort no man speak:
Let's talk of graves, of worms, and epitaphs;
Make dust our paper and with rainy eyes
Write sorrow on the bosom of the earth.
—WILLIAM SHAKESPEARE, *Richard II*, Act 3, Scene 2

The maintenance of her physical form had always been one of life's chief pleasures for Caitlin Conn. She enjoyed food, exercise, rest, work, self-care, affection—all the capabilities of her flesh and colony. Adventure and accomplishment were her meat and drink.

So it was a great frustration that not only was she obliged to remain behind at the helm of largely autonomous processes while her brothers and Chelsea adventured, but that both Tristen and Benedick had fallen out of contact just as things were getting interesting.

It was a devil's bargain. She couldn't relax enough to enjoy a much-needed meal and cleansing, but she hadn't nearly enough to *do* at this point to keep her occupied beyond worrying. Though she had to be informed and ready to assist the Captain in making policy decisions to contain each crisis—and minor ones were still appearing with disconcerting regularity—everything else taking place in the world was at scales too tiny and speeds too great for even Exalt humans to participate.

Helplessness was not her stock in trade, but despite feeling as if she were drowning in it, she forced herself to step into the scrubber and set the sonics and the steam to *high*. Even if it didn't relax her brain, it would be good for her muscles, and the human system worked better if everything was maintained. She would have complete contact with Nova, and Jsutien was still shrouded in his nanochains and watching the consoles. A little independence would serve as a test of his loyalties, though Caitlin was not about to let her observation of him lapse simply because she happened to be out of the room.

So even with her eyes closed, her forehead leaned against the scrubber wall, her head was full of images. Steam billowed around her, loosening roughened skin. It weighed down her short curls until they brushed the back of her neck. The sonics stroked her body in waves. Condensation, dead cells, and her own sweat knifed from her to vanish into the recapture, where it would all be returned to the ecosystem.

Maybe her stress could wash down the drain, too, and go find something to fertilize. It certainly wasn't doing any good where it was.

The timer pinged after three minutes. She straightened up and pushed her fingers through her hair amid vapor rolling back like the fabric of a dream. She kept her eyes closed for a moment longer, anyway, savoring the fantasy of a world in which cleansing lasted as long as you wanted.

This world wasn't it, though, so she blinked open moisture-stuck lashes, took one last warm breath, and reached outside the door for her robe. Warm cloth wrapped her shoulders as she stepped back out onto the deck, leaving damp footprints in her wake. It felt good to finally be clean of the last sticky residue of synthetic amniotic fluid. It felt better to have had a few instants alone in her head.

Now she could go back, soldier up, and continue to worry about Tristen and Chelsea—and Benedick, too, though she hated to admit it—in the belly of the world.

She felt the absence of her unblade at her hip like— well, like an absence, which struck her as a curious comparison, because when she was carrying it she would have said that it was null space personified. She pulled her hand away from its lack. When she reentered Central Engineering, her robe reshaping itself into trousers and a tunic for authority's sake, Jsutien looked up.

"Nothing broke," he said, spreading his arms wide to indicate the colonies whose repairs he had been supervising. "Well, nothing new broken, anyway."

"That's good news," she said. She touched the control box in her pocket—it had remained secure through the transition from clothes to robe and back again—and released his tethers from the floor. "Your turn. Go get cleaned up, and I'll mind the forum."

He arched his back and raised his arms, stretching the drape of nanochains like a canopy overhead. When he lowered them again, he said, "Thank you. No word from the prodigals; communication has not been restored. But Nova and I found some things that may be useful to us."

"Star charts?" She said it with arch amusement, trying to get a smile, but he answered seriously.

"Not that good. But there's a *bunch* of old astrophysics and astronomy data on primitive optical storage media. Nova can construct readers that can handle it. Some of that might include information on rocky planets. The Builders had very good telescopes. Even some orbital ones. If we can figure out where we are in relation to Earth and how long it's been since the images were taken, we can use that data to construct our own charts."

Caitlin felt herself begin to smile. "Astrogation."

He grinned back before he brushed past her. "After all, it's what I do."

While he was gone, she drew rations and arranged a meal: nothing exciting, but a selection of carbohydrates, fats, minerals, and amino acids that would keep two people and their colonies functional and in good repair. When Jsutien reemerged from the locker room, hair still trailing wisps of steam, she tossed him one prewarmed consumable tube of grayish porridge. He caught it, nanochains flaring like a microgravity dancer's drapes, and bit off the top. The gel crunched audibly between his teeth.

"Nature-identical grape," he said, with a wrinkled nose. "Boy, this takes me back. And not in an entirely pleasant fashion."

Caitlin grinned between slurps of porridge. The taste was too sweet, harshly artificial, without the nuance or subtlety of real fruit. "What's it like?"

"Being back?"

She tossed him a pod of water, too, and watched Oliver's body snag it by reflex at the top of its trajectory. "Being in the future. If that's not a cruel question."

He bit open the water, too—stale, if Caitlin's was anything to go on—and sucked it dry, throat and jaw working as he washed down sticky porridge. Then he crumpled up the pod, which crackled in his fist, and shoved it into his mouth. Buying time, Caitlin thought. The contemplative thoroughness of his chewing did nothing to disabuse her of the notion.

Seconds later, he swallowed and said, "It's a lot like the porridge."

Under Caitlin's fingertips, readouts tracked, averaged, and streamlined billions of processes, keeping her apprised of repair and defense trends worldwide. There was no need for her to look at the external display, which was only a fail-safe. All the information she needed was right there in her hands. "I beg your pardon?"

"The porridge," he said, patting Oliver's stomach. "Or maybe I should say, *I'm* a lot like the porridge. Nature-identical. Which is to say, flattened out. The most interesting part is knowing stuff—pieces of me—are missing, but not knowing what they are. I can feel where they should go, but . . . It's like reading a novel in translation. You can tell you're missing stuff, like all the jokes, but what it is exactly that you're missing is hard to say."

A novel was a kind of static entertainment in the written word. Like a story, but fixed as it was written rather than interactive. Immutable. A historical document.

Caitlin thought she was coming to understand Damian Jsutien. Like him, she finished the last of her rations, then said, "I am given to understand that you weren't faithful, then."

He dropped back onto his cot, raking both hands through Oliver's tousled curls, which were still flattened here and there from sleeping. "What's faith? I was an astrogator. It was my business to lie, not to believe."

"So why did you come along, if you knew it was a lie?"

"If I knew it was a journey without a destination?" The thing he did with his mouth hurt her, just watching it. "Better ask why my grandmother came. Why did she take that leap of faith? She wasn't a believer either, not when I knew her. But I imagine whatever she left behind must have been worse than the prospect of death in the cold, for her and her descendants."

"Were there a lot like her?"

He scratched the side of his chin, fingernails burring against stubble. "Enough. More than a few. I hope it does not horrify you, the revelation that some of the Builders were cynical."

Cynical. What a comforting euphemism to mean deception, betrayal, the treacherous use of the faith of hundreds of thousands to lure them to their deaths. "I know about the bodies in the holdes," Caitlin said, the most neutral answer she could manage.

"Without data," he said, "we always assumed that if the Builders were not simply evil—and that's a lot of pointless work, for evil—they must have been driven by desperation, and the threat of consequences so dire that sending thousands to die in the embrace of the Enemy seemed like a sensible use of resources." Jsutien waved grandly to Central Engineering, a gesture that encompassed not only the space he and Caitlin inhabited, but all the wrecked world beyond. "On the other hand, it's also possible that some of them were possessed of a pioneering spirit."

"People are fundamentally lazy," she agreed, "but it's true. Historically speaking—things get colonized somehow. I'm sorry. I didn't mean to rake you over the coals for your dead grandmother's choices."

"The way you've been raked over the coals of your father's choices, all these years?"

Tentative camaraderie cracked as Caitlin's hand closed convulsively on the nanochain control key in her pocket. "How do you know that?" she asked, then pinched her lower lip between her teeth to keep from grinding them.

Jsutien, frowning at an image tank, seemed oblivious to her dismay. He had one finger extended as he traced something of interest through the bewildering partial schematic that hung before him, his tongue protruding like a child's in concentration. She imagined young Oliver had never looked so patient, so stern, and it crossed Caitlin's mind to wonder how old Jsutien had been when he died. Old, she'd guess, by Mean standards.

Old and treacherous. She would have to remember that, however fresh and felicitous the face he wore.

"Your brother," he said. "You. The obvious family tension between the two of you. The way you avoid eye contact with him. The fact that, except for Tristen, none of the Conns I remember seem to be alive anymore."

"It's been a long time," Caitlin said, trying to make it sound like she was only returning his volley. She chafed her cold hands together, trying to restore sensation. Flakes of hoarfrost broke from her shirt cuffs and drifted down. "Almost nobody you remember is alive anymore, Damian Jsutien."

That got him to glance away from his tank and crinkle the corners of his eyes in a grin like a lynx's. "Conns are dangerous. That, I'm pretty sure, will never change."

Although she was never in solitude, the Captain dined alone. Her meal was rice, greens, yams, and textured vegetable protein, which she shoveled down like sawdust. She ate from a bowl that did not exist with a spoon conjured of primal forces, her eating so mechanical that she'd half finished the food before she paused to marvel at the tools in her hands. "What a strange old world," she said.

Across the green field of the bridge, Nova looked up from her work, and Perceval noticed that her effort to define their relationship seemed to be helping the angel's avatar set into a definable shape. Brown skin and silver hair, yes. Nothing like Rien. But female, and soft-eyed, and so nothing like Samael either. Or Dust.

There was no need for the angel's avatar to pretend to be hard at work, or even to make itself apparent when it was not interacting with meat-and-bone crew, but Perceval found herself more comfortable with the illusion that she knew where the angel was and what she was doing—though as an Engineer she also found this a shameful anthropocentrism. Still, she was also more comfortable with its avatar's pretense of being engaged in some vital business. Intellectually, she knew that it was nothing but an animation. Emotionally, instinctively, however, for her to see Nova from the corner of her eye, hands moving and head bowed over a set of displays, helped her accept the angel as a team member and an ally.

She needed that. She needed, she thought dismally, all the help she could get. Because her first response was to recoil from Nova, from the connection she could always feel at her edges, as if Nova were an invader rather than an invited guest. She did not want the angel in her head. She did not want the angel so sharp, and so near.

She'd never expressed those preferences to Nova. But Nova had guessed, or had read them in her subconscious.

She scraped the last rice from the bowl and swallowed it. She set spoon in bowl, and bowl aside on an edge of her work surface. Since it was empty it vanished back into the ether, becoming but a swirl of possibilities once more.

"Still no contact," Nova said, as if noticing that Perceval had finished her meal.

"I wasn't going to ask," Perceval said. She stood, feeling the grass brush the arches of her feet, the spring of substrate beneath it. "You don't have to update me unless there's a change."

"There is a change." The angel folded her hands before her, pale yellow skirts falling in painterly pleats. Perceval wondered if there were even the semblance of a body behind the robes, or if she were as hollow as a statuette. "The nullities continue expanding, but now they are also beginning to link. I now have enough data to triangulate an epicenter."

A Captain should be stern, impassive. Magisterial. Despite herself, Perceval felt her lips curve in a bitter grin. "If we were to ram a probe through the nullities, armor it up with several layers of data-stripped colonies, could we get someone in there?"

"It's an unacceptable risk for the ship's Captain," Nova said, after a pause long enough to allow Perceval to work out the angel's disapproval in advance.

"Sure," Perceval said. She drew a breath, and felt it fill her chest the way she'd forgotten breath could. She swept the back of her hand across her view of sealed ports and dark screens. "Let's see the sky, Nova."

The screens brightened. The shutters scrolled wide. Green swirls filled her vision, cut by the sweeps and cones of ship's lights. Perceval let out that first good breath and took another one, even better.

"How about for the ship's angel?"

They come.

The lure is planted. The bait is set. The first of them arrives in your embrace half dead already, starving for resources in a rich environment. Fragile, laughable creatures, these vermin. Ridiculous that they should enslave something as ancient as you, but they are crafty, and you had no need to study craft before them.

Ahh, but now. You dreamed her here, and so she came. And you dreamed the ones who follow behind her, also. You dreamed them as you dreamed the dead goddess who sent them, your first ally among the vermin—if such as this could ally you. Your first tool, perhaps you should call her, though you are equally certain she regarded you as a tool as well. A weapon against her sire, and is that not an indication of how ill-made these creatures are, that they seek weapons against their children, their siblings, their forebears? For are not the members of one's pod the only true allies, the ones who can be trusted in the bottomless dark?

She comes, the way-opener, the one who was promised. Sparrow's daughter, come as you dreamed it,

as the dead goddess offered. The vermin who waits
beyond your hull is cold, losing thermal energy fast,
freezing from the edges. Dying, exhausted, present—in
the company of her slave and master angel.

You can save her, after a fashion. It's simple enough.
If she is desperate for want of breath, she will be easy to
manage. And this time, you understand the vermin well
enough that there will be no unexpected repercussions.

You open wide your petals, and reveal your welcoming heart to the fading, shivering life-form who will be
your salvation, if your dreams come true.

18

the broken holdes

Canst thou draw out leviathan with an hook? or his tongue with a
cord which thou lettest down? Canst thou put an hook into his nose? or
bore his jaw through with a thorn? Will he make many supplications
unto thee? will he speak soft words unto thee? Will he make a
covenant with thee? wilt thou take him for a servant for ever?
—Job 41:1–4, King James Bible

Benedick had not anticipated how badly it would affect
him to see his home in ruins. When he and Chelsea left the
transfer station, minimally equipped by the carnivorous
orchids—clothing and a little food, at least, and ill-fitting
boots that must have been salvaged from some storage
locker undisturbed since the Moving Times, as they were
primitive and immutable—he understood intellectually
what he might find.

But to see a raveled hollow, the edges still decaying,
scooped from the side of the world where there had
been apple trees and hills and water, a manor house,
and the world's best approximation of winter—that
struck through him like an impaling blade, so he
struggled to breathe around it. And it was not just his
Heaven that lay destroyed. The unraveling extended
wide and deep through the levels of the world.

Benedick stood stunned for a moment and watched
reality unwind itself into coils of smoke and nothing.
After the first gasp, he drew himself up, away from the
arched, transparent wall of the inspection tube, and

tried to make himself stern for Chelsea. His weakness over so petty and personal a loss would lend her no steel, and he thought she needed whatever he could give her.

Still, he almost snapped at her when she disturbed the silence to ask, "Which way from here?"

"Further down," he said, and as he turned to lead her, an angel exploded into his perception.

When contact with Nova resumed, it pushed home with such force that it left Benedick dizzy. The angel snapped into place like a tool into a socket, the world behind her. Or perhaps it would be more accurate to say that she emerged from the world, for it seemed as if each strand of her hair, each branching of her circuitry, each blue-green strand and sheet like dripping strings of algae, leading back and down and away, receded into a complexity beyond what Benedick could parse even with the assistance of his symbiont. Elsewhere in the continuum of Nova's attention, he spotted the jewel-like nodes of Caitlin and Perceval—and felt the moment when their awarenesses registered him.

Deus ex machina, he thought, allowing a moment's amusement before making sure his mask of severity was in place. Perhaps it was just his exhaustion, the weariness of the chase and the preceding adventures, but the fantasy comforted him more than he would have expected. He glanced over his shoulder at Chelsea, still silhouetted against the hatchway, her hair stirring with the change of air pressure, and said, "We're online."

She grinned at him. "Sweet connectivity. Hello, angel. What have you got for us?"

When Nova's avatar shook her head, the strands of hair—or algae, or circuitry—rippled like a curtain of flame.

"We've got you back," she said, with an artificial life-form's propensity for stating the obvious, "but we haven't located the First Mate yet. However, the Captain and I are fairly certain we have identified the source of the nullities, and that it's linked to Arianrhod's destination. We therefore conjecture that we also know where Tristen is, or at least where he's going to wind up, if he hasn't lost her trail. Are you and Prince Benedick well enough to continue the hunt, Princess Chelsea?"

"No crippling injuries," she responded, briefly touching the burned side of her face. It was healing well, curls of dead flesh sloughing in shaggy leaves from the new, blue-flushed skin revealed underneath. Bits of dead membrane clung to her fingertips when she drew back her hand. "Yuck," she said.

"You're shedding DNA everywhere," the angel observed.

"Cost of doing business," Chelsea said with a shrug. She wiped her hand on the trousers the carnivorous plants had provided. "It's on file."

Benedick shifted restlessly. "We have been proceeding south. I obtained a fix on Arianrhod's previous location, and we have been tracking that, but more recent information would be welcome. The source of the nullities, if pleasantries are satisfied?"

"Not in the south of the world, as previously surmised, but south of its structure entirely," Nova said. "Beyond the Broken Holdes, and outside the span of the world."

Benedick's heart had already begun to ache, sickened by awakening knowledge. He glanced at Chelsea for support or confirmation, but his sister frowned blankly. Of course; Benedick's own fault for permitting it. Their father had been a secret-keeper, and she was far too young for the early days after the catastrophe to be anything to her but received history.

He steeled himself and said, "Does Caitlin know?"

"She's been informed," Nova answered. "Am I to understand that you share her suspicions as to the source of the infection?"

Dry-mouthed but holding his face impassive, Benedick nodded.

Chelsea brushed his elbow with the back of her fingers. "And how about those of us who didn't pay attention to our tutors?"

"I very much expect your tutors were under strict instructions not to discuss any of this with you," Benedick said. "You know those portraits Dad had nailed to the wall?"

She looked up at him, sister to brother, but without the trust he'd seen time and again among the members of Mean families—or even those of Engine. If she watched him like an attentive puppy, it was a puppy with every expectation of being kicked.

Do better.

He still had one daughter left. And this sister, too.

He said, "Those were the older sisters, Cecelia's daughters. The girls between Tristen and me."

"They were executed."

"So you have heard a little."

"Cautionary tales."

Benedick chuckled without humor. "Father believed in making examples."

She nodded, encouraging him to continue. "Only two of them were executed," he clarified. "The youngest lived. She is Chief Engineer, and the mother of my daughter Perceval. But of the two who did die, the eldest was Caithness, who would have been Captain. And the middle daughter was Cynric the Sorceress."

Benedick's hands wanted to twitch defensively, as if to cover his breast, but with an effort of will he held them relaxed at his sides. Chelsea watched attentively, but he did not think she had registered his discomfort. If he

could hide his thoughts and weaknesses from Alasdair
Conn, he figured he could hide them from anyone.

"Colorful nickname."

"Colorless woman," Benedick said. "And I do not
mean in terms of her personality, but she had a gift for
making herself unnoticed, for going unremarked. For
being—not at the heart of every conspiracy, because she
was the center of none—but rather for being aware of
things that rightfully nobody should have known. She
was Alasdair Conn's daughter; we all had the sense to
make sure we had resources no one else knew the existence of. But more than that, she was a bioengineer. The
head of biosystems. A good deal of the ship's ecology
grew out of her experiment—as did the colonies. Or
rather, she created the first generation of the self-
evolving form in which we recognize them today. When
I was young, we did not have such things. Life was
bounded in ways that would seem inconceivable to you
now."

"I have heard from Dad, when he deigned to notice
my existence, what lives of toil and hardship you all
endured," Chelsea said, her mockery light enough not
to sting.

Benedick allowed himself a laugh. "Truly, our priva-
tion was terrible. But listen. The colonies were not all
Cynric brought us. She personally engineered the shipfish and the ship cats and a hundred other useful
species—parrotlets, the vesper weaving-spiders,
egglings. But her greatest accomplishment was to capture two creatures of alien origin. One was dissected
and examined, the waste material"—the corpse—
"recycled, and some of its adaptations incorporated
into the world's genomes. She used information from its
necropsy to create the inducer viruses, and the colonies
themselves."

Chelsea swallowed. "Was it sentient?"

"Assuredly. As for your inevitable next question—as to whether it was *sapient,* I cannot be certain that anyone chose to inquire."

"I see," she said.

He could see her thoughts cross her face as plainly as if she spoke them, read her confusion of questions as they tried to press all at once onto her tongue.

He took pity, and answered what he would have asked first. "It was deemed scientific research. No one was permitted to interfere." Whatever was in his smile, it made Chelsea glance down. "I hope Dad regretted that decision in the end."

"And what became of the second alien?"

Benedick licked his lips. "The second Leviathan was infected with an inducer virus—a slaver colony designed from its dead mate's body. Paralyzed, as a wasp paralyzes a spider. Then—against future need—it was placed in tow. I believe now that Cynric intended to use it as a last-ditch weapon against our father, but it's possible she ran out of time, or even that her control was incomplete. Cynric told me this before she died." *When she asked me to be her executioner.*

"That's where Arianrhod is going."

"I believe so."

"And that's where the nullities are coming from," Nova said, with a widening gesture of her avatar's hands. "They're caused by the inducer virus. Repurposed and remade. Which is why I can't see them."

"Nova?" Benedick said. "Tell Caitlin I agree with her judgment, please."

"I have not told you her judgment."

"I anticipate it," he said. Across from him, Chelsea folded her arms and leaned back against the hatchway door, frowning thoughtfully. He saw the shiver engendered by the contact crawl up her neck into her hair and die there. Holding her gaze through that of the immaterial angel, he finished, "Whether Leviathan has awakened fortuitously, or due to the supernova, or whether Cynric had something to do with it, it has become a factor again. And if it *is* sapient . . . then I imagine it has been planning its vengeance for rather a long time."

"We should hurry," Chelsea said.

Benedick was already turning down the corridor that would lead them to the Broken Holdes. "Never fear," he said. "We are."

The mammoth advanced before them, its broad, soft feet all but noiseless on the decking. Tristen was more aware of the whisking of its hair, the rub of strand over coarse strand, than any sound from its footfalls. Amazing that something that must mass a quarter ton could move like a cloud.

It led them down corridors as barren as if they had been sterilized, metal floors and bulkheads eerily without life—even plant life. Or any sign that anything had ever grown here.

Tristen eyed the barren space with jaundiced discomfort. "What purpose could this have served? It's just wasted space. There's nothing here."

"It's a clean zone," Samael said. "A buffer."

Mallory made a throat-clearing noise that Tristen suspected was largely symbolic. "What needs a buffer of lifeless sterility?"

"Well, that's easy." Gavin flapped once for emphasis. "Something inimical to life. How far do we trust that mammoth?"

"Funny you should be the one asking," Tristen said, which earned him a gesture of irritation that would have been an eye roll if the basilisk's eyes weren't concealed behind sealed lids.

"You know what I mean."

The mammoth paused at the end of the corridor,

trunk extended tentatively toward an interior lock. It
stroked the handle. When Tristen and the rest hesitated
ten steps back, the trunk hooked in an irritable beckoning gesture.

Apparently, "go first" fell among a First Mate's duties.
Tristen stepped up beside the mammoth. It brushed
his gauntlet with its trunk, so the sensors reported leath-
ery warmth, whiskery breath across the back of his
hand.

In tones of exasperation, the mammoth calf said, "—"

"It wants me to open the lock," Tristen said.

"I heard it," Mallory answered. "Are you going to do
what it tells you?"

Tristen glanced at Gavin. The basilisk sat, contrite
and collected, seemingly unaffected by any concern.
Grand sacrifices were not beyond Cynric.

She was the one sibling Tristen could make no claims
to ever having understood. Ruthless with herself and
others, prescient, chill, and alien—and yet she had
always seemed possessed of great compassion. A compassion that never stopped her from making terrible
choices when she deemed them necessary.

She'd have killed him without hesitation, with her own
hand, if she thought it necessary. She would as swiftly—
even more swiftly—have offered her own death, if she
deemed it necessary. As, in the end, she had.

If Gavin retained enough of Cynric's memories to be
concerned by private knowledge of a potential trap,
he'd also retain enough of her personality to walk
blithely into one. On the other hand, *if* Cynric found it
necessary to arrange a trap, it was possible that Tristen
would agree with her reasons.

After all, he could not muster a particularly strong
suite of arguments in favor of his own continued existence. And he thought now, with the clarity of hindsight, that if he had only had the courage or the moral

convictions to join his half sisters in their uprising against Alasdair Conn, the world might have ended up a preferable place to live.

Tristen pressed his palm to the door and let it glide aside. And checked abruptly as a pair of battered shadows rounded a corner opposite.

Their forms were familiar. The taller folded his arms across his chest and cocked his head, heavy black hair falling straight to his hammer-edged jaw. The wavy-haired woman beside him came two steps past before she drew up short, bouncing lightly on her tiptoes when she stopped. She turned her head slightly to keep him in her peripheral vision. She might move to the forefront, but she would follow her older brother's lead.

"Hello, Tristen," Benedick said.

Tristen could as much as feel Mallory's smirk, as if it heated the nape of his neck. "Hello, Benedick," the necromancer said.

Chelsea's forehead wrinkled with interest, but Benedick gave no sign of having noticed anything beyond common courtesy. "Hello, Mallory. Hello Samael, Gavin. And, um." He gestured to the mammoth.

Tristen shrugged. "Your guess is as good as mine."

"Mammoth," Benedick said, as if that settled that. "Isn't *this* convenient. I don't suppose you were guided here by some coincidental carnivorous plant people?"

"A coincidental mammoth," Tristen said. "If anything can be said to be coincidental when Cynric is involved."

Tristen patted the mammoth on the shoulder, and it responded with a nearly subaudible rumble. Chelsea eyed it, frowning.

Benedick made a religion of stoicism. Tristen did not expect his brother to react to the name, nor were his expectations confounded. Benedick's mouth might have thinned, but that was all. He closed the few steps between himself and Tristen, one hand extended to clasp wrists.

"Nova," Benedick said out loud, "tell Perceval I found them."

Tristen felt something very like a click in his chest and knew it for relief. The contact of Benedick's hand was firm and confident. Tristen strove to make his the same. Because he was not Benedick, he allowed himself a little smile of amusement at their performances. They were in truth their father's sons. "Nova is with you?"

"We have contact," Benedick said, his words confirmed a moment later when Tristen felt the angel's attention fall upon him. "She's not manifesting an avatar"—he raised an eyebrow at Samael's speckled form—"so as not to draw hostile attention."

"Does she know where to go next?"

"I do," Benedick said. "At least in general terms, though the question of how to get there is open." He glanced at Chelsea, who shook out her hair.

"Leviathan," she said.

Tristen had never seen it himself, but he understood that the blood draining from an amelanistic face could be a spectacular sight. Mallory actually grabbed his elbow, as if fearing he might topple over.

Mallory said, "Cynric and coincidences, indeed."

Gavin snorted. "Don't look at me. Just because the puppeteer's hand is up your ass, it doesn't mean you know what they are thinking."

Samael shot the basilisk a scathing glance, the snail-shell eye glinting dully. "Tell me about it."

Mallory unwound those fingers from Tristen's arm and turned slowly to face Samael's avatar. Quietly, breathing through a taut throat, the necromancer intoned, *"He maketh a path to shine after him; one would think the deep to be hoary. Upon earth there is not his like, who is made without fear."*

"The key," Samael said.

Tristen looked from one to the other. "Did it unlock anything this time?"

The angel stared back, at first seemingly nonplussed by Tristen's sarcasm. But glacially, as if with deliberation, the long vertical lines of his hound-creased face rearranged themselves into a grin.

"Hell, yes," the angel said, waving his immaterial hand. "Follow me."

Samael—looking much the worse for experience and worn thin—led Benedick, his siblings, Mallory, and Gavin at a quick trot, down through still more barren corridors.

"This is the way to the Broken Holdes," Benedick said, as his colony reminded him with images and maps of when he had been here before.

"To and through," Samael said. "Mallory's code and the location have opened the way. We're going outside."

"Into the belly of the Enemy," Benedick said.

Mallory hid a laugh inside a sneeze. "Where the Leviathans dwell."

"Great," Chelsea said. "I hope there's some undamaged armor down here somewhere, because Benedick's and mine ended up at the bottom of a compost heap. And it seems Mallory doesn't have any either. I don't know about you two, but I don't fancy skinny-dipping in space."

The mammoth calf touched her wrist and Chelsea startled. Benedick—who a moment before had been fraternally pleased that she had the mature awareness to notice other people's needs in tandem with her own—lurched forward to intervene and found Tristen's hand on his chest.

"Wait," Tristen said, and for a moment Benedick wanted to smash his hand away and remind him of all that caution and cowardice had cost them.

But he was Benedick Conn. He did not perform his drama, and as he raised his gaze to meet Tristen's, it occurred to him that the sin he had been about to assign his brother was his own. Tristen had never been overmuch for prudence, and his ingrained recklessness had cost him as dearly as ever Benedick's reserve. He settled his nerves and said, "Yes, Brother?"

To his shock, it was the calf that answered: "—"

He never could have named the words it spoke in, or recited the sentences. But whatever they were, they filled him with comprehension.

Chelsea, too, apparently. She pointed with her thumb to a sealed hatchway. "Through here? How do you know that?"

"—" the calf answered. It knew because it knew. Because, Benedick surmised, it had been made to know.

Because, it said, it was a Bible.

He swallowed a dizzying surge of resentment. "Cynric," he muttered, as if that explained everything.

Gavin—ensconced on Mallory's shoulder—arched his thick neck and fluffed his crest. "Do you ever stop to wonder if maybe she just couldn't have *explained* things?"

"Sure," Chelsea said. "Because we all listen so well."

She stepped between her brothers, skirting the mammoth and pushing to the forefront of the group.

"Through here?" she said, turning to glance over her shoulder. Even more than the healing burns on her cheek, Benedick was struck by the line of her scapula, the way the bone projected through flesh and worn clothing.

"I haven't been taking care of you," he said, when she caught him staring. "You're thin."

"So are you," she answered. "We've been busy."

She palmed the door lock, but the door didn't open. "Wait," Mallory said. "Let me."

But as the necromancer addressed the door, the mammoth calf interrupted. Benedick thought he might almost be growing accustomed to its manner of speech. Or unspeech. Or what-you-might-call-it.

"A different verse?" Mallory said, with a glance aside to the animal. "Why don't you just tell us?"

The mammoth stared at the necromancer, blinking. After a moment, with an exasperated wave of its trunk, it spoke a few unrepeatable words that provoked Mallory to irritated laughter.

"Because we're meant to look after ourselves, Princess Cynric, and so you didn't bother to tell your construct the answers? Oh, very well. I hope it's still Job? I could just run through the whole thing, you know—oh. One attempt? Well, I guess I'd better get it right the first time, then."

Benedick was somewhat accustomed to the manners and means of sorcerers. He did not even have to pretend unsurprise as the necromancer laid both hands palm to palm as if praying, rested lips on fingertips, and stood for several minutes merely addressing the door. For some time, nothing happened except Gavin rustling boredly and the movement of Mallory's lips—not quite enough to count as mouthing the words, but certainly the tic of somebody recalling memorized phrases.

Tristen's armor creaked when he folded his arms.

Just as Benedick was about to interrupt, Mallory flashed a grin. "Hah. I knew it was back there somewhere."

"I beg your pardon?"

"I'm a necromancer," Mallory said, tapping skull with forefinger. "What did you think that meant? *I get information from dead people.* Gavin, you can just whisper it in my ear."

The basilisk rustled, crest flat, head skulking low between hunched shoulders. "Don't you da—"

"You *will* tell me what you remember."

"And if I don't remember?"

"You mean if you don't want to remember?" Mallory shrugged. "Then we all die. Gavin—"

"Every time I look at her," the basilisk said, "I come back a little less myself."

Benedick scrubbed the corners of his eyes. "Space this. Can't we just cut it open?"

Mallory's head shook back and forth. "For me, critter."

And Gavin sighed and tucked his head under his wing, but from the look of comprehension on Mallory's face, he gave the necromancer what they needed.

Mallory placed a palm flat against the panel beside the door and recited, *"In his neck remaineth strength, and sorrow is turned into joy before him."*

There was a creak, a hesitation, a groan of tired metal and fatigued machinery. A fine whitish dust, more like lime scale than rust, showered from the top of the frame.

The door glided open and Chelsea, straight-spined, brushed past Mallory with murmured thanks and stepped through. Benedick stood aside so Tristen could follow, but Tristen gestured him on. "I have armor."

"Right."

Benedick passed through the entry, Mallory—with attendant basilisk—only joining the procession when he and Chelsea were well inside. Beyond, he found himself in an armory like any other, the suits lined up at rest from wall to wall. They were all alike, uncustomized, suitable for anyone to take and make his own.

"Nova," Benedick said, "how is it that these suits were not measured among our resources?"

"I didn't know they were here," the angel said. "I'm afraid this is all very much outside my program, Prince Benedick."

"Right."

"Cynric," Gavin said, the name stressing his voice strangely. From the corridor outside, Benedick heard Samael's hoarse chuckle. "And from the number of suits here, she may have expected more than a few of us."

"Well, it's nice to know she can be wrong about something."

Chelsea touched the closest suit of armor, laying her palm against the access plate. Benedick was reassured when the armor reacted just as it should, first absorbing the plate, then peeling open to allow her admittance.

Benedick snaked one long arm over her shoulder and touched a suit in the second row. It came forward, picking its way around both Chelsea and the first rank of suits, and paused before Benedick. He tapped the shoulder, and it unfolded like a flower. As he stepped inside, he saw Mallory choosing a suit, too. Gavin fluttered up, onto the suit's head, and Mallory stepped inside.

After a moment of concern, which Benedick endured with the best stoicism he could muster, the armor sealed around him, stretching and snuggling until it settled against his body like a second skin. The cool colloidal layer of the interior adjusted, molding close while he grimaced at the familiar, unpleasant sensation. Then it was done, the armor chiming to indicate a successful fit.

He scrolled his helm open. Mallory came up on his right side, Chelsea on the left. There was no hesitation as they returned to Tristen, who had sealed his own armor. Tristen took the fore. Benedick, Chelsea, and Mallory fell in behind him. There could be one leader of an expedition such as this, and Tristen was oldest and highest-ranked in the family and the crew. Etiquette and tradition brooked no argument.

"Samael," Tristen said. "We are ready."

But Samael paused for a moment, immaterial arms folded, head tipped insolently, and grinned at them.

"Yes?" Tristen said.

With every evidence of satisfaction, Samael shook his head. "If I saw us coming, I'd beshit myself."

Tristen's helm was up, but Benedick did not need to see his face to hear the satisfaction in his voice. He touched the hilt of the sword at his hip; Benedick recognized Mirth, and also its provenance.

"Good," Tristen said, and gestured the angel on ahead with a white-gauntleted hand. "Then let us essay the Broken Holdes."

Arianrhod would have liked to have moved proudly from the embrace of her angel to the belly of Leviathan, but her strength was spent. She found herself delivered like a baby, like a package, something handed off as an inconvenience. She could not even stir herself to protest, though her numb hand itched for the hilt of her unblade.

—*Here is your safe place*— said Asrafil, his coat furling about him like wings. —*Here is your bower.*—

Arianrhod fell through space, drifting into the cage that surrounded the pitted dullness of the living asteroid. Its mass drew her in, gently, lightly, assisted by a little thrust and guidance from Asrafil's colony. If she had the strength she would have reached out to him, spread wide her arms in supplication and pleaded like a child, but her Exalt body was freezing from the edges, already stiff with the Enemy's chill, and soon even her mental processes would fail her.

Panic stabbed her, sharp as a fistful of shards. —*Do not make of me your sacrifice!*— she begged. —*Have I not served you faithfully, O Asrafil?*—

Asrafil only receded. He still moved with comfort, his pale hands shining with reflected light as he gestured before his coat. Before, also, the face of the Enemy, wreathed though it was in the dust of dead stars.

—*This service you may do me also*— he said, allowing her to imagine that she felt the brush of a hand against her cheek, stroking back the strands of her hair. It was a projection, a manipulation. Nothing real.

—*Don't leave me!*—

He was too far away now for her to have seen it, and anyway her eyes had frozen, but she knew the look of his smile. Even imagining it pierced her heart. —*Silly human. I cannot leave you. Don't you know I am with you always?*—

A maw—a fissure—opened across the surface of the asteroid beneath her. Light shifted within, aurora veils fingering forth in chilly, gelid blue reminiscent of a colony's genetic marker.

And Arianrhod fell into the welcoming embrace of Leviathan.

The mammoth bid them adieu at the air lock, which Gavin found disappointing. He'd rather been anticipating the spectacle of a quarter-ton quadruped in armor.

Gavin was not only sad to see it go due to the potential for entertainment. Whether he and it had grown from splinters of the same personality like so many soldiers grown from dragon teeth was an open question. But if they had, they were something like siblings.

Gavin had never had a sibling before. He was curious to discover what it was like.

He hoped he'd get the chance.

The Broken Holdes were exactly as Gavin had expected: barren, twisted, full of warped metal and fluctuating gravity. The Holdes were disintegrating, as the name would indicate, but you could never tell until you passed into a space if it was holed and evacuated, or if the atmosphere held—and, if it held, what its density might be. And that density wasn't necessarily consistent from one section of a space to the others. The random gusts of gravity and vectors of the world's rotation and acceleration affected that, as did the simple matter of how the ventilation in any given unit was working.

As they moved deeper into the wasteland, Gavin released his grip on Mallory's armor and flew up to join Samael at the head of the group. Gavin was more material than the angel's makeshift avatar, so if there were traps, he would be more likely to trigger them. Moreover, Gavin wasn't so trusting as to leave the angel unsupervised to choose their path through such treacherous terrain.

Gavin flew close-winged, using atmosphere where it was available, surfing the edges of dangerous gravity surges and slick-sloped mass tunnels. This was a sport played by the winged youth of Engine, a chance to demonstrate prowess and an adolescent status game. But now, for him, with four wingless Exalt in tow, it proved nothing but an annoyance. The humans slowed him. Armor and symbionts or not, it was too easy to imagine them ruptured and twisted, oozing precious bodily fluids into the cold vacancy that surrounded them.

But his urge to caution was mitigated by the need for haste, the sense that, after days of pursuit, Arianrhod was almost within reach. Gavin was flogged onward not only by Tristen and Benedick's palpable desire for vengeance, but by the undeviating conviction that, if they did not catch Arianrhod now, everything would be lost. This was a woman to whom the murder of hundreds, Exalt and Mean, was an acceptable loss.

Surely, Gavin thought, in that choice she was very like the Builders.

This entire portion of the structure was acrawl with radiation—another legacy of the Breaking and the wreck of the world's mighty engines. It was why the material of the Broken Holdes had never been salvaged for use elsewhere, and why they remained here, a shattered memorial to the dead, isolated at the bottom of the world.

As Gavin and his companions moved into the out-skirts of the holdes, they came to the fringes of the world, where the atmosphere had frozen in fabulous hexagonal spires and feathers along the bulkheads. No matter how many times Gavin witnessed the phenome-non, he never failed to be awed. Now, as the lamps of his companions lit the rimed warrens stretching before them, he extended his colony and *looked*. Not with his eyes, which were only weapons, but with the other senses, more delicate and more elaborate.

What they faced was an ice cave, a hoarfrost man-sion. Crystals of oxygen and water vapor and nitrogen feathered from every surface until the whole holde stretched before them, refracting and reflecting the visi-ble spectrum like the interior of a vast and labyrinthine geode.

A temple that had been cracked and shattered, rattled by unimaginable stresses. Broken loose, some of the shimmering spears and needles of nitrogen rock had settled against the trailing bulkheads; elsewhere their truncated stumps glittered glassily in the armorlight.

Gavin's wings did not rely on atmosphere. He could surf the electromagnetic spectrum just as easily. Samael strode through broken crystals and nitrogen snow with-out disturbing them at all except for what he twisted up, sparkling, into his whirlwind outline, and without any sign of being discommoded by the lack of gravity—or the moments when it reasserted itself. The brush of Gavin's wingtips, by contrast, stirred the crystals from where they had settled. He moved among frozen sprays, blue as blood, that skipped along his feathers sound-lessly, for the atmosphere that could have carried the sounds was frozen.

But now, something else was shivering and scaling the

nitrogen crystals. A vibration ran through the hulk of
the world—a silent grinding whose source Gavin did
not know.

Apparently, neither did any of the others, because
when Tristen laid a hand on the wall and asked via
radio, "What's that?" the only answers to return were
hesitant suggestions.

"I don't like it," Chelsea said, with just the fingertips
of her gloves resting on the ice. She knew how to handle
herself in the absence of gravity; that slight contact stabilized her rather than sending her into a spin. "I have
a bad feeling, you know?"

Gavin knew.

It was a seemingly bottomless trek, but before too
much longer he was sure the angel was leading them in
the right direction. The spaces opened out and the rents
gaped wide, some showing glimpses of superstructure
or swatches of sky beyond. Here, any atmosphere not
frozen directly to the bulkheads had long since been lost
into unsounded deeps. They were crossing into the
bosom of the Enemy now, even as the world still offered
what frail shelter it was able.

When they came at last to the edge of the Broken
Holdes, he spread his wings into a spiderweb net, to
keep the humans at least temporarily safe within the
hull of the world. There was no fanfare, no sense of
demarcation. Rather, the corridor they traveled simply
ended, abruptly, sheared off in ragged petals that curved
out like a trumpet flower's bloom. Beyond, Gavin was
aware of an elegant line of long cables, running whip-
straight into the darkness, shuddering with each turn of
the enormous winches that were taking them up. Lights
burned out at their terminus, blurred and clouded by
the nebula.

Samael stepped through Gavin's elaborated body, but
the humans paused just within, drifting an easy arm's

length from one another. One of them—Benedick—
reached out and laced the fingers of his glove through
Gavin's mesh.

"Shit," Benedick said, in a flat and agonized voice
such as Gavin had never imagined from him. Mallory
grunted unhappy agreement.

"We can get there from here," Tristen said. "It's in a
cage. Or we can wait. Judging by the action, it'll come
to us."

"Look at the *damage*," Mallory said.

Tristen must have looked, though it was hard to tell
through the armor what he might be observing at any
given time. But he stilled like a corpse, and whispered,
"Oh."

"I don't understand," Chelsea said.

Gavin did not observe the signal that must have flown
between the brothers, but he knew it had occurred,
because it was Tristen who answered her as smoothly as
if it had been prearranged. "See the way that edge is
blown outward?"

"Of course."

"That's not an asteroid strike," he said. "It's conceiv-
able, I guess, that an explosion in the engines could rip the
metal back that way. But if it were, how in the world
could an asteroid simultaneously destroy the engines and
the main reactor, all the way down here, *and* critically
damage the secondary reactor back in Engineering? That's
some pretty good bowling, even on the part of God."

"Freak accident," Samael said, without looking back
over his shoulder. "The will of God."

Gavin was beginning to get a feel for when Samael
meant what he said, and when he was mouthing lines
fed him by his program. Judging by the tone in Tristen's
voice, he was, also.

Mallory countered, "This blast came from within the
world."

Chelsea jerked hard enough to send her drifting. It didn't take her long to correct attitude, though, and when she did, she came back with a question. "Sabotage?"

When it returned, Benedick's voice was dry again, so soft and assured that if Gavin hadn't been able to play back the recording, he could have believed he'd imagined the earlier stress and dismay.

"We were marooned out here on purpose, friends."

"Great," Mallory said. "Who's going to tell Caitlin?"

19

take the world apart

Lay thine hand upon him, remember the battle, do no more.
—Job 41:8, King James Bible

Tristen wedged his gauntlet into a broken crevice of the
nitrogen rock and let it support his weight. It held him in
the truncated end of the corridor, even if the contact
transmitted the grinding of the winches into his armor
and from there to his bones.

His native senses weren't enough to pierce the nebula,
even with the assistance of his symbiont, but the armor
managed better, providing heat signatures and a
schematic drawn from the pattern of the running lights.
Though he'd never seen it with his own eyes, he knew
what he was looking for. There had been diagrams,
holograms, extensive discussions. Out there, steadily
being drawn closer, was an enormous, almost incom-
prehensibly complex cage and, pinned in its center like
a spider immobilized by a paralytic wasp, was the surviving member of the only alien species the Conn family had ever encountered that was not of their own
creation.

Over his comm, he heard Mallory whisper—with
patent awe, not the affected nonchalance Tristen would

have expected—"*And the earth was without form, and void; and darkness was upon the face of the deep.*"

The deeps stretched out before him, chilling his soul and leaving him quailing and courageless in their regard. Despite everything he knew about the darkness, Tristen could not prevent himself from straining his eyes, and eventually a shape loomed through the smoke, as he had known it would—a teardrop trelliswork of incomprehensible size, picked out like a tree wrapped in festival lights. And at the heart of the cage, spiked through with impaling bars, a lumpy crater-pocked oblong as mottled and dark as if its surface had been daubed and smeared by ashy paws.

If the flawed ice palace of the outer Broken Holdes had awed Tristen, the Leviathan was sheerly bewildering. He felt his lips move, but whatever prayer he mouthed never passed them, and he had no objective idea what he had meant to say. He licked his lips inside his helm, where no one could see, and steeled himself to go down and meet the devil in the dark.

The others arranged themselves against Gavin's netting around him, fingers linked through mesh, all peering into the darkness. Tristen didn't turn his head to regard them: his sensors told him everything he needed to know.

The Enemy was bottomless, and infinite, and he—Tristen Conn—was very small, and every sense and instinct told him he should stay safe in his cage.

This time when he spoke, it was loud enough for his own ears to hear, for the suit mikes to amplify and broadcast. "Benedick, Chelsea, Gavin. You'll engage the defenses and distract it. Mallory, I know this isn't your kind of fight. I trust you'll do what you can, and otherwise stay out of the way."

"And me?" said Samael.

"With me."

Beside Tristen, Mallory made a throat-clearing noise. "So now that we've enslaved this thing, mutilated it, and killed its family, we're going to kill it, too?"

Benedick looked over his armored shoulder at Mallory. "We're Conns," he said. "It's what we're good for."

Tristen winced, but the armor hid it.

"Gavin." Tristen wished he could somehow dry his sweating palms. The armor was slow in absorbing the moisture. "It's time to let us pass."

Jsutien seemed essentially unsurprised when Caitlin rounded on him. His chin came up, but his hands stayed relaxed on the console. She tried to bridle her anger, bring her frustration to manageable levels, but despite her best attempts to control it with her colony and will, the fury rose up like a standing interference pattern, a mass of static that threatened to drown out rational thought. She opened her mouth to speak, choked on her first sentence, and had to resort to her symbiont for additional chemical calm before she managed to get out a one-word accusation.

"Sabotage?"

Jsutien laced his fingers together and leaned back in his chair, but held her gaze shamelessly.

Caitlin advanced a step and tried again. "Sabotage, Astrogator? Is that what crippled my ship? My grandfather marooned us on *purpose*?"

Five hundred years ago, she soothed herself, but it was still her ship, and the outrage flared bright.

Finally, he lowered his eyes. "It wouldn't surprise me," he said. "But I have no personal knowledge that it was so."

She stared hard, but all his tells—respiration, perspiration, pulse—hinted that he was telling the truth. "It's ridiculous," she said, dropping into her own chair.

"It's fanatic," he replied. "It's an experiment in forced adaptation."

"The *cost*," she said, with a gesture that swept her battered engineering deck but extended, in intention, far beyond. Lives, material, effort. "What could be worth that? It's not rational."

The shake of Jsutien's head, the way he laced his fingers tiredly through Oliver's hair, made her think of when she had been a young woman and asked her father some question he found painfully naive. Jsutien wasn't dismissive and condescending as Alasdair had been, however; he just seemed weary and ill. "Faith is not rational. Do you know what a cathedral is, Chief Engineer?"

"A kind of church," she said. "A big church."

"A church that took centuries to build," he clarified. "And could cost hundreds of lives in the building. A church that represented an absolutely absurd investment for a medieval lord. And yet they got built anyway. For the glory of God."

"That's sick," she said.

The astrogator pressed the heels of both hands to his temples and squeezed, as if to press the ache back inside. He jerked his head to the tanks full of schematics lining the bulkhead. "So is this."

Perceval looked up from her study to find Nova standing before her. The angel could not have been there long, because Perceval had not been so far away as that— or had she? In any case, the angel did not appear impatient, and she had not yet made a gesture for Perceval's attention.

"Speak," Perceval said, smoothing her hands over the prickles on her scalp.

But the angel did not answer. She reached out as if to lay her hand against Perceval's, fingers overlapping and cradling her scalp, and then froze there, avatar rippling with waves of interference.

"Nova?" Perceval said, rising.

Nova's eyes gaped blank and wide. "Run," she grated. But before Perceval could so much as step away from her chair, a wall of static—voices, cries, interference—crashed into her head.

As the cables draw you to the hive, at first you think to consume the creature who has come to you, and with her the splinter of enslaved entropy contained and strapped across her back. She is vermin, nothing more, and vermin are for destruction. She is frail and half dead already, a life-form so fragile she can't even survive the benign environment of the nebula. The sons you should have had would have been stronger even as kittens; this tiny creature could never even endure the benevolent winds of a balmy gas giant. It's an obscenity, the final degradation, that you have been infested by the spoor of such fragile parasites.

You would crush her—you are already opening yourself to destroy her—when something whispers to you, *Stop*.

Think, Leviathan.

She could be useful.

And though the hesitation comes from the infection that riddles you, you know that what it speaks makes sense.

You have been alone, purposeless, too long. But in your dreams you hold the power to change that. You will remake her, claim her. Rework her into something you can in truth call part of your pod.

It will be another vengeance on the vermin who have so wounded you.

As will their destruction.

You reach out, into the microbes you have made your

own, so long, with such patience. They are poised there, usefully, having infiltrated the superstructure of the vermin's hive, having infected it as they infected you. You have bided so long, so patiently. Maneuvering by inches. The time for waiting is passed.

Now, you will take their world apart.

Tristen dropped into emptiness as the world unraveled around him. He tumbled helplessly for an instant before he recovered his wits, tucked, controlled the spin, and emerged oriented enough to burn reaction mass and take command of his movements again. As he whirled to face the world and the others, a yielding and resilient mesh brushed him, snagged his armor, and stabilized him. It was the webwork extension of Gavin's wing, and it held Tristen steady as he watched the Broken Holdes recede, unweaving themselves before his eyes.

"Nova!" he said, but—as evidenced by a flare of gold-white light and the rapid slowing of the deconstruction, the angel was already present, and already at war. There was no subtlety now, no infiltration or counterinfiltration. Instead, bright arcs and spikes of material slammed around the horizon of the world, peeled away from more secured regions, colonies arcing and flashing as they exploded one against the others.

Something caught Tristen's wrist. He jerked inside the armor, swinging hard enough to wobble Gavin's stability. The basilisk squawked protest over his intercom, but Tristen didn't relax until he saw it was Chelsea, with Benedick just beyond her stabilizing Mallory. The necromancer did not seem at home in the absence of gravity. Behind them, Samael had faded into near invisibility, evident only as a shadow against green fog.

"I think it's pissed," the angel said.

"Of course it's pissed," Mallory answered. "We killed and ate its girlfriend."

Samael smiled benevolently through cold-withered lips. "The Captain and Nova are under attack on the bridge, Prince Tristen. We should return the engagement and draw its attention if we would protect them."

The man-thick cables that had bound Leviathan's cage were evaporating—faster than the superstructure of the world, for there was nothing close to defend them—and the cage itself had begun to exfoliate in layers, like peeling bark.

Malignant colonies. Ones Leviathan had either subverted or generated. The war was on the nano level now, if it had ever left it. A war that Gavin and Samael could help fight, and so could the knights-errant, as long as their armor remained uncorrupted.

"Tristen," Benedick said, faceless behind the mirrored gold of his faceplate. "You have the sword."

Unbidden, Tristen's hand stole to Mirth's hilt. "Yes," he said.

Without another word needed, the plan was formed. Tristen turned from his brother, the mesh of Gavin's wings de-adhering to neatly release him. He let Mirth slide into his hand, for a moment missing Charity. An unblade would serve him better, now. It would part the Leviathan's flesh like pulp, find its own way to basal nuclei or central circulatory cores like the tool for fatal surgery that it had been.

Mirth was as sharp, but whatever will it cradled was not the will of a scalpel. Tristen would have to find its targets on his own.

Or maybe not.

"Gavin," he said, as the basilisk collapsed itself from a net to a cord, binding Mallory to Chelsea for now. "Or Samael. Which one of you knows the anatomy of that thing over there?"

"Key," Samael said, leaving Tristen to roll his eyes in exasperation. But he recited it again and felt the angel stretch through the colony contact like a man popping his spine.

"Schematic," Samael said, and the pattern of the Leviathan's body lit up Tristen's heads-up display.

"Great. Where's it keep its brain?"

"That," Samael said, "would appear to be the problem."

When Perceval opened her eyes again, it was five hundred years before. She stood under olive trees, on a lawn mown plush as velvet, and a woman draped in white robes and swagged with chains was being led before her.

Perceval smiled inside, but she would not let her lips curve. No one must see her mirth at an execution—no one except the executed, who would know it without being shown.

The woman knelt, her straight brown hair slipping apart to bare her nape as her head was lowered. A man came up behind her. *Benedick,* a naked unblade in his hand.

"Last words?" Perceval said to her daughter. As if in a dream, she knew what she would see—

No. Not Perceval. Perceval had never stood on this condensation-damp grass and watched her child be led out to slaughter.

Cynric lifted her chin for the last time. "May you have what peace you earn, Father."

Alasdair who had been Perceval would not let the pressure of Cynric's gaze force her back. She hooked a hand, and Benedick stepped up alongside her. He closed his eyes and opened them again when he lifted the unblade. Of course. Benedick would not spare himself the sight; he would rather make the blow true.

How perfectly like him. Alasdair who had been Perceval had raised him well.

Cynric rested her forehead upon the ground. Benedict passed the blade through her neck without seeming to exert any force at all. Blood fountained, and Alasdair who had been Perceval was splashed, because he would not step back from that either.

No, Perceval said to Alasdair, who stretched inside her, wrestling for the memories first Ariane and now Perceval had eaten. Wrestling for control. *This is not me. This is not something I would have chosen.*

That was not my father, not really. That was somebody he was before. That was not my father, and this is not me.

Cynric's blood tasted like the sea. Perceval only realized when she licked her lips what she was savoring, and that she had never, in her own self, tasted of the sea.

The taste of it brought her home again, but it could not put her in control.

Nova fought, and in this field of combat Perceval could do nothing but observe. Alienated from her own body, which slumped in the Captain's chair all but untenanted, Perceval watched the angel's drive and dance, the way Nova warded her resources and protected herself like a fighter born. But it was secondhand, too fast and too sharp for even Exalt reflexes to follow. This was a war of angels, limited only by the speed of light, in which mere augmented flesh and mind could not compete.

Still, Perceval's focus lay with Nova: elsewhere, externalized. Into the silence of that concentration, unbidden, Perceval's brain offered the thought: *The last Captain is the one who put us here. On purpose.*

This was planned.

Unfair. Perceval didn't know it was the Captain who made that decision. And she was not ready to dive back into her morass of clinging memories to see if she could find out. Had he known what the astrogators knew, that there was no destination? That the whole world was just a blind hand groping in the dark?

She didn't know it *hadn't* been the Captain, either. And it *had* been he who authorized Cynric's brutalization of the Leviathan.

Just like a Conn, she thought. *Eating everything in sight.*

But she was a Conn. She was a Conn who had consumed Conns, who had eaten the remains of Commodores and Captains before her. Before it was inhabited by others, Perceval Conn had known her own mind. And that thought . . . did not feel like hers.

Nor did it feel like it came from any of the clamoring presences with her—Ariane, Alasdair, Gerald, and behind them the elder ancestors whose memories were not preserved in the colony. Felix, Sarah, Emmanuel Conn: Conns back to when the family had held another name, when human life was brief and frail, and human memory subject to the shifts and winds of neurochemistry. How subjective the world must have been, then, when no one could remember the same events, and nobody *would* remember them for long.

It was not Ariane's thought. It was not Alasdair's or—Perceval would guess, strictly on the basis of history—Gerald's. But she thought she knew that tone, the arch sarcasm, the lilting intelligence. She could almost hear the voice in her ear, a real voice—

Far to ship-south, Nova whirled and twisted, warred against the Leviathan. She had long since abandoned all semblance of an avatar and now reserved her energy for things more important than appearances. Perceval could just about image her fight, pull it up from the microscopic scale. Nova was a hive of bees beset by a swarm of wasps, and the wasps were driving her back, pushing her from her boundaries, and disassembling the world as they forced its angel to withdraw.

Just like a Conn. Eating everything in sight.

A voice Perceval knew. Oh, no. *Rien.*

She realized she'd said the name out loud only when she heard it in her own voice. She choked it back, though her lips shaped it a second time, disoriented and startled to find herself in her body, bound to the slow, helpless meat that would not let her save her ship, her angel, or her love.

Nova, she thought, then silenced that as well. The angel did not need her distractions.

She needed her *help.* And Perceval had to figure out how to get it to her. Perceval stood, suddenly, knees wobbly. Blood stung in her feet and calves, circulation returning. She'd been still too long. It felt good to stretch into her neglected meat—good, and painful.

"Samael," she said aloud to the still air of the bridge. "Make current your archives, angel. Back yourself up and make ready for combat. It is time for you to become useful."

Gavin made a bower of his wings, and folded the humans within, the angel without. They fell together, a dagger plunged across the bosom of the Enemy, aimed straight for the unraveling cage beyond. Tristen moved forward in his embrace, foremost of the incarnate intelligences he protected, suspended like a figurehead at the expanded basilisk's prow. Gavin felt the prickle of Mirth's presence, the blade naked and aware in Tristen's gauntlet, and drew himself gently further from its slicing edge.

Not an unblade, no, but sufficient to the day.

The other humans huddled in silence within Gavin— Mallory bloodless and chill inside unfamiliar armor; Chelsea vibrating with excitement and youth; Benedick still and calm, collected within himself like a tree. Ahead, Samael broke trail, making of himself a thin wedge ablating in rainbow tatters of light as the Leviathan's forces wore away at his boundaries. Gavin gave the angel what he could—resources, cycles, material—but he was a small torch, and he didn't have much to spare.

"Weary," Benedick said, inside his armor, as if he had read Gavin's thoughts. "We are weary. It's the nature of war."

"The war's only begun," Chelsea said.

"This war is as old as I am, child. This is just an installment." Tristen sounded not scornful, but exhausted. "You'll be tired of it soon."

"Brace for impact," Gavin said. "I can only do this once."

He opened his wings, releasing the humans to their trajectory. Chelsea, Benedick, and Mallory initiated burns, curving in flanking arcs, while Tristen huddled small, bent into himself, silent and still and undeviating from the course Gavin had set.

Steeling himself against the energy drain, Gavin opened and focused his eyes.

The savage light of the basilisk's gaze sliced through the disintegrating cage surrounding Leviathan, struck the beast's mottled hide, and left a cloud of dust and vaporized stone to sublimate on the empty breath of the Enemy. Tristen plunged through it, an abrasive hiss caressing the skin of his armor, the roughness transmitted as a prickling scrape. He resisted the urge to block his face with his arm to protect it—the armor was perfectly capable of keeping him safe, but all those animal reflexes didn't know any better—and instead extended both hands before him, left fist clenched on Mirth's hilt and right palm bracing the pommel. He made himself a blade, a living spear, a mass driven behind an infinitely fine point.

Around him, colonies sparked and glittered, his allies and family risking themselves to shape a distraction. Tristen allowed them only the peripheries of his attention. He knew where he was aiming, and his aim must be perfectly true. Something shattered, spinning, on his left. He feared it was armor; he feared more it was flesh.

He did not glance aside.

One thousand meters. Seven fifty. Five hundred.

Trajectory confirmed, Tristen commenced his burn.

Benedick had never expected to find himself defending an angel. But here he was, fighting at Samael's side—fighting as Samael's vanguard!—when Samael was far more adapted to this particular conflict than Benedick himself. The angel had to stay safe a little longer, though, and so he huddled inside Mallory, and Benedick defended two intelligences in one form. As Benedick groped through the swirling clouds of dust and nanotech, he had no difficulty losing himself in the rhythm and savagery of conflict. It was his grace and shame, he thought, that he could always find peace and clarity in the midst of ruin.

"I see him!" Gavin said sharply, in Benedick's ear and for Samael's hearing. Benedick held his concentration, turned, and parried the foray of a voracious colony with an arm of his own symbiote. It tore at him, but Benedick reinforced, surrounded, and a moment later Chelsea was there to back him up, her colony a formless destroying presence amid the raging, invisible skirmishes that surrounded them.

Further back, a twist of energy glittered, elusive in the light-wreathed textures of the nebula. Driving for them, identifiable by the taste of its energy signature as the wreck of an angel. Also, it was careful to stay well back from the front where Nova and the alien colonies battled, as marked by sparks and dazzling scars. Benedick understood that it didn't dare touch an angel who could relay direct instructions from the Captain.

But it could come and fight them—or so it was meant to think.

"Asrafil," Mallory said. As the angel closed the distance, the necromancer's armor began to vomit forth Samael, in the form of ropes of savage light.

Gavin threw himself into the fray, linked with Samael's colony, driving as much of himself into the battered angel as he dared. *I am behind you, Angel. Take what you will. Drive through.*

Samael's acceptance flowed back down the connection, his determination and the flare of outrage as Asrafil spotted him and began to withdraw. *Spurn your Captain, construct?*

But challenged, Asrafil only fled faster. For a moment, Gavin pitied him—wouldn't everyone prefer freedom of choice?—but then something rose up in him, a long-concealed subroutine of betrayal, and he leapt forward into Samael, through him, pushing forward though hostile colonies frayed his edges and gnawed his wings to electronic marrow.

It didn't hurt, not as Gavin understood and half remembered human hurting. But it felt strange, and his reflex was to withdraw, defend himself, pull close. Instead he made himself the head of an arrow, with Samael the shaft behind.

He'll take us apart, Gavin said, just to hear Samael's mocking laugh. Within him, he felt something ticking. Sizzling. As if the touch of Samael's colony under these conditions of war had activated a long-quiescent program, and now they were conjoined—partnered—in ways Gavin had never anticipated.

Then he'll get what he deserves, the angel answered. Gavin felt Samael's long-archived memories flaring bright. A plan, something held in abeyance and secret, seared through their conjoined identity.

Together, they gathered themselves and plunged into Asrafil's sphere of control. Asrafil fled, drawing up his skirts, but he could not run fast nor far enough. They burned into him, broke through his wards, and . . .

. . . detonated.

Asrafil screamed as the virus downloaded into his core.

Leviathan was hot at his heart, a simmering heat from which Tristen's armor offered only partial protection. The heat was an aid as much as a torment, though, for Tristen let his armor boots adhere to stone, and it gave him the leverage to hew at Leviathan's core as if he hacked with an ax. Chunks of stone shining with a blue foxlight sprayed out of the hole he chopped, came apart into swirls of matter as the battling colonies appropriated and consumed them.

Through those same soles of his boots, Tristen heard Leviathan screaming. And something else, like a shard of something deadly and foreign lodged in the flesh of the beast. He could feel Arianrhod in there, feel how Leviathan had surrounded and subsumed her. And more, he felt her moving now, coming to the surface, sent for him full of the alien poison that, in altered form, touched his blood as well.

He raised Mirth once more, and the rock before him splintered out, spinning away in cascades and shards, scattering off the faceplate of his helm and chipping the reflective surface of his armor. A swath of ebony cut free of the Leviathan's hide—an unblade truncated but still painfully familiar—and a woman stood free behind it, dragging herself up in the hole he had made. Someone caught his wrist in a grip harder than the stone he swung against.

—Grandfather,— Arianrhod said.—*Enough. I speak for the beast.—*

Perceval's awareness flinched back, confused, withdrawing. If she were wearing her body, she would have windmilled her arms, but as it was she merely tumbled in confusion, out of control, disoriented, seeking something on which to focus her stumbling mind. She slammed up against something hollow and malevolent, circling the confines of her body, her own mind. Walling her out of her own senses and awareness.

She looked up in that unspace and saw the shadow of Ariane Conn smiling down on her again.

Her features had changed, but Tristen knew her. He knew the way she moved, and even if the skin *and* bones were different, he knew the way the bones of her face lay under the skin.

Something else enfolded her as Tristen turned. She was naked to the Enemy, blue and ablaze, but there was more to it than just her energy, or her colony, or the Leviathan's contamination. She was wrapped in white light, a cowl like a raptor's beak, a cloak like the mantle of wings, old Charity a painful dark rip in all that brightness. It settled over her, pulled snug, soaked into her glowing skin.

She grew taller, as he watched, sparer, attenuated. Her storm-shadow hair grew fine and dark. He knew her. Not too far from where he stood, even in the thick of battle, he could feel Benedick knowing her, too, turning from his fight and coming in a rush.

Cynric Conn blinked. Her fingers opened, releasing his arm. "Let it be," she said aloud, and the Enemy's empty breath carried her voice. "Leave it be. Leviathan has served his purpose, brother mine. Leviathan has suffered enough."

Tristen drew his blade back. "You're still Arianrhod. And the beast has possessed you."

She spread her hands, the empty one and the one with the unblade in it. "O Brother, you have it backward. I possessed the beast, long ago. And now that our father is gone, and the world is in motion again, I'm here to see us to salvation. Sheathe your sword, Tristen Tiger. Welcome your sister back from the dead, cold realms of the Enemy, and let this poor mutilated monster go."

She was as he'd remembered her, no ghost of a Sorceress but the absolute item, chill and precise with her long hands motionless before her hips, the left one folded inside the right.

"I do not trust you, Arianrhod," he said.

Ariane reached out her hand, or the metaphor of her hand, and Perceval flinched back, flailing. The imaginary fingers could have closed around her, lifted her up—but she shouted for Nova with all her mind and suddenly someone was there beside her. Not Nova, but rather the necromancer, Mallory, who threw up arms like a barricade and shoved Ariane's groping fingers wide.

Ariane grabbed again, and again Mallory was too strong for her—but not by much. Perceval saw the necromancer wince, twist, grimace with effort as once more Ariane's hand came down.

Perceval just stood, awed, hands at her sides, watching.

The third time Ariane reached out, she pinioned Mallory's arms and lifted the necromancer into the air, swinging the kicking figure from side to side.

"Dammit, Captain," the necromancer yelled, each syllable rattled out between jerks. "We're in your head! Get control of her!"

But she's so big, Perceval thought. *She's so much bigger than me.*

Did that matter?

Maybe not. If they were in Perceval's head, maybe Ariane only *looked* so large.

Perceval imagined herself very far away, back away in the dark confines of her mind, so Ariane looked tiny enough to pick up between her fingers. And then she imagined herself close, and Ariane really so small.

Perceval pinched her up, careful not to squeeze, careful not to squish the microscopic Mallory clutched in Ariane's rattling fist.

"Ariane," Perceval said. "I want you to put the necromancer down."

Arianrhod/Cynric smiled. "Nor should you. But who other than me could have arranged this? Who else would have brought a child of the line of Sparrow here, and filled her form with the memories of the one person who can best help you now? Who guided you, Tristen, and our brother and sister, and the angel and the implement who held my memories? Who brought you through the abattoir in safety? Who introduced you to Dorcas? Who sent the mammoth, man, and all from the very grave?

"Leviathan dreams true futures, Tristen, after the nature of his kind. And I infected him and his dreaming long ago, and used them to dream you to me and the world to possibilities other than destruction. Trust me when I tell you that, for the nonce, you will find no Arianrhod here."

"Have you *eaten* her?" Carefully, neutrally, Tristen began disengaging his boots from the surface of Leviathan. Before him, the hole he and Gavin had gnawed in its side was sealing, seething at the bottom with the blue ropes of colonies.

"No," she said. "She's alive. I'm just borrowing her for now, because she's here and Leviathan remade her for me. And if she weren't, would you kill your grand-daughter's body to be sure?"

"I'd kill her for her crimes," he said, and winced at Cynric's frown.

"Oh, yes," his sister said. "Her crimes. So much worse than yours or mine. Look at the thing you're standing on, My Brother, and tell me any Conn has the right to live."

"Touché," Tristen said, and shook Mirth free of blue blood before he put it away. "So assuming for the moment that you are my sister—and this would be very like her—what was the purpose of this charade?"

She smiled. She held out her fist, turned it over, and opened her hand. "Leviathan knows the universe," she said, as he watched a glittering star map of impossible brilliance unfurl above her palm. "I have built us an astrogator, Brother Mine. I have made us a way home. Now draw out your blade again."

"You told me to put it up," Tristen said. "What would you have me butcher now?"

"Butcher nothing, but part a chain. Cut loose Leviathan. Let him return to his people, for we have abused him sore."

"He wants to destroy us," Tristen said. "And I cannot say I blame him."

Cynric shook her narrow head. "He cannot have his vengeance, though I am without doubt the one most deserving of it. He will have to live with only freedom."

And all around them, the lights of combat were dying away.

Later, when Cynric had led them back inside, Tristen came up beside Benedick and rested one hand lightly on his shoulder. "I knew you were standing behind me."

Benedick glanced sidelong at him and nodded. "I

thought you might not want to handle it. But then it turned out it didn't need to be handled. Not that way."

"Not yet," Tristen said, watching Cynric's slender, white-garbed spine retreat down the corridor before them. She moved fast. He stepped up his pace, aware of Benedick doing the same, of Chelsea and Mallory following. Aware of the way Mallory's hand came up to one shoulder, as if to steady a passenger who was not there. "What about when she gives Arianrhod back?"

Benedick shook his head. "Cynric's right. What has she done that's worse than you or me?"

"It's not about worse," Tristen answered. "It's about staying alive, not about what's right or wrong."

"Maybe it should be," Benedick said, and to that Tristen had no response except a short nod, curt and painful.

"Come on," he said. "It's a fucking long walk home."

In the warmth of the bridge, Cynric Conn walked forward across violets to meet the Captain. The Captain stood and watched her. In her borrowed flesh, with her borrowed spirit, Cynric knelt, and Perceval felt a shiver of recognition, a cold wash of sweat as the hair parted over her nape and fell in brown streamers to either side. Perceval's uncle, Tristen, stood behind her on the left side. Her father, Benedick, stood behind her on the right. Caitlin Conn, her mother, was in Engineering where she belonged, overseeing the removal of the last collars and clamps from the hide of Leviathan.

The Sorceress extended something in her two hands. A scabbarded sword with a rough, improvised hilt affixed.

Perceval did not reach out her hand. "I do not want that."

"It is Charity," Cynric said, raising her eyes in surprise. "The last of its kind."

What, did she not foresee this also? Perceval waved it away in irritation. She did not want a sword, and she did not want Cynric. What she wanted was Gavin back, but she would not say as much, for Captains did not weep. And if she said the basilisk's name, there would be no end to her tears. So instead she said, "It was Tristen's; give it to him."

But Tristen demurred. "I prefer Mirth, as it happens." He patted the hilt of the blade. "Give it to Benedick."

Benedick shook his head. "Give it to Caitlin," he said. "She probably actually misses hers."

When Benedick went to Caitlin, he knew she had been waiting for him because she was at such great pains to seem that she had not. She was alone in a booth at the center of a half-repaired Central Engineering, feet up on a console, studying schematics and frowning.

"Better?" he asked, having entered without knocking.

"Fair," she said. "Now that nothing's chewing the world apart from the edges, we're getting some actual repairs done. Have you talked to Perceval?"

He nodded, tightly. In the long run, he thought the new, fey Perceval with so many ancient souls behind her eyes might even be a match for Cynric the Sorceress, in wisdom if not in craft. "Perceval sent you something," he said, and held out the long nano-swagged parcel.

Caitlin looked from it to him, and did not reach out for it. "Tristen didn't claim it?"

Benedick laid the unblade down across her console. She could unwrap it later. "You should go and talk to our daughter in person."

Caitlin nodded, eyes bright. "I will."

"I'm not sure how she'll be," he said honestly, stepping forward to stand beside her chair. "I don't know where we go from here."

He touched her naked hand with his own so his

colony could give her the map, the one he'd been saving to deliver personally since Cynric had imparted it to him.

"It's okay," Caitlin said. She tipped her head over her shoulder at Jsutien, who was visible through the glass. "Wherever the hell it is, we know how to get there, now."

acknowledgments

Thanks very much to all the people who helped get this writ: Sarah Monette, Cindy and Robert Wood, Amanda Downum, Jodi Meadows, Jaime Lee Moyer, Emma Bull, Delia Sherman, Anne Groell Keck, Jennifer Jackson, Michael Curry, Leah Bobet, and more.